COMMAND ME

MORE BY GENEVA LEE

CONTEMPORARY ROMANCE

THE RIVALS SAGA

Blacklist

Backlash

Bombshell

THE DYNASTIES SAGA

London Dynasty

Cruel Dynasty

Secret Dynasty

FANTASY & PARANORMAL ROMANCE

FILTHY RICH VAMPIRES

Filthy Rich Vampire

Second Rite

Three Queens

THE ROYALS SAGA: ONE

COMMAND ME

GENEVA LEE

ESTATE

COMMAND ME

First published, 2014. Fourth edition.

Print ISBN: 978-1-945163-25-8

www.GenevaLee.com

Cover design © Date Book Designs.

Image © sergvalen/AdobeStock.

For the girls who need a new fairytale.

CHAPTER ONE

My eyes skimmed the smoking room's ornately decorated walls as I gulped my glass of champagne. Overhead, a painting of a duke, or some other important character with a lacy cravat at his throat, glared down at me, denouncing me as a fraud. Being a recent graduate of Oxford didn't mean I belonged at the exclusive Oxford and Cambridge Club. Most of the other graduates were from old money, and while my family was wealthy by most anyone's standards, we didn't have a family name or a title like most of my peers at the Degree Day celebration. I finished my drink while cursing my best friend Annabelle for convincing me this was a good idea.

"Clara, there you are!" Annabelle swooped at me like a hawk and her perfect fingernails dug into my arm, preventing my escape as she dragged me across the room toward a group of young men. Other than the aggressive move, she was the picture of propriety, her blonde hair still tucked in a graceful chignon at the nape of her neck, and the clasp of her necklace resting below it in perfect symmetry. Everything about Annabelle was polished—from her three-inch heels to the three carat diamond sparkling on her left hand. "I want you to finally meet my brother John."

"I'm not looking for a boyfriend right now, Belle. I'm a career woman now, remember?" I reminded her. Even if my new job at Peters & Clarkwell hadn't technically started yet, I didn't need a man to distract me. Belle knew that, but it wouldn't stop her from insisting I meet him. Even with her education, she'd been bred to believe a girl's best prospects lay in marriage. I was familiar with this concept, my mother having harbored similar delusions.

Belle shot me a wink over her shoulder. "But you could have some fun. John works all the time anyway and he's worth a fortune. You could be a Baroness."

"Not everyone bases attraction on money and power," I said in a low voice, not wanting to offend the number of powerful and rich people surrounding me.

Belle halted in her tracks, causing me to crash into her. She leaned toward me, and she whispered in my ear, "Have you ever snogged a rich and powerful man? Gone to bed with one?"

I bit my lip and glanced around us, uncertain how to answer. Belle knew I had only been to bed with one man, my now ex-boyfriend, who was neither rich nor powerful. Daniel had the chip on his shoulder to prove it. Whereas I often felt inferior around the old money at Oxford, he only felt angry. I'd grown-up well-off, at least. A shiver ran up my spine, thinking of how ugly our relationship had grown toward the end. I'd ended it over winter holiday, but even months later the thought of him made me shudder. Belle noticed and sighed.

"Daniel doesn't count," she said. The perfect, porcelain skin between her expertly shaped eyebrows furrowed at the thought. She shook her head as if wiping away the distasteful memory and shot me a mischievous smile. "If you had been to bed with a man like I'm talking about, you would know."

"I'm deeply concerned that you're deeming your brother as suitable for this position," I told her, cocking an eyebrow suggestively. "How close are you two?"

"Stuff and nonsense." She swatted at my arm, but the impish grin stayed on her face. "I'm just looking out for you, Clara. You need a good shag."

I suspected as much, although she hadn't voiced this particular concern until now. She'd been my flatmate through the worst bits with Daniel. Not only had she approved of our break-up, but she'd been hovering over me like a mother hen since then, taking me shopping and introducing me to new people. It was only a matter of time before she tried to set me up on dates. I supposed I should be grateful that she'd waited until my final exams were over and I'd officially graduated before she pushed her matchmaking agenda.

"Belle, I really don't need a guy right now," I said as firmly as possible, hoping to put the issue to rest but knowing there was no way in hell that I had.

She dismissed my objection with a fluttery wave. "Need and want are two different things, love. Never confuse them."

Before I could object further, she beckoned for a tall and rather awkward man to join us. John was clearly her older brother, if his receding hairline was any indication, and there was no doubt he had money. Somehow he'd managed to pair the most expensive and the most boring elements of modern fashion into one garbled, but obviously costly outfit. A Rolex and Berluti loafers were combined with a Harris Tweed jacket straight out of the eighties. He looked as though he couldn't decide if he was off for a day of hunting or business.

And that's how he dressed for a party.

"You must be the famous Clara," John said, taking my hand. For a moment he looked torn between kissing it and shaking it. The result was a limp and sweaty squeeze. John might be worth a fortune and have a title, but he didn't strike me as a go-getter. "Belle has told me all about you. A degree in social studies, is it?"

"Yes." I wanted to draw my hand away, but I wasn't sure how to do it.

"Fancy yourself the next Mother Teresa?" he asked, dropping his other hand on top of our loosely clasped ones. It was not an improvement.

"And if I say yes?" My question was bold and Belle blinked in surprise next to her brother. It wasn't like me to be so confident, especially around a stranger. But that had been me in university. I had a degree from a top college now and a highly competitive new job. I wasn't the same girl anymore. I couldn't be. I wouldn't allow it.

"You're much too pretty to be a nun," John said. His chest puffed a little as he added, "I recently qualified for barrister."

"How fascinating," I said absently, pulling my hand from his and looking across the room. "If you'll excuse me, I see..."

I bolted into the crowd before Belle could produce a minister to finalize the engagement, noting that I really had to speak with her about attempting to set me up in the future. Despite Belle's education, her family had placed her on the fast track to marriage, a rather archaic result of being titled. She might have fought them on the issue, but she seemed quite happy to go along with it, especially since her fiancé was a favorite of the palace. But I couldn't see myself married, and I didn't want to, especially after Daniel. A career was a better path for me. Safer, more fulfilling and infinitely less messy.

The crowd swallowed me up as I fled, protecting me from Belle's matchmaking, but making it almost impossible to get out. By the time I pushed through to the hallway, my heart was racing. I sank against the wall and took a deep breath, tugging down the simple black sheath I'd borrowed from Belle despite her objection that it was too somber. It was one of the few items in her closet that was age-appropriate. My own closet consisted of jeans and jumpers and a handful of nice, tailored suits. It was nothing like hers. Most days, Belle looked like a movie star, flashing as much skin as she did money. But the rest of her wardrobe consisted of dress suits that looked as if they'd been stolen from the Queen Mother herself. I'd been lucky to find this, even though I suspected it had been purchased for a funeral.

An exotic spicy scent wafted toward me, tickling my nostrils. It was completely out of place in the stuffy, old building, which had outlawed the practice of smoking, even in the now inappropriately named smoking room. I'd seen the signs in nearly every room, but clearly someone had not. I looked up, realizing a bit late that the smoke meant I wasn't alone, and my hand clutched my chest reflexively when I caught sight of him. Where there's smoke there's fire, and good lord, was he smokin'.

The man lounged against a door propped open to a terrace, a thin clove cigarette dangling carelessly from his sculpted lips, which twitched into a bemused smile that rested comfortably in its place. His face was lined in shadows cast by the light filtering in behind him, but I noted the trace of his strong jaw and a hint of blue in his eyes. I didn't need to see more to know he was one of the rich and powerful men Belle had spoken of. He was what she'd been referring to in her earlier statements. It radiated from him—wealth and authority and virility—and my body responded to it, my traitorous feet stepping closer to him. I could see him better now and discovered he had another defining characteristic—he was also handsome, which hardly seemed fair.

He had a face that would make angels weep and gods go to war. Sharp, chiseled features highlighted by golden skin spoke of faraway, sunny beaches. His dark hair wasn't a result of the shadows he stood in. It was nearly black and tousled into a mess that made me imagine tangling my hands through it. For a brief second, I pictured grabbing it as my body pressed against his.

Get a grip, I commanded myself. I hadn't been laid in a while but reacting to a stranger like this was embarrassing, even if he didn't know what I was thinking. Of course, from the arrogant but seductive curve of his smile, he knew exactly what I was thinking. But the smile stopped at his eyes, which blazed fiercely. I felt the hunger in his gaze as though it was mine, and my own desire tightened across my belly. I needed to keep him at a distance. I could feel it.

Plus the whole smoking in the boys' club bespoke a general disregard for rules. Or other people.

"I don't think you're supposed to smoke here," I said. I sounded like a total snot, but I'd grown sick of the privileged class bending the rules at their whim, and something about the way he was looking at me suggested I was nothing more than an object—a toy that he wanted to play with.

"My apologies." He smirked, but his amusement didn't hide the cultured rasp of his voice. "Are you going to report me for conduct unbecoming?" He stepped back so that he was technically on the terrace, finding a way to loosely follow the restrictions. But I suspected he did it to please me. He didn't strike me as the type to worry about breaking a few rules.

Even though I couldn't see his eyes clearly anymore, I felt his gaze burn into me. It flustered me, my emotions waffling between annoyance and girlish excitement. "I wouldn't want you to get into trouble."

He turned toward me, revealing his striking face once more as his lips twitched and curved into a wicked smile, flashing me a row of perfect teeth. "We wouldn't want that."

Blood rushed to my cheeks in a hot flash of embarrassment. I wanted to kiss that wild smirk off his face, but I shook the fantasy from my mind. In the light, he looked familiar, like I had known him at some point. Perhaps a childhood schoolmate? I would have remembered him if he had attended my college. There was no way I wouldn't have noticed his crystal blue eyes or that shock of dark hair that skirted the line between propriety and pop star. Between the broad shoulders trapped in a well-cut suit and his good looks, he wasn't a man I would easily forget. So how could I know him—and not know him? My gaze lingered at his unbuttoned collar and loose tie, imagining what it would be like to unfasten the rest of his buttons and pull him free of it. My teeth sank into my lower lip at the thought.

Was I actually standing here, fantasizing about a total stranger—in front of him? Maybe Belle was right, after all.

His eyebrow cocked up as I continued to stare, and I looked away, ashamed that he'd caught me. Of course with his looks, he likely got stared at quite often. He didn't need to know he'd gotten my knickers in a twist, or that he could probably talk me out of them altogether. Although he probably knew that his crooked grin was practically a panty-dropping license.

"I think that I should warn you of the dangers of smoking," I said, wanting him to feel an ounce of the humiliation coursing through me, but also desperate to keep the conversation flowing. I didn't want him to leave.

"Poppet, you would not be the first." But he flicked out the cigarette and tossed it in a nearby can. The movement was smooth and self-assured, as though there was no possibility of missing—as if the world would merely shift to suit his needs.

I was increasingly sure that I knew him, and whoever he was, he was having a lark at my expense. "Have we met before?"

"I think I would remember you," he said, his eyes flickering as he spoke, the magnetic energy of them growing in intensity, sending a tremble quivering through me. "It's more likely that my reputation has preceded me."

"A ladies' man then?" I asked. That wouldn't surprise me.

"Something like that," he said, his words thick with implication. "What's an American girl doing in this snobby old place?"

I stiffened immediately, feeling some of the familiar defensiveness this observation usually produced. But I sensed he wasn't condescending, just curious, so I forced a smile onto my face. "I'm a British citizen actually. Although I grew up in the States. Mom's American. She met my dad when he was studying at Berkeley."

Stop telling him your life story, the tiny obnoxious voice that played critic to my every waking moment admonished me.

"And a California girl, too," the stranger said. "I can't imagine why you'd trade the beach for rainy old London."

"I like the fog." It was true but admitting it made me blush. It was a silly reason, but his head cocked, as if he were intrigued.

I took a step closer to him, holding out my hand. Perhaps he expected a formal introduction before he'd fess up. "I'm Clara Bishop, by the way."

"It's nice to meet you, Clara Bishop." His hand caught mine, and there was no hesitation as he raised it swiftly toward his lips. A surge of electricity passed between us, the air in the room practically crackling as the sensation seeped into my veins, spreading until I felt dizzy. Desire swam through my blood, pooling in my belly.

I wanted to pull away. No, I *needed* to pull away.

Belle's words echoed in my head. I didn't want him to stop touching me though. I wanted to melt into him and I was strongly considering it when a beautiful, blond woman sauntered into the hall and stopped to stare at us.

I had to pull my hand away if I wanted to break the electric connection buzzing between us, but when I tugged free from his grip he grabbed my arm and drew me roughly to him. His lips crushed against mine with an urgency I thought existed only in

films. Strong arms coiled around my waist, tightening possessively as he cradled my back. He tasted of cloves and bourbon,
wild nights and reckless abandon, and my lips parted instinctually as his tongue slid into my mouth. His kiss was forceful—
commanding—and I found myself slipping under his control,
my body molding against his as I softened under the heat of our
embrace.

His tongue flicked lazily against my teeth, and my mouth
spread wider in welcome. He accepted, thrusting his tongue
deeper, drawing my own into his mouth and capturing it with a
languid suction. My legs buckled weakly, my body ready to sink
to the floor under him, but he pressed me closer to him, the
hardness of his body bracing me. His hand slipped from my
waist to the hollow at the small of my back. The intimate
gesture spurred me to life and my fingers tangled into his silky
hair as I held on to the kiss, certain I would fade to nothing
without his body crushed against mine.

When he finally released me, it was too soon, even though
his hand stayed on the small of my back. I stumbled back a step,
but he held me steady, as if he'd anticipated my reaction. Of
course, a man who kissed like that probably had learned what to
expect. I couldn't help thinking he should come with a label:

Warning! Content is extremely arousing.

I searched his face for a clue as to why he kissed me, even as
my body craved the taste of him, but all I saw was the ragged
passion burning in his eyes. It sucked the breath from me and I
couldn't speak for a moment.

"Why?" The question slipped out, equal parts spoken
thought and accusation.

"My motives are less than chivalrous," he said, dropping his
hand from me at his confession. I shivered at the loss of contact,
wishing he hadn't. "That woman is a particularly horrible
mistake of mine."

"You kissed me to avoid your ex-girlfriend?"

"I would not call her my ex, but my apologies all the same." There wasn't an ounce of regret in his words. His eyes cooled, the molten blue fire now hardened to sapphires. He took a step towards me, but then hesitated, changing direction toward the terrace.

I deflated at his shift, and it was then that I realized I wanted him to kiss me again—a desire I knew was written all over my face. Silence fell between us, but even though he didn't speak or touch me again, my heart continued to beat rapidly like a caged animal trying to break free.

"Congratulations on your matriculation," he told me.

I blinked at the change of topic, remembering where I was and why. The world had faded away when he touched me, and it was only now that I recalled that I knew nothing about this man who could have taken me up against the wall moments ago if he'd wanted to. "Did you graduate as well?"

His hand covered his mouth quickly but not before I caught that smirk flash across his face once more. "I took a rather different career path. Are we playing twenty questions?"

"Will you tell me who you are?" I asked.

He winked at me. "I think the point, poppet, is to figure that out."

My eyes narrowed, my lips still stinging with the memory of his kiss. If he wanted to play games, I could play games. "You took a different career path? But you're here—" I gestured around us "—at a prestigious club, so you're either a well-dressed waiter or you come from money?"

I waited for him to answer, but he shook his head, wagging a finger at me. "That wasn't a yes or no question."

"If you don't want to play..." I shrugged, surreptitiously checking the hall behind me.

"I merely want to play by the rules, unless you'd rather I ask you the questions," he suggested.

I swallowed, struggling to keep my body under control. "Do you come from money?"

"You could say that," he said with a shrug.

"Yes or no," I prompted.

"Yes," he said, leaning in and catching a lock of my hair between his fingers. "Is it my turn yet?"

"I haven't asked all twenty questions," I whispered, aware of the proximity of his lips.

"Don't spend them all at once," he advised me as he tucked the strand behind my ear. "It's best to leave some anticipation."

"You already know who I am," I reminded him.

"But there are lots of things I'd like to know about you." His breath was hot on my neck as he spoke. "And I'm dying to hear you say yes."

"What if the answer is no?"

"Trust me, it isn't." His lips brushed across my jaw. My eyes closed to the sensation of his five o'clock shadow rasping across the delicate skin.

He stepped away, and I choked back a pant of longing, adjusting my dress in an attempt to look nonplussed.

"Last question," he said, "and then let's see if you can guess."

One last chance to unravel him and I was no closer than I'd been when we met. And now my body hummed with arousal, distracting me from my objective. There was only one thing for it. There was only one question I could ask.

"Who are you?" I asked, calling his bluff.

He shook his head and mouthed yes or no. Clearly he wasn't going to be less cryptic, even after using me to avoid his ex. I'd been a convenient pawn, and the thought sent shame rippling through me. I didn't think I could calm my racing heart if I stayed near him.

Had I imagined the electricity in that kiss? I was certain that I hadn't. As sure as I was that he wanted me, too. My mouth went dry at the idea. I thought of what Belle had said about snogging a man with wealth and power, and I forced myself to ignore the throb of ache traveling through my body. I wasn't interested in being toyed with by a man like this. I refused to be.

"I should be getting back," I said, aware that I had to make a move before his scorching presence turned me into a puddle of want on the floor in front of him.

His eyes blazed as he nodded, smoldering through my body, but this time it wasn't my cheeks on fire. "I hope to see you again, Clara Bishop."

He didn't wait for me to leave. Instead, he disappeared onto the terrace, vanishing into thin air. It wasn't until he was out of sight, freeing me from the heady affect of his presence, that I realized I'd kissed a man without knowing his name.

And I wanted to do it again.

CHAPTER TWO

S linking back to the cocktail party, completely distracted by the stranger and his kiss, I didn't even see Belle until I was back in her clutches. She beamed as she grabbed my wrist and dragged me toward the bar. Most of the people around us wouldn't notice the slight pinch of her eyes as she smiled, but I knew it meant I was in trouble. Considering how dazed and infuriated I was after that kiss—that incredible kiss—I wasn't going to put up much of a fight.

"What in the bloody hell was that?" she asked, shoving a bowl of mixed nuts at me.

"I'm not hungry." Food was about the last thing on my mind.

"Are you pissed already? Don't make me force-feed you."

"I'm not drunk," I said, even though I felt like I was. His lips. The taste of them on mine. The press of his body. A wave of heat rolled through my body and I resisted the urge to fan myself.

"Clara." Belle snapped her fingers to get my attention. I shook my head and stared at her dumbly. "I *said* that you could have at least have had a drink with my brother."

"I'm sorry," I said. I did feel genuinely bad for ducking out so gracelessly in front of her brother. But the only way she was ever going to learn not to set me up was if I made it an embarrassment to her. Belle was fluent in humiliation from a family disgrace years before. I hated to play that card, but it was the only thing that got through her obstinance. Still it was our graduation day.

"I thought I saw my mother," I fibbed.

Belle's face softened and she snatched a few nuts out of the bowl, holding them out to me. "Protein. You're going to need your strength."

Truer words were never spoken, even if my excuse had been a lie. My mother was supposed to be here today, and I had little doubt she'd come. The Oxford and Cambridge Club was hardly a place she could expect to visit without an invitation, and today some of Britain's most elite families were present to celebrate a graduation. Madeline Bishop wouldn't miss that for the world. The press wasn't welcomed since it was a private party, but there was always the chance there would be paparazzi outside, if she got lucky. Our family generally didn't warrant such attention but she'd been seeking it ever since her and my father had made their initial fortune fourteen years ago. It was a little embarrassing, and I wasn't exactly eager to see her. Belle understood this all too well.

"Thank you." I popped the nuts in my mouth. Their saltiness made my mouth water, and I realized I was famished. My gaze landed on a nearby mantel clock and I groaned. It had been over six hours since I had last eaten.

"I won't be held responsible for you fainting on your degree day," Belle said, giving me a wink. She knew me well enough to know that between the stress of the ceremony and this party I would forget to eat. "Don't look now, but the Bishops have arrived."

"God save the Queen," I muttered, taking a deep breath and snatching up a few more nuts. I would be sure to follow them with a nice bourbon. Turning around, I caught sight of my mother decked out in a stunning but short peacock-blue garden dress that hugged her impressively athletic body but was hardly appropriate for her age. It didn't seem fair that she was probably in better shape than I was. Of course, she considered looking fit to be her profession.

I saw her searching the room, her hands artfully resting on a string of pearls at her neck. She might not have been born British but she could hold her own with any of the aristocrats in this room. Her head was high, her nose tipped slightly up, and her gaze scathing as she looked around her. There was a smile of benevolence on her lips as though she was deigning to enter a room of her subjects.

Taking a deep breath, I raised my hand to wave her over.

"Last chance to run," I told Belle.

"And leave you alone? Not a chance, but you do owe me a bottle of wine later." She slipped a rocks glass into my hand, knowing exactly what I needed to get through this encounter before I even asked.

"Deal." Although by the end of the day we'd probably need more than one bottle.

"Clara, my dearest girl!" Mom flew through the crowd to me, kissing me delicately on the cheek. Affection from her was always as fragile as a butterfly wing. Feelings were so easily broken, she'd once told me, so it was better to be cautious with them. I'd watched the same delicacy infiltrate her marriage since I was a child.

Dad held out a hand, and as soon as I took it, he pulled me into a bear hug. "Clare-bear, you did it!"

I flushed a little at the nickname from my childhood. Dad

had never believed that love was fragile, even if he did treat my mother like glass.

"A university graduate," Mom said, thrusting her chest out in pride, and causing none too subtle looks of appreciation from the men around her. "An Oxford graduate at that."

"To my little girl." Dad raised a glass to toast and I felt the slightest tug of emotion at the gesture.

There'd been little doubt I would attend university, even though my father had fought to graduate years ago. My mom hadn't been so lucky. It felt strange to know she was here celebrating the person that had kept her own ambitions from being fulfilled.

"Future Nobel Prize Winner. Britain's great hope," Dad continued.

I rolled my eyes at him. "More like Future Nobel Prize Winner's errand girl."

"Everyone starts somewhere," he reminded me. "Even small stuff is important. Gandhi started somewhere."

I had no doubt of that, but just the thought of the job I'd landed made me feel slightly nauseous. Thankfully, I had over a fortnight until I had to actually begin my work there, and plenty of things to do in that time to occupy my mind. "No hunger strikes from me," I promised him.

Beside us my mother froze. "That was in poor taste."

"I'm sorry. It was just a joke," I reassured her.

But my mom had begun to fan herself while casting glances around her. "It's stifling over here."

Dad smiled softly. "Then let's find another spot for you, love."

It was passive-aggressive tactic number one of my mother's playbook. She had to be constantly moving. It didn't matter how lovely her view was, how fascinating her dinner partners were, or the exclusivity of the party she was attending, she was always convinced that she was missing out. She was sure that around the corner there might be a better opportunity or a more important person. This meant that my family had hopped from house to house for the first several years after they'd sold their internet business. My dad had finally put his foot down and informed her this was it when they moved from Los Angeles to Kensington six years ago. It was the poshest home we'd ever owned, with the poshest address, right across the street from the former pop singer who was married to the famous soccer player. My mom had been game for it for the first few years but had been dropping hints for a while that she was ready for a change. Or rather, she wanted to seek greener pastures. Dad, to his credit, had not budged on the issue. But that hadn't stopped her from engaging a real estate agent. Every few months, I would be dragged to look at properties. She'd hinted that she wanted to buy one for me but I was not about to let that happen. They'd paid my expenses at university and I'd managed to deal with my mother's demanding and sometimes stifling curiosity regarding my life, but I was an adult now with a proper job and no desire to continue living under her thumb.

"Clara, have you considered where you will live now that you're back in the city?" she asked, linking her arm through mine as she displayed her uncanny knack for guessing what I was thinking.

Not with you, I thought. London was still a strange beast to me, having only moved to the UK shortly before heading off to school, and my mother knew it. That didn't make me want to live with her though. "I told you I was going to stay with Belle."

"But Belle is getting married," Mom reminded me. She turned and flashed a brilliant smile at my friend. "I must hear every detail about the wedding."

Belle returned the smile, briefly raising a knowing eyebrow when my mother turned her back. She knew that my mom had just invited herself to Belle's wedding. Mom would probably be game to take my place as a bridesmaid if I would let her.

"Not for another year," I said calmly. At least I sounded calm. This was actually a huge concern for me. I didn't do well living on my own, something both Belle and my mom knew. I wasn't certain what I would do when Belle got married and moved in with Philip. I was trying not to think about it.

"Don't worry, Mrs. Bishop," Belle said, her eyes twinkling. "I've got a long list of men that are dying to take Clara on a date, and they are all excellent long-term prospects."

I willed the floor to open and swallow me up. I hated the idea of being set up, as though I needed someone to arrange romance for me. It made me feel undesirable, and this afternoon had proved I was anything but that. "Are we talking about men or investments?"

"They're the same thing." Mom tossed the thought at me and returned her attention to Belle. "You're such a good friend to set her up, and you must start calling me Madeline. We'll be seeing each other all the time now."

Visions of lunch dates and high teas swam in my head. I'd never quite succeeded in reminding her that I was going to be busy with a job soon. My mother hadn't needed to work in so long that I wasn't sure she had a good hold on what a career actually required—like work.

"I hope so," Belle said. She found my mom hilarious, but even I knew she was lying. Madeline was best served in small doses.

We'd relocated closer to the door I'd fled from earlier, and my thoughts drifted back to the kiss. Part of me wanted to slip away and look for him, but then would I be any better than the girl he'd been trying to avoid? Likely not. How would I feel if I found him only to have him grab the nearest tart and snog her?

The new Clara Bishop doesn't have time for playboys or baggage or drama, I reminded myself.

But still, I couldn't help but replay the kiss, slowing down each moment in my memory until I could almost feel the brush of his lips again. My hands clenched at my sides as I fought against the tremble of arousal that rolled through my body.

My mother's high-pitched giggle broke me out of my reverie. It was unlikely that anyone had said anything truly funny, but I smiled anyway, as though I was in on the joke.

"Your father and I have been talking." Mom glanced over to Dad, who was shooting her a frustrated glare, which she ignored. "Why don't you move in with us? Surely, Belle will want to be alone with Philip, and we have more than enough room."

They did have more than enough room but there was no way I was taking my mom up on her offer. "We've already signed a great lease on a flat," I lied.

"You have? Without consulting me?" My mother wore pouts like some women wore hats. Often and with lots of ceremony. This was no exception. She looked at me as if I'd totally betrayed her.

"I'm sorry. We couldn't pass it up," Belle said, stepping in to help me sell the lie.

"I just know so much about real estate." The pout deepened, revealing the fine lines she paid to hide. It wasn't a good sign if she'd take her sulking that far.

"We only have a lease," I reminded her.

"But that's still a contract. Do you know that I read in the Sun that more and more landlords are spying on their tenants?"

The second play from Mom's playbook was to make something sound scary that would never normally be so. It had succeeded in terrifying me the first eighteen years of my life, but now that I was twenty-three, the attempt only made me weary.

"I'm certain it will be fine," I said.

"We're renting from a nice old lady," Belle jumped in.

I shot her a warning look. This lie was growing so quickly I wasn't sure I could keep up. I'd been lying for my mom's own good for such a long time that I knew it was much easier to feed her small lies than to expound on one until it was too big to swallow or, for that matter, remember.

"Is that Doris?" Mom asked, clutching my father's arm. It was a boon for her to see someone she knew today, and I guessed there was no way she'd pass on the opportunity to be spotted at this event. "Let's go say hello."

Dad looked like that was the last thing he wanted to do, but he nodded and gingerly took her arm.

I smacked Belle in the arm as soon as they were out of earshot. "We do not have nice little, old lady or a flat."

"Actually," she said, drawing out the word dramatically, "we do."

My eyebrows popped up in surprise. "We do?"

"My great aunt Jane owns a building in East London."

I wouldn't have thought it possible she could surprise me more, but that certainly did. "Your great aunt lives in East London?"

"Oh, just you wait." Belle took a long sip of her cocktail and shrugged, as if it weren't strange to have an older relative living in one of London's hippest areas. "You're going to love her."

"I don't know," I said. "I haven't even seen it yet."

"Trust me on this. We're meeting her tomorrow. Besides, can you imagine moving back in with your parents?" Belle asked, clutching her neck like she was being strangled for good measure.

"Yes and no," I admitted.

"Yes?" It wasn't a question, but a statement of incredulity.

"You know I don't like living alone," I reminded her. But the thought of going back to my parent's homes was hardly a comforting one. I'd been independent at university, and apart from a few bad decisions—mostly related to Daniel—I'd done well since my sophomore year.

But there were people to fall back on now. Most of my friends would be moving to London soon. Still, Belle was my closest friend—and the only one I could imagine moving in with. Maybe in another year the independence I'd felt in my first year of school would recover from the damage dealt it by Daniel enough that I would no longer feel the compulsion to share a flat, but I wasn't there yet.

"I know, and that's okay." Belle laid her head on my shoulder. "But this means you have to let me set you up. I would feel terrible if I had to send you back to your parents next year."

"Who knows where we'll be in a year's time," I reminded her.

Belle squeezed my shoulder. "That's the right attitude."

"You think this means you can set me up, don't you?"

"One date," she pleaded with me, adding, "with my brother."

"I don't think he's my type." I wanted to spare her feelings. It really wasn't her fault that her brother was obviously a drip.

"I know he would probably bore the life out of you," she said. "But I want to see you taken care of."

"I can take care of myself."

She looked like she seriously doubted that, and I hadn't given her good reason to believe me over the last year. But despite her concern, I wasn't going to relent on the issue of dating her brother. Barrister or not. Thankfully, I was saved from more of her fawning by the arrival of her fiancé before she could continue to plead her case.

"There's Philip," she said, jumping up and smoothing her skirt. She turned to me for approval.

"You look fabulous, as always." I didn't have to fib. No matter how much she'd drank or how long she'd been on her feet, Belle always looked freshly pressed and carefully polished. "Tell Pip I said hello."

Belle stuck her tongue out at me as she sashayed toward him. Philip acted a bit too serious for my taste, and that was saying something. He hated the nickname Pip, which made me love it. Not because I didn't like him. He was fine—classically handsome with a sharply angled face and dusty blond hair, tall and well-spoken. And the fact that he came with a title and loads of money didn't hurt either. He was exactly what Belle wanted in a man: financial and genetic security. I couldn't blame her for that. We'd both felt lost in our lives, so I understood seeking a safe spot. I only wished she could respect my safe spot would never be with a man like him or her brother or any of the other old friends I was likely to suddenly meet in the next few weeks.

I watched as Philip caught her hand and pulled her to him. Her face lit up as soon as she was in his arms, and a sigh escaped my lips. They looked perfect together, like a fairytale come to life. Maybe I was wrong about why they were together. Perhaps he was more than just a soft landing after all.

THERE ARE SOME PLACES YOU WALK INTO AND immediately feel at home in, as though it had been waiting for you to show up all your life. For me, most of those places had been libraries and cafes, quiet spots on secluded beaches and under shady trees. I'd never really felt at home in any of the houses my parents had purchased when I was a teenager. They were too big and too cold. It had been more like living in a museum and I hated to feel like I was on display. But I'd known as soon as I walked into the flat Belle's aunt owned that I would be happy here.

More than happy: safe.

"What do you think?" Belle asked me, twisting her engagement ring around her finger.

I wasn't sure I could find the words, and there was a little part of me that hated to admit I was wrong about the idea of renting from her aunt. But I turned to face her, unable to keep a silly grin from sliding onto my face. "When can we move in?"

Aunt Jane swept by us in a blur of flowing tunics and scarves to open a window. "That's better! I can't stand stuffy rooms." She sighed into the breeze floating in through the window. "It's vacant, and that's not good for a house's soul. I have the keys right here. It's yours when you want it."

I took a set from her outstretched palm without hesitation. To deal with end of term stress, I'd systematically made a list every day that included all the things I needed to worry about after exams. Finding a flat had been one of the items I'd still lost sleep over. Now it felt like the pieces of my life—my real, adult life—were falling into place. And the rent she'd given us would be easy to cover even after Belle got married so long as she offered what was clearly a family discount. I wouldn't even have to dip into my trust fund.

"It will be nice to have young blood in this house," she continued. "The last tenant was a musician, who I fear was going slightly tone deaf."

"Aunt Jane has a soft spot for musicians," Belle informed me with a wink.

"They make excellent lovers," her aunt confirmed. Her face was deadly serious, as though we were merely discussing a business item like what to do if the toilet overflowed. "Please tell me you've gone to bed with a musician."

I choked back the laugh that bubbled into my throat and

shook my head. Aunt Jane's expression suggested that she thought this was a great loss. She turned hopefully to Belle who answered in the negative, as well. Her petite shoulders slumped and she shook her head sadly.

"And with you getting married. Ah well, you can always have an affair. Musicians are excellent for that, too."

It seemed to me that the breath of fresh air in this flat was Aunt Jane, and I followed her from room to room as she pointed out the small quirks of my future home. Nothing about her screamed old money, although I knew she was if she owned this building. Her gray hair was spiked in a sort of punk rock pixie that suited her slight frame and elegant face. She had aristocratic bones, that much was certain, but she felt worldly and exotic. Nothing like the stuck-up types I'd encountered at university functions. I'd known that I liked her instantly and my gut was never wrong.

The flat was perfect. It had been updated recently with gleaming, stainless steel appliances and an overlarge Jacuzzi tub. But the walls were a combination of exposed brick and carefully maintained plaster with delicate woodwork that framed the doorways and windows. The oak floors had been refinished and polished. The only thing it lacked was a fireplace, but I'd hardly miss that during the upcoming summer months. Once we had furniture, I'd be able to check off most of my to-do list. I might even have a few days to explore London before I began work.

"Do you have a room preference?" Belle asked me as we took a final stroll through the flat.

"Either is fine."

"Liar." She linked her arm through mine and dragged me to the smaller but cozier of the two rooms. "I know you want this one."

I chewed my lip, afraid I would be stepping on her toes if I admitted she was right. With its bay window, it was exactly to my taste.

"It is nice," I said slowly.

"It's yours. The other one has a door to the loo, so I can beat you into it every morning."

"How devious of you." I laughed, not because she was clever, but because the idea that Belle would rise before me seemed unlikely. Belle's primary job for the next twelve months was finalizing the details of her wedding. If there was ever a career that allowed for schedule flexibility, she'd found it.

"I'm going to thank Aunt Jane." She disappeared, leaving me alone in the room.

I could already see where the bed would go and my bookshelf. I could probably even squeeze in an armchair or at least a bench under the large window that overlooked the bustling street three stories below. Everything was falling into place, thanks to a stroke of luck and my careful plans over the last academic year.

But deep down, I wondered when it would all change. Staring out my new window, I noticed the spring sky had gone gray and clouds hung low—a storm was coming.

CHAPTER THREE

Faint noises crept into my dreams from the street below my window, but I clung to the unconscious state. I was dreaming of a handsome man with the slight scruff of next-day stubble, his face cast in shadows, and the sultry scent of cloves hanging in the air between us. His fingers were on my collarbone, tracing down to my top button as his lips found my jawline. The honk of a horn distracted him, and he pulled back even as I fought harder to stay asleep. But then he was several feet from me, a knowing smirk on his face. He shrugged as the morning light seeped through my eyelids, dissolving the final fragments of the dream. But I refused to open my eyes, desperate to sink back into the fantasy.

It was the rich scent of coffee that did me in entirely, forcing my eyes to open as Belle sauntered into the room. She crooked her finger at me. "Sit up, darling, and you can have this."

"What time is it?" I asked, still searching for the strings of consciousness to connect me with the all important where and when of my early morning state.

"Time to unpack," Belle said, releasing the mug to my custody, "or are you off to be a grown-up already?"

"I don't start until next Friday. You have me at your mercy for a while yet, which is why you should let me go back to sleep." I took a sip of the coffee, surrendering to the fact that I wasn't going to have a lie in.

"Did you get anything unpacked?" Belle asked as she read the list of contents scrawled across the nearest box top.

I patted my mattress. The four-poster bed was fully made up with a down comforter stuffed in a creamy duvet and a half dozen feather pillows. A good night's sleep had been my top priority after a week of crashing on couches and trips to and from Oxford. But that meant that all around us boxes were still taped shut. My walls were still bare, save for a coat of steely-blue paint. I'd even have to dig to find clothes, although, from the looks of it, Belle had already unpacked her closet. Despite the fact that it was the crack of dawn, she was fully dressed in skinny, dark jeans and a loose, draping t-shirt that fell artfully across her slender figure. She looked like a model with her shiny blond hair tied back from her perfect, naturally sun-kissed complexion.

Outside, a series of honks shattered the somewhat peaceful bustle of early morning traffic. Belle leapt to her feet to peek out the window, frowning when she caught sight of the street below.

"What in the hell is going on down there?" I asked.

"A bunch of gawkers. They look like reporters," she said with a dismissive wave. "Maybe there was an accident."

I groaned and shoved myself out of bed, depositing my coffee mug with a sigh on a nearby box. It was disgraceful how reporters flocked to any gruesome scene in London, as though the public wanted to see photographs of mangled cars on the nightly news. Even the protection put into place after Princess Sarah's death hadn't stopped them from finding new ways to stalk their bloody headlines. My stomach turned over just thinking about it. I had no idea what had their attention now, but no doubt I'd be subjected to all the sordid details at every newsstand for the next few days.

"I don't see anything happening." Belle wrinkled her nose in annoyance, obviously put out to not know what was happening on the street.

"I'll never be able to lay in now," I said, shifting boxes around until I found one marked clothes. "Let me get a shower and then we can unpack."

Belle nodded, slipping toward the door. "I might pop down and have a look while you get dressed."

I shook my head, doing my best to look reproachful.

"What if there's an emergency? Or a murderer on the loose?" Belle asked. "We're new to the neighborhood, Clara darling. We should take precautions."

"Don't you mean we should catch all the gossip first?"

Belle mashed her lips together, trying to hide a grin, but only appearing more impish for the effort. "You won't even know I'm gone."

It took nearly five minutes for the shower to heat up, but when I slipped in, my shoulders relaxed and I let the water wash over me. Shutting my eyes, I thought of my dream and the mystery man from earlier in the week. Something stirred in my belly, tightening in my core, and I wished I could finish the dream. *Or better yet,* I thought as I lathered soap across my body, *I wish I could see him again.* I tried to convince myself the desire was innocent. That I only wanted to know what his name was and why he'd used me to avoid that girl, but honestly, more than anything, I wanted him to kiss me again. My hands had slid further down my stomach, making their way for the pulse growing more demanding between my legs.

"Don't be stupid," I said to myself, turning to rinse off the rest of the soap in the hot water before I shut off the shower. Hopefully, I wasn't desperate enough to get myself off alone in the shower yet. By the time I had towel-dried my thick, chestnut hair and found a pair of comfortable old jeans, I could hear Belle in the kitchen.

"Uncover all the sordid details?" I asked as I joined her. There was fresh coffee in my mug, and I sipped it as I waited for her to spill.

Belle met my eyes, her face both pale and flushed at the same time. Her fingers drummed against a stack of newspapers on the counter.

"Is there something you forgot to tell me, Clara?" she asked.

My eyebrows knit together as I tried to decode her question. Belle and I had been flatmates through our years at Oxford because, apart from generally liking each other, neither of us pried. We didn't have to. Belle never separated personal from private, meaning she had no secrets from me, and since my life was far less interesting than hers, she knew it all.

"What's going on, Belle?" I asked in a low voice. My stomach twisted into a knot. "You look like you're going to be sick."

She let out a nervous laugh that evolved into a fit of giggles as she tried to speak. "It's...just...so...absurd!"

I grabbed for a paper, but Belle snatched it away, shaking her head with a coy smile.

"You might want to sit down, darling," she instructed me.

I sank onto a kitchen stool, dread creeping up my limbs and turning my blood to ice. I'd never done a single thing wrong in my life. There was absolutely no reason to suspect that what-ever had Belle in a tizzy had anything to do with me. But it did. I was certain of it. I could tell by the way she was acting.

She was positively gloating.

"Out with it," I said with impatience, feeling sicker by the minute.

She flipped over a tabloid so that I could see the cover photo of two people snogging. This is what she was freaking out about? I raised an eyebrow at her and she shoved another tabloid under my nose. This photograph was cropped closer to the subjects, but it took me a moment to process what I was looking at. I recognized the paneling of the hallway and the terrace behind the couple. It wasn't just any two people. It was me and the mystery man from the party at the Oxford and Cambridge Club. The photograph jolted me back to the moment.

His silky hair.

The taste of cloves and bourbon on his lips.

My body responded to the memory with a pang, aching for his touch.

It had been a legendary kiss, but that didn't explain why we were on the cover of a tabloid.

"I don't understand," I said, but even as the words left my lips, the attached headline began to sink in. "The reporters outside?"

Belle nodded.

How could I not have recognized him? Apparently I'd been more out of it the last few months than I thought. The tiny voice in my head clucked at me, tossing around words like idiotic, naive, innocent. Then I remembered what had woken me this morning and I grabbed Belle's arm to steady myself.

"Me?" My mouth went dry as I asked.

"You were the one snogging the fucking prince," Belle said, her words a curious mix of jealousy and admiration.

"But I didn't know it was him," I said weakly, memories flashing so quickly through my mind that everything became a tangled jumble of thoughts and emotions. My pulse raced as I realized the mystery had been solved. I knew who he was, and the excitement of that bubbled through me until I realized the terrible price of that information. It was no longer my mystery, and I could no longer claim the innocence of ignorance. Not knowing who he was? It wasn't much of an excuse, and it certainly wasn't going to grant me a reprieve from the reporters out for whatever piece they could get of me. And knowing who he was? It wasn't going to get me back in his arms. My stomach dropped as the full implications of this mistake hit me, and I choked back the bile that rose in my throat.

"How on Earth did you not realize it was him?" Belle asked.

I paused to consider this, trying to ignore the tongue-lashing that my overly critical, rational side was giving my subconscious. Like most girls my age, I'd grown up on a diet of the royal family, particularly the two handsome princes that weren't much older than myself. They'd even graced the cover of a few popular teen magazines in the States when I was younger. But they'd all but vanished from public life. At least Alexander had, not long before my family had moved from California to the UK, and then I'd gone off to university. A crush on the crown prince hadn't exactly been my top priority for the last few years.

"He seemed familiar," I admitted. "I thought I knew him from Oxford. I haven't even seen a photo of him for years. Are you sure that's him?"

"Have you been living under a rock?"

"I have been studying and going for jobs," I reminded her, pacing through the kitchen as though I could walk off the embarrassment. Lack of a social life was a foreign concept to Belle, who thrived on being at the center of a group as often as possible. I hadn't even been to see a movie in months.

"He's back from Iraq," she told me, her fingers tracing the photo longingly. "He got a medal of some sort and has been celebrating by shacking up with every vagina in the greater London area."

I winced at this revelation, feeling surprisingly hurt. Not only was the guy I'd been fantasizing about for the last few days completely unattainable, but I was just another girl in a long line. "Should I be flattered or horrified that I'm counted in the throngs of his conquests?" I tossed the tabloid I was holding in the rubbish bin. Then immediately pulled it back out to stare at the photo more. "Why is this even news?"

"Because the press thinks you're different."

I snorted at this, shaking my head in disgust. "I guess I didn't actually let him fuck me. Does that make me different?"

I didn't add that I would have let him or that I'd been fantasizing about him for days. It was foolish of me to even think about him after that day. I'd known he was trouble the moment we'd met, so why had I toyed with the idea of seeing him again?

"It's not that." Belle wrinkled her nose in frustration. I couldn't exactly see why she was the one getting annoyed when it was my face on the bloody magazine cover. "It's the circumstances. He's been photographed at clubs with plenty of women."

I raised an eyebrow. "You already mentioned the throng."

She continued, ignoring my color commentary. "He's only been seen in public places. No one's caught him doing anything or anyone."

I groaned, starting to feel frustrated myself. "You said he'd shagged half of London."

"That's what I've heard—"

"That's what you've read," I corrected.

"Look at him!" She thrust a paper at me to make her point. "Tell me you don't want to get your knee-pads out for that!"

Even with the slight blur from a photo clearly snapped on a camera phone, he was stunning. But then I could fill in the details lost in the fuzzy picture—the curve of his jaw, the twist of his mouth, the perfect darkness of his ink-black hair. Forget the knee-pads, I'd kneel on hard stone.

"He has a total god complex," I told her, ignoring that my

body agreed with Belle. "What that photo doesn't tell you is that he just grabbed me and kissed me."

Belle collapsed against the counter, folding her arms over her head. "I...can't...take...the...hotness."

"Only you would find that hot," I shot back, but I was glad she couldn't read my mind.

"Only you could kiss Prince Alexander and not know it," Belle said with a laugh. The jealousy had dissipated from her voice entirely now. This had just become another of my silly mistakes, but that didn't mean she was going to let it go. Instead, she started in on a series of questions, barraging me with each new one so quickly that I could hardly keep up with her, especially with the dizziness permeating my head over the revelation.

Until one question filtered through the haze. "Was he an amazing kisser?"

"Yes," I said without hesitation, recalling his strong and powerful arms around me. "He was in total control, which makes sense now."

"More!" Belle cried mock-orgasmically.

"Down girl," I said, but I couldn't help myself. The kiss had been my delicious secret before, but now...it was more. It was confusing and exhilarating and terrifying—hot as hell, of course —but I needed Belle to help me filter through my feelings.

"All I could think when he kissed me was that I wanted him on top of me," I continued.

"Oh my god," Belle moaned. "Are you going to see him again?"

A thrill shivered through me at the thought, but I pushed it away. "I doubt it! He only kissed me to avoid an ex-girlfriend."

Belle's mouth twisted into a smirk and she waved the front page at me. "He looks like he's enjoying it, and I know you enjoyed it."

I stuck my tongue out and hopped off the stool. Belle's one-track mind wasn't helping me understand my feelings at all. She had my back, but I wasn't sure she could keep from pushing me on him if she ever got the chance.

Thankfully, Belle took my cue and began unpacking dishes to the cupboards.

"Your mobile is ringing," Belle called from the hallway as she carried a mislabeled box to her room.

I froze when I saw the caller ID, immediately silencing the phone. Realization crept through me, washing away the arousal I'd felt as I relived the kiss for Belle and replaced it with the grim awareness that more than reporters knew about this now. By tomorrow everyone I'd ever met would know. The butterflies in my stomach evolved into a swarm of angry bees. I didn't like attention. It wasn't good for me. It wasn't...healthy. Would they all start calling me? Texting me? After considering that I was about to be deluged by friends and family, I set my phone to vibrate.

Belle peeked into the kitchen. "Who was it?"

"My mom," I answered with a groan.

"Oh Christ, she's probably planning the wedding."

"You're right. I should call her back and set things straight." But I couldn't convince myself to do it. Instead, I knocked my head against the wall a few times.

"Whatever you do, don't bludgeon yourself to death. Most girls would kill to snog Alexander, not kill themselves for getting to."

I stopped and stared at her. Most girls would, but was I most girls? Alexander must have thought so. Just another girl to use and throw away. Of course, kissing a girl to piss off your ex made sense to a guy like that, but now I was the one dealing with the fallout! He'd thrown my world majorly off-course for the last week, leaving me hot and bothered and curious, and now I had to clean up the mess.

And how the hell had they tracked me down anyway? It sounded like Alexander left a trail of women in his wake. Why had they focused on me?

"You know what I still can't figure out? How the reporters discovered who I was. Consider the paparazzi karmic retribution for the privilege," I retorted.

"That's some SIS shit for sure," Belle agreed. "Someone must have seen you and recognized you. Probably whoever took that photo."

"If I know them, they better hope I never figure out who they are," I said. Dropping my silenced phone back onto the counter, I grabbed a box. My mother and everyone else could wait until I'd gathered my thoughts on this matter a little bit more.

"Back to work?" Belle asked.

I nodded. Maybe continuing to sort out my new life in London would help me sort out my conflicted feelings about what had happened. It was a long shot.

Belle caught me around the shoulders and squeezed. "It'll blow over."

I smiled gratefully. That was exactly what I needed to hear.

It soon became clear that Belle's mission had shifted from getting the flat set up to distracting me. By the time we were arguing over what to put on the bookshelves—I stubbornly believing it should be books—we'd all but forgotten the maelstrom waiting for us outside until we realized there was nothing but half a bottle of wine in the fridge.

"I'll grab some curry from the corner," Belle said, grabbing her pocketbook.

"You shouldn't have to go," I said, feeling badly. "Maybe we could order up?"

"I might starve before then." Belle clutched her stomach for emphasis, but I could see the real reason she didn't want to wait any longer hiding behind her eyes. "I'll think of a proper way for you to repay me later and I promise it will be cruel and embarrassing."

"It can't be more humiliating than having my photo all over the Daily Star," I pointed out.

"I'll think of something." She winked and disappeared through the door.

Belle's laptop was on the counter and I grabbed it, curiosity winning out over common sense. One Google search later and I had dozens of celebrity blogs and gossip magazines to wade through. I checked out some of the Prince's recent photos and found there had been no mistake. The unbelievably sexy man I'd stumbled upon at my graduation was exactly who the papers claimed that he was, and Belle was right. He'd been photographed with too many beautiful women to count. Every recent photo of him came complete with a leggy blond or buxom redhead or even identical twins. I doubted he'd been giving them tours of London.

I slammed the laptop closed, annoyed that I'd even looked, but turning, the mass of papers on the counter confronted me. I reached to crumple them up and toss them in the garbage, but found myself interrupted by a buzz on the flat's intercom.

"Forgot her keys again," I muttered as I hit the call button. Apparently things in London wouldn't be too different than they were at university.

"Miss Bishop?"

Or maybe not. The man's tone was clipped and formal.

"I have no comment," I said, anticipating what the man wanted. How long could this possibly go on before people lost interest? A week? Maybe two? Could I hide out in my flat that long? I had to start work in a week, but surely that wouldn't be interesting to a bunch of environmental lobbyists.

"I'm not here from the press," the man at the other end responded. "I'm here to collect you."

"Collect me?" I repeated in surprise. My thoughts flashed to my mother who was probably foaming at the mouth by this point. I checked my phone, discovering ten missed calls from her.

"Prince Alexander of Cambridge wishes to speak with you."

My mouth fell open and I was eternally grateful I was alone in that moment. "I'm not sure that's a very smart idea. In case you haven't noticed, there's a small swarm of reporters down there waiting to devour me alive."

"I am Prince Alexander's personal guard. That's why His Highness has entrusted me with bringing you safely to meet with him," he said. "I can assure you that no one will even know that you left this building.

"Give me a moment," I said. Whirling around the room, I tried to think of a reason not to go, which turned out to be pretty easy given that I was being stalked by a couple dozen reporters, I was hungry, and the prince hadn't even bothered to share his name with me when he'd casually ruined my foreseeable future with his kiss.

But the memory of Alexander's lips hot on mine and his hands on my waist holding me in a firm, confident embrace made my knees buckle and I found myself reaching for a pencil to scrawl a note to Belle. I told myself I was being thoughtful. I told myself I deserved an apology after getting dragged into this drama. I told myself a lot of things as I met Alexander's personal guard near the lift, but I refused to consider whether I was making a mistake.

I told myself I wasn't.

CHAPTER FOUR

Norris, the Prince's personal guard, fell squarely into the strong and silent type, but as he promised, he managed to sneak me out of my building and past the horde of reporters hoping to catch a glimpse of the latest royal scandal. Namely me.

Perhaps his unassuming appearance was part of his job, but I'd expected the Prince's personal guard to be a trifle more tough. Norris looked average with a stocky build and a nice, but not expensive, suit. His salt-and-pepper hair was smoothed past ears that stuck out a bit too far. I wouldn't have thought of him as intimidating. Then again, considering how easily he'd bypassed the paparazzi, his ordinary appearance might have been a blessing. But the one thing I really wasn't expecting was to be taken somewhere public to meet Alexander. Norris had promised me a private meeting, so I barely swallowed down my surprise when he pulled past London's hottest nightclub, Brimstone, to the rear alley, which came just short of the last of the winding line of people hoping to be let in to the exclusive club.

"This is where I'm going to avoid being seen with Alexander. I mean Prince Alexander," I stammered, cursing silently.

My nerves had finally kicked in, and I couldn't hold back my babbling. "Or should I call him His Royal Highness?"

Norris's eyes darted around us as he escorted me to the back door, but he spared me a glance of pity. "I wouldn't be nervous. His Highness is merely a man, after all."

I might have bought that if he hadn't referred to him as *His Highness*.

At the door, I realized I hadn't even grabbed my purse. I'd only shoved my keys and phone in my pocket, which meant I didn't have ID, and to top it off, I was wearing jeans and a t-shirt to the hottest nightclub in town where I was meeting the Prince of England. What a cock-up, as Belle would say.

The American in me had a few more choice descriptors for the situation.

The muscle-suit at the door barely spared a glance at me. He simply nodded to Norris and opened the door to us, but as we passed, I saw the guy's mouth twitch. Further proof that I looked ridiculous. I tugged at my t-shirt and threw my shoulders back in attempt to look poised. I hoped that it worked for those on the outside, because it did little to enlarge my self-esteem. At least I had showered today and my ponytail was respectable. It was the only facts I had to comfort me as we stepped into the back room of Brimstone.

The faint pulse of the club pumped through the walls, mimicking the nervous beat of my heart. Even behind the scenes, there had been attention to detail. Torchieres breathing red light meant to look like flames lined walls papered in a black and metallic linen pattern. The crimson light caught on the strands of silver, making the walls sparkle and throb with life, and as the dulled music seeped further into my bloodstream, raising goose bumps along my arms, my anxiety shifted to inexplicable excitement. Norris led the way, passing a hall full of people waiting for their chance at the loo.

"Hey mates," a man called to us from line. "There more toilets back there?"

Norris ignored him and I shot the guy an apologetic smile, slightly embarrassed by my guide's snub, only to be met with a mixture of dirty looks and confused glares. Their expressions said it all: who is this girl and why is she so important? Two questions I was asking myself at the moment as well.

Two more bouncers waited at the end of the hallway, blocking a set of stairs, but once again they parted for us without so much as a word. The steps led to a skywalk over the club—the kind reserved for half-clad dancers, but it was vacant tonight. Below us, a mass of sweaty bodies fought in rhythm to the music, a turbulent mix of dance and electronica being spun by a deejay in the corner. The interior of Brimstone was cast in the same crimson light as the back hall, and flaming murals licked across the walls. I wasn't the type to go out to clubs. I felt too self-conscious. But right now I wished I were part of the chaotic hive of activity below. It seemed easier than facing Alexander.

"Miss Bishop." Norris stopped in front of a large mirrored window and bowed to me. As he stepped away, the mirror slid open to reveal a hidden room.

I entered alone, feeling instantly out of place in the lush setting. There was a privately stocked bar but no one tending it, a leather couch and chair clustered around a low coffee table inlaid with gold leaf, red velvet draped over the walls and my fingers reached out instinctively to run my fingers over the silky fabric. But the sexiest thing of all stood with his back to me, peering out the floor-to-ceiling windows on the other side of the room. As the door shut behind me, he turned to face me. A slow smile spread across his face, and I swallowed, knowing he was taking in my very casual appearance. Tilting my chin up, I walked toward him, hoping that I could put on the cool, confident attitude that I needed to get me through this meeting. But the closer I got to him, the more my legs felt like jelly.

He was dressed for this atmosphere in a perfectly tailored pair of black trousers and a slate-grey button down. Even in the dim light, his blue eyes sparked mischievously at me. His jawline still sported the same perfect five o'clock shadow that screamed sex. How did he manage to keep it so perfectly even? I couldn't help but imagine how it would feel against my bare flesh, between my thighs. My body throbbed at the thought and I nearly tripped on my feet. He was steps away and his arms shot out to steady me, but I righted myself on my own.

Enough of that or you'll make an ass of yourself. Of course, considering how I was dressed, it was a little late for that.

I'd read enough about the prince's exploits on Belle's computer this afternoon to know I was in real danger of winding up on that couch with my panties off. And if I was being honest with myself, part of me was hoping that's where we would end up. But the sensible part of me—the part that still controlled a majority of my brain—knew that was a terrible idea.

"I'm fine," I said to him, side-stepping his second attempt at assistance. I paused for a moment. "Should I curtsy or something?"

"Please don't," he said, not bothering to hide his amusement.

"I wouldn't want to offend you, Your Highness," I explained.

"Can I get you something to drink?" he asked, ignoring my taunt. The invitation was coated in sex, smooth as honey and dripping with temptation, and my conscious mind tried to find the most polite way to say no.

"Yes," I said instead. *Oh, fuck it all.*

"What is your poison, Miss Bishop?"

You, I thought instantly. Okay, perhaps getting out of here with my dignity was going to be harder than I imagined. "I just graduated university, so I'm not picky."

"Used to the old plonk then?" he asked, flashing me those perfect teeth. "Sadly, Brimstone tends toward—"

"Real booze?" I offered.

"Exactly."

"Then I'll take what you give me."

Something dark flashed across his light eyes and he sucked in a breath that hissed past his perfect lips. The sound sent a shiver racing down my spine. The air between us sparked with the intensity of his gaze until he finally turned away and strode toward the bar.

I took the opportunity to check out the scene below as he poured the drinks, needing to distract myself from the dangerous pull Alexander had on me. It was quiet in here, but if I closed my eyes, I could make out the faintest *boom boom boom* of the club's music. It was marvelous to think we could be up here, secluded and enjoying a private drink, while it looked like a can of live sardines down there.

"Can they see us?" I asked as he handed me a crystal tumbler.

He shook his head. "It's like those mirrors on police procedurals. To them, it reflects back the club."

I took a long sip of my drink as I took in this information. For all intents and purposes, I was alone with one of the world's sexiest men—an accolade that was actually awarded to him by *People* magazine, according to my research earlier today. I had to agree with their assessment.

"You must come here often," I said. He had to if they afforded him private rooms and exclusive access.

"I've been told to go to hell a number of times," he said. "I decided to take the advice."

"Ahhh," I said, laughing despite the nerves that left me feeling jittery in his presence. "Brimstone."

"My natural habitat."

"I doubt that." The words slipped carelessly from my mouth. How was it possible for him to put me at ease and make me so nervous at the same time?

"I owe you an apology," he said, moving to stand so close to me that his shoulder brushed against mine. Our skin didn't even touch, both our arms still covered, but a thrill trembled down my arm.

"No harm done," I said, tacking on an awkward, "Your Highness."

He laughed at this. "Alexander please. Norris informed me that no less than *two dozen* members of the press are camped in front of your flat."

"Alexander," I said, testing out the name. It felt strange to directly address the man that would one day be the King of England by his proper name. "Once they see how boring my life is they'll go away."

"They'll make your life hell until then." His voice was low, but it seethed with hatred. It was no secret that he had good reason to hate the press. They'd been vicious after he'd been involved in the fatal accident that killed his younger sister.

"Is that why you went to Iraq?" I asked and then immediately wished I hadn't.

"Back to our game? I suppose I advised you to save a few," he said humorlessly.

My heart thrilled at the reference to the cat-and-mouse game of twenty questions he'd engaged me in during our first meeting, but his lack of amusement at my presumptuous question told me he didn't really want to answer me.

Alexander's smile was tight-lipped as he turned away from me.

"Yes," he finally answered in a distant voice. "Yes, it was."

"I'm sorry. That's none of my business. It's only..." My words trailed away as I realized it didn't really matter what I thought. Why couldn't I shut up? Because he made me nervous and it wasn't awkward date jitters. It was as if every nerve in my body was firing at the same time, warning me I was in danger, like feeling the caress of heat before accidentally touching a flame, except every piece of me wanted to embrace the fire.

"Only?" he prompted, watching me with cautious, if curious, eyes.

"I wish you hadn't gone," I whispered. I had no clue why I said it. I hadn't even thought of Alexander's infamous, highly-debated exile from home before today, but I knew that I meant it with every fiber of my being.

He didn't respond, instead he turned his attention to the window overlooking the club and downed the last of his drink quickly.

"I can handle it. It's very kind of you to be concerned," I added. Taking a deep breath, I set my glass down and looked toward the door. He had apologized. I had reassured him. Our business was done.

"Clara."

I stopped, waiting for him to continue, and I knew then that I wanted to hear my name on his lips again. I wanted him to whisper it. I wanted him to command it. I wanted him to cry it out.

"Yes," I said, swallowing hard on this realization.

"As much as it pains me to say this—and believe me, it pains me—for once, those leaches did me a favor. I tried to find you at the party, but no one knew who you were."

No surprise there. I might have graduated at the top of my class, but I'd done so by keeping my nose to the grindstone. My circle of friends was small, and other than Belle, most of them weren't rich or titled. But someone there had known who I was and told the press. Whoever it was hadn't been doing me a favor, which must have accounted for why he or she hadn't told Alexander.

"I've thought about you a lot," he continued.

His confession took my breath away, and I stared at him, dumbstruck.

"Since last weekend?" I blurted out when I could finally speak. He'd made it sound like an eternity had passed instead of a few days. But hadn't I been thinking about him in the shower this morning and trying very hard not to think about him this afternoon?

"Is that so hard to believe?" He moved closer until our bodies were a mere breath apart, and I was glued to the spot. It took everything I had in me not to melt into him.

Alexander circled around me, and I felt like prey under his ferocious gaze. He could protect me—or tear me limb from limb —and from the faint smile playing on his lips, I wasn't sure he'd decided which he was more likely to do. He stopped behind me, leaning close, his lips brushing against my ear. "If you knew what was good for you, you would run."

My mouth went dry even as my panties grew wet. "Am I in danger?"

"People around me tend to get hurt," he whispered, his breath hot on my neck.

My thoughts flashed to the dozens of women he'd picked up since he'd returned home. I couldn't recall seeing any of them photographed with him more than once. Had he charmed them into his bed only to discard them by morning? Something about his words struck a warning chord in me though.

"Will you hurt me?" The words felt like a dare rather than a question.

"You've been reading the tabloids," he said. "Don't believe

everything you read, Clara. I have never done anything to a woman that she hasn't asked for...*begged* for."

I spun around to face him. I wasn't certain if I was angry with him for being so cocky—or if I was mad at myself for being so turned on. But my questions died on my lips as I found myself fighting hard against the dizzying effect he had on me. It was unfair that his power was coupled with such a godlike face.

I took a deep breath, refusing to look away from him. "Do you like that? Do you like women to beg?"

He loosed a low, gruff laugh that made my core clench. "I enjoy making women ask for more. I enjoy making them whimper and cry out and call my name, and I'd very much enjoy making you beg."

"I'm not really the begging type," I said, even though my words were as weak as my resolve was becoming.

"You could be," Alexander said. "I can see it in your eyes: the desire to be commanded and taken. You'll enjoy it when I fuck you."

Yes, please.

Alexander trailed a finger down to my collarbone, and my body tightened in anticipation, recalling my dream. Then his fingers curled around my neck, his touch light but assertive. He was in control, and when he drew me closer, I molded into him instinctively. I could feel his cock pressed against my belly, and my body responded with a twinge that tingled through my nerves until my sex felt swollen and ready. I waited for him to make a move, no longer a slave to conscience or rational thought. Instead, a hundred scenarios played out in my mind. Over the table. On the couch. Against the glass window. He could have me any way he would take me.

But instead he withdrew from me. "You should go."

His sudden rejection rocked through me, nearly knocking

me off my feet. I swayed, momentarily disoriented by the abrupt shift in his demeanor. "I probably should."

A man like this—one that confused me and mesmerized me, thrilled me and terrified me—was no good for me. I forced myself to consider that even though I was crushed, Alexander was bad news. I'd known that all along, so why was I here now?

Alexander turned from me, hiding his blue eyes and the deep secrets reflecting beneath their smoldering surface. "You asked if I would hurt you, Clara. I can't lie and say that I won't. I want nothing more than to strip you bare and pin you to that wall. Hold you there until you beg for my cock, and when I finally give it to you, you'll beg me never to stop."

Again he moved closer and I felt his heat radiating from him. It seeped into me, making my blood broil. The passion coursed through my veins, heating my flesh and slowly engulfing my senses until there was only him.

He ran a hand through his hair and shook his head. "But if I do that, it will only ruin you."

"This isn't an old novel," I snapped, hoping he didn't catch the break in my voice. "I'm not a hapless virgin."

His hand flew out and caught my arm, pulling me against him roughly. "I've thought about your lips all day. I've pictured you on your knees with that pretty little mouth wrapped around my cock sucking me off. If I had you now, I would want more. Once wouldn't be enough. But more is something a man like me can never have."

"Because I'm not royalty?" I asked, feeling daft for even suggesting something so antiquated. I knew this wasn't a game. He wanted me—almost as much as I wanted him. A man like Alexander could have anything he desired, so why push me away now?

"I think they'd be more pissed that you're American, but really no one cares about that," he said with a dark smile. It faded from his lips, but the darkness remained in his features. "Because nothing beautiful can survive around me. Do you understand that? They'll destroy you, and if they don't, eventually I will."

His assumption that I couldn't handle him had me furious at a level I found hard to express. Apparently, he wasn't only arrogant when it came to his conquests, he was also full of himself when it came to all women.

"Maybe I can take care of myself." I twisted away from him, but his grip remained firm.

"Maybe you can," he admitted. "But don't tempt me into risking it. I can't be held responsible."

He dropped his hold of me then and I saw the dare in his crystal blue eyes. He wanted me to run. He expected me to run. Instead my hand shot out, grabbing his shirt and pulling him down until our lips met. A growl vibrated through his body as our tongues met, and I shivered both at the sound and at the primal urgency of his touch. His hands slid down, cupping my ass and lifting me off the ground as the kiss deepened, his tongue sweeping across my teeth before it thrust inside my mouth, drawing out mine. He sucked it slowly until my legs wrapped more tightly around his hips, my body desperately searching for relief from the mounting pressure in my core. Despite our clothing, I circled against his hard cock, rocking against it when I found the right spot. Somewhere my sensible side, no longer able to stay silent, began admonishing me, her tone shocked and her eyes wide.

Shut up, I commanded her.

Still holding me up, Alexander's hand drifted up and caught my ponytail, tugging it back so that my lips broke from his.

"This is your last chance," he warned. His eyes burned into me, but once again I felt frozen—totally under his control.

And it was then that I realized control was the one thing I could never, ever give him.

"No," I whispered.

Disappointment flashed through his still blazing eyes, but he released me gently to my feet. The ground was shaky beneath me, but when I took a step back, it was my legs that trembled.

"You're a smart girl." He hesitated, searching my face for a reason I couldn't give him. Then he dropped his lips to brush across my forehead. "Norris will see you home safely, and I'll have my people work on getting rid of those reporters."

The fire that had roared between us moments ago had cooled into business, and I wished I were still kissing him.

"Thank you." The words were thick on my tongue, anticipating the words I knew would follow. Words, that despite my show of resolve, I didn't want to hear.

"Goodbye, Clara Bishop." Alexander's eyes lingered over me and I sensed he was holding back, as though he wanted to say more.

I took a deep breath and backed my way toward the door—and the safety of the club outside. "Goodbye."

But when I stepped out of the room, the relief I expected to flood through me didn't come. Instead I felt something else entirely—an emotion I couldn't quite place. It ached and plucked at me, familiar and foreign at the same time. Norris met me at the foot of the stairs before I realized what was swirling through me, leaving my body numb and my center hollow.

It was regret.

CHAPTER FIVE

Tears blurred my eyes as Norris took my elbow, guiding me back toward the exit we'd entered through. I felt ridiculous for crying, but it had been a trying day: hiding in my flat, sneaking out to meet up with Alexander, avoiding my mother's calls and my friends' text messages. I could have been hit by a car crossing the street and received less attention. And to top it off, Alexander had rejected me. Or I had rejected him. I wasn't really sure. It felt like such a mess now that I could only be certain of one thing—I was done with it all.

Pulling free of Norris's gentle hand, I darted away from him, slowing to a stride as I passed the line of people waiting for the loo. There was no way I was going to spend this week—or even this night —hiding. Alexander said he would fix things, but I wasn't going to wait around for that to happen. I didn't think I was imagining eyes swiveling to follow me. Then a few girls snapped my photo on their mobile, and I knew I wasn't being paranoid. I had been recognized.

But that was the point.

I needed this to end now. Even if Alexander called off the reporters, there'd be suspicions that something was going on between the two of us. Suspicion had to be laid to rest. I was about to start a job in this city. I couldn't very well have photographers following me everywhere I went.

The floor of Brimstone was packed so tightly that I barely managed to push through the sweaty crowd, although I was able to entirely lose Norris in the process. As it was, I got groped by guys too pissed to know better. At least I hoped that was their excuse. But now that I was out on the dance floor, it felt like I was actually in hell and stuck in a giant swarm of the damned. It was certainly hot enough down here, and I was miserable too. My eyes flashed past the flaming murals on the wall and the dancers surrounding me to the giant mirror that lined the loft above the dance area. Was Alexander watching me? Did he even care?

The thought was enough to spur me forward until I forced my way out of the crowd. As a bouncer opened the door for me to exit, I realized that it didn't really matter if Alexander was watching. The security guard cast a sideways glance at my strange attire, no doubt wondering who had let me in dressed like this.

"Wash day," I called over the din. His mouth split into a grin that dropped from his face a moment later when the first flash bulb went off. Confusion replaced amusement as the first burst was followed by a dozen more.

I didn't have much of a plan for how to deal with this. My entire experience with the paparazzi until this morning had consisted of photographs in the tabloids. A celebrity would hold a hand over her face and walk quickly away, but I wanted their attention. I needed to prove that I wasn't worth their time. Although now that I was actually in the situation, I wasn't sure how to make that happen.

"Miss Bishop! Smile, love!"

"*Miss Bishop, how long have you been involved with the Prince?*"

"*Miss Bishop, is it true that the King has condemned your relationship?*"

"*Were you secretly married in Oxford?*"

It was like that childhood game *telephone*. From one silly picture they'd managed to spin an entire love affair. The truth had been entirely distorted in favor of headlines. Something twanged in my chest as I thought of how Alexander had to deal with this every day. No wonder he'd been so hot and cold. It was a coping mechanism to help him survive. And now these leeches had their hooks in me, waiting for the next juicy moment they could exploit in the name of news.

Stopping in front of the crowd and pushing my shoulders back in an effort to look serious, which was quite difficult considering my ensemble, I addressed the crowd.

"I'm sorry to inform you all that I have no relationship with Prince Alexander. Someone has made a dreadful mistake. I do not know the Prince. I am not in love with him. And I highly doubt the King gives two figs about me." The words rushed out of me, even as I tried to stay calm and collected. I was running on adrenaline now, which meant I was lucky that I was even coherent right at the moment.

I didn't expect them to stop taking photos or run away or even apologize, but I certainly didn't expect the reporters to cluster closer to me after I'd explained that I was a dead end. They didn't seem willing to believe that. A few jostled against me, screaming questions in my ear. I was nearly blinded by the flash of their cameras. They all spoke so quickly that I wouldn't have been able to answer one of them if I wanted to. I wished I'd let Norris take me home as the crowd pressed closer and closer. Club-goers had joined the chaos. A few men attempted to fight the reporters in the name of chivalry, which would have been laughable any other night. And a few others were simply trying to take photos with their mobiles. They probably didn't even know who I was. It only mattered that there was news of some sort. No doubt the whole scene would be spread all over Facebook by the morning.

I fought against the crowd, pushing my way past one group, only to have another wave surge on top of me. Bodies pressed in on every side of me, drowning me, until I couldn't breathe. The air squeezed from my chest and I gasped, trying to inhale but choking as the mass pushing against me prevented me from catching my breath. Panic trembled down my arms and legs, rolling through me in tiny quivers as my eyes darted around, looking for a means of escape. I had to get away. I had to breathe. I had to protect myself. But with each passing second, I grew more terrified, more desperate, until I tripped over someone's legs.

The crowd parted only far enough for me to stumble to my hands and knees before the frenzy set in once more. Dozens of flashes popped and sparked around me. My arms wrapped around my head reflexively, trying to block out the gawkers and their shouts.

"Enough!" The command bellowed so loudly over the crowd that even I lifted my eyes to see who had called out.

Alexander stood a few paces away, his face contorted with barely controlled rage. He'd pushed his sleeves up to his elbows, making him look like a man eager to get down to business. Fury blazed in his eyes as his gaze traveled from person to person as though he was silently daring any of them to defy his order. He took a few steps forward, and as he came closer, the anger radiated from him like a heat wave. The crowd around me backed away, unable to tear their eyes from him. It might have been because he was the Prince of England, but I knew there was something more primal to this scene. Even I responded to it, my heartbeat racing faster instead of calming until he dropped down and pushed my hands from over my head.

"Are you okay, Clara?" he asked quietly.

I managed a nod. Behind me, a few of the girls with cameras had started filming again.

Alexander took my hand and helped me to my feet, but as soon I was standing up again, the questions began.

"Alexander, is this your girlfriend?"

"Alexander, is it true that your father doesn't approve of your relationship with a commoner?"

I winced at that one. True, I wasn't royalty, but it felt a bit hypocritical to call me out as a commoner. It was meant to be an insult, I could feel it as I could feel the daggers being cast at me from many of the women nearby. I had to get out of here. My throat constricted even though no one was shoving against me now. I forced myself to breathe, but the result was the quick, shallow pants of another panic attack. Alexander fell into step beside me. Ignoring the reporters, he glanced down at me, concern shining through his fiery eyes. He shifted closer, placing his hand on the small of my back. It lingered there, scorching through the thin fabric of my t-shirt, as he guided me past the reporters and onlookers. His touch steadied my nerves, and warmth spread through my body from the spot where his hand rested possessively, settling in my chest.

Without a word, he calmed me.

Norris overtook us, rushing to the car to open the door, even as the crowd followed us. Alexander's hand dropped away as soon as I bent to enter the backseat, but to my surprise, he ducked inside himself. The door slammed shut behind us, and Norris slid into the driver's seat moments later. It felt like an eternity had passed since Alexander had lifted me to my feet in front of Brimstone. Time had slowed under his protection, but in the silent car, it sped back up as cameras clicked outside the tinted windows. My eyes found the ground, and I became heavily invested in a snag on the mat at my feet until a confident arm slung over my shoulder and pulled me close, encouraging me to bury my face in his shoulder. I inhaled the indescribable scent of him: cloves and soap and bourbon. It sank into me until the world around us faded away and I relaxed in his embrace.

Without a word, he claimed me.

WE RODE SILENTLY THROUGH THE CROWDS BACK TO MY flat as I tried to keep it together. I wouldn't cry in front of Alexander. I wouldn't show him my weaknesses now that I'd glimpsed his brutal strength, because I didn't want him to see me as vulnerable. Peering up at him, I felt his power rolling over me. He was powerful and commanding—he was unlike any man I'd ever met and I didn't want him to see how much that scared —and excited—me.

"Clara." My name rolled off his lips with ease and I savored how it sounded. "Are you okay?"

I nodded, a lump stuck in my throat. Did he sense the shift in our connection? The thread that had drawn me to him had been invisible—inexplicable—when we'd met. I'd felt it when I saw him again in Brimstone. But now that tenuous, elusive connection was gone, replaced by a firm, unyielding bond of trust. He had stood by me. I had to give him credit for that even though he'd gotten me into this mess in the first place. Was he thinking the same thing? Did he feel it, too?

"I'm sorry you had to go through that. I should have known better than to kiss you." The arm he had casually draped around my shoulder withdrew and he ran a hand through his messy black hair.

I was torn between wanting it to be my hand tangling in his

hair and disappointment. I had misread everything. I imagined the link between us. And did he mean the first time he kissed me or when we had kissed at Brimstone? Somehow, despite the terror I'd already experienced, I didn't regret either kiss. In fact, more than ever, I wanted more. I wanted his lips on mine, and his body pressed so hard against me that I could feel his arousal jabbing into the soft flesh of my belly.

But that was never going to happen. I couldn't let it. I couldn't let whatever was happening between us go on. I straightened up and took a deep breath, twisting to meet his eyes. "I'm fine," I lied. "Things got out of hand. I'm afraid you're more experienced with this sort of thing than I am."

"Unfortunately, you're right." He paused, watching me so intensely that I squirmed in my seat. "I know I should be sorry that I kissed you, but I'm not. In fact, I'd like to do it again."

My doubt washed from me when he spoke, and I found myself powerless against his suggestions.

"I'm not stopping you," I said in a soft voice, surprising even myself.

Alexander sucked in a breath and tore his gaze from mine to look out the window. "You said *no*."

I had said no, and I could no longer remember why. "I didn't mean it."

"What mixed signals you give me, Miss Bishop. That's a risqué thing to do with a man like me."

"And what kind of man is that?" I asked even though I already knew the answer—a dangerous man. A dangerous but beautiful man. Not just because of who he was or the life he lived. I'd seen glimpses of what he hid beneath the mask of control he wore—glimpses of something wild and untamed.

"A man who takes what he wants," he answered ominously. He paused, regarding me as if to ascertain if he'd scared me.

But what I felt was far from fear. I pressed my legs together as the heat between them increased, a tiny pulse beginning to tick anxiously. Even his words were sexy, and I wanted more. "You haven't taken *me*."

"We met under unusual circumstances," he pointed out, dropping a hand to rest on my knee. The contact sent a shudder of desire up my thigh, ratcheting up the throb in my clit.

"You weren't looking to pick anyone up?" I asked, doing my best to ignore his touch and completely failing. "Not your usual scene?"

His mouth twitched into a bemused smile. "I rarely find such exciting company at the Oxford and Cambridge Club."

"Why were you there?" I asked, my rational side getting the better of my flirtatious one.

"My friend Jonathan received his degree. He conned me into coming," he said.

"I have a hard time imagining you being conned by anyone."

"Then you must not know Jonathan."

"Wait," I said, a realization dawning on me, "do you mean Jonathan Thompson?"

"The one and the only. Do you know him...well?" The question was strained, as though he dreaded the answer.

"By reputation only," I assured him. Jonathan had also taken a degree in social studies, but we'd had little contact outside of a few shared courses. I only knew more about him because Belle had slept with him in our second year. She wasn't the type to kiss and tell, but Jonathan had turned out to be a major asshole. I'd steered clear of him socially after she'd warned me about him. Not that I'd had much of a social life at university. Without the old family connections, my focus had been on my studies. I couldn't count on landing a respectable position any other way, even with my parents' money. People like Jonathan didn't have to concern themselves with such things.

"Jonathan claims he bedded every girl in his class," Alexander said. "I'm glad to see you had higher standards."

"Says his good friend," I added.

"Some people you should keep close," he advised, darkness flickering through his eyes as he spoke, reminding me how much I wanted to unravel his mystery.

I scanned the streets outside the car in effort to calm my rapid pulse. Everything about Alexander, from the words he spoke to the company he kept, screamed at me to run. But I'd been running and hiding most of my adult life, so I couldn't bring myself to turn away from Alexander now. He drew me to him with an energy that was as magnetic as his smile.

You owe him your gratitude and nothing more, my rational side lectured me. She was right and I knew I should listen, but I also knew I didn't want to.

"Where are we going?" I asked when we passed the entrance to my building.

"There are reporters following us. Norris will lose them before I take you home." His hand slid further up my leg, gripping my thigh possessively as he spoke.

I closed my eyes, pushing away all the analysis and doubts clouding my thoughts, and reveled in the warmth of his touch and those words. I wanted him to take me. Take me home. Or take me here. A horrified voice began whispering in my head.

Mistake. You are making a mistake. You aren't strong enough for this. You can't attract a man like him.

I shushed her and concentrated on the sensations thrilling through my body, aware that he had edged closer to me and that our bodies were now pressed together.

"Clara," he said in a low voice.

"Hmm," I replied, lost to the moment.

"I need you to know that no matter what happens next—if

you get out of this car and never speak to me again—I will see to your protection," he promised.

I closed my eyes and took a deep breath. "Why?"

"Because you are the only person who wished I'd never left," he said in an even voice.

But I saw through his careful control and his measured words, past the wild, untamed side of him I'd glimpsed earlier, to the broken boy that had never healed. And I knew then that the next words I said would be the first time he had heard those words spoken, too. "I'm glad you came back."

"I want you." His words were final. A command, not a question. It was in his voice. He wanted me, and he would have me. I could find no strength to fight it because I wanted him more than I'd ever wanted anything in my life. The thought left me dizzy. His hand slipped up until it was nestled against my sex and a soft moan escaped my lips. "But not tonight."

My eyelids flew open as I stared at him accusingly. "Is that what you do? Toy with girls until they drop to their knees for you?"

He could take me now and I wouldn't object. He knew that, and I could see that knowledge reflecting from his eyes. So why the games? "Do you need me to beg for it?" I asked.

His fingers rubbed against my jeans, teasing the bundle of nerves that was already throbbing at his mere presence. "Need? No. Want?" He hesitated. "I want to hear you beg for me. Beg for my cock. Beg for me to fuck you, and you will, poppet. But. Not. Tonight."

"Why?" I wasn't proud of how desperate the question sounded, but a girl can't be held accountable when her clit is pounding like a war drum.

"Because your entire building will be surrounded by the morning, and I'm not interested in sex, Clara. I want to explore you. I want to rip those clothes off of you and take you to bed. I'm going to fuck you until it hurts, and I want to hear you beg me to do it." He paused to let this sink in, giving me enough time to visualize exactly what he was proposing. "And I need more than a few hours for that."

I had stopped breathing, hanging off each of his promises until I thought I would melt into the seat. I didn't think I could wait that long, and part of me longed for him to take me now, even with Norris only a few meters away. But I wanted to know a night like the one he promised more.

"I get what I want," he reminded me, and I knew the matter was settled.

"When?" It was the only thing I could think to ask with his gaze scorching through me.

"Tomorrow."

"And the reporters?" I managed to ask.

"I'll deal with them." Alexander settled into his seat, a pleased smile sweeping across his perfect face. He knew he had me. He had been victorious, although there was never any doubt that he would be. How could I have resisted him? Resisted his godlike face or his chiseled body or the unshakeable pull that drew me to him? "Norris will pick you up at eleven."

"Then I'll see you tomorrow night," I said as the car came to a stop. I hoped my excitement wasn't as obvious as I felt it was.

"Oh, no. Eleven in the morning." Alexander leaned over and caught my face in his hands. "I told you I need time, poppet."

His lips whispered across my mine and I opened my mouth in welcome, but he pulled away, his azure eyes flashing. "Until then."

CHAPTER SIX

The living room lamp flicked on as soon as I turned the lock in the front door. I whirled around, my eyes still adjusting to the dark, to discover Belle sitting cross-legged on the couch, glaring at me. Any other night I would have laughed at her for being a mother hen, but tonight it felt more like I'd just been caught by the prison warden.

"How long have you been sitting in the dark?" I asked her.

"Since I got home and decided to wait for you." She pointed to a bag still crammed full of take-out boxes. Guilt crept over me as I realized I'd been gone nearly an hour and a half.

"I'm sorry," I began, but I had no idea what else to say. So much had happened since she went to grab dinner, and now that I was out of Alexander's intoxicating presence, I was beginning to feel a tad foolish. But then I remembered his lips dancing across mine and the now familiar but still uncontrollable longing returned.

"Earth to Clara."

I shook my head and forced myself to meet my best friend's gaze.

"I asked where you were. I thought you were just in the loo at first, but then you never came out."

"I left you a note," I said defensively, but it was clear she hadn't gotten it.

"But," she continued, ignoring me, "I know you can't have been *stupid* enough to go out with all those paparazzi waiting for you." She paused, obviously waiting for me to jump in and explain, but I was still trying to sort out where to begin. "And yet, here you are, dragging your sorry bum in without a word of explanation."

I held up a hand in surrender. "Give me a minute."

Dropping on to the couch next to her, I tried to collect my thoughts. Belle sighed impatiently and grabbed a takeout box. It had to be cold but she flipped open the carton lid and began twirling noodles around chopsticks. Instead of eating them herself, she held them up to me. "Eat."

I knew better than to argue with her over this. I slurped the noodles down, savoring their coating of rich, salty sauce despite their coldness. She shoved the box into my hands and I took over the process of feeding myself, grateful for the chance to sort through my thoughts as much as I was for the food. We ate in silence until my belly was sated, and I had to admit my head felt much clearer after food.

Setting my half-empty carton down, I shifted to face Belle, who watched me with curious eyes, her mouth hovering over her own noodles.

"When you left I got a call." She was silent as I filled her in on the insane chain of events that had transpired while she was out grabbing takeaway, but as soon as I finished, leaving off at the part where Alexander helped me to his car, she let out a long, extended sigh.

"If you don't shag that, I will never forgive you."

I couldn't choke back the nervous laughter that bubbled

from me. My eyes darted away from Belle's too serious face, worried she would figure out that I'd already agreed to meet him tomorrow. I wasn't entirely sure why. Perhaps because Alexander's and my relationship was already too public, part of me wanted to keep something for myself. But despite my attempt to avoid that tidbit, Belle's narrowed into catlike slits.

"What aren't you telling me?" she demanded.

"Nothing. I...just..." My fingers twisted the tassel of a throw pillow, and Belle swatted at it. I pulled it away from her reach and clutched it to my chest.

"Out with it, Bishop."

"I'm...seeing him tomorrow." It was actually a relief to admit it.

"Tomorrow? Bloody hell!" Belle jumped up from the couch and began rapidly pacing the living room. "That doesn't give us much time."

"To do what?" I asked, although I wasn't sure I wanted to know the answer.

"What will you wear?"

"He couldn't keep his hands off me in this," I reminded her, plucking at the hem of my t-shirt. "I think anything will be an improvement over this."

Her eyebrow crooked up, suggesting that she seriously doubted that. "You can wear a burlap bag for all I care—although I won't let you—what are you wearing *underneath*? Oh bollocks, when did you get waxed last? It's too late to do it now."

"Everything is in order down there," I assured her, not bothering to inform her that although I'd never waxed before in my life that didn't mean that things weren't neat and well-kept down below.

"Knickers? Bra?" she asked.

Her pacing was starting to ratchet up my nerves again. "I also have those."

"I've seen yours," she said in exasperation. "You can't wear cotton knickers to shag Alexander."

"I don't imagine I'll be wearing them long." Just the thought distracted me as I remembered Alexander's strong, commanding hands. By tomorrow, I'd know what it was like to have them all over my body, and a ripple of anticipation shivered over my skin, raising goose bumps.

"Focus, Clara!" Belle snapped her fingers, drawing my attention back to the state of emergency she'd declared.

"He's picking me up at eleven in the morning," I told her. "There's nothing I can do about it now."

"We live in London now," she said, grabbing her purse from the floor. "Shops are open late. You're a 36B?"

"C," I corrected. "But I can't go out there." Norris had driven us around the front of the building earlier, and although I'd been too focused on Alexander to check things out, I had no doubt that the paparazzi were still camped in front of our building.

"I'll go."

"You already went out for dinner." I knew Belle's intentions were noble, but she'd nearly worked me into a frenzy at this point. It was too much. "I shouldn't go."

"That's why I'm going—"

"No," I stopped her. "I shouldn't go *tomorrow*. It's a terrible idea. Do I really want to wind up on more tabloids?"

If I kept getting caught with Alexander, the rumors would only swirl more. I could almost picture the headlines: *Tasty Tart! Her Royal Whoreness!*

Getting involved with someone like Alexander, even for a fling, could destroy my career before it even got started. I didn't harbor any delusions about my position at the nonprofit, but I wasn't ready to commit career suicide before I'd had my first day.

"No, no, no," Belle ordered. "I know that voice. You aren't going to talk yourself out of this. For once, you need to let go."

"And what good will it do me?"

"I love you," she said, her eyes soft as she spoke, "but you need a good fuck. You've spent the last six months under a stack of books—"

"Some of us needed good marks."

"And before that," she continued as though she hadn't heard me, "you were with Daniel, and let's face it, darling." Belle lifted her pinkie finger and wiggled it.

I smothered a giggle with my hand. "How do you know that?"

"Because I saw you in the morning after he slept over," she said, "and you always looked tired—and not in a good way."

I seriously doubted that my sex life could be judged based on my morning-after appearance. "Daniel was perfectly adequate."

"Exactly. Beans and toast will feed you, but you can't pretend it's a steak."

I shook my head at her. "None of this means that I need new underwear."

In the end, Belle won out, and to be certain that I'd be too busy to overthink my date—or whatever it was—she left me with a list of things to do while she was out. I resisted the list at first, but some of the items made sense. My toenails were fine, but maybe a fresh coat of polish would be nice. Painting them, as it turned out, had the odd effect of calming me down and exciting me at the same time. When I was a teenager, I would have gone through all this obsessing before a date, but I had to admit that it had seemed less important in college. I didn't exactly want to be the kind of girl that spent hours and hours preening before she saw a guy, but it had been too long since I'd really pampered myself.

Belle could run a beauty salon with the amount of product she kept on hand, and before long, I had freshly pedicured feet. I padded through the flat, careful not to stub my still-drying toenails, and headed for her room. She'd given me carte blanche access to her closet to find something to wear, *because as she put it, you are leaving the house in a pair of jeans over my dead body.*

I couldn't help marveling at how organized her closet was already. I liked my things neat and well-ordered, but there was no way I could have unpacked my belongings as quickly and efficiently as she had, even though I had a quarter of the clothing.

I ran my fingers down the assortment of dresses that hung according to their length, stopping in the middle near the closer to knee-length dresses. Most of them fell under the family celebration category, meaning they looked a little too much like something a British monarch might wear.

Alexander's grandmother, I realized.

That definitely wasn't going to work. I knew Belle would push me toward the shorter dresses, but the last thing I wanted was to feel self-conscious right off the bat. I'd never arranged anything this close to a booty call before, and as aroused as I was over Alexander's promise that he needed to screw me all day, it was getting harder to silence my rational side. Without his presence—without the inexorable pull I felt around him—I could see more clearly the reasons I should stay away.

One time, I promised myself. *And then it's over.*

It was late spring in London, which meant the weather was a little fickle but tended toward warmer temperatures. I rifled through the hangers, discovering Belle had a serious ball gown problem. No one could possibly need this many fancy dresses. Shoved between a Jenny Packham evening gown and a Vera Wang in champagne silk, I found exactly what I was looking for.

Stripping down, I tried on the flowing maxi dress. It was

sleeveless, but its sweetheart neckline would support my bust, a problem Belle didn't usually need to worry about. It was a soft shade of blue—romantic and dreamlike, which was a reflection of how I felt. With my freshly painted toenails, I'd be able to rock a pair of sandals for the first time this season. It wasn't the amped up ensemble my friend would pick out for me, but with its low neckline and figure-skimming fabric, it was plenty sexy enough.

Belle arrived back half an hour after I'd completed her checklist, holding an Agent Provocateur bag triumphantly over her head. To my surprise, she wholly approved of the dress I'd chosen.

"It will go perfectly with this." She opened the carefully wrapped tissue to reveal a pale lace bra and panty set that sparkled silver when she held it up. The set was delicate and feminine, managing to scream sex and wealth at the same time.

I took one look at the price tag and knew why.

"I'm paying you back for this."

Belle waved off my declaration, her lips curving as I held up the sexy lingerie. She knew I wouldn't have bought it for myself. Not because I didn't have the money, but because I'd never had a reason to before. She grabbed the bra out of my hand and snapped off the price tag.

"No going back now," she purred.

I snatched it away, pressing it to my chest as I imagined what it would be like to wear it, which only resulted in me thinking about why I would be wearing this. Heat flooded my cheeks as I pictured wearing this in front of Alexander. I'd worn lingerie before, but nothing as exquisite as this. It was beautiful and sexy and *delicate*—as delicate as the arrangement between him and me.

. . .

THE NERVES HIT ME AS SOON AS I WOKE UP IN THE morning. My stomach rolled at the thought that in a few short hours I was going to possibly be making the biggest mistake of my life or maybe the best decision of my life. The jury was still out on how bad an idea it was. Grabbing a shower, I tried not to look in the mirror as I finished my usual morning routine. But when I finally was forced to look up as I began applying the little bit of makeup I planned to wear, I discovered I was already flushed. I looked excited and slightly crazed. All in all, it actually didn't look that terrible.

Belle was making a racket in the kitchen by the time I joined her, still in my robe. She was dressed in tiny pajama bottoms and a nearly sheer tank top, and for a second, I wished I had her body—toned, athletic with perky breasts and defined abs. Despite running several days a week, I was curvy and slightly too tall. I'd been told more than once that my voluptuous figure had scared a boy off.

She was cooking up a storm. There was already a plate of sausages and sliced tomatoes, and she was frying eggs next to a pot of what I suspected was beans.

"Are you cooking for Philip?" I asked, amazed by the sheer amount of food she was readying.

"I wanted to make sure you ate before your date," she said, shooting me a wink. "It sounds like you're going to need your strength."

"Don't remind me." I grimaced as I lifted the lid of the pot and discovered I'd been correct about my guess.

Belle spun toward me, spatula pointed at my chest. "Uh-uh, Bishop. You are not going to psych yourself out."

I shrugged, grabbing a piece of English bacon and popping it into my mouth as I dropped onto a stool. "I already have. Remind me exactly what was I thinking again?"

"You were thinking that you had a chance to screw one of the world's sexiest and most powerful men," she reminded me.

When she said it like that, I nearly understood.

"Clara, this is the opportunity of a lifetime," she added.

I raised an eyebrow at her. "Having sex with someone is the opportunity of a lifetime? Spoken like a true prostitute."

She stuck her tongue out at me and turned her attention back to the eggs. "Having sex with a prince is," she said. "Remember when you were a little girl? Didn't you want to be a princess?"

"This is hardly the same thing." I smirked at the thought. "My pretend play didn't usually include the *Kama Sutra*."

"Didn't you miss out then?" she said dryly. "Seriously, though, this is the closest you'll probably ever come to living that fantasy. The thing no one admits is that we don't give up our childish fantasies, we just accept they're out of our reach. You're an adult now, but that doesn't mean you don't want to snag a prince. Or shag one, at least."

"You're hopeless," I said, "and I don't mean a hopeless romantic."

"I'm a realist, darling. And a very *real* opportunity presented itself to you. Don't back out now."

I hadn't said anything about backing out, but I'd been thinking about it and obviously my best friend had caught on. No surprise there. "I'm just not sure that it's a good idea. I'm not the type of girl that just screws around for fun."

That was the truth. I'd always been a girlfriend-type, even during my more experimental years. The last time I'd let a guy pick me up, it had been Daniel. I'd gone home with him hell-bent on finally going wild for a night and wound up stuck in a crappy relationship.

"And how is that working out for you?" she asked. "Daniel treated you like shit. Relationships are overrated."

"Remind me to use that line in my bridesmaid's toast."

"I'm in love with Philip," she countered. "You weren't in love with Daniel, and look how awful your relationship was. It's a much better idea for you to keep this casual."

I threw my hands up in surrender. "Okay, okay. I wasn't going to cancel anyway."

I didn't add that part of me knew canceling on Alexander would be impossible. If I managed to do it, despite his insanely sexy voice, he'd find me. I got the impression he wasn't the kind of man who took no for an answer. Not twice. And I used my one go at it.

And despite everything, I didn't want to say no to him. In fact, I was counting on not saying no to him all day long.

"Earth to Clara," Belle called.

I blinked my eyes, drawing myself out of my daze as she placed a plate piled with food on it in front of me. "I'm going to be too full for sex."

"Pish-posh." She grabbed her own plate and hunkered down next to me. "Think of this as fuel. I expect you to be able to keep up with him."

"You do, huh?"

"And I want to hear all the sordid details."

Rolling my eyes, I cut into my egg, spilling yolk across my plate. "Have you met him before?"

"Sadly no. My family was never a favorite of his parents, especially after daddy..." She trailed away. I knew better than to push it. "We didn't get invited out to the country or anything. And he was gone for so long after the accident."

Thinking about the infamous wreck that had killed Princess Sarah and nearly claimed Alexander's life made it difficult to eat. "He mentioned that. Going away after the accident, I mean."

"Were you in America at the time?"

I nodded, pushing my food around my plate. "It was all over the news. Although I had other things going on at the time."

"It was so sad." Her voice grew distant as she recalled the incident. "People broke down crying on the street, even my mother. I went to her funeral. Everyone did. There must have been hundreds of thousands of people lining the streets and when her casket passed, there was absolute silence."

"She was our age. It's hard to imagine," I said. "Were there paparazzi involved?"

"No one really knows," Belle said grimly. "The rumor was that they'd been drinking. Alexander was twenty, but she was underage. There was another person in the car, but the press never uncovered who it was."

"I still don't understand why Alexander left," I admitted. He'd been as much a victim as his sister.

"Sarah was beloved. I think it was partially because she looked so much like her mother. Her mom died in childbirth with Prince Edward and that was such a shock. The idea that she died tragically as well was too much for most people." Belle shrugged. "It's funny how people act like they know famous people."

I couldn't help wondering if Alexander had left to escape recrimination or because he couldn't handle the loss of both his mother and sister. It felt like too much for one person to endure.

"You need to eat," Belle said, changing the subject.

Despite Belle's clucking, I couldn't finish more than half of the breakfast. My stomach was too nervous, churning too quickly for me to stomach the food. It was already ten o'clock, which meant I had an hour to get myself ready—or to back out. Despite my promises to Belle that I wouldn't run from my chance with Alexander, I remained unconvinced that I could actually go through with our date the closer I got to it. If I could even call it a date.

I dropped my robe on my bed and picked up the bag of Agent Provocateur lingerie that Belle had brought me, only to discover that she'd bought more than one set. Tucked under the paper that wrapped the set she'd shown me last night were at least five more and a few pairs of stockings. Clearly, she had higher expectations for how today would go than I did.

I stuck with the set she'd given me last night, especially after checking out the others in the bag, some of which included garters. And one pair with a slit up the already negligible crotch of the thong. She'd been right to give me the silver gray set. It was the prettiest, but it was also the most traditional. Nothing about today was ordinary, so I was glad that at least I wouldn't feel completely out of my own skin.

Fastening the bra, I turned to check myself out in the standing mirror in the corner of my room. The delicate lace glistened over my pale skin, creating an almost ethereal affect. The bra pushed together my breasts without giving them any extra padding, something I didn't need. The lingerie definitely showed off all my assets, right down to my full hips and ass. Thanks to Belle's intrepid online stalking after her shopping trip, I'd seen a few more pics of the girls Alexander had been spotted with since he had returned from his military duty. They were mostly blond, tall and lithe. Alexander would have been better off to ask Belle out it seemed. It wasn't hard to see a pattern to his pictures—beautiful, model-esque blondes—although he'd only been photographed with one girl more than once, and she was the prettiest of them all. The papers claimed she was his girlfriend, but there was a coldness to the photos. Alexander was always turned away from her or walking away from her. There didn't appear to be any proof that they were together other than the tabloids' speculations. But speculating about who might be the next Queen of England probably sold a lot of papers.

For a second, I wondered how it would feel when that day inevitably came and he assumed his role as King. The pictures and stories would be everywhere. As they would be when he eventually married. Could I really handle watching his life unfold? Was I even capable of a casual fling with him? My body wanted him, but my heart was already in the balance. He'd protected me from the reporters, giving me the safety I'd craved so often as a child and a teenager. Of course, if chivalry survived anywhere in the modern world, it better survive in the Prince of England.

After all, as Belle had pointed out, little girls needed fairy tales to rely on.

I'd just slipped my dress over my head and pulled my sandals out of my crammed closet when my cell rang. I froze, positive it was him calling. He'd come to his senses. He'd give me an excuse about a prior engagement or a sudden emergency. He was, after all, chivalrous. But it would be a lie.

But when I saw the screen, I felt a mixture of relief and annoyance to see my mother's number on the call display. Realizing I had to deal with this before she showed up on my doorstep, I hit the answer button. "Hi, Mom."

"Thank god, you are answering the phone! I've been worried sick about you."

Translation, she'd been dying to pry every detail she could out of me.

"I'm fine, Mom," I reassured her. "I've been unpacking and had my phone on silent."

There was a pause. "You've seen the news?"

"I'd hardly call it news," I retorted. I clutched the phone to my ear as I buckled my Prada sandals.

"Well, it's news to me. Why didn't you tell me you were dating anyone?" It was more admonishment than question.

"I'm not dating him."

"That's too bad."

For her, I thought. "It was all a misunderstanding."

"Misunderstandings don't usually result in lips locking."

"This one did," I said simply. I couldn't imagine trying to explain this to her any further.

"Actually, I'm glad to hear it," she said, and I froze as she continued. "All that attention might not be healthy for you. There's a lot of pressure when you're dating someone who's in the media spotlight."

My parents had endured their fair share of media attention during the dot-com boom, and she'd been chasing it ever since, so it was a surprise to have her warn me away from the spotlight. The more attention I got, the more she would receive. But I had to give her credit. Despite her many vices and weaknesses, she's always looked out for my sister's and my interests.

"You have nothing to worry about," I promised her as I stashed a few condoms in my purse. Just in case. I didn't feel badly lying to my mother. Lying was the natural state of our relationship. I'd learned long ago to hide anything from her that could upset her fragile happiness.

"That's not the only reason I called."

I held my breath, hoping she only had more gossip to dish.

"Your father's going to be out of town for a few days," she said. "I thought we could have a girls' day. You've been so busy studying the last few months, I think you deserve a spa day and some shopping."

"That's very tempting—"

"Now before you give me some silly reason as to why you can't possibly come, let me reason with you," she stopped me. "You are about to start your first real job. You'll need the right clothes for it."

I got the sense that she didn't think I was up to finding those clothes for myself. "I have plenty of work-appropriate dresses. You don't need to buy me anything."

"I know that dress you were wearing in those pictures belonged to Belle. I know you're frugal, but, Clara, you don't have to be. Johns says you've barely touched your account."

"Johns is giving you updates on my accounts?" I asked in a strangled voice.

"Of course he is. We're still listed on the trust fund until you turn twenty-five."

"I didn't know that." I couldn't quite keep the accusation out of my voice. I hadn't known because they hadn't told me. I'd assumed the trust fund that they'd given me access to on my twenty-first birthday had been my personal safety net. They'd failed to tell me that access still had strings attached.

"Don't take that tone with me. Johns only reports once a year and in case of a discrepancy." She paused before adding, "If it's that important to you, I can ask your father about changing the conditions."

"I'll talk to him myself." If either of my parents were going to be reasonable about this, he would be. I had no doubt that my mother had been the one to insist on staying on the account until I was twenty-five, so she could be certain I was handling it properly. Of course, she would see its purpose as funding a flashy lifestyle while I wanted to keep it invested so I could focus on starting a career that allowed me to do something I cared about.

"How's Tuesday?" Mom asked.

I blinked and clutched the phone tighter. "Tuesday?"

"For our girls' day?"

I'd almost forgotten why she had called. "Sure."

The line stayed silent and I waited for a response. "Mom?"

"I will see you on Tuesday," she said finally. I didn't think I imagined her voice breaking as she spoke.

I said goodbye, still puzzled over her bizarre behavior. But I didn't have long to think about it before Belle appeared breathless in my doorway.

"There's a Norris waiting for you downstairs?"

"Personal security," I told her as my stomach flipped over.

"Hot," she moaned, following me to the door.

"Wish me luck?"

"You don't need luck." She kissed my cheek, and I tried to believe her as I made my way toward the lift. As soon as I saw Norris, I realized today was one of those days that would forever divide my life. I wasn't sure how I knew that exactly, but I saw the dividing line clearly. When I looked back on my life, every moment up to this one would be *before Alexander*. How long would it be until every future moment became *after Alexander*?

No regrets, I decided. My life was already divided, and after today I would be able to say I'd done it—gone wild and bedded someone way out of my league. Wasn't it what Belle was always saying I needed? It would be worse to always wonder what it would have been like—what he was like.

I pushed the doubts out of my head as Norris bowed slightly to me, extending his arm and leading me into the unknown.

CHAPTER SEVEN

I hadn't been able to appreciate Alexander's private car the other night, which I suspected had something to do with his presence in it. But since he wasn't waiting in the back seat for me, I had plenty of time to explore it now. I'd always found Rolls Royces to be thoroughly sexy and British, and this one was outfitted with privacy glass that I suspected was also bullet-proof. Between the security and size of the car, I was already imagining him taking me in the backseat. My hand reached toward the leather seat cushion as though it was searching for him and the release I'd needed since our first meeting.

But I was all alone, and it felt a bit snobby to have the glass up between Norris and me, so I pressed the button to lower it.

"Is it alright if I put this down?" I asked.

"Whatever you wish, Miss Bishop."

Of course. The British were always so damn polite that it was impossible to tell what they really wanted. It drove my American half a little crazy.

"It's strange," I said, thinking out loud, "I didn't think it was common for the royal family to use drivers." As soon as the words were out of my mouth, I wanted to suck them back down.

Alexander had already explained that Norris was more than his driver. He was his personal security guard who also drove his car. I wasn't certain why he required near constant personal security, and I guessed that Norris wasn't likely to tell me. That's why Alexander trusted him.

"His Highness does not enjoy driving."

I nodded as though this was perfectly reasonable, but, of course, it wasn't. I'd spent my formative years in America, where I'd learned that a guy's car was almost as important an extension of him as his dick. I supposed that might be different in England, but I suspected things weren't that different. And this car with its sleek silver body and luxurious interior suggested that I was right.

"I would think he'd like to drive this," I said, feeling obligated to keep the conversation going now. I wished that I hadn't opened the divider, but if I closed it, I actually deserved to feel like a snot.

"He appreciates his car and trusts me to drive it." Norris's response was simple, and there was only a hint of double entendre to it, but the clue was there all the same. I was suddenly glad that I hadn't bit my tongue. If I had, I might have asked Alexander about it at some point. Now I knew not to.

"Thank you," I said with meaning. Norris must have known he was giving me the information I needed even though he hadn't said much.

"Of course, Miss Bishop. I'm happy to drive for Alexander."

He was professional, that was for sure. No wonder Alexander trusted him.

We'd barely been in the car ten minutes when Norris pulled up to a set of private gates near the heart of Westminster that opened to us at once. I swallowed, my nerves getting the better of me, as he drove forward into what looked like a very exclusive parking garage. This wasn't an American parking garage though, which were usually monstrous in size and structure. Here there were less than ten spaces, most of which were empty, and the entrance made it clear this was a bit more than a permit-only garage. Where were we exactly?

Norris opened my door to help me out and led me toward an elevator that dinged as we approached. My breath caught as the doors opened, revealing Alexander. He wore a three-piece suit in charcoal gray that was tailored to precisely fit his chiseled body. He looked good enough to eat, and I was ready for my taste.

"Clara." He held out his hand. There was no hesitation in his gesture, although I saw it for what it was: an offering. By placing my hand in his, I was accepting whatever happened next between us. I could still run, but I knew I couldn't do that, and from the smug grin plucking at the corners of his perfect mouth, Alexander knew it, too.

I took his hand without a backwards glance. The elevator doors slid shut behind us, snapping me back to the present moment and I whirled around, letting go of him.

"Is something wrong?" Alexander asked, concern in his voice.

"I should have said thank you to Norris. It was rude of me."

The smile playing across his mouth broke through. "I'm sure the salary I pay him makes up for any perceived impoliteness on your part."

"It was still rude," I said, a frown tugging on my lips. "Please give him my apologies for my behavior *as well* as my thanks."

Alexander's head tilted, a funny look replacing the amused one, but it was gone as quickly as it came. "I thought perhaps you'd come to your senses."

My body responded to the rasp in his voice, blocking my ability to appreciate Alexander's warning. "Have you come to yours?"

"You're not the dangerous one." He stepped closer to me, and I drew in a sharp breath of anticipation.

"Maybe I'm a wolf in sheep's clothing," I answered, not missing a beat.

"I guess I'll have to strip you and find out," he growled, and I had no doubt what I'd find when I finally rid him of his clothes. There was no lamb lurking under Alexander's savage sensuality.

"Where are we?" I asked, eager to have something else to talk about. The air crackled between us, distracting me with thoughts of Alexander's lips on me. We both knew why I was here, but I wanted to play it cool as long as possible. Although I suspected Alexander knew he was getting to me.

"The Westminster Royal," he told me.

"Swanky hotel," I murmured. It was the sort of place where movie stars stayed when they filmed in London, and judging from the exclusivity of the parking garage, they did so for security reasons.

"They appreciate their guests' privacy, which is something I appreciate."

"Do you check in under a false identity and leave under the cover of night?" I asked.

He laughed at this. "It's not quite so clandestine as that. Although most of the staff only knows me as Mr. X."

"Does that make me Mrs. X for the day?" I asked, then realized what I had said. I covered my mouth in horror.

"I rather like the sound of that," he purred. His head cocked, drinking me in. "Mrs. X. She sounds rather wicked."

I licked my lips, surprised to find myself nodding.

"Are you okay with that?" he asked. "With this arrangement, I mean."

"I hadn't expected..." I let the thought trail away.

"A hotel?" he guessed.

"Yes." I couldn't bring myself to meet his eyes. I was too awed by his presence, too overwhelmed that I was standing in a private elevator with this god in a three-piece suit who wanted me. And if I was being honest, too nervous that I was heading up to a hotel room with a man I hardly knew.

Alexander moved closer to me, his hand cupping my jaw and raising my face so that I was forced to look up at him. "I wanted to be certain that no one found out about this."

His words sucked the air from my lungs like a punch in the gut, and I pulled away from his grasp, wondering what would happen if I hit the red button on the elevator panel. Considering that the heir to the throne was in the lift with me, I imagined SIS might be involved. Scotland Yard at the very least.

"What is it?" Alexander asked, stepping close enough that his body pressed against me. "Why are you looking like I've got you in a corner?"

"I have a little self-respect, you know," I snapped, turning to face him. I tried to ignore the magnetic pull of his body as my breasts brushed against him. But they betrayed me, beading tightly and obviously through my lace bra and thin cotton sundress. "If you're worried about being seen with me, perhaps it's best that you let me off."

"I can't," he said.

I stepped back, breaking the contact between us, and crossed my arms over my chest, hoping he hadn't seen the way my body reacted to his. "Try."

"This lift only goes to the Presidential Suite. I can't let you off until we reach it, but..." He reached over and pressed the red button that had been tempting me before and we came to a sudden stop, jolting me against him. "I think you've misunderstood me, and I'm not interested in taking a woman to bed who thinks I'm a liar."

I swallowed hard on this statement. "Then explain it to me."

"With pleasure." He wet the bottom of his lip and loosened his tie. "I was under the impression you wanted the paparazzi to leave you alone."

He left this statement hanging in the air as though it were a question, so I shrugged, not willing to commit to anything until I heard everything he had to say.

"I wanted to respect your desire for privacy," he said. "By now, you'll have done your research on me."

Another unasked question, so I nodded.

"Reporters love to take photos of me with women and speculate on our relationships. Old friends become new flames. Waitresses become flings."

"So you didn't sleep with all those women?" I asked.

His mouth twitched as he shrugged. "Not *all* of them."

"Lovely."

"I believe you told me that you weren't a hapless virgin," he reminded me. His body shifted closer, backing me against the elevator as he pressed his hands to the wall, caging my body as he surveyed me like a panther preparing to pounce. "I assume we can be open about our sex lives."

"We can," I said, setting my jaw firmly.

"Good, because I want you to be open with me, Clara. I'll have you either way, but you'll enjoy it more if you aren't busy thinking I'm a dick."

I couldn't help but smile at this.

"A smile," he said. "Now that's *lovely*. I wonder if I'll see that after you come when you're still full of me."

There was a dark undertone to his words and I shivered in expectation. I imagined I would smile and possibly cry. He struck me as the type that might produce both emotions equally.

"So are we agreed?" he asked.

"To share our sex lives?"

"I need to know the women I sleep with are discreet. That they use good...judgment."

I rolled my eyes at this. Hadn't he been the one flitting about town with a new woman every night? "I've been with one guy. My college boyfriend. And I'm on The Pill."

I didn't feel the need to go into further details about Daniel. It wouldn't do anything for our relationship to reveal the uglier bits of my past. I'd made the mistake of sharing too much of myself with Daniel, and he'd used it against me. What would a man like Alexander do with such information? A man trained to be a political leader? A man who met a woman he barely knew at a hotel to fuck her? He obviously had flexible morals. I just didn't want to test how flexible they were.

"What about you?" I asked.

"More than one," he said simply. "I'm always cautious, and I can assure you that I'm clean."

I frowned at this, not only because of the implication but also because of his non-answer. "And that's important because?"

"I felt it should be addressed before I took you to bed, and because I don't think I can wait until we reach the suite." He stepped closer, pushing me harder against the mirrored wall of the lift, and I felt his cock pressing into my belly. The caution I'd felt moments before disappeared entirely in favor of the feeling of his hands as he tugged down the straps of my sundress. He caught sight of the lingerie and a growl rumbled in his throat. "Your breasts are more perfect than I'd imagined."

I melted at his words, desiring pooling low in my belly, and leaking between my legs. But the sensible side of me peeked out. "Should we do this in the elevator?"

Alexander flashed me a wicked smile, brushing a finger across my lips. "Oh poppet, I know what's worrying you. You're worried that I'll get my quick fuck in the elevator."

"I don't want you to get bored with me before you even get me to the room," I said with a shrug.

"That won't be a problem," he said, his finger dropping lower, trailing along my collarbone and leaving a trail of fire in its wake. "Your body was made to fuck, Clara. Has anyone ever told you that?"

I shook my head, my mouth too dry to answer him.

"It is," he continued. "I find it very inspiring. I don't know if there are enough flat surfaces to ride you on in the suite. But if it would make you feel better—" his hand pushed up my skirt then dipped below the band of my thong, seeking its way lower until it found its prize "—we can wait and go upstairs."

My eyes clenched shut as his finger manipulated my clit with expert strokes. "We should..."

But I couldn't even force the rational thought out of my mouth. I couldn't think clearly with him pressed against me, with his hand touching me like that. Hell, I couldn't think clearly with him in the same room as me.

"Perhaps I can offer a better solution," he said, his breath hot against my neck as his fingers continued to knead. "I need to taste your sweet cunt, Clara. I've been thinking about it for days. Will you let me do that?"

I moaned a yes. Alexander didn't wait for more encouragement. His fingers caught the waistband of my panties and ripped them away. Somewhere deep down, the price tag associated with the underwear flashed through my mind, and I realized I would buy a hundred more pairs if it meant he would rip them all off me.

Alexander dropped to his knees and urged my legs apart. "Spread wider," he ordered, and I widened my stance. "Beautiful."

His hands stroked along my thighs up toward my seam, and when he reached it, he spread it wide and studied it for a moment, a look of appreciation on his face, before his fingers found my cleft. My eyes snapped back shut as he pushed two fingers inside of me.

"Are you always this wet?" he asked.

I shook my head again. I wasn't this wet in a bathtub.

"Do I do this to you?" he asked, fucking me slowly with his fingers.

I nodded.

"Say it, Clara."

"Yes."

"Yes, what? What do I do to you?"

"You make me wet," I moaned.

"Good girl," he murmured with approval. He continued to tease me with his fingers for a few seconds and then the warm rasp of his tongue sent a series of shivers trembling through my body. He licked across my sensitive bud leisurely. Back and forth. Back and forth. Back and forth as his fingers continued to plunge into me. I began to shake as I neared the edge.

He pulled away. "Not until I say, poppet."

I whimpered at the command but felt helpless to resist him.

Then his mouth was back on me, tonguing me with quick, circular motions punctuated with bursts of suction. I grabbed the rail behind me, trying to keep my orgasm at bay even as it bubbled toward release. I cried out half pleasure, half plea as he began to fuck me harder with his fingers.

"Come," he commanded, and I unraveled around him, shattering to pieces that melted back together only to shatter once more as a new wave of intensity rolled through me. When only the after-tremors remained, Alexander withdrew his hand. But he continued to suck gently on my clit until I wasn't sure I could take anymore. My thighs clamped protectively against his head, but he continued his oral machinations on my swollen, sensitive cleft. It felt impossible but my body responded immediately, building toward another orgasm, but before I reached the peak, he pulled away, hitting the red button on the elevator control panel as he stood up.

"Now you're ready for me to fuck you," he said. It wasn't a question, but I answered anyway.

"Yes," I whimpered, barely able to stand.

All he did was smirk.

CHAPTER EIGHT

The elevator doors slid open, and Alexander stepped into the suite, shrugging out of his jacket and dropping it over a silk sofa in one fluid movement. I followed him, still weak-kneed and tongue-tied from his attention in the lift. The surroundings were as impressive as I expected though. A wall of floor-to-ceiling windows looked out over the Thames River with Big Ben sitting catty-corner to the suite. From up here, the traffic below looked more like a child's play set, but London still buzzed with energy. Across the river, the Eye spun cautiously, a seeming contradiction to the old world stylings of the buildings surrounding it. That's what I loved about London—the old and the new clashing one moment and merging into something organic the next. Few cities in the world had managed to maintain their history while innovating the way this one had, and everything about this place seemed different from this vantage point. Pressing my hand to the glass, I couldn't help but feel dizzy. I was in a whole new world—in more ways than one.

Alexander came up behind me, pressing his taut body against mine. Suddenly, it wasn't only London that was humming with life. "Enjoying the view?"

"I am. You?"

"Very much. The city isn't bad either." His lips dropped to my neck and I felt the painful but pleasant nip of his teeth. My body responded with a sigh, my limbs going weak as I sagged against him. His hands dropped to my skirt and lifted it up. I remembered then that I was bare underneath the thin sundress, and now I was on display as much as the city below. No one could see us up here, few buildings even rose to this height in the city. But I still felt exposed as his hand slipped between my thighs, urging them open. Alexander stroked a finger along my seam and my sex grew slicker with my want.

"I'm going to fuck you in front of this window," he said in a gruff voice. "I'm going to show the whole city that I take what I want."

My core clenched at the dark edge to his words even as I still marveled that he wanted me, even if he couldn't possibly want me as much as I wanted him. It wasn't humanly possible. Tomorrow I would be some girl he'd screwed, but he would always be Alexander. The thought made me long to draw today out. I wanted to relish every second, every touch, but I wasn't sure I could wait much longer.

"I'm going to make you come in front of the busiest street in London." His thumb brushed circles lightly over my clit as he spoke, taking me near the edge but refusing to let me fall over it.

"Please," I said, offering myself to him. The bustling city below us vanished as he continued his gentle but precise massage. There was only him. Only the rough sweep of his fingers. Only the sound of his ragged breath in my ear.

"Soon," he promised. "But not yet. I need to see how far I can take you. How much that beautiful cunt of yours can handle."

Feeling his erection pressing through his slacks against my backside emboldened me. "I can handle anything you give me."

Alexander growled, and in a flash, I was in his arms as he carried me through the sitting area toward a door. I only had time to register a bed before he dropped me on it.

"Take that off," he ordered.

I did as I was told in too much of a hurry to honor his demand than to make it into a show. I slipped the dress over my head, leaving me in only my lacy silver bra. It hadn't been too long ago that I would have been too self-conscious to show this much skin to a man, but with Alexander's eyes on me, I felt anything but. His gaze fucked me with such intensity that I believed his claim that he would make me beg.

"I almost wish I hadn't destroyed those panties," he remarked, standing at the foot of the bed, one hand stroking his cock through his pants. "I'll have to get you a new pair so I can fuck you in that sweet lace."

A shiver raced through me at the idea that he was already talking of a future encounter. I'd thought it impossible that he'd want to see me again after he'd had me. But I already suspected that I'd come whenever he called—and I suspected that I would come more than once at that.

"Spread your legs."

I dropped them open as he began to unbutton his shirt. My breath caught as he shrugged it off, revealing a thin v-neck that exposed his muscular arms and the top of what I was certain was a beautiful chest, but to my disappointment, he didn't remove the undershirt. The disappointment was short lived as he began unbuckling his belt. He tugged it free of his pants and stared at it for a moment, darkness flickering in his light eyes. I wondered briefly what he was thinking. Had I gotten in over my head? But he dropped it to the floor, leaving him in only his undershirt and boxers. I watched, mesmerized by what I was about to see, as he tugged off his shorts. His cock sprang free, the broad crown glistening with proof of his arousal, and I understood why I'd been able to feel it so clearly through all our clothing. It seemed impossibly unfair that he should be powerful and handsome and that well-endowed. I'd never thought I could be so wildly excited by a piece of anatomy, but in a split second, I had imagined all the things I could do to that beautiful cock. I wanted to wrap my lips around it, so that I could pleasure him as he'd done for me in the lift. I wanted to feel it pressed between my breasts, but most of all, I wanted it inside of me.

It was thrilling and terrifying to imagine him fucking me. I wasn't certain that my rather small experience with sex had prepared me for him.

Alexander fisted his cock, running his hand along the thick shaft from tip to root as he regarded me with hooded eyes, as though contemplating what to do with me. "Since I'm not certain your tight little cunt can handle me, I think it's best if we try a more...traditional style."

Despite myself, a giggle broke past my lips. It was girlish and nervous, the product of being both insanely turned on and well outside of my comfort zone.

"Are you laughing at me?" His lips curved into a wicked smile. "Don't be naughty or I'll have to take you over my knee." He spoke with the air of someone who was teasing, but the amusement didn't reach his flashing eyes.

I bit my lip, my body at war with wanting to please him and my mind in total shock. I didn't think I could take a man spanking me, and yet the idea had made my clit throb with such violence that I thought I might come just from the thought. I was completely at his mercy, and he knew it.

I watched as he ripped open a foil packet and sheathed himself with a condom. Then Alexander dropped onto the bed and crept over me. He hovered there, and I reached up to slip my hands under his shirt. One hand flew, catching mine as he lost his balance and dropped on top of me, his massive weight pinning me to the bed.

"No," he said.

I blinked at the harsh denial, rawness creeping toward my throat. There was no way I was going to cry in front of him—or let him spank me, come to think of it. The rational side was waking up and she was none too pleased to find herself in this situation. I pushed against him, trying to get him off me, but he stayed in place, not moving as I fought to extricate myself from the embrace.

"Clara, stop."

It was obvious I was going to get nowhere by trying to physically free myself, so I stilled and stared at him defiantly.

"This can stop now. We can stop now," he said, and I relaxed a little. "But I don't want it to, and I don't think you do either."

"I think I do!"

He nodded. "Let me say one thing and then you can decide. If you say stop, that's it."

"That's it?" I repeated, unable to keep the suspicion out of my voice.

"I only have one rule when it comes to sex."

"Only one?"

He gave me a look full of rebuke, and I clamped my mouth shut.

"I don't take off my shirt, and before you ask, I don't explain why."

"That's your only rule?" I had at least a half dozen of my own, including what was and was not okay to put or not put where, as well as what positions I was absolutely not going to do. But I had no doubt that those strict rules would fall victim to Alexander the second he asked me to bend on one.

It seemed that I didn't have quite the same effect on him.

"My only rule," he repeated. "I don't like women to touch me there."

My head and body warred over this revelation. "You want to put me on display for all of London, but I'm not allowed to touch your abs? That hardly seems like a fair trade."

"I promise that you won't feel that way by this afternoon," he said. "I don't think you'll have any doubts about my generosity then. But you can say no now and leave. I'll understand."

"I assume others have said no to this then?"

"You know what they say about assumptions, Clara."

I took that as a *no*. Of course, no other woman would be stupid enough to turn Alexander down. They probably didn't have the strength. I wasn't sure I did.

Alexander's hand slipped between my legs and his thumb found my clit once more. The rough pad of it circled slowly, reminding me how turned on I'd been moments ago. "Perhaps I could convince you?"

My eyes shut as he continued the sensual massage, and I felt my resolve melting away. I wanted him, even if I didn't understand his rule. Who was I, of all people, to judge someone for having body issues? Although I couldn't see what he could possibly want to hide. Everything I'd seen of him so far had been perfect—*beyond* perfect. He was the essence of masculinity. Virile. Commanding. He mesmerized each time I looked at him.

"You don't have to tell me why," I managed to say between pants. "Just tell me one thing—do you not take it off for throwaway fucks?"

Alexander's hand stilled and he grew so silent that I opened my eyes to make sure he was still breathing. "Throwaway fucks?"

"Girls like me," I continued, despite the tiny voice in my head telling me I should shut up. "Girls you fuck and forget."

"I don't like that term," he said in a low voice that chilled my heated blood. "I've had casual sex before, Clara, but always with the understanding that that was what it was."

"We've never discussed it," I reminded him, the tiny voice in my head now screaming. "Look, I've never had a fling. I don't know how this goes. I'm usually a relationship girl, so help me understand. Do you keep your shirt on to keep your distance?"

His jaw clenched and a vein throbbed on the side of his neck. "I thought I made my intentions clear. I wasn't under the impression this was a fling."

My eyes popped open wider. How could he not see this as a fling? I'd spent less than two hours with the man and I was spread naked under him. It was the definition of a fling.

"Do you want a fling?" he asked.

Something in his tone plucked at me, but I shook it away. "I assumed..."

"There's that word again. I'm not interested in you as a throwaway fuck. Why would you think that?"

I stared at him as though this was the most preposterous thing I'd ever heard. "If it walks like a duck, and it talks like a duck."

"I think this is one time where you could use fuck in that statement." He released my hand and pushed up over me. "I don't know what to do with you, Clara Bishop. I've been thinking about fucking you since I saw you in that tiny black dress at the party. When you said no to me at the club I thought that was it and then you changed your mind and agreed to a date."

My heart leapt at his words, even as I struggled to wrap my head around what he was saying. "This is a date?"

"Isn't it?"

"The Royals really are fucked up," I muttered, but I wasn't able to keep myself from grinning.

"Don't I know it?" His smile twisted ruefully. "So did you expect flowers? The cinema?"

"Usually, I expect a little more conversation on a date," I admitted. I flushed as my embarrassment grew over the misunderstanding. But it wasn't just humiliation staining my cheeks, it was hope—hope that I'd see him again after this. I wanted to believe him when he said I wasn't just a fling, but it felt dangerous to do so.

"Maybe we should start over," he suggested.

But I didn't want that either. I was too tightly strung, ready for him and what he had promised me. I was afraid I might snap if we stopped now. Wasn't I thrilled by the idea I might see him again moments ago? Why had I even brought this up?

"I don't *court* women," he continued. "There wouldn't be a point."

"But we're on a date," I pointed out.

"Dating and courting are two different things. You and I could go to dinner or to the country or we could stay here and fuck. That's dating to me. Courtship implies expectations. I don't do romance and I don't do long-term. If you're looking for more, I can't give you that. What I can give you is pleasure. More pleasure than you've ever known in your life. I will spend every moment I have with you taking you to the edge and holding you as you spill over." He paused to let this sink in. "Isn't that what everyone is looking for when they go on dates? Why pretend we're after something else? You're attracted to me, and I'm attracted to you. I want to fuck you all day long and then I'd like to see you again and fuck you again. Could you agree to that?"

I bit my lip, trying to hold back the questions I had about this arrangement. What would happen when he grew tired of me? What if I wanted out? And as if to help vanquish all those tumultuous thoughts, Alexander lowered until his cock pressed against my seam.

There were a million reasons to stop this now, but none of them felt as compelling as the want coursing through my body. "Yes."

Alexander's lips closed over mine, effectively ending the conversation. Without breaking the kiss, I felt his hips coaxing my legs back open. I parted for him and his cock nudged against my swollen sex, but he held it there. A gasp escaped me as he teased me with the promise of fulfillment, and his kiss deepened in response, his tongue invaded my mouth, capturing it and sucking more moans from me. All he had to do was thrust and he would be inside me, ending the delicious agony I felt and laying to rest all the questions that had nagged us moments before. But Alexander took his time, his hips moving in circles, his thick cock rubbing against my throbbing clit before he nudged the tip back inside of me.

"I want you inside me," I whispered and Alexander's head lifted so that our eyes met. He pushed slowly in, not breaking our gaze, and I arched against him into the exquisite fullness I desperately sought. My body made precious contact with his hard muscles, my nipples brushing against his cotton shirt and tightening to beads. His hand slid under my back, supporting me as he rocked me toward the precipice of fulfillment.

His gaze bore into me like a dare, and I couldn't look away, even as the strings of my body tightened, winding taut as coiled wire.

"Say my name," he commanded.

"Alexander," I gasped, breathing hard as the tension seeped through my muscles and took control.

"Again," he ordered as his hands slid to my hips, pinning me to him as his cock drove into me with relentless strokes.

"Alexander." I cried his name as my orgasm splintered through me in violent waves that spasmed through my limbs, but my eyes stayed trained on him. He continued his thrusts, hard and fast, as he raced toward his own. Alexander's hands clenched my hips, and his gaze smoldered into me as he came. He was in total control, but I could feel my own slipping away with each second his skin was on mine.

He wrapped his arms around me and collapsed onto the bed, holding me close to him. I was too stunned to move, so I focused on my breathing, trying to calm my racing heart. That didn't seem possible with him still so near to me, and when he pressed a kiss to my forehead, an ache burst through my chest that had nothing to do with the fear or anger I felt during our earlier argument. With that one small gesture, he'd washed away all the rational questions I'd had about getting more involved with him. I only wanted to touch him again and see him come undone.

CHAPTER NINE

An hour later, I rolled out of bed, popping up on my tiptoes to stretch out the delicious ache in my muscles. Alexander watched from bed, his perfect body half-tangled in the sheets. The thought of his eyes traveling over my flesh sent a wicked thrill up the back of my neck, and I decided to put on a little show for him. Reaching for the wall, I bent down on the pretense of stretching, arching my back and thrusting up my hips. A low growl rumbled from Alexander and I couldn't help feeling a trifle smug that I could elicit such a primal reaction in him. I sashayed toward the bathroom and stopped at the door, posing for him.

"I'm going to take a shower if you care to join me," I offered.

Alexander's eyebrows lifted, but he shook his head. "Tempting, but I'm going to order room service. Any requests?"

"I'm not picky." But then I thought better of it. Sex like that should be commemorated. "Actually, get some champagne."

"Your wish is my command." He jumped up, still wearing his undershirt and nothing else, which did nothing to hide his powerful legs. He looked like something out of a Greek myth, carefully carved to perfection for the pleasure of women. I couldn't take my eyes off him. I was as fixed on him as he had been on me moments ago.

Alexander strode over to me, a cocky smile tugging at his lips. His black hair had a just-fucked tousle that immediately recalled how it had felt to tangle my hands through it. He held out a hand as he reached me, and I took it cautiously, unsure what to expect. I was surprised when he drew me to him, wrapping an arm around my waist. He leaned to kiss me, and despite our half-clothed state, the kiss was tender with a touch of longing hidden in it. It took my breath away and I felt another tug in my chest, as though that invisible string was reeling me closer to him. Alexander broke away, and as our eyes met, I saw the same desire and confusion reflecting in his.

But then he smacked my bare ass and dropped his hold on me. "What would you say if I suggested you only wore that around me?"

"I'm not wearing anything," I said, willingly stepping into his trick. I needed to break the tension hanging in the air between us as much as he did. I wasn't supposed to feel like this —I wasn't supposed to feel anything at all except mind-blowing orgasms. Things were moving too fast.

"Exactly."

"You're a bit of a fiend, aren't you?"

"I'll show you just how much," he warned, lunging at me.

My heart raced, fueled by equal parts lust and turmoil, so I sidestepped him and wagged a finger. "You promised me food and champagne."

I didn't add that I knew if he got his hands on me I'd never get a shower or a snack. Or have a chance to think about the heady cocktail of emotions swirling through me. It would be easier to fall into his arms, where I could forget all the reasons that I was in over my head. Part of me wished he would grab me and fuck me until I forgot how irrational and reckless I was being. I couldn't hide from the facts for long.

"Food and champagne." Alexander held his hands out in surrender, but then he crossed them over his chest and looked me up and down. "But then I'm going to have my way with you."

A shiver raced up my spine. "Promise?"

"I promise that you're going to spend the rest of the afternoon screaming my name."

My knees buckled a little at the thought and his hand shot out to steady me, his smug grin spreading to a full-blown smile. The effect was dazzling with his straight white teeth and movie star good looks, and I couldn't help but think of those lips and the things they were capable of.

"You're testing my resolve, poppet," Alexander said.

I blinked and stared at him. I was testing his resolve? He had to know the effect he had on me. It was written all over my face—and my body.

"Standing there, biting your lip, with your hair down. I give you ten seconds to get out of here or I'm taking you back to bed."

I squealed and scampered away, closing the bathroom door behind me. My heart pounded at Alexander's promise and the remembrance of what he'd already done to me. Catching my reflection in my mirror, I studied it for a second. My breasts hung loose, still swollen with arousal, my nipples beading tightly at the thought of Alexander. But I refused to let my focus linger on my body. Instead, I counted to ten and forced my gaze up. My liner had smudged a little, giving my eyes a smoky touch. It was kind of sexy, especially in combination with my wavy, loose hair and kissed-pink lips. Between my legs I felt the slick proof that I wasn't just dreaming. The girl in the mirror looked like a total sexpot. It wasn't a side I'd ever seen in myself, but I had to admit I liked it.

The hotel bathroom was stocked with more than the average shampoo and conditioner. It was practically a small convenience store, and inside the medicine cabinet, I found a package of hair ties. I tugged my messy hair off my neck, piling it onto my head, wanting to keep the sexy, just-bedded look I was rocking.

But when I stepped into the hot shower, I felt lonely. Whatever had prompted Alexander to refuse to remove his shirt in bed also kept him from joining me in here. I thought about this as I ran soap across my body and washed between my legs. Of course, that's why he didn't want to shower with me, removing his shirt would have been unavoidable, which meant that it wasn't just a measure of intimacy—he was hiding something. But what? Every bit of him that I'd seen up until now was stunning. His body literally left me breathless from my desire to touch him. I'd been too hurt at the time to see the harsh rejection for what it really was: fear. I understood body issues better than most though, and I knew better than to push it. Maybe in time, he wouldn't feel the need to hide from me.

I found myself hoping he would. But I shook the thought from my head as I rinsed the last of the soap off my body and turned off the water. I didn't need to get attached to Alexander. This was supposed to be casual. I had other things to worry about—like my new job and settling into life in London. There wasn't time for me to get involved with someone, especially not someone as complicated as Alexander. We were both looking for a good time, and if we were going to make that happen, I had to set aside my curiosity.

Tying a soft robe around me, I discovered the room service had already arrived. Alexander lounged in his shirt and shorts in the living room, his feet propped on the coffee table. A cart, crammed with dishes and glasses and a bottle of champagne, was parked next to his chair.

"Did you order everything on the menu?" I asked.

"Personally, I worked up an appetite," he said with a shrug, "but if you need to work on your own, I still want to screw you against that window."

I held up a hand. "Stop. I'm famished but maybe after?"

Alexander's eyes sparkled as he nodded. "You continue to surprise me, Clara Bishop. One minute you're running away from me and the next—"

"You have my panties off in a lift?" I finished for him. "Be honest, this isn't the first time a girl has dropped her knickers for you."

"Well, no," he admitted. "But you hardly *dropped* them. That reminds me that I need to buy you another pair."

I waved off his offer nonchalantly even as heat pooled low in my belly at the memory. Where had he stashed my panties when he ripped them from me? From the wicked gleam in Alexander's eyes, he was thinking about the same thing. I bee-lined to the room service cart in an attempt to stay focused. It wasn't healthy to screw like bunnies without eating for hours. To my surprise, I lifted the silver lids to discover two hamburgers, French fries, and small but fancy bottles of ketchup.

"I hope it's okay," Alexander said, coming up behind me. He gripped my hips with his firm hands and peeked over my shoulder. "You aren't a vegan or something? I haven't mortally offended you?"

"It's fine," I said, twisting to face him. "I love meat."

It took me a second to realize what I'd said, but from the close contact of his body, I could tell his cock got the message much faster.

"Tell me more," he breathed.

"After we eat," I said, ducking from his grasp and grabbing a plate. "I had no idea the Royal Family ate things like hamburgers."

"Oh yes, usually it's only crown roast and leg of lamb and mint jelly." His words were covered in thick coating of bitter amusement. "Actually, my family dinners are terrible. Stiff. Too many courses. Too many forks. Someone's always picking a fight, usually me. Maybe that's why I skip so many of them."

I'd just taken a bite of my burger but I had to do my best not to choke on it. Alexander was opening up to me. I swallowed hard on my food, suddenly more interested in learning about the mystery man in front of me than in what I was eating. "I can relate to that."

"Ah yes. Your parents are web entrepreneurs," he said. "Lots of dinners alone?"

I lifted an eyebrow in surprise. "Checking up on me?"

"I was interested, and if I have to spend my whole life in the public eye, I might as well enjoy the perks of my position." He joined me on the couch. The whole thing felt so normal, except for the revelation he'd just sprung on me.

"Translation: it's okay for you to spy on me."

Alexander laughed. "It was not nearly so clandestine. You probably learned more about me on the internet than I did from MI5 files."

"I have an MI5 file?"

"Not really. Hence why I didn't learn much. I wanted to know how the pretty American girl wound up at a boring British graduation party," he admitted.

"I'm not American. Not really."

"That did catch my attention," he admitted, taking a bite of his food and chewing it quickly. "You chose British citizenship. You could have chosen dual citizenship. Why?"

I hesitated at the question, uncertain how to answer. "There's nothing for me in America."

Nothing good, I added silently.

"That sounds like a story."

"How about you?" I asked, deflecting the attention back to him. It was better if my past stayed put. Neither of us gained anything from bringing it up.

"I'm an open book. You only have to go as far as the nearest tabloid to learn everything you need to know about me."

I wasn't buying that for a second. The gossip columns might make educated guesses about Alexander and his personal life, but as someone who'd spent a little bit of time with him in private, I knew they hadn't even scratched the surface of what he was really like. And despite my firsthand experience with him, I knew I hadn't either. The thought scared me as much as it excited me. "I doubt that. Tabloids seem to think rumors are facts, after all."

"Yes, they do." Alexander set his plate down and stood up, moving to look out the window. "What do you want to know, Clara?"

"What will you tell me?"

He flashed me a humorless smile before he turned back to stare out over London. "Nothing. I'll tell you nothing you want to know. I'll crack a joke or distract you with a kiss."

The honesty of his answer struck me like a blow and I couldn't respond. The pain in his voice was palpable. It lived and breathed as much as the sexy, broken man in front of me. But his directness couldn't tell me the one thing I ached to know: what had broken him?

It was the only way to know if I could fix him.

"You'll like me better if you believe the tabloid headlines," he added after a long silence.

The air was so heavy between us now that I thought it might crack the room in half, separating us forever. I couldn't let that happen. "Even the one that claimed you had an orgy at Brimstone last month?"

"Wouldn't you rather believe that one was true?" he asked, and to my relief, he smiled. "It promises inhuman stamina."

I already knew he had inhuman stamina. "I will admit I don't like the idea of you screwing a whole room full of women."

"Ahhh. The jealous type?"

I'd never been the jealous type, and I found it to be a big turn-off after my screwed up relationship with Daniel. But the thought of Alexander with another woman twisted my insides. I couldn't exactly tell him that though. It sounded too crazy after the short amount of time we'd spent together, and I guessed Alexander had dealt with his fair share of crazy over the years. "How would you feel if I screwed a room full of men?"

His hand flew out, striking the window and making me flinch. "Touché, poppet. But I should warn you I'm not good at sharing."

"No doubt that comes from never having to share much as a child."

"More than I would have liked," he said darkly, advancing toward me. His face was unreadable, cast in shadows. "While I'm fucking you, no one else will. Do you understand?"

My mouth fell open, but I shut it again. Setting down my plate, I stood so that we were on an equal level. "Is that an order?"

"You didn't seem to mind my orders earlier." His finger pushed between the layers of my robe and probed my stomach. "You liked being told what to do."

"In bed," I said, stepping away from him. I sensed a fight coming on and I couldn't think clearly when he was touching me. "I don't like being ordered around."

"I wouldn't dream of ordering you around *outside the bedroom*, Clara." He tilted his head and studied me for a moment. "But asking you not to sleep with other men seems to be on point, no?"

"Am I allowed to sleep with other women?" I asked.

"No, but that's an interesting idea."

"Okay, down boy." I rolled my eyes. "I'm just trying to prove that you're being irrational."

"It's not irrational," he said, grabbing the tie of my robe and yanking it so that it fell open. His gaze burned into me, and my nerves crackled, smoldering with desire. He wasn't going to fight fair. "I have many things I plan to do to this body. I want to take my time with it. I need to, so I'm not interested in playing games. If you want to be with me, I expect loyalty."

He stepped closer and slipped a hand between my legs. I choked back a whimper of pleasure at his touch and forced myself to keep eye contact with him.

"I have no issue with exclusivity, but you don't do relationships," I reminded him.

"I don't court. I'm not looking for romance or marriage. I want to fuck you, Clara. I want to make you come, and I want your perfect cunt to be mine exclusively." He'd begun to probe my seam with his long, powerful fingers. It was enough to make me dizzy, but I fought to maintain control. Reaching out, I gripped his cock through his shorts. It was rock hard and so very thick, and I fought the urge to drop to my knees in front of him. "This is mine then."

Alexander's lips twitched and I felt his cock pulse in my hands. He pressed against me, thrusting his cock fully into my grasp. "It's all yours, Clara."

His lips found mine then, kissing me until I no longer cared about what I'd really wanted to know: how long? How long was he mine?

It didn't matter. A week with him was more than I could ever ask for, and as his fingers slipped inside me, fucking me toward another earth-shattering climax, I pushed the question completely out of my mind.

CHAPTER TEN

I was on my stomach, buck naked and fantasizing about Alexander's hands kneading much more intimate parts of my body, when a text alert buzzed on my phone, which sat on a chair in the corner. My masseuse, Tyrone, clicked his tongue disapprovingly over the interruption.

"You're all tense now, girl," Tyrone chastised me. "Relax."

I tried to, but after last weekend, there was only one man my body obeyed. I focused on the new age music drifting through the room and slipped back to my fantasies. When I pried my deliciously limp body from the table at the end of the session, I grabbed my phone, surprised to see the text I'd received was from Alexander.

There's a window in this room that would benefit from having your naked body spread across it.

I fumbled as I typed a response, half dizzy from my near comatose state. The fact that I could hear the sexy rasp of Alexander's voice in my head reading the message didn't help.

After I was dressed, I stepped into the hall to discover my mother waiting for me. She looped her arm through mine and sighed. "Wasn't that wonderful? I didn't even know I was so tense."

"Me either," I said.

"Are you ready to shop?" she asked.

I nodded, stifling the urge to groan. I was going to need another massage after spending the day shopping under my mother's critical eye. Pocketing my phone, I smiled at her. "Lead the way."

A few hours and a small fortune later, we stopped to meet my sister for lunch. The afternoon crowd at Hillgrove's consisted mostly of ladies who lunch, like my mother, and a few tourists who were busy snapping pictures of their high tea sandwich assortment. My mother gave them a distasteful look, adjusting the brim of her Stephen Jones hat while we waited for my younger sister to join us. Our shopping bags were piled on an empty seat and Mom had taken the liberty of ordering already. Just as she had taken the liberty of choosing a dozen new dresses for me. I'd managed to convince her to let me pay, and I'd even gone so far as to buy a few pairs of heels. Although I wasn't likely to get much use wearing them around the office of Peters & Clarkwell, but since my social life had taken a surprising upturn last Friday, I knew I'd have plenty of opportunities to wear them.

I hadn't even fought her when she thrust a selection of short, sexy dresses at me in Yves St. Laurent.

"I'm so glad you picked up some new things," she said, sipping a martini. Most of the women here were drinking out of teacups, but Mom was on her first cocktail. It was the little things that showed she was American still, whether she liked it or not.

"I want to make a good impression at my new job." I shrugged as if this was perfectly obvious. I didn't tell her that at least half of the things I'd purchased I planned to wear for

Alexander. I kept this to myself not only because I wasn't ready to tell her I was seeing him, but also because I wasn't sure how long the relationship would last. Alexander and I had struck a tenuous agreement—one I wasn't entirely comfortable with—and I didn't think my mom would understand that I was screwing him with no commitment on his part. Exclusivity meant nothing to her if it wasn't coupled with a diamond on the finger.

"And you'll look fabulous on dates," she said.

"Sorry I'm late!" My sister Charlotte said, arriving in time to save me from Mom's curiosity regarding my love life. She flashed us a winning smile as she dropped her purse on the floor and took a seat.

Dressed in a sleeveless cream-colored shell that hung loosely over black leggings, Charlotte looked as if she'd stepped from the pages of a fashion magazine. The ensemble might have been plain on someone without her eye for style, but she'd paired it with a chic, yellow scarf and gold studs. She pushed her large, movie star sunglasses up to hold back the dark hair that waved over her shoulders.

"How was your meeting, Lola?" our mother asked, calling her by her pet name.

"Fine. Over." Lola shot me a conspiratorial wink, and I did my best not to groan. I'd had no doubt that her sudden scheduling conflict had more to do with sleeping off a late night than the cushy summer internship she'd landed at a marketing firm in Chelsea.

"We're just glad you're here now." Mom patted her arm.

"What did I miss?" Lola asked.

"I was telling Mom about my new job."

Lola blinked, the smile still plastered on her face. "Oh."

My mother didn't seem to notice Lola's obvious lack of interest. She smiled broadly as the waiter brought a selection of tea sandwiches to us on a tall tray. Picking one up, she bit into it delicately. "But I was really curious about whether Clara is seeing anyone."

There was a slight break in her voice, which gave away her true feelings. I had to give her credit, she'd managed to avoid bringing up the recent scandal I'd been involved in the whole morning. That had to be some kind of record. But with Lola here, I'd expected the subject to come up sooner rather than later. I considered her question, taking a large bite of a cucumber sandwich to buy me some time. If I continued to see Alexander, it was very likely I'd find myself on the cover of another gossip rag. But Alexander was being discreet about our relationship, and there was no reason to suspect anyone might find out if we continued our cloak and dagger routine. Plus, we had Norris. Alexander had made it clear that our relationship wasn't going further than dating and sex. If there was no future, why should I tell her? I ignored the flutter of anxiety that thought produced in my stomach.

"No," I lied. "Although Belle has her sights on every single man she knows."

"Annabelle is a good friend," Mom said. "You're so lucky to have her."

Actually, I was lucky to have her around, even if my mother didn't know the real reason. Belle was such a good friend because it meant I didn't have to hide my true relationship to her. She wasn't going to tell anyone, but it also meant I didn't have to put up with her blind dates.

"I saw in the papers that you were seen with Alexander again." Lola fluttered her lashes innocently as she abandoned her sandwich in favor of her newly-arrived martini.

I swallowed hard and took a long drink of water. Of course, she would have seen the photos from Friday night outside of Brimstone. "I agreed to meet him. That's all."

"That's all?" My mother laughed, shaking her head. "My daughter met the Prince of England, but no big deal."

"He's just a man," I said, hoping she couldn't see through my lie.

"He's far from just a man," Lola opined. "He's the most eligible bachelor in the world."

The vibration of an incoming text betrayed me, and my mother's eyes flickered to my mobile. Obviously she'd been aware of the number of text messages I had received today. I grabbed it and dropped it in my purse.

"That man is going to rule this country some day," Mom said in a soft voice.

"Mom, we're really more of a democracy," I reminded her. "Maybe I should set my sights on Parliament and sleep my way through them."

Lola choked on her martini, but Mom's eyes narrowed to slits. "Don't be filthy, Clara. Is it wrong that I want to know details? You don't tell me anything about your life. I only read about it in the papers."

"There's nothing to tell. He asked me to meet so he could apologize." At least I wasn't lying about that part. They didn't need to know I'd spent Saturday in his bed. Memories clouded my head for a moment and I was brought back to the present by the vibration of another text message. I snatched my phone out of my purse and read it.

I need to have my mouth on you. I need to make you come.

.My thighs clenched together at the thought and I had to shake my head a little to clear my thoughts. *Now's not the time for this*, I reminded myself. Mom was already suspicious, and when I looked up, her eyebrow was raised.

"Who's been texting you today?" she asked.

I turned to my sister, hoping for some distraction, but Lola was glued to her own mobile. I obviously couldn't count on her to come to my aid.

"Belle. She's having a fight with Philip." I hated lying. Now I'd gone and sullied my best friend's relationship, but if anyone wouldn't mind, it would be Belle.

"I hope it's nothing serious." Mom sipped her martini, her eyes still on me. I didn't think I imagined the double meaning to her words. She didn't believe me. She knew something was going on with Alexander, but how far would she press the issue? I needed our relationship to be secret for a while, even from her. At least until I'd figured out what our relationship was exactly. Without that, I wasn't certain I was strong enough to continue seeing him.

"It's not," I reassured her.

"Good." She gestured to our server for another drink. "Because I'd hate to see you get hurt."

"I'll be fine," I said with a sigh, somewhat relieved that we weren't skirting the issue any longer.

"I want you to be taken care of, Clara, but a man like Alexander...you're too fragile for him."

I gripped my fork and stared past her. She meant well, she always did, but that didn't mean that I wasn't tired of hearing how breakable I was. "I'm not a child anymore."

"I didn't say you were. But Clara, you're fiercely independent," she said gently, "so much so that you don't always see what the rest of us see."

"You mean Daniel?"

"Daniel, and other things."

I couldn't hold back a sigh. "I'm healthy, Mom. That was a long time ago."

"Clara, darling." She stretched her hand across the table and took mine. "I want you to stay healthy. You're an adult now. Just be sure that your decisions are made with your head and not your...heart."

I hated to think she might be right. Hadn't my head been warning me away from Alexander all along? I'd let myself be led around by my body, and somehow now my heart had gotten mixed up in this mess too. But the last person I could talk about this with was my mother. Alexander made me feel alive. In university, I'd been focused on my studies or Daniel. I'd learned to push down my emotions and lock them away so that I could make it through the day. And I'd hated it. Graduation had been about more than a degree. It has been about liberation, and the arrival of Alexander into my world had reawakened me to life, even if it had been primarily on the physical level.

My father had been protecting my mother from feeling too much for years. She couldn't possibly understand.

"Excuse me, I need the loo." I stood, surreptitiously pocketing my phone.

"I'll go with you," Lola said.

"I guess I'll stay here with the sandwiches," Mom snapped, obviously aware that I was avoiding this topic.

"I'm sure the gin will keep you company," I said sweetly.

Lola followed me to the bathroom, chattering away about her weekend and her hangover and some boy she'd brought home. The basics filtered in but my thoughts were elsewhere.

As soon as we were in the bathroom, I found a stall. Shutting the door behind me, I checked my messages.

I need to hear you crying my name as I fuck you.

Yes, please, I thought in reply. I heard the words spoken with his deep voice as I read them, tinged with a rasp that betrayed his physical yearning. It had barely been forty-eight hours since the last time I'd been with him, but I ached with desire reading his message.

I shot back a response.

But how can I scream your name with my mouth busy sucking you off?

A trio of responses arrived lightning-fast.

You won't know until you've tried.

Christ, I'm so fucking hard for you.

Finish eating and get your pretty ass over to me.

When I emerged from the stall, Lola was leaning against the bathroom counter. "So who's really texting you?"

"Belle," I said, deciding it was best to stick with my lie, especially since Lola held the world record when it came to gossip. She continued to watch me as I washed my hands and checked my makeup.

"You're glowing," she accused.

I bit back a grin and shrugged.

"Who screwed that smile onto your face?" she pushed. "C'mon, you have to tell me. We're sisters!"

"I don't kiss and tell." I headed for the door, but she blocked me.

"Was it Alexander?" she asked.

I went around her, ignoring her question. It was best to neither confirm nor deny, and I didn't know if I could pull off a convincing lie when it came to the subject of Alexander and sex. That was something I was definitely going to have to work on.

Lola pouted the rest of lunch, ganging up on me when Mom brought up the subject of dating.

"And your father says that his new associate is single," she told me. "He's working on an app that allows you to follow people all over the world and text them."

"Sounds like Twitter," I said dismissively. There was no way I was going on a blind date with one of my father's web developer friends.

"Clara's seeing someone," Lola said. She took a bite of cookie and smiled smugly as she chewed.

"You said you weren't!" Mom looked at me accusingly.

"And I'm not. Not really," I added.

"What about you, Lola?" Mom asked, and the two of them fell into a discussion about the numerous men vying for my sister's affection.

"I do hope your sister meets someone nice soon," Mom said to her when they'd finished their gossip.

"I had a lovely afternoon," I said, shifting the topic away from my personal life. Flattery always distracted her.

Her hand clutched at her necklace in mock humility. "It was nice, wasn't it? We need to see more of each other now that you're out of school. Your father is working all the time. I've been lonely."

"I start work on Friday," I reminded her for the tenth time today.

She hesitated then took a deep breath. "You know you really don't need to work. At least not doing something like social work."

I flinched at the audacity of her suggestion. I knew she disapproved of my choice of vocation, but this was the first time she'd really suggested that I not work.

"You're worth twenty million pounds," she said in a low voice, so that the other diners couldn't hear her. "You don't need to work."

How could I explain to her that she was the reason that I needed to work? I'd watched my mother flit from charity event to charity event for years. She'd been deeply involved with the start-up when I was a baby, but as soon as it sold, she'd abandoned the notion of needing a job altogether. I had been too little to really know much about my mother before her and my father had sold their online dating site, *partner.com*, for two hundred million dollars in the mid-90s, but I'd heard stories. She'd been ambitious once, and she'd given it all up for a life of shopping and lunch dates. I might not have known my mother back then, but I knew her now and it didn't take much to see she wasn't happy. "I'd rather use my degree."

My degree was my one trump card, the one thing my mother always agreed with. The thing she felt I had to have to succeed in life. Maybe because it was the only thing that Madeline Bishop didn't have and couldn't buy.

"Of course, you would," she said, her eyes growing glassy. She looked away, pulling back her hand and I felt a pang of sympathy for her. How would things be different if she'd graduated herself? "And when you finally meet the right man, you won't have to worry about money."

That struck me as an odd thing to say. I know her and dad had struggled the first few years of their marriage, but at least they'd been happy. It was strange that she couldn't see how unhappy she was now that she had money. Of course, she was right. I would never have to worry about money. It was a bit of a relief, even if the money sometimes felt unwelcome. I'd toyed with giving it all away before, but there were provisions that prevented that in the trust fund arrangement. I wouldn't have full custody over the money until I turned twenty-five.

After the bill was paid, we rose to say goodbye. My mother flung her arms around me in an awkward show of emotion, which I wasn't fully comfortable with, but I accepted the gesture all the same.

"Call me and tell me how your first day goes," she said as she collected her bags from La Mer and Louis Vuitton.

"I promise."

"Lola." Mom shifted her attention to my younger sister. "I picked up your eye cream."

We walked out of the restaurant together, and I braced

myself as soon as we hit the front door, but there were no reporters outside. Mom squeezed my arm and gave me a knowing smile, before she kissed my cheek and got into a waiting taxi.

As soon as it pulled away from the curb, Lola slipped her sunglasses on. "Have a fun afternoon."

"I'm heading home to an empty flat." I paused, at war with myself, before forcing myself to add, "You could come over."

"I'm sure you'll find something more interesting to do," she said suggestively, pushing her sunglasses down to shoot me a wink.

I clutched my phone and shook my head as she walked away. She wasn't sprinting into adulthood, she was crashing into it.

The weather in London had started to grow warmer, so despite my collection of shopping bags, I decided to walk to the Tube. I could only imagine what my mother would think of that, but it seemed silly to take a cab all the way to East London, and the weather was gorgeous. In a few more weeks, summer would arrive bringing heat and stickiness along with it. I might as well glory in the few remaining days of spring we had left.

My purse vibrated and a thrill ran from my head to my toes when I saw it was another message from Alexander.

I need to see you now. The Westminster Royal.

At least my job wasn't starting until Friday, which meant I could play as much as I wanted to now, and I'd been waiting all day for Alexander to ask for something more concrete. His texts had kept my body humming with barely repressed sexuality this afternoon. Now he was going to make good on that, and I couldn't wait. I could use the stress relief after a day with my mom too. I texted him back and changed my direction, heading to the hotel where I'd last seen him. I couldn't keep a somewhat silly grin off my face as I walked. Thankfully, I'd gotten made up for a day shopping with my mom, although I suspected Alexander would like me in anything. My phone alerted me to an incoming message and I checked it, excitement turning my stomach over. I would be with him soon. I would feel his hands on me soon. But when I saw the text, my heart dropped.

Belle: I think you should see this.

CHAPTER ELEVEN

I read the post twice while standing in the lobby of the Westminster Royal, but it was the attached image that I couldn't get out of my head. Alexander's arms were around a beautiful blonde woman, the kind of woman that would make any other woman irrationally jealous. There had been no effort to hide it. Whoever had snapped this photo had been close enough to capture the full spectrum of what had been going on. I'd seen her before, in other photos that Belle had shown me, but the worst part was that from this angle I knew without a doubt that she was the woman Alexander had dismissed as a past mistake on that fateful day at the Oxford and Cambridge Club. She was obviously someone important because the caption read: *Alexander spotted once again with the stunning Pepper Lockwood.* She was all legs and blonde hair and bee-stung lips. She looked like a model, and her golden blond beauty complimented Alexander's dark hair and muscular build.

You have no claim over him, I reasoned. But didn't I? Hadn't he insisted—no, *demanded*—exclusivity? Apparently he didn't hold himself to the same expectations. I shouldn't be surprised, but still, I was, and more than that, I was hurt. I'd spent all day dreaming about being with him, but now I felt hollow, gutted by my foolishness.

"Miss." A porter came up to me and hesitated. "May I help you?"

I'd almost forgotten that I was standing in the lobby of a five-star hotel. I started to shake my head, but then I made a decision, sliding my phone off. "The Presidential Suite."

"You must be here to see Mr. X," he said. "This way, please."

The *ex* part certainly seemed fitting at the moment. I wanted to kick myself. He spent so much time here that he went by an alias. How had I gotten myself into this mess?

The lift ride to the top floor was excruciatingly slow despite the private car reserved for guests of the suite. The photo had been taken last night at a private function. I wasn't angry at him for not taking me, not when we were trying to keep our relationship quiet, but I was pissed that he held me to different standards than himself. If he thought I was going to sit around and wait for his calls while he screwed around with half of London's female population, he had another thing coming.

But what really scared me was that he clearly knew this girl. It was obvious from the embrace and from the story attached, not to mention his reaction to her presence on the day we met. The gossip site pointed out that the two were old friends but then speculated that something more was going on. Maybe he'd changed his mind about seeing me. He'd only been back in London a short while after all. He'd kissed me once to avoid her. Was he screwing me now to get back at her?

It clawed at me not to know. It wasn't healthy to be this attached already. I knew that, but I also couldn't help it. My attraction to Alexander was inexplicable. While most women would have seen his godlike money and title and sexiness, what was underneath was even sexier. Underneath all the control and power, there was a soul so human and fragile that I'd been lucky to glimpse it only once or twice. But he'd shown himself to me. I was sure of that much. I had thought that meant something. Now I was no longer sure.

Maybe it was all a game with him. He'd warned me he was dangerous. He told me that he would hurt me.

Mission accomplished.

My stomach twisted and I felt a too familiar rawness creeping up my throat, the tears swelling there as I tried to hold them back. I wouldn't give him the satisfaction of knowing he had gotten to me. Maybe he got off on that, too.

I was barely holding it together when the elevator stopped at our floor. *His floor*, I corrected myself.

Get it together, Clara. I focused on channeling my hurt into anger and stepped through the sliding doors with my fists clenched.

Alexander was on me before I could react. He lifted me up, hands cupping my ass as his lips crushed into me. I couldn't think. I was intoxicated by him, my body betraying me, anger melting into desire as he slid a hand up to grip my neck. He pressed me against the wall and my legs wrapped more tightly around his waist. I didn't want this moment to end, although I knew it had to.

One last kiss.

I couldn't hold back the tears anymore, and they spilled down. I tasted my sadness on his lips and he gasped, pulling back to stare at me in confusion.

"Clara." He caught my chin in his hands and tilted my tear-stained eyes to meet his. "What's wrong?"

I turned my head from his and pushed against his chest until he set me on my feet.

"What's going on?" he asked in a low voice.

"This, *Mr. X!*" I held up my phone, so he could see the TMI article.

"I'm not sure I understand what's happening here."

"What's happening is that you're an asshole!" The words exploded from my mouth.

Alexander ran a hand through his dark hair and walked over to the bar. "Drink?"

I shook my head. It was intoxicating enough to be around him, I didn't need to further jeopardize my good sense.

"So TMI is reporting that I was seen with Pepper last night?"

Hearing him say her name was like a punch in the gut. It confirmed all my greatest fears. He did know her, and he wasn't even going to lie about it. I supposed that should have made me feel better, but it made me feel worse. As though I should have known this was going to happen.

"Weren't you the one that said tabloids report rumors as facts?" he asked. "Because I rather appreciated the truth of that statement. Sit down, Clara."

I folded my arms over my chest and stared him down. So he was going to use my own words against me. Fine. He could play it that way, but I didn't have to obey him. "I'd prefer to stand."

"Suit yourself." Alexander dropped into a leather armchair and sipped his drink thoughtfully.

"So you know her?"

"Of course, I know her. I've known Pepper for years."

"You aren't making me feel any better."

"Are you jealous?" A slow smile carved onto his lips.

I refused to meet his eyes. Yes, I was jealous, and I didn't like it one bit. "Who is she?"

"A friend of my sister's." Alexander's voice caught on the final word of this statement, and he took a long swig of his drink.

"And that's it? Wasn't she the girl at the club?" Suddenly all my feelings felt confused. In a very real way this girl had brought us together, but I needed to understand why, especially if she was actually a part of his life.

"She was," he confirmed. "You're wondering if I'm using you to get to her."

How did he do that? How did he know what I was thinking even though we'd known each other such a short time?

"We're connected, Clara. Can't you feel it? At first, I thought it was just sexual." Alexander set down his glass and stood to come over to me. "The way your body responds to mine. How it feels when I'm inside you. But it's more than that. I know you feel it."

I did and that was what scared me. Alexander had made it clear there were no long-term options for us, and this feeling—this connection—was far from casual. "Why even bring it up? You don't do commitment, remember?"

"I remember." Alexander's mouth twisted into a frown. "I don't understand it either. I don't even know why I'm explaining myself to you—"

"Because you want exclusivity, remember? You demanded it from me! But apparently not from yourself!"

"Do you think I fucked her?" he asked, taking a step closer to me. His proximity raised goose bumps all over my body, and I had to consciously keep myself from closing the small gap between us. I hated myself in that moment. I hated him for making me want him so badly.

"If it walks like a fuck and talks like a fuck," I said. *This* was definitely a time to use the real term.

"I don't lie, Clara," Alexander said in a quiet voice. "And if you accuse me of doing so, I will take you over my knee."

I gasped, backing a step away from him. He'd threatened to before, but I saw now that he meant it—and not playfully.

"You'd like that," he continued, prowling toward me. "I see it in your eyes—the hunger."

I held up a hand, shaking my head, forcing my rational side to prevail over my hormones.

Alexander's hand shot out and grabbed mine, bringing it to his lips. "I'll never lay a finger on you without your permission, but the sooner you accept the truth, Clara, the better."

"What truth?" I choked out the words, willing myself to ignore the blaze of longing igniting in me.

"You want to submit to me. You want me to tell you what to do with that sweet little mouth. The way your body responds to mine. It wants to be controlled. Dominated. *You* want to be dominated. You're so incredibly strong, Clara." Alexander trailed a finger across my belly and my core clenched. "But you need to lose control. You want to."

I shook my head, but his words had struck a cord. I wasn't telling him no. I was telling myself no. "No, I don't."

"You'll be safe with me." Alexander caught my shirt in his hands and pulled me roughly to him until our bodies pressed close together. "I'll never take you further than you can handle, but I will take you to the edge. I will give you more pleasure than you ever thought possible."

I swallowed, trying to comprehend these promises and the strange effect they had on me. My rational side began painting a picture. I'd had a bad relationship before and it was clear this one was headed in the same direction. "I'm not like that."

"I don't think you understand what I'm offering you. *Release.* My only thought is of your pleasure. When you give yourself to me, I take that responsibility seriously, Clara."

I turned away from the intense gaze of his eyes, trying to clear my head. "What are we talking about? Ropes and safe words?"

"Small steps, Clara, but yes. A safe word is a necessity. For now I want you to trust me. I want you to trust that I will give you pleasure."

"And you'll punish me too?" I demanded. "Threaten to spank me if I misbehave?"

"Only when you don't trust me," he said coolly even though fire sparked in his eyes. "Without trust, you can't give me control, Clara, and then we can't have what we both need."

"You mean what you want!" I couldn't believe we were having this conversation.

"Need," he said in a low voice that was anything but soft. "What *you* need."

"I...don't..." I choked on the words, too astonished to rebuke him.

"Yes, you do." He said the words gently, as though he was explaining to a child why she needed to eat her vegetables. "Let me show you."

I balked at him, but my body reacted to his words with a shiver of dangerous arousal. Shaking my head, I forced myself to reject the suggestion that I wanted this. "I can't. I'm sorry."

Alexander took a step back and stared at me. "Someone tried to break you before."

I bit my lip, tears stinging my eyes. *And no one would again.*

"I'm not him, Clara. That's not what I want to do to you."

"You warned me," I cried. "You told me you would hurt me!"

He'd shown me all the warning signs and I'd still come running to him. To his bed. Suddenly it became clear that it wasn't Alexander who was sending mixed signals.

"I did," he said in a soft voice. He turned away from me.

"I should go." There was nothing for me here. That much was clear.

"You probably should," he said, "but I wish you wouldn't.

Go to bed with me one more time. Let me show you. Let me give you pleasure."

I thought of how I'd felt when I saw that article earlier today, and I heard my mother's warning echo in my head. I was too confused. Alexander had me all mixed up, and spending more time with him—going to bed with him—was only going to make that confusion worse. I'd given him the wrong idea about me, about what I wanted. I hadn't walked into a trap. I'd led the predator to my door with breadcrumb promises spilled from my lips. "I can't."

Alexander stiffened, but he didn't turn to look at me, instead he bobbed his head curtly, but as I tuned to leave, he said. "You won't."

There was a note of accusation in his voice. He could see right through me. He hadn't been lying about that connection. Why then couldn't he see that the intensity of our relationship was terrifying? But he knew that. He also knew that I found it exhilarating. He'd counted on that being enough and it almost had been, but I'd seen the darkness in his eyes and it scared me.

It scared me almost as much as it aroused me. That's why I left.

CHAPTER TWELVE

The next few days passed in a blur, and I found myself, despite my best intentions, checking the email alert that Belle had set up for me. It didn't matter though. Alexander was flying low under the radar. The only contact he seemed to be making with the outside world was the texts he sent to my mobile. He was making it hard to stick to my decision to end our brief relationship before it got out of control. I took to repeatedly reminding myself it was better to end things now to get through the day. We barely knew each other after all, but the fact that Alexander hadn't given up suggested maybe I wasn't crazy for having a hard time calling it quits.

There was still so much I wished I knew about him; however, I knew my fascination with him wasn't healthy. Alexander came with baggage that I couldn't carry. The fame. The darkness. The control issues. It was too much, too fast. *He* consumed me when he was near me and occupied my mind when he wasn't. Ending it was the only option.

So why couldn't I let him go?

But this morning I had bigger things on my mind. At least, I was trying to keep the fact that I was starting my new job at

Peters & Clarkwell my top priority. In actuality, the fact was that I was failing miserably.

"You should block him," Belle suggested as she poured me a cup of coffee.

"He has access to SIS," I reminded her. "I'm not sure it will matter if I block him." I didn't add that I'd already tried and couldn't bring myself to do it.

"I don't like seeing you this way. Are you sure this girl is really something to get so miffed over?"

Belle's heart was in the right place, because I hadn't been able to tell her the truth. That the real reason that I'd walked away from Alexander had nothing to do with the tabloid photos of him with Pepper Lockwood. How could I explain to her that he scared me? She knew I'd attracted the wrong men in the past. She would completely understand my compulsion to run if she knew what he wanted, and maybe that's why I couldn't bring myself to do it. Belle would never look at Alexander the same way again. What I couldn't figure it out is why I cared so much. He wanted to dominate me. He claimed only in the bedroom. He claimed it would be safe. But was that a risk I was capable of taking?

"I don't know," I said, not able to lie to her. At least, not entirely. "Maybe I'm just hurt, but I think it's better if we get some distance."

As if on cue, my phone buzzed with an incoming text. I snatched it up before she could see what it said. Alexander's texts ranged from reasonable to wildly sexual, although I expected the overly dirty ones came from a night spent drinking too much. He'd managed to keep them respectful for the most part, which made it even harder not to respond.

"Whatever he did, he isn't trying to hide that he's thinking about you." Belle flipped her hair over her shoulder and shot me a meaningful look.

"He's thinking about sex, like most guys," I corrected her.

"Most guys don't bother thinking at all, let alone texting you repeatedly."

I turned my attention to my coffee, hoping it would steady the agitated beat of my nerves. "I can't worry about this. I start work today."

"And you look fabulous," Belle said, switching topics on my cue. At least, I could count on her to know when to drop something.

I looked fabulous because Belle had organized my new wardrobe for me and helped me pick out my first outfit. She'd abandoned two days of catering appointments to focus on distracting me, and I was grateful. As it turns out, I wasn't hopeless in the fashion department because this morning she only had to correct my choice of shoes. I still wasn't sold on wearing three-inch Jimmy Choos to work, but who was I to argue with Belle? I'd knotted my hair into a loose bun at the back of my neck, not wanting to look too young or too frigid, and put on just enough makeup to give my pale skin some color.

"Do you think this dress is okay?" I smoothed down the simple linen shift as I stood, wondering for the tenth time if I should wear a jacket. Summer was fast approaching and I expected the walk to be warm. The last thing I wanted was to show up sweaty on my first day, but then again, I wasn't convinced a sleeveless dress was work appropriate.

"Stop obsessing." Belle shook her head. "You look great and you do not need a jacket, before you even ask. They're damn lucky to have you. You don't need that job, Clara."

"That doesn't mean I can do whatever I want," I argued.

"No, but it does mean you don't have to worry about what they think of you—or at least what they think of your clothes. But even so, you look like a sophisticated career woman, and they're going to die over your accent."

I hung my head dramatically. "I don't have an accent."

"You're an American in London, honey."

"I'm not American!"

"If it walks like a duck and talks like a duck," she said with a wink.

All the enthusiasm drained from my body, and I lurched forward to clutch the countertop. Was this how it was always going to be? Little things reminding me of Alexander. Little things driving me crazy. All the what-if's and might-have-beens chipping away my sanity.

"What is it?" Belle cried, setting her mug down so quickly that its contents splashed over the rim. She caught my arm and peered at me with concern.

I could only shake my head, forcing a small laugh to lighten the mood. "It's nothing."

"You were thinking about him, weren't you?" There was no accusation in the question. It was soft and welcoming, practically begging for me to confide in her. "I know there's more going on here, Clara. Bloody hell, if I'd known he was going to have this effect on you, I would never have encouraged you to go out with him."

"Why would you think he has an effect on me? I barely know him." But my words were hollow. There were a lot of things I didn't know about Alexander. The trouble was both that I wanted to know them and that I had glimpsed enough to feel bound to him. In fact, I knew it wasn't just a feeling. I was bound to him, but I couldn't explain that to Belle. I could barely explain it to myself.

"Oh darling." Belle brushed a stray lock of hair behind my ear and wrapped her arms around me. "Today is not about him. You worked really hard to get here."

She was right. I couldn't let Alexander ruin this for me. If I really wanted to prove I was independent, that I didn't want him, I had to stand on my own two feet and do it.

"I'm going to kill myself in these heels," I said, ready to talk about anything else.

"Nonsense. Those heels are tame," she reminded me.

I laughed when I considered the sky-high stilettos she'd convinced me to purchase for nights on the town. Apparently she didn't fear mixing alcohol and footwear as much as I did.

"I need to get going."

"Here." Belle shoved a bag in my hand. "Lunch."

"Thanks, Mom," I said, pecking her on the cheek.

"No excuses. Take a lunch break. I don't want you to work yourself to death!"

Smiling as I closed the door to the flat behind me, I realized I had someone watching out for me after all.

MY DESK CONSISTED OF A SMALL TABLE CRAMMED INTO A cubicle as far from the window as possible, and I loved it. I had earned that desk and the small name plate that my new boss had presented to me upon my arrival. That was what I couldn't explain to my parents or to Belle: the sense of pride at having worked for something. I loved them all dearly, but it was something they just couldn't fathom.

"The facsimile machine is in here," Bennett explained to me as I followed him through the office. I was pleased that hardly anyone gave me a second glance. My brief moment of notoriety seemed to be a distant memory to everyone. Of course, maybe they weren't as in tune with the breaking stories of TMI and other less dignified news organizations. Serious work was done here.

"We're about to start a campaign with Isaac Blue's foundation to raise awareness about drinking water safety in Africa. I know you have some experience working with the well-known..." Bennett trailed away as soon as he saw my face.

"Sorry," I choked out, gesturing for him to continue.

"When your parents sold their company, you spent some time in society circles," he prompted, and I immediately felt foolish. Of course, that's what he meant. We'd discussed my parents' company during my interview. He would have done follow-up research.

"I was a little too young to really remember that," I admitted.

"Don't worry about it." Bennett waved it off. "I'm just trying to warn everyone now because Isaac might be sitting in on some meetings and well..."

"I get it," I said with a smile. I couldn't exactly blame the boss for wanting to let everyone know we were going to be working with one of the sexiest actors alive. A year ago, that news might have thrilled me. I probably would have rushed to text Belle as soon as I had a moment alone, but now it barely made a dent.

Bennett welcomed me into his office and took his seat. I smiled when I saw the photograph he had of two identical blond-haired girls on his desk.

"Abby and Amy," he said with a broad smile. His affection for them was obvious. "They're six going on eighteen."

"You must have your hands full," I said, thinking of how much trouble Lola and I had caused when we were kids. We'd been born so close together that we'd acted like twins up until secondary school.

Bennett tucked his hands behind his head and frowned. He was a good-looking guy in his early forties with salt and pepper hair and age lines that made him look distinguished. He was lucky to be aging well, but I guessed the twins were keeping

him young. "When I was your age, I did this job because I
idealized the world. Now that I have them, I do it because I
don't."

I nodded as if I understood.

"Who are you doing this for?" he asked. "Do you have a
significant other?"

I swallowed against my dry mouth and shook my head. At
least I knew he hadn't heard about me and Alexander. There
was no way he would have asked if he had. "Nope. I'm doing it
for me."

"It's as good a reason as any." He shook his head and smiled
at me. "Sorry, I didn't mean to get all deep on you. I think I've
been a little too philosophical since my wife died."

I stifled a gasp, even as my hand flew to my chest. I wasn't
sure if I hurt more for him or for the girls. I had a trying relationship with my mom, but at least she was around. "I'm so sorry."

"Thanks," he said sincerely. "My therapist wants me to talk
about it casually to others so that it becomes more real to me."

I couldn't keep my face from screwing up at this bit of information. "Your therapist sounds like a dick."

As soon as it was out of my mouth, I wished I could swallow
it back down, but it was too late. To my relief, Bennett dropped
his head back and bellowed.

"You know, Clara. You're right. I thought the same thing,
but everyone kept telling me I had to go and see him," he said. "I
should probably cancel my next appointment, huh?"

"I guess if that's the best he can do," I said apologetically.
"I've been here all of an hour, and I'm already butting into your
personal life. I'm sorry."

"Don't be. It was a refreshing change of pace. Everyone else
here," he dropped his voice to a whisper, "was around when she
died. They treat me like I'm made of glass."

I knew what it was like to be deemed fragile. It became

impossible to tell if you'd really break if you fell after a while. "I won't treat you that way."

"You're going to be hard on me then?" He looked at me hopefully.

I cracked a smile. "You have no idea."

DESPITE BELLE'S GOOD INTENTIONS, MY LUNCH LEFT something to be desired, namely in the flavor department. So I grabbed my purse, thinking I might check out the chips shop on the corner. As soon as I stood, I felt eyes on me. The girl in the cubicle across from mine looked away as soon as I turned toward her. Two more people whispered in the corner and didn't bother to hide their gaze. My cheeks flooded with heat. Maybe I'd been wrong about not being recognized. Digging my phone out of my purse to text Belle, I discovered I had a new email in my personal account. My heart stopped when I saw the subject line.

The TeXXXts Prince Alexander Doesn't Want You To See

Eyes bored into me from every direction, and I willed the floor to open and swallow me alive. This was what I'd been desperate to avoid: attention. I scrolled through the story, fighting the urge to throw up. Bile rose in my throat as I saw the posted messages. They were all there, in all their explicit glory. Not only had someone hacked his account, they'd tracked the recipient of the messages: me. And to make certain there was no doubt that I was the Clara Bishop that had the Prince in a frenzy, they'd included a photo they must have snapped this morning when I left for the office. How hadn't I noticed them there? Had I been that oblivious?

Stuffing my phone back in my pocket, I lifted my head, determined to make a dignified exit. I would get lunch. I would forget this happened and it would all blow over. The first story had, after all, and there weren't going to be any more. It was over between Alexander and me. But I hadn't gotten two steps when my confidence faltered and I stumbled. Standing at the door to Peters & Clarkwell was Alexander.

CHAPTER THIRTEEN

I t took me a few seconds to recover, but I regained my footing and strode toward him. What was he doing here? How did he even know I had started work? It had been days since I had seen him, and I'd never told him where I was going to be working. But despite his unexplained presence, I wasn't surprised that Alexander had found his way to me. Behind me, the office buzzed as people realized who he was.

So much for a normal work life.

"What are you doing here?" I hissed under my breath. Crossing my arms across my chest, I did my best to look unhappy to see him. Inside I was anything but. God, he looked sexy. His hair disheveled, although I noticed that he had circles under his eyes like he hadn't been sleeping. Most likely he'd spent the last few days partying. He was dressed casually in a fitted t-shirt and jeans that hung off his hips like an invitation. My thoughts flickered to memories of us in bed and I caught my breath, hoping to calm my racing nerves, so he wouldn't see his effect on me.

"You've had long enough. I need to talk to you." He stepped

forward and took my arm in a gentle but assertive hold, leading me toward the building's lift.

Was he fucking serious? I'd had long enough?

"Couldn't you text me?" I asked with a sarcastic note to my voice.

"I guess you saw that too." Alexander dropped his hold on me as we entered the elevator, but as soon as the doors slid shut behind us, he pinned me against the wall.

"Alexander!"

"Why haven't you answered my texts?"

"The whole world can read that you want to go down on me on a gossip site and you're worried about that?" I didn't bother to hide my disbelief, because I was too busy focusing on keeping my body in check, even as it rebelled against me. It was all I could do not to arch into his embrace and kiss him. I wanted to brush away the fear I saw in his eyes and tell him everything would be okay. But it was as much a lie as my pretending I didn't want him here with me.

"I don't give a damn what they can read!" he exploded, pushing off the wall and clenching his hands into fists. "Why do you care what they think, Clara?"

"Me?" I touched my chest for emphasis. "You were the one who wanted to meet me in secret at a fucking hotel!"

Alexander stared at me a moment, wheels turning in his head. "I did that to protect you. You were scared of the paparazzi."

"They were reporting we were in a relationship," I reminded him. "And I didn't know who you were at the time."

"We are in a relationship," he said.

My mouth fell open. I was torn between the bubbly, bouncy feeling of joy this produced in me and total confusion. Never mind that I'd called things off between us, things had never really gotten started. "We broke things off."

"You were overwhelmed and I gave you space, but did you think I would allow you to end things like that?" he asked. "I made it clear that I hadn't had my fill of you."

"But you didn't want to be seen with me," I argued. "You can't pick and choose when to be in a relationship!" I knew it was more complicated than that. I only wished it were that simple. There was too much for us to work through, especially when everything between us came on his terms.

"I wanted to protect you." Alexander turned back to me, trailing a finger down my face. "I didn't want to scare you. I can do that all on my own."

I barked a short, humorless laugh as the lift doors opened. "You can at that."

"So is that what's going on?" he asked, pulling me into a deserted alcove off the lobby. "A misunderstanding?"

I wanted it to be that and nothing more, but the truth was there was a lot more going on. First of all, there was the mysterious Pepper Lockwood. He still hadn't explained what was really going on with her to me, and then there was the proposition he'd put forth the last time we spoke. He wanted to dominate me. He wanted me to submit. I wasn't sure I was capable of that. I wasn't sure it was healthy.

I shook my head, tears welling in the corners of my eyes. "I wish it was."

"You're scared of me." He spoke this like a realization not a question and dropped his hold on me in resignation. "I tried to warn you."

"Maybe I don't understand," I said softly. I couldn't deny that I hadn't stopped thinking about him, and I couldn't deny how I felt now that he was here. Somewhere my rational side was shaking her head, but where had my rational side gotten me romantically? My body knew what it wanted, but could I trust it? Maybe it was time to listen to my heart.

Alexander's hand gripped my hip tightly, kneading into the flesh through my skirt, as though he was considering tearing it off me. I trembled at the touch, hungry for contact from him after so long. How could I deny how he made me feel? But I needed to think. I needed to know what I was getting into. There was no way I could choose whether or not Alexander had a place in my life until I did.

"When I told you that I was protecting you from the reporters, how did you feel?" he asked.

I was taken aback by the change in conversation, but I considered his question for a moment before answering. "I guess that—" I paused, breathing in deeply before I answered "—I felt safe."

"Why?" The question was a challenge. He was trying to help me understand his own reasoning. But it was more than that though. I could see in his eyes that he *needed* me to understand.

"Because you care," I realized.

It was hard to explain to him that my parents often had been too caught up in business ventures to worry about how their lifestyle affected me. Instead, they knee-jerked, trying to control me. And then there was Daniel, which was a whole different mess. But there was also an element that I didn't fully understand. The thought of Alexander protecting me publicly and privately didn't stress me—not yet, at least. Not when I really considered it. Instead, it flooded through me like sudden heat. The more I thought about it, the more the warmth spread until I felt secure and safe.

"I do care, Clara." He leaned in so that our faces were at the same level and he stared into my eyes, unflinchingly. "I didn't want you to experience being trashed by the press."

"So it wasn't that you didn't want to be seen with me?" I asked.

"Have you looked in the mirror lately? I can only assume you haven't, so let me describe what you look like right now. Clara Bishop has large, gray eyes with fluttering lashes and a button nose. That would be enough to make her pretty, but then she has these pouty lips that make me hard. Her hair is silky and soft, and no matter how much she tries to control it, there's always some locks that escape to drift down her neck or blow across her face. I can't help imagining letting it all down, watching it fall over her shoulders as she comes on my cock." Alexander shifted, pressing me against the wall, so that I could feel his erection pushing into me. "She drives me crazy, and I honestly don't care who knows it."

"But you don't do relationships, Mr. X," I said in a soft voice.

"I don't do romance," he corrected, "but if you'll let me, I will do pleasure."

"There's no one else then, Mr. X?" I purposefully called him by the moniker he used at the hotel.

"Too formal, poppet."

"Okay, then. There's no one else then, X?"

"I'm true to my word, Clara." Darkness glinted in his eyes, turning the crystal blue to flinty steel.

I shivered, remembering the last time I'd questioned his word. He'd threatened to spank me—one thing I knew that I couldn't allow. "But you want to dominate me."

I couldn't claim to be an aggressive person. At times, like so many women I knew, I took the passive route, preferring to avoid confrontations. But I could be assertive, too. The one thing I couldn't choose to be was submissive.

"I want to give you pleasure. When you found out I was protecting you, it made you feel safe. That's what I want to do," he explained as his lips cruised along my jawline, providing evidence that he meant what he said. "I want to show you that I can protect you while showing you the heights of pleasure you've never known."

I swallowed at the thought of Alexander being in control of my body—at the thought of his hands exploring me and his voice commanding me. He'd proven he was an excellent lover, but could I really give myself to him? Could I trust him not to break me again?

"I don't know," I said, because I didn't. I couldn't count on being able to keep my head when it came to Alexander, which meant that I couldn't count on not making a mistake.

Alexander's head dropped to my shoulder in resignation, but when he lifted it to meet my timid gaze, the passionate fire that burned moments earlier still blazed. "You win."

"I do?" I didn't quite understand.

"We'll do it your way, Clara. I want you. I want you any way I can have you."

He was relenting—or was this a compromise? I couldn't fathom what he was offering me. "You agree that I'm not your submissive?"

"I agree not to push you, Clara—unless you ask me to..." His voice trailed away, leaving something left unsaid. But if he wasn't going to push me on this, I couldn't push him either.

My pulse raced at his confession even as the shock of it wore off. And while my heart thrilled, desire for him pooled in my belly. How long did I have to wait until I could have him again?

"Soon, poppet," Alexander promised, tucking a strand of hair behind my ear and kissing the hollow of my neck. "What are your plans this evening?"

If I was being honest, my plans tonight had involved a good amount of red wine and renting a movie. Now it appeared I was going to be given another option. A familiar voice told me to play hard to get, but I ignored her. I was a starving woman in

Alexander's presence. Only with him here could I see how much I'd missed him.

"I'm flexible," I answered.

Alexander's mouth curved into a smile. "There's a thing this evening. Would you go with me?"

"What kind of thing?" I asked, instantly suspicious.

"A ball." He held a finger to my lips. "And before you say no, it is for an excellent cause. We're raising money for endangered animals. And furthermore, I don't want to go either."

I hesitated. This was more than a date. This was stepping out in the limelight in a very real way. There'd be no denying our relationship after it. Alexander had to know that.

"There's no going back after something like this," Alexander said, voicing my thoughts out loud. "If you want a chance at normalcy—at privacy—you should say no. But if you want a relationship, it seems as good a place as any to start."

"What about you? Do you want normal?"

"I don't even know what those words mean. I never have." There were ghosts echoing in his eyes, and I stroked his cheek as if I could chase them away.

I wasn't sure what to say, torn between my desire to claim Alexander as mine, but knowing that doing so meant opening myself up to judgment. Not only as the woman I was today, but also my past. How long would it take before every secret I ever had was splashed on the cover of a tabloid? How long before the paparazzi lost interest in me?

"I can protect you from this. We can meet privately if you prefer," he offered. "If you don't want to come tonight, I understand, but please understand me when I say—" his eyes gleamed as he spoke "—you *will come* tonight in other ways."

My lips twitched. "Is that so?"

Alexander's hands slid from my hips to my waist as he leaned in, kissing me hard on the mouth. Our tongues tangled together, dancing around each other like I was dancing around this question. It was an unfair means of persuasion.

"But they know about us," I reminded him, breaking away. "They have the texts."

"By Monday morning, MI5 will know who hacked my account, and they'll be in jail."

"And that will be another huge story. The kind that links back to this one," I pointed out. "An arrest won't erase that."

"No, but it will send a message," he said firmly. "And don't worry, I've devised other ways of contacting you."

"Carrier pigeons? Smoke signals?"

He smirked. God, I wanted to kiss that cocky grin. "That can be arranged."

My body hummed in response, charmed by his smile, by his laugh. He turned me on when he was serious, when he was demanding, but he thrilled me to the bone when he was light-hearted, and I realized I would give anything to see him that way as often as possible. I knew that meant I couldn't walk away from him, even if I tried. "I can't keep pretending you mean nothing to me. I don't like the hiding or the secrecy, but I still want my privacy. Is that something we can make work?"

But even as I asked, I knew it wasn't possible. Alexander had lived his whole life under scrutiny. Why would it be any different for me?

"Of course." To his credit, he said it sincerely. But maybe that's how one got by in a world like this, by believing things could be changed for the better. Maybe it's how I would survive.

"I'll go," I said at last. As soon as it was out of my mouth, I realized there were other implications to saying yes to Alexander. Namely, I was going to a ball tonight. With nothing to wear. With no clue how to act. With the sexiest, most sought after man in the world on my arm. But Alexander's lips kissed me until I forgot about all the whos and whats, only remembering the why.

"You are my fairy godmother," I said as Belle held up a pair of shoes that perfectly matched the Alexander McQueen she'd found for me. Having Belle as a flatmate was like having access to Harrods at home.

"And next week, I'm taking you shopping." She wagged her finger like I was in trouble.

"Ugh." I flopped back on her bed and pulled a pillow over my head. "I just went shopping."

"You should have thought of that before you started banging His Royal Hotness."

I stuck my tongue out at her but couldn't keep a goofy grin from sliding onto my face. I couldn't help it. Since I'd returned to my desk I'd felt lighter, as though I was full of air—relaxed and carefree. I hadn't even cared that half the office was whispering behind my back and I didn't bother checking my email alerts the rest of the day. I'd call that more than progress.

"Are you sure it's okay if I wear that?" I asked for the tenth time.

"Yes!" Belle shouted, pretending to throw a shoe at my head. "I'm wearing something else. Philip wouldn't like that dress."

"Why not?" I asked.

"Too sexy," she said with a shrug.

Of course, staunch Philip wouldn't want his perfect future wife to look too hot amongst the royal crowd. It wasn't his style to draw attention, something Belle had been acclimating to slowly. Thankfully, I couldn't imagine Alexander having similar hang-ups. Mostly because my plan was to distract him with the dress and tempt him to leave early. I knew there was no way he'd be able to keep his hands off me while I was wearing it.

"I'm so glad you're going to be there," Belle said, redirecting my attention from my fantasies back to the task at hand.

I for one couldn't believe I was going to be there. It felt a bit too much like a fairytale. In fact, it was a fairytale. The same one little girls were still told when they went to bed at night. The same story sold to women in movie theaters. Except it was happening to me, and I was having a hard time accepting it.

"I'm nervous," I admitted to her. After having a lot of very personal messages on display for the world to see, I was about to go out publicly with Alexander for the first time since he'd saved me in front of Brimstone. This time, I was stepping out and asking to be judged, and I had no doubt that all of England—and most of the world—was up for the challenge.

I had a sneaking suspicion I would be found wanting by most people.

"Why?" Belle asked. "You're going to look hot as hell. The whole world knows that Alexander is mad about you."

"That's part of the problem." I clutched the pillow tighter and tried to steady my nerves.

"So everyone who reads TMI knows that you're a sex goddess. I wish I had your problems." She winked as she laid out a pair of silky undies next to her gown and nothing else.

"Will Philip approve of you wearing so little under your dress?" I asked.

She slipped off her shirt, laughing as she reached for her robe. "He won't mind that part. It's all about appearances to him."

Was that my problem? Was it all about appearances to me? Alexander had reassured me repeatedly that he didn't care what anyone else thought, but did I care? What did it matter what they thought of my looks or my clothes or my personality if he wanted me? Except that it did matter, because I'd suffered from self-doubt before. I didn't want to let it get to me, but if it did, I knew Alexander wasn't going to like what he saw. I was determined to keep my personal demons at bay, not just for him but for myself as well.

"Do you want me to get that?" Belle asked, interrupting my thoughts. I stared at her quizzically. "The buzzer!"

"You're half-naked. I'll get it." I jumped from the bed and headed to the hall. Hitting the button, I braced myself, still convinced that my next encounter with a reporter was just around the corner.

"Delivery for Miss Bishop."

I hesitated. There was no reason to suspect that anything was up, but all it would take was one time to get burned. Then the perfect solution occurred to me.

"She's not home," I lied. "You can leave it with Ms. Hathaway in Apartment 1. She's the landlord."

"Thanks, miss." The delivery guy didn't seem to think this was odd or push his case, which meant I was probably being paranoid. He was just a delivery guy after all, but I knew it was okay to be cautious.

I debated going down and retrieving the package for a few minutes before I finally went back into Belle's bedroom to discover steam pouring from the bathroom. Poking my head in, I discovered her busily plucking her eyebrows while the shower water heated up.

"What was it?" she asked.

"A delivery."

"Ohhhh!"

"I had them leave it with Aunt Jane."

Belle blinked at this revelation and then continued her pursuit of errant eyebrow hairs. "That's smart. We should probably do that with all our packages from now on."

I nodded as I digested her words. *From now on.* Because things were going to be different after today. I was going out in public, finally revealing that the speculation was true—that I was dating Alexander. Of course, what they didn't know was what our relationship was really like, the darkness that tinged our lovemaking. The control Alexander so desperately needed. I couldn't help but be glad that Alexander had kept his lascivious texts to topics of a rather more tame persuasion in comparison. But not because I was embarrassed that Alexander had a dark side, but because it was his. I suppose we did have one thing that was only between us. One secret that we'd managed to keep private. It was hardly a secret though, after I'd made it clear I wasn't interested in submitting, but it was something.

"So spill. What is he really like in bed?" Belle asked as she washed her face. "After reading TMI, I get the feeling that you left out some details."

"You should get in the shower," I said, skirting the question. The only way it was going to stay a secret was if I kept it to myself, which meant keeping it from everyone, even my best friend.

"Go get your package," Belle ordered.

I darted downstairs, knowing that we had less than an hour to get ready. It occurred to me about halfway down that I might have to say something to Belle about hogging the shower, but then I shrugged it off. It wouldn't take me that long to get ready and I'd done most of my necessary primping before starting work today.

Knocking quietly on Jane's door, I realized I was still unsure I really wanted her to answer. But answer she did. Today she was clad in a summery dress that billowed around her in a riot of colors. Despite her age, she looked like a love child, and I half-expected her to say she was on her way to a Beatles concert.

"Oh Clara, darling!" She welcomed me with a kiss to the cheek. "I have a package for you."

"I know," I admitted sheepishly. "I asked them to leave it down here. There's been some more...articles and I wasn't sure if it was a real delivery man."

"Well, he didn't ask a thing about you. In fact, he didn't look like a delivery man, more like a...oh, police officer," she said as she paced over to the table in her living room.

"Maybe a security guard?" I asked. It hadn't been Norris's voice, but still.

"Yes, more like that, dear." Aunt Jane thrust an envelope toward me and my heart skipped a beat as I took it. It was a letter, hand-addressed to me, bearing no postage. I turned it over, anxious to see if there was a return address. There wasn't, but it was stamped with a glossy red wax seal that bore a dragon.

"That looks like a love letter," Jane remarked.

I didn't have to open it to know it was, just as I knew it was from him. "I think you're right."

"From Alexander?" Jane guessed.

I blushed. I wasn't sure why it hadn't occurred to me that she would have heard about my relationship to Alexander, but it still surprised me. Mostly because I hadn't put my guard up as I had with all the others. "I think so."

"This is much classier than those little snippets on the phone." Jane moved to pour tea into two cups on the table and then offered one to me.

If anyone else had offered me tea after admitting they knew about the most recent tabloid fodder involving my personal life, I would have run screaming. But there was something about Jane that I trusted. For one, Belle trusted her, but more than that, Jane struck me as a kindred spirit. I couldn't explain it, but I implicitly trusted her. I took a seat and accepted the cup.

"How are you holding up?" she asked.

"Surprisingly well." I took a sip of tea, wondering how much Belle had told her about my past.

"I can't imagine what it's like to have your personal life selling papers." Jane shook her head, taking a slow sip from her own cup. "There have always been scandals, my dear. But in this day and age with all the computers and smart phones and Wi-Fi, everyone knows about everything. It's impossible to keep things quiet. Let me tell you, there would be a number of royal families just ruined if they'd lived in this day and age. After all, illicit romances have been around forever."

I choked on my drink, burning my tongue in the process. "Illicit romances?"

"Well, there was Harold who had to abdicate his posi-tion...what was it? Thirty years ago. Fell in love with a girl from France. Not royal."

"I didn't think they cared if you were royal anymore," I said in a small voice. The truth was I didn't know. But it was the twenty-first century for fuck's sake, there couldn't be a huge number of royal suitors available to meet and marry.

"That was ages ago," she said, waving it off. "I think they were more upset that she was from France. Bad blood there."

"And what about a girl from America?"

Jane sat down her cup and I saw her jaw tighten. "Sadly, I'm not sure England is ready for that."

"Even if I'm a British citizen?" My stomach turned over, and I fought against a wave of nausea.

"I'm afraid they'll hear the accent and well, that will be that." She patted my hand comfortingly. "But can I give you a bit of advice?"

I nodded, desperate for even a scrap of hope if she had one.

"Fuck 'em. The whole lot," she said. "Those phone messages or whatever they were, they might not have been

Shakespeare, but he sounds like a man who's willing to put a lady's needs first."

This time when I choked on my tea, it was from laughter. Embarrassed, giggly, girlish laughter—and I didn't care.

"Men like that are hard to come by. My second husband was a grand giver in that sense." Jane winked at me and I caught a flash of Belle in the gesture. Maybe that's why I felt so comfortable around Jane, even when the subject matter was uncomfortable. It was more like looking into the future than talking to a stranger.

"I'll keep that in mind."

"Enjoy yourself," she said, "and remember your heart."

I stood and placed my cup in the sink. "Remember not to let it get broken?"

"Remember to take chances with it," Jane said as she saw me to the door. "Otherwise, what's the point of having one?"

I thought about that as I climbed the stairs back to my apartment. Being with Alexander was dangerous, like taking a leap into the unknown. But maybe that was just what I needed.

CHAPTER FOURTEEN

My fingers trembled as I broke the envelope's seal, spotting the words "for your eyes only" scrawled across the bottom. I stood against my bedroom door, my heart pounding, unsure what to expect. The letter was penned on a thin sheet of elegant cream stationary with bold masculine strokes, and although I'd never seen Alexander's handwriting, I instinctively knew it was his.

Clara,

I know I've scared you. I have no right to ask you to be with me. There are risks, more than I've let on about, but I can't release you. I'm afraid that even if you tried to run now I wouldn't let you go. I crave your body. The touch of your skin. The sweet silk of your thighs against my face and the taste of you on my lips. Even as I warn you away from me, know that you are mine and I protect what is mine. Even from myself.

X

I ran my fingers over the X, a smile tugging on my lips. His words left me aroused and perplexed. It was nearly a love letter —the first I'd ever received—and yet its romance was tainted with his self-doubt. The self-doubt I wished I could wash away. If only I could show his past sins were behind us, but I feared doing so might lead us down a treacherous path.

A shiver ran unbidden up my neck at the thought of Alexander in control of my body. How could I want that and be scared at the same time? It didn't make any sense. Of course, nothing about our relationship was rational.

Could I follow him into the darkness to save him? I wasn't sure.

ALEXANDER PICKED ME UP AT THE DOOR AN HOUR LATER, which was a surprise since he usually sent Norris to bring me quietly out the back. Since Belle had already confirmed that there were reporters outside, I let her get the door while I took a moment to focus on my breathing, willing calm to overtake my body.

That calm vanished the moment Belle opened the door. Instead my breath hitched at the sight of him dressed in a classic black tuxedo tailored to his perfect body. He was clean-shaven for once and his black hair, although wild, had been combed into an appropriate level of control for the event. Looking like this, it was impossible not to see him as the powerful man he was. Some men wore tuxedos, but Alexander owned it.

He carried a dozen red roses that popped against the black backdrop of his jacket, the scarlet providing a direct contrast to the darkness while still emanating a fierce sensuality. But the thing that made my heart speed up was how he looked at me, staring at me with hooded eyes. The lust was obvious as his gaze raked across me possessively.

I'd picked the right dress. At first glance, the silver, silk gown fell in billowing wisps down my curves, but underneath, a bustier caged my waist and pushed my breasts into the plunging, strapless neckline. Two nearly concealed slits allowed my legs to slip free as I moved. I felt like a movie star as soon as I put it on, and from the way Alexander watched me, I looked like one, too. Belle had twisted my hair and pinned it so it spilled over my shoulder, and I hadn't fought her on the scarlet lipstick she'd suggested.

"It's nice to meet you," Belle said, breaking the silence. She stepped aside and he strode into our flat, his eyes never leaving mine.

Finally, he tore his gaze from me and extended his hand to her. "Alexander. You must be Belle."

Belle looked torn between accepted his hand and curtseying. Thankfully, she took his cue, nodding as though this was a normal introduction. "Are you looking forward to this evening?"

"Yes," he answered, although his response was too stiff to be believable. "That is, I'm looking forward to the company."

Belle gave him an approving look, her eyes darting to me. "Excuse me a moment."

As soon as she left the room, Alexander stepped forward and handed me the flowers.

"I thought you didn't do romance," I teased.

"Consider that a consolation prize," he said. "If you're going to put up with my family for the evening, you deserve a reward."

I considered this as I searched the cupboard for a vase. Of course, his family would be there. I'd been so obsessed with the idea that we were about to make our relationship public—in a big way—that I hadn't really thought about meeting his entire family.

Alexander moved behind me, gripping my hips. "Don't think about them."

"That's easier said than done," I whispered. "I barely know what's going on between us and now I'm going to meet your family."

"It's not a big deal. Just remember that if they're jerks it's because of me and not you," he reassured me. But as he spoke, his grip on me tightened.

"That doesn't really make me feel better." They were going to judge me, and my American accent was only going to make the situation worse. I was following Alexander into a viper's nest and we both knew it.

"Don't think about it," he ordered, pulling me against him. "Right now, I want you to think about what I'm going to do to you in that dress."

Despite my anxiety, this brought a smile to my lips. "I don't know how I'm supposed to concentrate with you looking like that."

"She does look fantastic, doesn't she?" Belle flitted back into the kitchen. She didn't bat an eyelash to find us pressed close together even though she had to have heard what he'd said to me.

Alexander murmured his agreement, and Belle swept past us. She reached to the highest shelf and retrieved a vase. News that his family was going to be there tonight had distracted me from my search. "Here. Oh wait!"

Belle whirled around and grabbed a pair of scissors from a nearby drawer.

"Sorry!" She clipped a rose from its stem. It was in full bloom, its petals spread into velvet leaves. Belle tucked the beautiful blossom into the loosely pinned hair above my ear.

"Perfect," Alexander said with approval. Lust glinted in his eyes, and it made my knees weak.

"I need to go. Philip will be downstairs." Belle air-kissed my cheek. "See you there!"

I breathed a sigh of relief and waved her off. Of course, I would have Belle there, and no matter what happened she would have my back. While I hoped I didn't need an escape plan, if I did, I couldn't do better than Belle.

"Shall we?" Alexander crooked his arm, and I took it. "If we don't get going, I'm going to spread you across the kitchen counter."

Yes, please. I bit my lip in attempt to cover my excitement.

Alexander groaned, his eyes flashing darkly, and shook his head. "Let's get to the car before we miss the party, Miss Bishop."

"Lead the way, X."

By some miracle, Norris had managed to get around the back without catching the attention of the paparazzi camped outside the flat. The fact that they had missed the limousine idling behind my building proved how indispensable Norris was. Maybe they had all packed up and headed over to the scene of the actual event this evening. Not that they had any way of knowing I would be there with Alexander. He'd been careful about not using his mobile phone to message me; instead, I'd been given instructions to contact Norris if there was any trouble.

Alexander placed his hand on the small of my back, guiding me toward the car. His touch didn't waver until I was safely inside. He disappeared behind the closed door and I took a look around. The low seat wasn't ideal in a ball gown, but it was much more spacious than the Rolls.

"Do you know what I love about London this evening?" Alexander asked as he slid fluidly into the seat beside me.

I cocked my head in curiosity. Right now I loved everything

about London because it was, in *this* city, where Alexander was with me.

"The traffic. I never appreciated it before tonight." Alexander moved closer to me, taking my face in his free hand. He drew me to him but stopped short of kissing me. Instead he lingered for a moment, and I breathed him in, losing myself momentarily to his touch, his scent, his nearness. When he finally crushed his lips to mine, my hand flew up and caught his, holding him to me, greedy for the taste of him. It had been too long since I'd felt his body against mine. We'd known each other such a short time, but I'd felt his absence like the ache of a ghost limb. He was meant to be with me. He was meant to be part of me.

"Poppet," he murmured. "I've thought about you all week."

My breathing shifted to panting as he bent to grasp the hem of my dress. He lifted it over my knees, giving him leeway to slide a hand across my thighs. The gown's silk made it impossible to wear even a scrap of underwear, and I'd been counting on its length to hide that fact. Alexander's hands urged my legs apart and he slipped his hand against my sex.

He groaned when he made contact with my bare flesh. "That's hardly playing fair."

"This dress doesn't work with panties." I shrugged apologetically, but the smile on my face was anything but sorry.

"Personally I'm of the opinion that no dresses actually work with panties," he said with a wicked smile. He shifted in his seat and withdrew his hand, leaning forward as if to kneel before me.

"No," I said, stopping him.

"I don't like that word from you, poppet," he growled. "I have a very hard time listening to it."

I ran my tongue across my lips and shook my head. "No, *I* want *you*."

"And you can have me."

"No, I want to taste you." I'd imagined how it would feel to wrap my lips around his luscious cock since I'd first seen him, and the thought of having him at my mercy sounded even more delicious.

Alexander didn't resist me. Instead he sat back, propping his hands behind his head, lust written across his face. Occasionally the car jolted from a bump in the road, but I didn't care. Hitching my skirt higher to allow me freedom of movement, I dropped to his feet. My hands trailed along his slacks, sliding up his thighs as I reached for his zipper. I tugged it open, and Alexander moaned as his cock fell into my hands. Despite its softness, it was heavy and hot as I began to stroke it tenderly, and it then grew thick and firm in my hand. Bowing down, I dipped my mouth to his heavy sac and tongued his balls, sucking one carefully into my mouth. Then the other. Alexander shifted forward to allow me more access as his breathing increased.

He groaned when I ran my tongue up the length of his shaft, and I was pleased to see he was fully erect now. His cock was a thing of beauty—virile, primal, unabashedly masculine. I teased him, licking and sucking, for a few more minutes until his hands had fallen to his sides and clenched into fists. Feeling him harden and lengthen in my mouth made my sex swell with desire. I was so ready for him, but all I wanted right now was to watch him fall over the edge. I sealed my lips over the wide crown of his cock and then lowered my mouth to its root. Hollowing my cheeks, I sucked him hard, drawing my mouth hungrily up his shaft before plunging back down.

"You look so fucking hot with your red lips wrapped around my cock." A growl rumbled through his chest and he caught the nape of my neck as my lips engulfed his length once more. "It makes me want to fuck you."

But I wasn't about to let him. I needed to watch him come. I wanted it. Increasing the pressure of my suction, I was rewarded with the first warm drops of pre-ejaculate. I moaned, sweeping my tongue across the glistening pearls, and sucked harder as Alexander's hand tangled in my hair.

"Oh Clara, you are so beautiful." His breathing grew ragged as his head fell back against the seat. "I'm going to come."

But I didn't budge as he spilled hot across my tongue. I swallowed each thick spurt greedily as he pumped into my mouth. Drawing my tongue up leisurely, I savored the taste of him that lingered in my mouth, and when I pulled away, Alexander's eyes were wild.

He scooped me off my knees and lifted me toward his lap, bringing his lips to mine and kissing me hard before he pushed me onto my back on the seat. His hands slid recklessly up my legs, shoving my skirt up to my waist. He traced my slit with deliberate but tender strokes, finally nudging a finger between my swollen lips. "Sucking me off made you wet."

I nodded, knowing the proof of my arousal coated his finger.

"I need to be inside you. Nothing between us. Is that okay?"

I moaned a yes and closed my eyes, my breath lodging in my throat as I anticipated the delicious stretch of my cleft around his cock. I couldn't believe he was still hard after the orgasm he'd emptied into my mouth, but a moment later, I felt the proof that he was nudging against my slick entrance. He sank into me slowly, giving my body time to relax against his rigid cock, and I gasped as he pushed inside me entirely. I circled against him, savoring the beautiful agony of his impalement, but Alexander grabbed my hips and held me steady.

"Not yet, poppet." I could see the struggle in his eyes. His desire to control my pleasure and his fight to control himself.

I whimpered, desperate for him to take me.

He found my clit and flicked it with his finger, sending a wave of anticipation rolling through my body. "Think of a safe word, poppet. You don't need it now, but you might later and when we're in that moment, you won't be able to think of it."

I shook my head.

"I'm trying to control myself, poppet, but I want to make you feel safe. Choose a word that makes you feel safe," he ordered.

"How about *majesty*?"

"Your safe word shouldn't be something that you might have to use for other reasons," he said.

"Oh X, do you really think you're going to get me to call you *Your Majesty*?"

He smirked. "With what I'm planning to do to you, you might."

The man couldn't be any more infuriatingly sexy, and it was hard to think clearly when he touched me. How could I ever say no to him? I'd tried to before. I'd walked away from him with barely a backwards glance, not realizing that soon my life would spin completely out of control and that he would become my center of gravity. And there was one word I associated with denying him. "Brimstone."

"You could just say go to hell," he suggested dryly.

"I thought you wanted me to pick a word that I would remember."

"Brimstone, though?"

"It was the last time I said no to you," I explained in a quiet voice.

"You've said no to me since then," he pointed out.

"But I didn't really mean it those times."

His smiled returned as I confessed this, and he rolled his thumb over my aching clit. "Whatever you wish, Clara."

"Then fuck me." It was all I could think of, feeling him inside me. Alexander responded with a thrust, massaging circles on my pulsing clit. My cleft stretched, blossoming open as he pounded ferociously into me. His heavy sac smacked against my ass, and I trembled under him.

"Look at me," Alexander said. "I want to see you as you come."

I opened my eyes and met his as he hammered relentlessly. The hunger I saw reflected there melted through me, and I shattered against him, bursting into a million fragments. Alexander arched back and drove into me as I felt the first lash of his hot seed. He came with my name on his lips.

"I love knowing that you're full of me," he whispered as I clung to him. "All night I'm going to be thinking of being inside you, knowing that I've marked you. Knowing that you're mine."

I licked my lips and pressed them to his, too awestruck for words. I'd given myself to him fully—bared my body and soul—and he had left his mark.

"And I'll be thinking of your hot, naked cunt under this sexy dress. I want it to be ready for me if I need it," he added

"It will be," I promised him.

I sagged across him—boneless and limp—but I forced myself to take his offered hand. We would be there any moment and I couldn't get out looking like this. Alexander buttoned his slacks and tucked his shirt in. Then he helped me smooth my skirt out, dropping kisses along my bare legs as he moved downward.

"Stop, you fiend." I smacked his shoulder.

"I can't help it. I can't keep my hands off you." He shot me the wicked smile that made me want to drop my panties. Except I had none to drop.

"I'm not wearing underwear," I reminded him. "You don't have to work so hard."

"We'll see about that." Alexander settled onto the seat next to me, brushing a few stray hairs into place and adjusting the rose that Belle had placed in my hair.

I opened my clutch and fixed my lipstick, which thanks to

Belle, had barely budged. The girl knew some cosmetic voodoo, that was for sure. Wiping away some slight smudges from under my eyes, I was relieved so little damage had been done. Of course, my cheeks glowed with the flushed heat of a recent orgasm, but there was nothing to be done for that. I could only hope it was written off as nerves or excitement, but I didn't really care. The whole world already knew about our sex life, thanks to the hackers who'd released Alexander's texts to me earlier today. *This will give them something real to talk about*, I thought smugly.

"Are you ready?" Alexander asked, knitting his fingers through mine. My heart leapt into my throat, refusing to budge. He'd offered me his arm before or wrapped one around my waist, but holding my hand felt personal in a way that nothing we'd experienced so far had. I swallowed hard on the unexpected emotions this produced as I tried not to cry.

Stop it, I ordered myself silently. *You are here as his date.*

There was nothing more to it than that, but even as my head warned me against getting my hopes up, my heart continued to race. He didn't release my hand until the limo had stopped and he slid smoothly out of the backseat. But as soon as he was out, he leaned in, offering it to me again. I took it along with a steadying breath, unsure what to expect. As I exited the safe confines of the limo, I was blinded by the flashes of dozens of cameras. I blinked against the glare as the reporters began shouting their questions for Alexander. I suddenly wished I'd come into this situation a bit more prepared. My first instinct was to look to Alexander, hoping for cues on what to say and do.

Alexander stared straight ahead, a charismatic grin plastered on his face and then he led me forward without a word.

CHAPTER FIFTEEN

Alexander's fingers stayed knitted through mine as we maneuvered through the lobby, but I couldn't stop shaking. The cameras. The questions. The number of women staring at my man. It was a lot to take in. Beside me, Alexander smiled, returning nods of welcome and calling out hellos, but his posture was stiff and his movements became automatic. After a few minutes, he pulled away from me, placing his hand on the small of my back. This small gesture usually made me feel safe and protected, but right now, it only felt mechanical. He was going through the motions as he put on a show for those around us.

"Are you okay?" I whispered when we reached the ballroom.

"I'm fine, Clara," he said in a clipped tone. "Excuse me one moment."

He left me standing there, alone, in a crowd of hundreds of people, and I wasn't sure what to do. My eyes skimmed the room for Annabelle, my would-be salvation. She should have gotten here already. I scanned the room until I spotted her lithe figure. Saying a silent prayer of thanks that she was so tall, I bee-lined toward her as quickly as dignity would allow—or this skirt for that matter. Belle caught sight of me and lit up, waving me toward her, but I hesitated as I realized that she wasn't alone. But relief flooded through me when Belle's companion turned, and I caught a glimpse of her face

"Stella!" I exclaimed, rushing forward to give her a hug. Immediately, I remembered where I was and stepped back, feeling embarrassed. "We probably shouldn't be hugging at something as formal as this."

"Nonsense! Hug me again!" Stella gave me another squeeze, grabbing my hands in the process. "I'm just the caterer."

"You look fabulous," I told her, and it wasn't a lie. Stella had always been pretty, but now her sleek, black hair was bobbed short, jutting to a flattering angle that emphasized her glamorous cheekbones and sloe eyes. On anyone else, her electric blue evening gown might have looked flashy, but as one of London's hottest up-and-coming chefs, she had the attitude to pull it off.

"Doesn't she?" Belle agreed. "Totally unfair that she spends all day around butter and lobster and she still looks like that."

"I keep my figure by dealing with a kitchen full of cocky jerks. It's hard work kicking their asses all day," Stella said dryly. "Speaking of, I should check on my new partner. I've left him in charge of the plating, and he's probably screwing it up." But instead of leaving, she shook her head in exasperation and returned her attention to me. "How are you, Clara?"

Stella had been a year ahead of us in school, earning a business degree that made her a double threat in the culinary world. I hadn't seen her since she'd graduated, although I'd planned to look her up when I got to London.

"I'm so sorry I haven't called you," I said. "I've had a lot on my plate."

"That's one way to put it," Belle said with meaning.

"Don't embarrass her." Stella shushed Belle and then gave me a sympathetic look. "You should come by and let me put something delicious on your plate to distract you from all this crap. Although from where I'm standing, you've found yourself something tasty already."

"If I knew where he was," I said. My eyes darted around the room, wondering if Alexander had come looking for me yet, but he was nowhere in sight.

"He probably went to get you a drink," Stella said. She'd always had a way of making me feel at ease since I'd met her in a nutrition class my freshman year, and I couldn't have been more grateful to see her right now.

"What are we raising money for again? Endangered animals?" I asked, taking in the event's decor. Lush ferns and vines transformed the space into an exotic jungle. Movement overhead caught my attention and I looked up in time to spy a dazzlingly brilliant yellow bird swoop overhead. Someone had gone a little over-the-top for this event.

"I thought you knew," Belle said, passing me a drink from a serving tray.

"I do not," I said, taking the drink gratefully. If Alexander was getting me a drink, he was slacking.

"And it's moments like these that you remember that she was raised in America," Belle teased. "It's the King's birthday. He chooses a charity every year to celebrate."

"Shit," I said. "Really?" Alexander had mentioned endangered animals, but he had obviously left out some important details. How in the world had I wound up here and what was he thinking? Maybe the King was particularly gracious on his birthday. I really hoped that was it.

Belle held her glass up in a toast. "To getting this over with."

Stella and I clinked our glasses against hers, but as I brought mine to my lips, heat flooded my cheeks, awareness rippling through my body. I knew he was there before he spoke, because my body responded as if it were being pulled backward.

"Clara," he said in a low rasp. "I see you found a drink."

I whirled a little quickly toward him, causing champagne to fly over the rim of my flute. It splattered on the dress of the statuesque blonde standing next to Alexander. She gasped, dabbing it gingerly from the delicate fabric.

"I'm so sorry!" I wished there was a table nearby that I could crawl under and hide.

The blonde shook her head even as she continued to fuss over the spot. "Don't worry about it."

She smiled warmly at me, and now that I wasn't focused on my faux pas, I managed a good look at her. Bee-stung lips and blond waves, complete with a willowy body and a short skirt. I couldn't believe it—she was even more stunning close up than she had been in pictures. If she weren't so nice, I would definitely hate her.

"Clara, may I introduce you to an old family friend, Pepper Lockwood?"

I smiled, hoping my nerves weren't showing, and extended my hand, but Pepper stepped past it and kissed both of my cheeks. It was so chic that I found myself hating her a little more, and hating myself for bring so shallow.

"It's nice to meet you, and I am so sorry," I repeated like a broken record.

"It's just a dress." She dropped her voice conspiratorially. "That's why you should always wear black. Nothing shows."

This was the girl I'd been worried about. Now that I'd met her, I felt silly.

"I should be going," she said. "I brought a date and I've lost him."

I knew just how she felt, and to my frustration, Alexander

gave me a cold kiss on the cheek and disappeared with her, leaving me to my friends.

"Wow, that was awkward," Belle said as soon as they were out of earshot.

"At least she was gracious about it." Despite a somewhat humiliating first meeting, I felt better having met the girl Alexander had been linked with by the tabloids. There'd been no spark between them. That much was clear. She really was a family friend and nothing more. I exhaled, releasing a sigh of relief I didn't realize I'd been holding.

"Sure," Belle said, but her eyes didn't meet mine as she spoke, and I made a mental note to pry whatever she was hiding out of her as soon as we got home.

"I can't believe you've hit that," Stella said with a sigh, her gaze still glued to the spot Alexander had stood in moments ago.

I smacked Belle on the shoulder.

"Ouch!" She rubbed the spot and frowned. "What was that for?"

I tilted my head, giving her my best *what-the-fuck* face.

"I did not say a thing," she said in a dramatically offended voice.

"Sorry, Clara," Stella said with a sheepish smile. "I saw TMI this afternoon and assumed, which makes me a terrible person."

"It's okay." I shrugged before downing the last of my champagne.

"And she is hitting that," Belle added.

I shot her another look, but she responded with a coy smile.

"Sorry, darling, it is written all over your flushed face."

I blushed deeper, which made them both laugh.

"It's certainly nothing to be ashamed of," Stella said. "I'd offer to body swap with you, actually."

"I'm pretty happy in this one," I admitted.

"Yeah, you are." Belle clinked her glass one more time.

We chatted for a few more minutes about Stella's restaurant and how she landed this catering gig, but my attention was divided between the girls and the crowd surrounding me. I'd come here with Alexander and I'd spent less than five minutes with him since we arrived. Pepper caught my eye and she waved at me. I returned it half-heartedly, disappointed that Alexander was still missing.

"I really have to get back to the kitchen and deal with Bastian," Stella said finally.

"Speaking of, I should go find Alexander." I excused myself as well and began searching for my date. Now that I'd had some liquid courage and discovered that Pepper wasn't the threat I thought she was, I felt more comfortable in my skin. It was clear that Alexander didn't though. Did he even want me here? He'd warned me of what to expect, but I'd expected the coldness from his family, not him. The fact was that it stung for him to disregard me while the slickness between my legs reminded me of what we'd shared hardly an hour ago in the limo.

I spotted him by the bar, still talking with Pepper, but now he was frowning. Her hand was draped over his and she spoke passionately. Something twisted in my chest, but I pushed it back, unwilling to allow jealousy to prevent me from being with Alexander. But I stopped when I saw his frown deepen. He began to speak, the wildness in his eyes visible even from a distance, before finally pulling away from Pepper and stalking off.

By the time I maneuvered through the crowd, I'd lost track of him again. Slumping against a column, I considered giving up. Why was I looking out for him when he'd abandoned me in the first place? What had he been discussing with Pepper? Whatever it was had upset him. Of course, he'd been on edge since we arrived. Releasing another long sigh, I struggled with the idea that Alexander was always going to raise more questions that he would give answers. Which raised the biggest question of all: could I handle that?

I was debating this when a strong hand caught mine and pulled me away from the party. Alexander's lips were over mine, his body pressing mine into a marble arch before I could process what was happening. I pushed against him at first, but then I weakened, melting into the kiss, craving physical contact with him as I wrestled with the enigma of a man who seemed to be constantly slipping through my fingers. His cock was hard through his pants and my body responded with trembles. We were only steps away from his father's birthday party and he was going to take me. I wouldn't stop him. I couldn't. But as quickly as the embrace began, it ended. Alexander stepped away and straightened his bow tie.

"I needed that," he said.

The kiss had rendered me speechless, struck dumb by the mixed signals of the last hour. One moment Alexander was open and bold, and the next closed and suspicious—and tonight I'd been passed between his two sides so often that I was developing whiplash.

He crooked his arm and offered it to me as I dabbed at the corners of my mouth, hoping my lipstick wasn't all over my face.

"You look beautiful," he said, but the lust that usually accompanied his compliments was absent from his voice. His words were even, carefully measured, and far too polite. I longed for his dirty mouth and wicked smile.

I took his arm and allowed him to lead me back to the party. We reentered the ballroom, and I immediately felt eyes on me. Nearly everyone had arrived, and they were all eager to get a peek at the girl behind the latest royal scandal. I tried to remember what Alexander has said in the limo. They were judging him and not me, but it was hard to think that when eyes narrowed as they met yours and tongues wagged behind hands everywhere you turned.

"Your Highness." A man approached us, bowing to Alexander and then giving me a stiff nod. "Your father requests that you join the family for the toast."

"I showed up," Alexander said with a grimace. "That should be enough."

"I'm afraid he's quite insistent," the man continued. "I suspect he'll just call you up in front of everyone if you don't—"

"Fine!" Alexander threw his hands up, dropping mine. I could feel the barely controlled fury rolling off of him and I stood stock-still, afraid to add fuel to his rage.

"I'll see the young lady to a table," the man offered.

"She stays with me."

"But sir—"

"She stays with me," he repeated in a firm voice that left no room for further questioning. Alexander grabbed my arm and strode quickly toward the front of the ballroom. He moved so quickly that I was practically running to keep up with his pace as he dragged me along.

His family was clustered together, taking turns speaking and ignoring one another, and I inhaled sharply, knowing this was the moment of truth. Alexander's father had chosen a tuxedo for the festivities as well, but it didn't help him blend in. He was undeniably handsome, despite his age, which was only apparent in the hair graying at his temples. The lines around his sharp eyes and mouth only served to make him look more distinguished. He was simply in a class by himself.

But he wasn't the most untouchable man in this room. That I knew.

Next to the King, a man who looked like a lankier version of Alexander gave him a funny look. It looked like a warning. But

Alexander kept going, stopping just short so that I could catch my breath.

"Remember, this is about me, Clara," he whispered.

I nodded, but my eyes were glued to the group of people in front of me. The blood pounding in my ears made it hard to process what he was saying. Alexander cupped my chin and turned me to face him. His eyes were cold—distant and dead—but I felt his control radiating out from him. It was as though he'd compartmentalized all his emotions in order to deal with tonight. I nodded again, this time giving him the eye contact that he so obviously desired.

"Good girl," he said, brushing a soft kiss over my lips.

"Alexander," a voice boomed, startling me away from him. "You've kept us waiting long enough."

"I'm sorry, Father," Alexander said stiffly. He ran his hand down my bare arm before he turned away from me. "I lost track of my date."

"How careless." The King gestured for him to approach. "May I speak with you?"

The implication was clear—the King wanted to speak with him alone—and Alexander moved to join his father.

Their conversation grew heated, voices raising high enough to be heard by those of us waiting in the vicinity. I did my best not to listen, but there was no mistaking the words "slut" and "shame." Holding my head up, I tried not to wince as the accusations flew between father and son.

The younger version of Alexander approached me, extending his hand. "I'm Edward."

Of course he was. Edward wore his dark hair longer and it curled past his ears, making him look boyish in comparison to his older brother. But he wore a tux well and he was almost as handsome as Alexander. He grinned at me, and I noted he was quicker with a smile. I shook his hand weakly, unable to speak for fear I would start to cry in front of him.

"Father's in an awful mood, which is unfortunately quite common." Edward clasped my hand tightly, searching my face as though he was looking for a clue as to how to make the poor girl he'd just met feel better. I wanted to tell him there was no use, but I knew I would never get it out. "Come over here."

Edward led me toward a nearby table. "Everyone please allow me to introduce Clara Bishop, my brother's girlfriend."

"Oh, I—" My protest was silenced with a warning squeeze.

A tall, sandy-haired man rose, buttoning his dinner jacket and offered his hand. I recognized him at once and fought the urge to check the party for Belle.

"It's nice to see you, Clara," Jonathan said as I took his hand. Rather than shaking it, he raised it to his lips.

"You know her, Jonathan?" a petite redhead dressed in ivory asked him. Most girls with such a fair complexion couldn't have pulled off her gown, but it only made her pale skin seem delicate and elegantly fragile. Her eyes traveled down my body calculatingly before she folded her hands primly on the table.

"Clara and I went to school together," Jonathan said, but when he raked his gaze across me, he didn't bother to hide his conclusions. His eyes sparkled like a man who'd discovered he'd been invited to sport.

If Jonathan Thompson thought I was going to play with him, he had another thing coming. My skin crawled where he had touched me, and as soon as I had the chance, I planned to scrub it with soap under scalding hot water.

"This is Amelia," Edward said, when the girl didn't introduce herself.

"*Princess* Amelia," she said flippantly.

Seriously?

"It's nice to meet you, Your Highness," I hissed. Everyone

here had been born with a silver spoon in their mouth and a stick up their ass.

"Perhaps you'd care to dance," Jonathan suggested, gesturing to the nearly deserted dance floor.

I did want to dance with Alexander. There was no way I was going to risk being seen with Jonathan, especially since I suspected he saw me as a bit of a challenge. "I'd rather wait for Alexander."

"Of course," he said with a nod, averting his eyes from me. "Alexander doesn't like to share."

There was a story here. I could feel it, but the last person I was going to ask to share it with me was Jonathan.

"Amelia?" Jonathan held out his hand and the sulky redhead took it, allowing him to sweep her toward the dance floor.

"Then let's get you a drink," Edward suggested as we watched them waltz. He looked over my shoulder to the other man at the table. "David?"

"I'll look after her," he said stiffly.

Edward pulled a chair out for me and I took it, grateful to be off my feet even if the company was less than welcoming. I glanced at David and realized we were in the same boat.

"You look like you're enjoying this as much as I am," I said, not bothering to hide my sarcasm.

A corner of his mouth tugged up, but he only shrugged. "My friends and I have different ideas on how to spend a Friday night."

"Maybe you should get new friends." My eyes caught Jonathan's as he spun Amelia on the dance floor, and he winked at me.

David snorted at me. I turned to face him, finding upon closer inspection that he was very handsome. His ebony skin and closely cropped hair showed off the strong lines of his face, and despite his sullen appearance, his coffee-brown eyes were warm. He was exactly Stella's type—quiet, brooding, and hot. "Actually," I said, "I have a friend here that you should meet. You'd like her."

Guys always do, I added silently.

"Are we setting David up?" Edward asked with a smile, returning with drinks in hand.

"I think he'd hit it off with my friend, Stella." Taking my drink, I raised an eyebrow. "What do you think?"

Edward debated for a moment longer, but when he opened his mouth, he was interrupted by the appearance of an older woman that I immediately recognized. The Queen Mother carried herself with the grace and bearing of a woman who bore kings. Age had touched her, turning her dainty curls silver, but there was nothing frail about her. Sweeping up to us in a modest, beaded gown, she stood nearly a foot shorter than her younger grandson. Although the contemptuous look she wore made her seem much larger.

Her eyes narrowed as she assessed me, and her nose pinched as though she'd caught a whiff of something rotten. "So Alexander brought his little tart to ruin his father's birthday."

My mouth fell open and I tugged my hand away from Edward, who appeared nearly as shocked as I was.

"Grandmother!" Edward's tone admonished her, but I didn't wait around to hear what else she had to say about me. It was bad enough that half the UK was reading my private messages right now. I didn't have to stand around being insulted by people who thought they were superior to me. Pushing through the crowd, I escaped as quickly as possible. I'd hide out in the loo until Alexander finally came looking for me.

He'd warned me, but he hadn't *prepared* me.

Tears stung my eyes, spilling over before I finally risked turning around. Edward was nowhere to be seen, but his grandmother had joined the argument that was still going strong between Alexander and his father.

He hadn't even noticed I was gone.

I felt foolish for coming here—for thinking things couldn't get more complicated between us.

But I was stuck here with no money and now my feet were killing me. I wasn't used to the sky-high heels Belle had insisted on.

Belle.

She was here, and therein lay my lifeline if I could just find her. Philip was boring but he could be counted on for chivalry, and right now I needed someone to rescue me. I had friends here, and I had to remember that. I could make it through this evening.

Turning to look for her, I bumped into Pepper.

I opened my mouth to apologize again, but she beat me to it.

"Stupid bitch," she hissed. "Are you purposefully trying to destroy this dress?"

The urge to cry vanished, replaced by shock, and I gaped at her.

"Oh, you're as stupid as I assumed," she continued, her green eyes flickering like a snake's tongue around the room in disinterest before they came back to glare at me. "Did you really think I wouldn't mind you ruining my Ralph Lauren?"

"I'm sorry," I said dumbly, my mind not quite caught up to the surprise, even as my heart began to pound like a war drum in my chest.

"So am I. Sorry that you're about to get dumped," she said with a smirk, tossing her blond waves over her shoulder. "Don't look so surprised. I could smell sex on you the second we met. Do you think Alexander is the kind that keeps girls around for second helpings? Where is he anyway? Or did he already drop you like the rubbish you are?"

My hands clenched at my side, forming fists that I was dying to use even as I fought the urge. "Alexander isn't the one calling the shots here, and don't concern yourself with our sex life. We're both very fulfilled."

My rage simmered as I neared my boiling point, and I wasn't sure how long I could contain it. In the last ten minutes, I'd been called a slut, a tart, and now trash.

"All of England is concerned with your sex life," she said. "Tell me," she lowered her voice, a wicked gleam in her eyes, "did you give them that story? Did you sell those texts to make a buck or two while you can?"

I didn't need money or fame or influence. A fact which was obviously lost on her. Pepper might have ties to the Royal Family, but from the way she was pouting over her dress, she didn't have my trust fund. What would be the point of showing her up? Now I understood Belle's look earlier. She'd been warning me. Trust Belle to spot a snake in the grass a mile away when I had to step on its tail and get bitten first.

"If you're done," I said, shoving past her, "I was leaving."

"Running away?" she asked in a mocking voice. "Make sure you drop your glass slipper on the way out, but don't count on Alexander coming to find you."

I swallowed on that and shot back. "I don't want him to."

And I didn't. This wasn't a fairytale and Alexander was no Prince Charming. More than ever, I wanted to go home and transform back into simple, loner Clara. I didn't bother looking for Belle. All I wanted to do was get out of there, but Pepper's words lodged in my brain. This was the end of my story. There'd be time to cry about it later. For now, I just wanted to escape.

CHAPTER SIXTEEN

The marble columns of the ballroom loomed over me like the bars of a cage, and the crowd of partygoers crushed against me. Panic overtook me, and I struggled toward the entrance. Turning one last time to look for Alexander, I caught Pepper watching me. She raised her drink in farewell, not bothering to hide her smug smile of satisfaction. Ignoring her, my gaze swept the room for Alexander, but he was lost in the crowd, and I didn't want to search him out. I wanted to get away from here as quickly as possible. I grabbed my clutch from our table, thinking I might catch a cab, but as soon as I was outside, I decided to walk. I needed to clear my head.

The spring air was cool on my skin, which felt feverish and flushed after my confrontation with Pepper. Just the thought of her made my fingers curl tightly over my embellished clutch, so tightly that the beads dug painfully into my flesh. The pain actually felt good after feeling totally numb for the last ten minutes.

What was I thinking? I'd learned to avoid people like that after watching my parents be burned many times by so-called friends. What was the point of friends who tore you down or competed with you? I'd done a fantastic job of being my own worst enemy for long enough. I really didn't need any help.

This whole night had been a mistake. Not because I felt inferior to Alexander's family and friends, but because I had no interest in playing into their delusions. Part of me wanted to go back and tell them what I really thought of them, but I resisted the urge. There was no cure for being an asshole.

By the time I got back to the flat, my feet ached from the effort of hiking halfway across London in four-inch Jimmy Choos. Aunt Jane's flat was dark when I entered, which was just as well, because I didn't really feel like talking. Rather, I felt like I should talk, a throwback reaction from my therapy days. But I was more than happy not to. Slipping off my heels, I took the stairwell up the three flights to our floor, rummaging through my purse for my keys as I came around the corner.

"Clara."

I jumped at the sound of his voice, dropping my shoes. But my momentary surprise quickly shifted to white-hot awareness. Taking a deep breath, I cursed my traitorous body for its reaction to Alexander's presence.

"Where have you been?" Alexander demanded, cornering me against the door as I neared him. His tuxedo jacket was gone and the sleeves of his button-down were rolled up. If Alexander in a tuxedo was impossibly sexy, Alexander half out of a tuxedo was devastating. A pang of longing shot through me, but I resisted the impulse to touch him, knowing what would happen if I did. Anger flickered in his cobalt eyes, and I felt barely controlled rage seething from him like steam from boiling water.

"Walking," I said, too tired for playing games or being witty.

"You leave without a word and then you *walk* home?" Alexander ran a hand through his black hair, and I noticed that it was already mussed, as though he'd done this a lot this evening.

"You pushed me away," I whispered, but my words weren't timid. I wanted him to hear me. I wanted him to stop and listen, so that he would know that I hadn't run tonight. "I didn't run. I made the choice to leave."

"You came with me. I expected you to leave with me. I need to know where you are. That's not a request, Clara," he barked.

I stared at him, waiting to see if he even heard what he was saying, but from the smoldering look he gave me, he did. "I'm not a child. I can take care of myself," I said.

"That was before," Alexander said, stepping close enough that his heat surged across my skin. "You made a choice, Clara, and when you did that I assumed the responsibility of taking care of you."

How could he be so dense and infuriating and sexy at the same time? Was it a trick of evolution: the ability to distract a girl with charm while you were being a total asshole? "I didn't ask you to do that!"

"No, you didn't. But you *chose* to come into my bed. You *chose* to stand by my side this evening."

If he thought that was going to be the extent of my choices, he had a big surprise coming. "Yeah, but we're not married or anything—"

"What message do you think it sends for me to bring a date to my father's birthday?" he interrupted me.

My breath hitched in my throat, caught on the lump rapidly forming there. I wasn't sure if I wanted to cry or shake him. Possibly both. "We barely know each other."

"That might be true," he conceded, "but we've been linked publicly, and after those texts were published today, people are going to make assumptions."

Between all the drama of Alexander showing up on my first day of work to the shit-storm that was this evening, I'd managed to forget about the hacked text messages. Adding that to the rest of today's events was too much to bear and I snapped, "What kind of assumptions? I really don't give a fuck what people who read TMI think of me!"

Alexander's head tilted, a glimmer of sympathy mixing with his anger. "It won't just be TMI's leak for long. There will be more legitimate news sources reporting on it. *I* live in the public eye, Clara."

The implication was clear. Alexander lived in the public eye, but I didn't have to. He was offering me a choice: one I thought I'd already made. He was giving me a second chance to walk away. But that didn't explain his actions tonight. "Why?" I asked in an effort to understand. "Why did you bring me tonight? You knew that assumptions would be made. It's hardly the first time you've been caught with your pants down. Why give them more to gossip about?"

I couldn't understand why he'd draw more attention to a relationship that was already tabloid fodder. Surely that would only make things worse, and he had to know that.

"Because I want to protect you." Alexander's voice broke, and when his eyes met mine, the intensity of his gaze pierced through me, drawing a gasp from my lips. "I need to protect you. I can't explain it, because I don't understand it. Maybe it's a compulsion."

"Compulsions generally aren't healthy," I whispered, barely able to produce words after his confession. The look he gave me —it shattered me. And in the moment, I didn't care. I didn't care that we'd been lying to ourselves about what was happening between us. I didn't care that my heart lay in a thousand pieces at his feet, because I couldn't bear the thought of him suffering that pain alone.

Alexander stroked the back of his hand down my cheek longingly. "This compulsion is. You can push me away, Clara, and I'll still devote myself to protecting you."

Emotions surged through me, flooding through my twisted perception of our relationship and washing it away. I had no words to drown the anguish reflected in his eyes. None that could reach the broken parts of him that I glimpsed. There was only one way to show him how I felt and only one way to free him from his demons. I crashed into him, my lips locking against his with brutal need as we collided. Alexander responded with hunger, lifting me off my feet and slamming against the wall in the process. He pivoted, still kissing me, and pressed me against the brick. Lowering me to my feet, he dropped to his knees and pushed up the flowing skirt of my gown. Alexander held it against my belly, leaving me exposed from the waist down.

"Spread your legs, poppet." Alexander held me firmly to the wall as he trailed kisses up my bare thighs. He took his time, sliding his lips along the sensitive flesh devotedly. His tongue licked softly down the hollow where my leg and cleft met. My hands tangled in his hair, clutching him to me as his kisses moved inward.

"I'm going to fuck you with my mouth, and I want to hear you come. I want you to let go," he growled, and I whimpered, already powerless to his demands. Alexander pushed my legs wider and thrust his tongue inside me, fucking me with powerful strokes. As pleasure welled in my core, tightening my limbs in anticipation, he pulled back only to close his mouth over my throbbing clit. Sucking it hungrily, his hand stroked my thigh but went no further. I longed for the feel of him inside me. His hands. His tongue. His cock. I was empty and only he could fill me.

"I...I need you inside me," I gasped as a tremor of ecstasy rippled through my body.

But Alexander didn't stop, instead the hand on my stomach pressed me harder to the wall. His tongue stroked across my sensitive clit again and then dipped lower, spearing me once

more and pushing me to the brink. I unraveled, moans spilling
wantonly from my mouth, as his tongue plunged inside me with
relentless passion.

Without a word, Alexander stood and took my clutch.
Sagging against the wall, unable to form words, I released it to
him, and a moment later, the door to my flat swung open. He
scooped me into his arms, carrying me over the threshold as his
mouth found mine, kissing me even as I fought to form coherent
thoughts. He'd never been inside. Should I point him in the
direction of my bedroom or opt for whatever flat surface he
found first?

Alexander answered for me, laying me across the kitchen
counter.

"You are so fucking beautiful." The low rasp of his voice
sent a shiver over my skin.

And I believed him, feeling his desire for me as acutely as I
felt my own. "Wait."

He stepped back, his gaze skimming my body, his eyes
hooded by lust. I pushed up and dropped to my feet, standing
with shaky legs before him. My fingers fumbled for the zipper of
my gown as he unbuttoned his pants. When I found it, I tugged
the zipper down and let the dress fall away. A growl rumbled
from Alexander and he advanced on me, lifting my ass from the
ground and carrying me to the wall. I wrapped my legs around
his waist and rubbed my aching sex against him. With my heels,
I pushed his pants down to his ankles. He stepped out of them,
kicking them to the side as I rocked against his liberated cock.

"Slowly," Alexander ordered, gripping my hips as he positioned his chiseled body between them. "*Now*, poppet."

I lowered onto his cock carefully, feeling the pleasant strain
as my body welcomed the substantial girth of his shaft. I bucked
against him, impatience winning out over restraint, but his
hands clutched my hips in warning.

"I don't want to hurt you," he cautioned.

My fingers slipped into his hair, knitting through it and tugging slightly. "I thought you liked that," I whispered.

His eyes flashed to mine, and I saw my face and the offer written across it reflected in his clear blue irises.

"Tread carefully, Clara." He dropped his forehead against mine, his eyes clenched shut as if he were struggling to control himself. My own breathing became shallow, my resolve resting on the tip of a knife. I wanted Alexander. I wanted all of him, even his dark side. Even if my desire scared me.

Alexander didn't open his eyes but he pressed a soft kiss to my lips. Pulling back, he pushed farther inside me until I sheathed him to the root. "This is enough."

His words were strained, but when he looked at me, he smiled. We stayed like that for a long moment, relishing the delicious sensation of joined flesh.

This could be enough, I thought as he held me. *For now*. But he needed more than this, and he needed me to give in to his darkness.

"Clara," Alexander whispered, "stop thinking."

"I—"

He stopped me with a kiss. "Be with me. Feel me."

Alexander shifted his weight, crushing me against the wall as he began to thrust, and I lost myself to him. My fingernails sank into his shoulders, anchoring me as he drove his cock savagely inside me. A cry escaped my lips as I swelled around him, pleasure taking root and traveling slowly through my body until the dam burst and my orgasm surged violently from my core, spreading to my limbs. "Alexander!"

He came at the cry of his name, pumping his thick cum into me.

I collapsed against him, his cock still twitching as my sensitive walls pulsed around him. Alexander's arms cradled me against him as he carried me from the kitchen into the hallway. He paused there and I managed a weak, "Right." He gently laid me on the bed as though I were fragile, then stripped off his tuxedo shirt and climbed in next to me with his undershirt on.

"About the party—" he began.

I held up a hand, unwilling to let talk of this evening's tension spoil a perfect moment. "Don't worry about it. We both knew they weren't going to like me."

"They shouldn't have been so rude." Alexander's eyes narrowed at the memory.

My mind groped for something positive to takeaway from our disastrous evening. "Edward was nice."

"Yeah. Edward understands what its like to be an outsider..."

Alexander trailed away as if there were a lot more to this statement, but I didn't press him for it. Right now, I wanted to focus on the beautiful man in bed with me, not the drama that accompanied being with him. But being with Alexander meant certain sacrifices.

I couldn't pretend to like or understand his life. He'd hinted at what was expected of him, and my heart hurt for the pain his lack of choices caused him. Whatever had torn his family apart haunted him. I could see its ghost in his eyes. I couldn't deny that I wished he would share it with me, but I knew pushing him to do so would only drive him away. Maybe the only way for him to find peace was to face his demons.

"I'm home safe, and you've damn near screwed me to sleep," I told him. "You should go back to your father's party."

"I don't want to go back to the party."

"X, it's your father's birthday," I pointed out.

"Exactly, and he has hundreds of people there to kiss his ass," Alexander said. "He won't even miss me."

"I doubt that."

Alexander shook his head. "You're right. He might miss me if he needs someone to yell at."

"I'm just going to go to bed," I told him, stretching my arms over my head as I unsuccessfully attempted to stifle a yawn.

"I want to go to bed with you," Alexander said, propping himself up on an elbow and brushing a kiss across my shoulder. He was impossibly beautiful. "Earlier wasn't enough for me. I have things to do to your body."

"This body," I yawned, "needs to rest. I have no idea how you've got that much stamina. It shouldn't be physically possible."

"We can sleep," he offered, and I froze.

"You want to sleep here?" I asked slowly.

Alexander frowned, brushing hair from my face. "Is that not okay?"

It was more than okay. Inside my chest, a dozen celebratory fireworks burst through me. But I couldn't exactly reveal my excitement and risk him pulling away again. The request was just so...*normal* that I wasn't certain how to process it. "Sure. Of course, it's okay."

Alexander pulled me to him, curving his body protectively around mine, as he cradled me to his chest. His lips nuzzled my ear, saying more with the show of silent affection than words could. A mix of emotions swirled through me, bringing tears to my eyes one moment and then forcing me to bite back laughter the next. How had we gotten here? I had no idea. All I knew was that I wanted to stay in his arms. No matter the cost.

"Alexander," I said his name softly, knowing I was treading into dangerous territory. "Earlier when you said you didn't want to hurt me..."

He stilled behind me, drawing in a ragged breath as I searched for the right words.

"I had my reasons for saying no before," I said finally. "But—"

"There's nothing more to say, Clara. You don't owe me," he said in a measured tone. "I don't need that."

But I knew he was lying. I saw it in his eyes, his desire to dominate me. I sensed how he fought his need to control my body when he fucked me. "What do you need then?"

"You," he said after a moment. "Sleep, poppet. All I need is you."

CHAPTER SEVENTEEN

His screams woke me, yanking me from my sleep like a fire alarm. Flipping on my bedside lamp, I discovered him curled in a ball beside me, clutching a pillow so tightly that his knuckles had turned white. I stared, trying to decide what to do. It wasn't safe to wake a sleepwalker, but this was clearly a nightmare, and I couldn't ignore his cries that clawed painfully from his lips.

My first mistake was putting a hand on his shoulder. Alexander reacted with force, elbowing me in the gut and knocking the wind out of me. I lurched up and swung my feet over the edge and planted them on the floor. Trying to stand was my second mistake. I hit the ground with a crack and crumpled, still trying to catch my breath.

"Alexander, wake up!" I yelled once my breathing had returned to normal. I stood again, unsure what to do. Grabbing a pillow, I smacked him with it, unwilling to risk more accidental injury. I could already feel the soreness of a bruise forming on my stomach from his blow. It didn't work, so I padded over to the wall and switched on the overhead light, contemplating if I should actually throw cold water on him or wait it out. Thankfully, his eyes opened as the room brightened.

His breathing was shallow and ragged, and as he panted, he turned to look at me with wide eyes.

"Clara?" My name was a plea on his lips. He blinked, disoriented from sleep.

I stood back, rubbing the injury he'd given me. It had been an accident, but I kept my distance. I wasn't frightened of him exactly. I was more stunned at having been awoken in such a violent manner.

"Oh god," he panted. "What did I do?"

He was on his feet instantly, starting toward me, but I backed away. Alexander paused, realization flashing across his eyes. "I hurt you," he said flatly.

He didn't wait for my confirmation. Instead he crossed the room and grabbed his pants. He pulled them roughly on and reached for his shoes. My mouth opened, looking for the words to ask him to stay but not finding them. He hadn't meant to hurt me, but it had still happened.

"I'm sorry," he said in a defeated voice. "I warned you. I'm so, so sorry."

I drowned in the sadness reflecting in his eyes, and there I finally found my voice as he reached the door.

"What were you dreaming about?" I asked in a small voice.

Alexander spun toward me and shook his head. "I won't ask you to carry my demons, Clara."

"Maybe you could just let me hold them for a while." I stepped toward him then, walking slowly as much to steady myself as to not frighten him away. His demons didn't scare me. Not when the alternative was losing him.

"It's too ugly for you. You're beautiful, pure—"

"I'm far from pure," I teased, but the air between us remained thick and we didn't laugh.

Alexander's hand wrapped around my throat softly, holding me in place as his eyes burned into mine. "*You* are my beautiful, Clara. That's why I want to protect you from the world. That's why I want to protect you from me."

Tears pricked at the corners of my eyes, but as I blinked them away, they fell hot on my cheeks. "You told me once that you wanted to hear me beg."

Alexander drew in a ragged breath and shook his head, letting go of my neck. "No. Not like that."

"Please," I whispered. "Please, X."

"Do you want me to tell you that I dream about screeching metal and fire? That I wake up holding a pillow because I'm dreaming that I'm cradling my sister's broken body?" he demanded. "And that every time I wake up, I'm no closer to knowing what the hell happened that night? I can't tell you anything, because I don't know anything!"

My thoughts spun out of control, trying to take in everything he was telling me. I knew about the accident, everyone did. But it had been years ago. "Have you spoken to anyone—"

"I'm not going to talk to a goddamned shrink. My sister would be alive if it weren't for me. Period. End of story."

"This isn't your fault." I dashed in front of the door, refusing to let him past. "It was an accident, everyone knows that."

"Everyone knows what they were told. Don't be stupid, Clara."

The remark, coupled with the coolness in his eyes, stung like a slap across the face. I shook my head, grabbing hold of all the confidence I could muster and crossed my arms over my chest. "You are not the first person to have been in a car accident."

"It was a little more than a car accident." His words were spoken softly, but the hard edge under them pierced through me.

His admission shocked me. What did that even mean? Every time I thought we had moved forward, something pushed us right back. We were both dancing around our issues instead of moving on, and then I realized that it didn't really matter. Alexander's perception of that night, what actually happened—none of it mattered. He needed to move forward and I had to help him.

I held out a hand to him. "Come back to bed."

Alexander's eyes narrowed, and he shook his head. "You're not safe around me."

"I'm only safe around you," I murmured.

"My life is dangerous," he warned. His hands ran through his sleep-tousled hair. "*I'm* dangerous."

I stepped closer to him, tipping my head up to meet his downcast eyes. "And I'm not going to break."

Alexander took my hand and drew me against him, wrapping a hand around my neck once more. "You are fragile, Clara. Delicate. If my life doesn't break you, the things I want to do to you might."

I sucked in a breath but forced myself to hold his gaze. "I'm not scared of being with you, X. I'm only scared of being pushed away."

A low growl vibrated as he collided into me with such force that I tasted iron as our tongues wrestled hungrily. His hands closed over my wrists, clamping them tightly and forcing them behind my back, showing his desire to dominate me. I folded into him, submitting to his overpowering will, and he swept me off my feet, carrying me back to bed.

Alexander moved between my legs, thrusting inside me without a word, and I gasped as his thick cock spread my sex roughly open. There was no tenderness to his touch. He'd been overtaken by something primal, and I responded instinctually, raking my nails across his covered back, clinging to him as he rode me. His hips ground savagely, pumping tirelessly like a piston inside my channel.

Holding his weight up with one arm as he rammed into me, his other hand grabbed my neck, forcing me to look at him.

"You are mine, Clara," he snarled, his grip tightening over my throat. "I claim you. Do you understand?"

The ferocity of his body and the weight of his words settled in my chest, but I took both with a feeble nod as a tear spilled down my cheek. I was his. I knew that. Alexander owned me, and my tears were a curious mix of joy and sorrow and fear. The fire in his eyes blazed brighter as I wept and his hips rolled in wild, raw circles as he tormented my body and soul.

"I'm hurting you now," he said gruffly, "like you wanted, Clara. Do you want me to stop?"

A "no" escaped my lips instead of a yes, and I groaned as he slammed his cock into me.

"You like it, but you think you don't," he grunted. "I expect you to come, Clara."

"I can't," I moaned. I was nowhere near release. My sex stung from his powerful thrusts and the tension coiling through my body had nothing to do with arousal.

"Accept the pain," he ordered. "Let go."

He released my neck and dropped his mouth to my breast, sucking my nipple hard into his mouth and swirling his tongue over the furl. Then he bit down, catching it in his teeth and tugging it until I cried out. Alexander's fingers plumped my breast as blood rushed to its sensitive flesh, and then he bit down again, dragging his teeth across the delicate tip. Something shifted inside me, and I relented to the torment, allowing it to overtake my shredded nerves, and in that moment, the pain transmuted to ecstasy.

I arched forward, weeping and screaming, as pleasure rocked through me, painting the world black. There was nothing but the stinging smack of his flesh against mine. The iron on my tongue and swollen lips. The sharp bite of his teeth on my breast. There was only him. He was my light in the darkness.

Collapsing with a sob onto the bed, I drew back, covering my face with my hands, as ashamed of the arousal I still felt as I was of the pleasure I'd taken from the brutal exchange.

Alexander slowed his movements, continuing to circle gently against my throbbing cunt. His body enveloped mine as he slid his arms under me, cradling me to him as he pressed kisses along my tender, swollen breasts. Rolling to his side carefully so as to keep our bodies entwined, he stroked slowly in and out of me.

He pushed my hands away from my face and brought his mouth to mine. The kiss was warm and deep, and he took his time, parting my lips gradually until a sigh escaped me. There was no clash of tongues or nip of teeth, only a languid, deliberate kiss that melted through my tested body.

"Clara?" He said my name in a silky voice, calling me back to him.

I opened my tear-stained eyes and met his, discovering that the smoldering fire in them had cooled. There were no ghosts lurking there. We had chased his demons away, but it had almost broken me.

And yet, I felt alive. My skin sang with the memory of agony and bliss. The feelings overwhelmed me, and I brought my hands to his chest, holding my palm flat against his heart. It beat steadily, evenly, his primal urges finally sated, and I counted the beats until my pulse matched his.

Alexander's hips rolled against me, still filling my sex, but the strain and torment were gone. Despite everything, he hadn't come, and I searched his face, suddenly fearing I'd done something wrong.

"Your pleasure is mine," he whispered. "I will push your body until it nearly breaks, but I will never hurt you."

And he hadn't. The pain of the encounter had ebbed from my body, leaving only a persistent, aching rapture in its place.

"And can I break you?" I murmured, stroking my hand down his face.

He sighed and shook his head. "I'm already broken."

"Then maybe I can fix you." My fingers trembled as I moved my hand lower until it found the hem of his shirt. Alexander's eyes stayed focused on mine as I slipped under the fabric and softly brushed my fingertips across the taut stack of abs he kept hidden from me. His body stiffened, his cock still pulsing inside of me.

A ragged moan escaped his lips at the contact, but he didn't turn away and he didn't stop me. I pressed my hand cautiously to his stomach, relishing his firmness, and then allowed my hand to drift further.

Alexander sucked in a sharp breath. "Don't."

But there was no anger in his words, only fear, and something else that he kept concealed. I closed my eyes, breaking the heady contact of his gaze so that I could think clearly. And that's when I saw what he was hiding.

Desire.

Opening my eyes, I stared at him, finally understanding, and spoke softly, "I claim this body. You are mine, Alexander. All of you."

And as I spoke, my fingers strayed upward, running across his ribs to feel the scars that marred his beautiful body. I paused, lingering over the knotted skin, but I didn't pull away, even as a shudder racked through Alexander's body.

Slowly, I began to circle my hips against his shaft as I grew bolder, exploring the part of himself that he'd kept hidden for so long. His breaths came quickly and he buried his head against my breast, trapping my hands to his chest. He clutched my ass as I ground against him until his desire won out over his shame, and he thrust fervently into my raw entrance, his cock erupting and filling me with surge after surge of his seed. The sensation overwhelmed me, splintering and rushing through me in an intense deluge that electrified me even as I felt the cold salt of tears on my breasts.

CHAPTER EIGHTEEN

As the first light of dawn stole through my bedroom window, I woke with a start. What had I forgotten? Then it hit me—Alexander was in my bed. He was still sleeping, breathing softly, his eyelids flickering slightly as he shifted and rolled onto his side. Biting my lip, I brushed a finger down his cheek. He'd taken off the mask he always wore last night and showed me the monster behind it, but all I had seen was him. Alexander was beautiful but broken. He was sexy but jagged. And although he'd revealed part of himself to me, I knew now that I'd only skimmed the surface of his darkness.

Before last night, I'd felt torn between unraveling his mystery and running as fast as I could from his brutal sensuality. Now I no longer had a choice. Not only because I'd seen past his facade, but because he'd forced me to see past my own. What he'd shown me should have terrified me, but it only made me crave him more.

I slipped from the bed, gliding across the floor in bare feet, so I wouldn't wake him. He was at peace for the moment, and I knew his demons waited for him when he awoke.

Belle was in the kitchen, sporting pajama shorts, as she

pushed eggs around a frying pan. Even with her hair piled messy on top of her head and no makeup, she looked gorgeous. After my decidedly rough night, I didn't even want to look in a mirror.

"I was worried when you left the ball early," she said, blowing me a kiss, "but when I got home, I realized you didn't leave alone."

My cheeks flamed and I reached into the cupboard for a glass. I'd been so caught up in Alexander last night that I hadn't considered she might be home. This building had survived the Blitz, so I could only hope that meant it had sturdy and *thick* walls. Turning on the faucet, I filled the cup with water, hoping that the nonchalant gesture would hide my embarrassment.

"You want some birth control to go with that?" Belle asked. "'Cause judging from the sounds coming from you bedroom, you need it."

"You're hilarious," I said, the rosy glow on my cheeks staining deeper.

"Don't I know it? And I haven't even started on all the puns I came up with when you kept me awake with your moaning last night." She scooped some eggs out of the pan and onto a plate.

I groaned. "I can't wait."

"You'll see, it's going to be a real scream," she said with a wink. "Oh wait, you already did all the screaming."

"Make sure you get some of 'your mama' or 'that's what she said' jabs in there when you're coming up with this ground-breaking material," I advised her.

"Pass me the beans," she said.

I slid the bowl to her and she ladled some next to the eggs.

"Thanks," I said, "I'm starving."

Belle wagged a finger at me, her eyebrow arched sugges-tively. "I bet you are, but these aren't for you. I'll make you some next. Believe it or not, you weren't the only one who got some action last night."

I tugged at the hem of my thin tank top. "Is Philip here?"

"Yep, I left him in bed."

"So maybe all that screaming you claim occurred wasn't just me," I teased.

"Philip's not really a roller coaster ride," Belle said, adding quickly, "not that I'm complaining."

Now her cheeks were flushed, but I smiled at her. "Hey, no judgment."

If every man were as amazing in the sack as Alexander, no one would ever leave bed. Society couldn't handle that level of virility in the standard package.

"Crap, I forgot the sausages." Belle threw some into a pan and flipped the hob back on. "So you couldn't even find time to say goodnight last night before you had to rip his clothes off, huh?"

I hesitated, unsure of how much to tell Belle. On one hand, she was my best friend. On the other, explaining the complexities of my relationship with Alexander wasn't exactly going to be easy. Still trying to hide what was really going on was by far the most unhealthy thing I could think of, and I needed a confidant. "Actually, I did leave alone."

"I guessed," Belle admitted. "Alexander found me when he was looking for you. He seemed worried, although it is hard to read that man. What happened?"

Tell me about it. I was only beginning to understand him myself. But last night's sudden departure actually had very little to do with him. My stomach churned as I thought of how I'd been treated last night by his friends and family. "I don't know. It all seems so silly now. Let's just say I met his family and they aren't very nice."

"Imagine that," Belle said dryly. "The Royal Family is a bunch of assholes."

Despite feeling sick, this made me laugh. "I know, right? Someone alert the media."

"I can't believe you just made an alert the media joke after making fun of my jokes earlier," Belle said, sticking her lower lip out in a well-practiced pout.

"I'll admit it's not my freshest material," I said.

"And that blonde—what was her name again?" Belle asked.

I wished I could forget her name. If there was one thing I didn't want to even think about, it was Pepper. How could someone so beautiful be so incredibly ugly? But I knew the answer to that. Pepper could have any man she wanted, but the trouble was that she wanted mine.

"Pepper Lockwood," I said, releasing a pent-up sigh of frustration.

"She was the one in the tabloids, right?"

"The one and only."

"Oh god. I suppose it doesn't help that she's even prettier in person," Belle said, throwing an arm around my shoulder and leaning against me. "She looks like a bitch."

"That's not just a look." I recounted to Belle that after Pepper's fake friendly introduction, she'd revealed her true colors. Belle's eyes narrowed a little with each new piece of information. They were slits by the time I finished.

"What a capital B," Belle said.

"You totally knew it, too," I said, referencing Belle's warning look the night before.

She shrugged modestly. "I hoped I was wrong."

"You were right," I admitted. "And the worst part is that I can't tell Alexander what she said or how she acted, but it's clear she's done a number on the entire family."

"Someone has to be smart enough to see past her little act."

"Morning!" Philip said he shuffled into the kitchen.

Belle and I startled apart, and she glared at her fiancé as though he was to blame for our skittishness. I knew exactly why we were on edge. It could just as easily had been Alexander walking through the door.

"Lovely to see you, Clara," Philip said, seemingly unaware of our reaction to his entrance. He rambled over and grabbed the kettle from the hob, pouring some hot water for his morning tea. "I didn't get a chance to say hello last night, although I heard you looked fabulous."

"That's not all he heard," Belle said as she handed him a loaded plate.

He frowned at her, obviously not as impressed with her wit as she was. "Thank you," he said stiffly.

"Of course." She shrugged as if this was no big deal, but I saw the gleam as she turned around. There'd been some question as to her ability to be a proper wife, but certainly having breakfast ready proved a thing or two about that. "Should I make a plate for Alexander?"

I hesitated, torn between making certain that he felt welcome and not wanting to disturb him. There was also the fact that I had a hard time imagining Alexander sitting down to Saturday morning breakfast. It was too normal.

"Alexander is here?" Philip asked, abandoning his fork and knife to stare at us.

"Who on earth did you think was making that noise last night?" Belle asked.

"A neighbor," Philip responded in a clipped tone. His gaze flickered over me before returning to his plate, but I caught the flash of disgust—and pity—in his eyes. I'd never been a huge fan of Sir Philip Abernathy, but this was the final straw. He had no right to look at me that way.

"Ignore him," Belle ordered me under her breath. Out loud

she said, "What does Alexander like?"

I wasn't sure. I'd seen him eat a burger, but I had no clue how he took his eggs or if he preferred coffee or tea with his breakfast. These were the kinds of things you were supposed to know about a guy *before* you slept with him. At least I'd known all of them about Daniel.

"Tea. No milk," Alexander said, coming into view. He was dressed in his undershirt and tuxedo slacks but his feet were bare. I ached to tear the clothes off him and take him back to bed where things between us actually made sense. "As for breakfast, *everything*. I'm starving. I worked up an appetite last night."

Alexander flashed me a sly smile that suggested he wasn't simply hungry for food. If he wasn't careful, poor Philip was going to be eating eggs while watching me mount Alexander on the counter.

I expected a smart-ass comment from Belle, but none came and when I turned to goad her, she was staring at Alexander with a dreamy expression plastered to her face.

"I'll get it," I said, snatching the plate from her hand and filling it up before she'd even turned to see what was happening.

Alexander took a barstool next to Philip, and they sat there quietly. I'd been under the impression they knew one another, but if they did, then they certainly weren't on friendly terms. My thoughts jumped to the bedroom. I wished I were in there with Alexander instead of watching the cold war at the counter.

Belle handed me a mug of tea and shrugged, as if to say *what can you do*? "What do you want, Clara?"

"Oh, I'm fine." There was no way she'd made enough for the four of us.

"Absolutely not. What do you want?" she repeated.

"Some eggs and toast, I guess." There was no use fighting her on it. She'd see the food got in my mouth whether she had to force it down my throat or not.

Belle shot me a *what now* look, glancing toward the bar, and I frowned. Philip struck me as a type who often disapproved of people and how they spent their free time. If I had to guess, Alexander's past wasn't something he took lightly, and if he had read half the stories that were posted about Alexander to sites like TMI, I couldn't blame him. But he didn't know him. They were related in some distant way, but that didn't mean they were family.

"What are your plans today?" Belle asked me, obviously desperate to break the tension in the air.

"Not sure," I said.

"Let's go shopping."

I looked to Alexander without meaning to, as if to see if this was okay. But as soon as I realized what I was doing, I shook myself. I didn't have plans with Alexander, which made me free to make other plans.

Alexander saw the look and spoke up. "I have a family thing, and I'm certain my father will require a few hours of explanation as to why I left last night."

I mouthed *sorry* to him, but he shook his head, dismissing the apology, and smiled reassuringly.

"Then let's go!" Belle clapped her hands in excitement. "There's a new boutique in Notting Hill."

"Notting Hill on a Saturday will be a mad house," Philip threw in, but we both ignored him.

"I need to shower and then we can go," I promised her. "Are you sure you don't want to come?"

"I would love to, but duty calls," Alexander said grimly.

Next to him, Philip guffawed.

"Is that funny?" Alexander asked.

"I find the idea of you and duty rather amusing," Philip admitted.

"Philip!" Belle protested, but it was too late.

"I served in Afghanistan and Iraq for seven years," Alexander said in a low voice, radiating with contempt. "I know more about duty than the average Englishman can fathom."

"And what of honor?" Philip asked. "Did you manage to find some over there? Or is it too late for that?"

Belle's shocked face mirrored mine, but neither of us spoke. We could only watch as Alexander stood and stormed to my bedroom, appearing again a moment later, carrying his jacket and shoes.

"You don't have to go," I said in a quiet voice.

"I have things to do," he responded gruffly, moving past me toward the front door.

But he pivoted at the door and grabbed me around the waist, crushing his lips against mine in a possessive display that clearly wasn't meant for me. He was marking me for Philip to see. I knew that I should stop him, but I'd already melted into him. When he broke away, he brushed a finger over my bruised lips and smiled grimly.

"Have fun today."

I swallowed and bobbed my head, doing my best to look chipper. "We will. Notting Hill is my favorite place in London."

Alexander paused as if he wanted to say something, but he opened the door instead. "See you soon, poppet."

It was hardly the farewell I was hoping for. With the integrity of his phone compromised and this morning's disaster, I had no clue when *soon* might be. A cold chill rippled up my spine as I considered that I might not see him again at all. We hadn't spoken about what had happened last night in bed. Had things gotten out of control?

Belle appeared at my side as I shut the door and whispered, "It'll be okay."

Part of me wanted to spin around and yell at her for what

Philip had said, but it wasn't her fault. I wasn't feeling so forgiving of Philip though.

By the time I'd showered and pinned my hair back, I was eager to get out of the house and do something normal. Just because I didn't consider shopping a career like my mom didn't mean I couldn't appreciate its ability to distract. Right now, I needed to shut down my overworked brain and more than that, I needed to spend some time with Belle. I needed her to make me laugh. I needed her to distract me from the mess I'd found myself in.

"You ready?" I yelled, knocking on her door.

"Five minutes!"

I plopped onto the couch and grabbed one of her magazines. Paging through it, I felt like I should take notes. I wasn't accustomed to being trendy or fashionable, but now that I had a real job, I couldn't get by on t-shirts and jeans.

Philip came whistling around the corner, but the tune died on his lips when he saw me. I'd assumed he'd gone after the spat, but apparently not. I stood, a scowl deepening on my face, and headed for my room.

"Clara, wait!" he called after me.

For some reason I couldn't quite explain, I stopped. Crossing my arms over my chest, I waited. Nothing he could say to me would make up for what he'd said to Alexander.

"I apologize for my behavior," he began, "but you have to understand that I grew up around Alexander."

"That's some apology," I hissed.

"Let me explain," he said, ignoring my jibe. "Alexander isn't what you think he is. He's a dark soul and he has secrets."

"But let me guess—you know them?" I already knew Alexander had darkness in him. Unlike Philip, I'd not only seen it, I'd experienced it.

"No. I've heard the rumors. The ones that get passed around at official functions."

"Didn't your mother ever tell you not to believe everything you hear?"

"I suppose she did," Philip said, "but she also told me to be careful whom I trust. I trust the people who told me about Alexander and what he does to women. How he uses them. How twisted he can be when he gets them alone." He took a step closer to me. "So let me ask you this, Clara, do you trust Alexander?"

This was hardly news to me, but the question of trust—that was an entirely different story. I considered it for a moment, thinking of the back and forth I'd experienced since I began seeing Alexander, but then I thought of his face as he revealed himself to me last night, of the fragile control he'd exhibited when I offered my body to him in any way he needed, and I had my answer. "I do trust him."

"Then I hope for your sake that I'm wrong," Philip said. "Be careful, Clara."

He disappeared back into Belle's room, leaving me to question my sanity. Could Philip see what I couldn't? Had I turned a blind eye out of lust or...I shook my head. The alternative was far worse. I forced a smile as Belle appeared in the doorway.

"Are you ready?" she asked.

I grabbed my purse and gritted my teeth. "Absolutely."

THE WEEKEND FLEW BY WITHOUT WORD FROM ALEXANDER, and I began to feel the first tendrils of doubt rooting in me. He'd broken his rules and shown a part of himself to me that he'd sworn to keep hidden, and then I pushed him further.

It was this thought preoccupying me as I got to my desk on

Monday morning. I'd purposefully headed in early so as not to deal with the swiveling heads I knew would follow my entry. Thankfully, the few people who had magically gotten there even earlier than me merely mumbled sleepy hellos as I passed.

But when I got to my desk, the answer I'd been waiting for was there already. In the form of another hand-delivered note-card. I picked it up and flipped it over, my heart thrilling as I brushed my fingers along the smooth wax seal. Plucking the flap open, I withdrew the card and read:

Poppet,
    Have a less dramatic week at work. I'm tied up with family business, but I will see you soon.
    X

I'd rather he was tied up with me, but I held the card to my chest, then glanced around to see if anyone noticed. It was thrilling to know his words were for my eyes only. I tucked the note into my desk drawer, but thought better of it and stuck it in my purse. Not only did I want to ward off rumors that could affect my working relationships here, but I also didn't know if I could trust any of these people. Not when private information about Alexander was worth a premium.

Bennett's curly head popped around the corner of my cubi-cle, curiosity glinting in his chocolate eyes. "You had a delivery this morning."

"Yeah, I got it. Thanks." It was best to leave it at that even though my new boss was a teddy bear.

"And I saw you on *Entertainment Today* this weekend," he teased. "Did you feel like Cinderella?"

Yeah, I thought, *especially the part where she runs away from the ball*. But I didn't tell him that, instead I shrugged, letting his good-natured ribbing roll off my back. "I came home with both of my shoes, so sadly no."

"Fine, don't give me the sordid details." Bennett pressed a hand to his chest. "I'm wounded, really."

I rolled my eyes and grabbed a notebook. "Don't we have a meeting to prep for?"

"Yeah, Isaac Blue's publicist called to confirm him for next Tuesday."

Within seconds, he'd switched to full business mode, giving me a reprieve from the questions about my personal life. We settled into a lengthy discussion, strategizing how we'd pitch the new campaign and what responsibilities I'd have for the presentation. By the time Bennett stood to leave, it was already noon.

"I should order something up," he said, checking his watch. "I promised the girls not to work this weekend, so now my inbox is full."

"Actually, I'm going to go grab something to bring back to my desk. What can I get you?" I asked.

A relieved smile spread across his face. "Clara, you're a saint. There's a fantastic curry place around the corner, but it gets packed at lunch. You might want to call it in now."

I found the curry counter online and placed an order. Sliding my purse onto my shoulder, I left, ready to get away from the desk.

London buzzed with Monday afternoon energy, everyone rushing to get a leg up on the week ahead. The temperature had risen, as had the humidity, announcing the near arrival of summer. I pulled my hair up off my neck, unsticking a few sweaty strands, and pinned it into a quick French twist. Despite the heat, I welcomed the sun soaking into my skin. May had been rainy up until this point, and I was ready for the change of season.

The aromatic scent of coriander wafted from the kitchen as

I waited for my order, making my stomach rumble. Twenty minutes later, I was on the way to the office with two bags full of Tandoori chicken, rice, and lentil soup. I crossed the street to avoid the surge of foot traffic coming off the Tube, which is why I saw it:

My face staring at me from the cover of a magazine. More specifically, my fifteen year-old face.

Starving for His Love: Bishop's Devastating Secret

The past I'd worked so hard to forget was splashed across every tabloid in the corner news stall.

CHAPTER NINETEEN

The day became a checklist of things to do. Normal people wouldn't need to be reminded to go back to work or check email or drink water, but then again, normal people weren't on tabloid covers. I had a variety of therapeutic tools I'd been taught in counseling, many of which I hadn't used for years. Today I used them all. I shut out the negative influence, which meant turning off the wireless on my computer and silencing my phone. I ate lunch with Bennett, who had no idea what was going on. I focused on completing important tasks. Above all of that, I tried to be kind to myself.

That proved to be the hardest. It always had been. I'd come a long way since I was fifteen, but I knew how easily I could backslide. The thing no one understood was that not eating wasn't always a choice. Now when I was stressed out, I some-times forgot. It became less important than all the other demands on my time. The problem was that mentality had grown from rotten roots. Simply forgetting to eat was one thing. Having a body that didn't recognize it needed food was another.

And now, despite all the work I'd done to weed the negative beliefs from my body, this was news. Actually, it wasn't. The headlines, the old photographs—they all accused me. No one was interested in the true story. They wanted to sell papers, and that shredded me. Alexander had lived with it his whole life, but it was new to me. My building had become a hot spot for hopeful paparazzi. I'd seen my sex life discussed on gossip blogs. I should have known it wouldn't be long until they dug deeper. Now my past had been resurrected in the name of entertainment, and if I thought about it for too long, I was going to fall apart.

By the end of the day, I'd finished several days worth of work. The Isaac Blue presentation was complete and ready for Bennett's approval, and I'd begun work on the new company email newsletter. But even as I drafted and edited at a mind-bending pace, my anguish smarted dully in the background. This time I couldn't put it behind me, because as soon as I stepped out of this office, I would be reminded.

Bennett knocked on my cubicle and stuck his head in. "Hey, you okay? You seem off."

"I'm fine." I forced myself to smile. "In fact, I finished the Isaac Blue presentation."

"Even the graphics?" Bennett asked in surprise.

"I just emailed them to you."

Bennett fist pumped the air, giving me a glimpse of what he must have been like when he was younger. The gesture, so boyish and genuine, made me like him even more. "I don't know how you do it."

"I'm working on the newsletter now," I continued. "I thought—"

"Clara," Bennett stopped me. "I think you're a bigger workaholic than me. It's half past five."

"No!" Spinning in my chair, I checked the time on my desktop. My pulse spiked when I saw he was right.

"Time to go home, or do you have a fancy ball this evening?"

Knowing he meant that as a joke, I forced a laugh. "I need to finish this up and then I'm out of here."

"Okay, I'll see you tomorrow then." Bennett paused. "Or I can walk you out."

I waved him off, doing my best to look casual and hide the slight shake of my hands. "Get home to the girls. I'm leaving in five minutes, I promise."

Fifteen minutes later, I couldn't procrastinate any longer. I got to the elevator before the panic kicked in and with it the questions. What if I couldn't get past them? What if the photographers followed me home? I told myself these were practical concerns, but by the time I reached the lobby, the hypotheticals had shifted to more dangerous matters. What would my mother say? Could I lose my job?

What did Alexander think?

There was no doubt in my mind that he knew. Just as there was no doubt that this was a deal-breaker. No matter how much I'd overcome or where I was in my life, my past would be a liability to him. He didn't need any more scandal or embarrassment to contend with from the press, and I was proving to be both. After today, he'd be forced to break up with me and I understood. There had been no more letters from him since lunch. He hadn't shown up my office Alexander had already begun distancing himself from the Clara Bishop train wreck. He could have his pick of women, why choose the damaged one?

I pushed the sting of this realization down and locked it away. Outside the lobby doors, I had to face my past. There was no time to despair for my future.

Twenty-eight steps to the revolving door. I counted each one in an attempt to focus on something mundane, but my heart continued to race as my heels clicked across the polished marble floor. Sun peeked through the door, and I was reminded of something my therapist used to say: "Why wait for the sun to come out from the clouds when you can turn on the light?"

Easy advice to give, I thought as I exited the Clarkwell Building and pulled out my sunglasses. As I came face to face with the swarm of paparazzi waiting for me, I wished I could turn out the light. If only I could escape into the comforting darkness of anonymity, but there was nowhere to turn. Photographers clustered around me, making each step I took toward home difficult.

Clara, are you currently in treatment?

Does Alexander know about your anorexia?

Is it true that you sought counseling as recently as last year?

I clamped my mouth shut as I pushed through them toward the sidewalk. A short guy about my age, wearing a Yankees ball cap, jumped in front of me, iPhone in hand. "Smile, love! I know you don't want any double chins in this shot."

Something snapped inside me and I rushed toward him. He tried to back away but I pressed forward until I was in his scruffy, unshaved face. "This is a joke to you, isn't it? Do you even have feelings? Because from where I'm standing, you've all forgotten that you're humans too! Tell me your secrets! Share that with me. You can't, can you?"

"I just wanted a picture!" The man held up his hands in surrender. If he thought he was getting away that easily, he wasn't.

"You're a piece of shit. You all are. Did you ever stop to think that I have feelings? Did you consider what a story like this could do to someone in recovery? Or what it tells people too scared to ask for help?" I whirled around, finger in the air, no longer directing my anger at only one person. "You're all sick. This isn't news! Get out of my life!"

A brunette with too much lipstick and not enough sense

stepped forward, frowning sympathetically. "Clara, we just want to help."

"Help? Help!" Manic laughter poured out of me. "I don't need your help. Don't you get that? I don't need you to fix me."

She moved closer to me, reaching out as if to pat my arm.

"Stop," I said in a quiet voice. "Don't you fucking touch me."

She gasped, whipping around to the cameraman standing behind her. "Did you get that?"

I watched in amazement as she proceeded to record a sound bite right in front of me. They really had no shame. They were just a bunch of soul-sucking leeches. I opened my mouth to give her a few more sound bites when Norris appeared at my side.

"Miss Bishop." He dropped a protective arm around me and steered me toward the street. Reporters crushed against us, elbowing one another as they shouted more questions. I turned my face into Norris's shoulder, grateful that he had shown up. But where was Alexander?

Norris forced open the car door against the drove of photographers, and I climbed into the back, sagging with relief after the door shut. But my peacefulness was short-lived. The Rolls Royce pulled away from the curb, dodging people on the street, before settling comfortably into evening traffic. Now that I'd made it out of there, fury seized me. Part of me wanted to cry, but I was too numb to produce tears. There would be repercussions for what happened today. I'd made a mistake by confronting them. It only gave them new material. Tomorrow the stories would tell of Crazy Clara Bishop attacking reporters. Still, I couldn't bring myself to regret it. Someone needed to call them out and people like Alexander couldn't risk it. My infamy would pass, replaced by the sins of his next girlfriend. In a month, I would be a nobody. In a month, he'd still be the heir to the throne.

I couldn't blame him for not coming. He'd sent Norris to fulfill his promise to protect me even as he realized I wasn't worth the effort.

The flat was dark when I entered, and a dam burst inside of me. I sobbed as I found a note from Belle on the counter saying she was staying at Philip's for the night. It was selfish to want her here, but right now I needed my best friend. Digging into my bag for my phone, I realized I'd turned it off and stuck it in my desk. I had no mobile, no friend, and Alexander had sent his security guard to escort me home. Humiliation flooded through me as fat, hot tears hit my cheeks.

I shuffled toward my room and the promise of my bed. I wouldn't berate myself, but maybe I could afford to feel a little self-pity. I'd done my best to not misstep since I met Alexander, but no one cared about that. They wanted drama and juicy secrets. I wasn't cut out for this life. Alexander hadn't come because he knew that. Now I knew it too.

At the door to my room, I stopped, realizing the light was on. I hadn't turned it on this morning before work. That might have scared me once, but now I pushed the door wider and stepped through, knowing what I would find.

Alexander filled the armchair by the window, his eyes turned to the street below. My heart lurched, drinking in the sight of him. His arms hung imperially on the armrests, his mere presence commanding even in the empty room. He was dressed in a faded black t-shirt that hugged his biceps, but even the casual attire did nothing to dull the brutal authority emanating from him.

He didn't speak and I didn't have the energy to engage him. Instead I dropped to my bed and clutched a pillow against my lap. A few minutes passed, and I lost track of time, before he stood and moved to the edge of the bed. He loomed over me, regarding me with practiced coolness. I met his gaze, noticing for the first time the slight tick of his jaw.

"Is it true?" he asked in a measured tone.

I swallowed, knowing that I was about to destroy the bond we shared. Had I really thought it was unbreakable? Maybe I was as delusional as the tabloids painted me. "Yes."

This time his jaw visibly tightened as he turned away. I blinked against tears, refusing to cry again until he was gone. But Alexander didn't leave, he took two steps, stopped, and put his fist through the wall. Jumping to my feet, I watched as he drew back his bruised knuckles. Plaster crumbled to the ground from the gaping hole he'd left.

"I'm sorry," I yelled, no longer able to hold back my tears. "I'm not perfect. I'm sorry you didn't know. But you need to leave."

Alexander pivoted to stare at me. "You think I'm angry with you?"

"I have no idea how they found out about it," I continued, my confession streaming from me in a nervous torrent. "I was in therapy before university, and I saw a private counselor my first year of college. There was a relapse a year ago, but that was all confidential."

"You no longer have secrets, Clara."

"I realize that now. I realize I owe you an explanation, but—"

"You owe me nothing." The gentleness of his tone stopped me more than the words, and Alexander seized on the moment of silence to approach me. "Do you understand that? You *owe me nothing.*" He cupped my chin as he repeated those words, holding my eyes to his.

His perfect face swam in front of me as I fought the tears. I shook my head. I didn't understand him. I didn't understand anything about today. I only felt him slipping away from me.

My life was spinning out of control and there was nothing to grab on to.

"I need you to understand," I whispered, but I couldn't bring myself to speak aloud the rest of my thought. *Before you leave me.*

"If you need me to, I will listen. But you don't owe me an explanation. Nothing you say will change anything between us."

I tore myself away from him, his words wrenching through me. He'd made his choice. "Then go."

"I don't want to go." Alexander took a step closer to me and then paused. "What do you think I'm saying to you?"

"I understand," I said, unable to look at him. "You don't need more drama in your life. You don't need a girlfriend who has to actively construct positive thoughts about her body and set alarms to remind herself to eat. I don't blame you for that."

"I'm not leaving you," he said in a soft voice. "I never wanted perfection. I wanted you."

I swayed on my feet, and his hand shot out to catch me. Alexander gathered me in his arms and carried me to the bed. Sinking down, his hold on me tightened as the tears I'd held back poured from me. I breathed him in—the scent of soap mixed with spicy cologne and something indescribable that belonged only to him. His grip didn't relax until I was calm enough to pull away, but I stayed in his arms.

"I still want you to understand," I murmured. We both had secrets and I understood now that I couldn't keep mine from Alexander.

Alexander nodded but stayed silent.

Taking a shaky breath, I focused on what I'd learned about sharing during group therapy. *No one here is out to judge you*, I told myself. That had been true then and I felt it was true now. Alexander didn't want to leave. That should have reassured me, but until I told him everything, I couldn't be certain he wouldn't change his mind if he found out more later.

"It started at school. My mother insisted that I attend an exclusive academy in California, and as usual, my father gave in. I didn't want to go. I was fourteen and my friends were my life, but I had no say in the matter. I guess that made the transition worse, and I had a hard time meeting people." I paused to take another calming breath before I continued. "Finally, an older girl took me under her wing. She taught me about makeup and boys. For some reason, I thought she was really popular. Probably because she seemed happy. And then one day, she went into the bathroom and threw up after lunch."

Alexander's arms stiffened around me, but he nodded for me to continue.

"She pushed me to try it, and when I wouldn't, she started dropping little hints. There was a roll around my bra strap. She slapped my thigh in the locker room and laughed as it jiggled. So one night, I went with her after dinner and threw up. It was hard for me and it took so long for me to do it while she stood there and teased me. When I finally did it, I decided I couldn't do it again. I hated it, but she was my only friend.

"After all these years, I still feel stupid when I tell this story," I admitted.

Alexander's finger flew to my chin and tipped my eyes up to his. "You are not stupid."

"I wasn't smart though. I believed her when she said my parents had sent me away because they were ashamed. I believed her when she said the thinner I got, the more popular I would become. By the time I went home for Spring Break, I weighed less than a hundred pounds. My mom—" my voice broke and I choked back a sob at the memory. Alexander pressed a reassuring kiss to my forehead and waited. "My mom started crying when she saw me. They pulled me out of school, and she drove me to therapy every single day, because she wouldn't let them admit me. That summer we moved to England. Dad thought it would be a better environment for me. Maybe he was right."

"He *was* right," Alexander agreed, burying his face into my neck. "Because you're here with me now, poppet."

The ache in my chest spread like wildfire as he spoke, but I forced myself to continue. "I've done really well with therapy. I learned my eating disorder was a coping mechanism that I used when I was stressed or lonely. I stayed in therapy until my second year at university and then I met Daniel."

"The one who tried to break you?" Alexander remembered with barely restrained disgust.

"I should have seen through him," I said.

"Don't make excuses," Alexander ordered.

"It was fine for a while, but then things changed. He changed. One minute he made me feel like the most important person in his life, and the next, I was the reason he was miserable. He criticized how much I ate, pointed out how little I exercised. He competed with me for grades. When my parents gave me access to my trust fund, we came home after my birthday party and I told him I was tired. He didn't like that. He accused me of being superior to him. He said I was being elitist and that I was too snobby to fuck him. Things escalated quickly and he almost—"

Alexander vaulted from the bed and began to pace, motioning with an impatient wave for me to continue.

I chose my words carefully, aware of the edge Alexander teetered on. "But he didn't," I said. "Belle came home. She saw what was going on and threatened to call the police. That night should have been enough for me to see what he was doing to me, but still I thought I was in love with him. I refused to go to therapy even though Belle pushed. I was fine. Things were under control, and then I fainted during class. At the hospital, they asked me when my last period was and I couldn't remember."

Alexander froze, his expression unreadable.

"I honestly thought I was pregnant, and the thought of having a baby with Daniel made me so scared that I got sick. They had to put me on oxygen and give me a feeding tube." My voice broke as I recalled that day in the hospital and the whirl-wind of emotions I'd suffered. "I realized that I wasn't scared of having a baby, but I was terrified of being permanently bound to Daniel. When it occurred to me that my child would have him for a father, there was a sadness deeper than any I've ever known."

"So you ended it," Alexander guessed. He'd stopped his furious pacing to hover next to the bed.

"I didn't have to," I said, a humorless laugh spilling out. It was impossible now to understand how I could have been so naive. "The results came back negative. I wasn't pregnant. I was malnourished. My liver was barely functioning. I was shutting down. I hadn't purposefully stopped eating. I hadn't even real-ized I was doing it. The doctors quizzed me and suggested I go back to therapy, especially a support group. It was there that I realized I'd been clinging to an idea of control that didn't exist. Not eating was something I chose. Maybe because of the awful things he said about my body. Maybe because subconsciously I desperately needed to control something. My group helped me see that I'd given him control over me instead. So when I say he broke me—that's what I mean. I loved him and he nearly killed me. At least, I thought I loved him."

"And now?" Alexander asked.

"Now..." I trailed away, no longer certain that was the case. Now I had someone to compare Daniel to, but I didn't dare tell Alexander that. "Let's just say that distance has given me perspective. Although after today, I feel like I've been thrown back in time. I suppose no matter how far I've come, I can't change what happened, and that means sometimes I have to face it."

Alexander's eyes grew distant as he considered this. He understood what I was saying better than most. I'd witnessed his nightmares and caught the self-deprecating comments he threw into conversations. Even though he hadn't laid open his soul to me yet, I knew that I could trust him with what had happened to me. I could only hope someday that he felt the same way. "That's why you ran when I brought up submission."

I nodded. I hadn't wanted to bring it back to him, not after how far we'd come in the last few days, but avoiding it wasn't going to help.

"I can't believe I..." he searched for the words, a familiar expression of self-loathing on his face.

"No, X," I stopped him. "It wasn't just that. It was the idea of any relationship."

"My predilections certainly won't help you," he growled.

"I thought that at first too. But you aren't him, and I'm stronger now."

"And your body?" The rasp in his voice arrested me with its implication, and I couldn't speak. "How do you feel about your body?"

Pushing the words over my dry tongue, I forced myself to answer him. "Most days I don't think about it. I eat. I get dressed. I walk or run. Other days, I catch myself wishing I had a body like Pepper's."

His eyes flashed at the mention of her name, but he didn't speak. Instead he lifted me into his arms, without so much as a word. I wrapped my arms around his neck as he cradled me against his chest. Alexander kicked open the bathroom door with his foot and carried me to the mirror. Setting me gently on my feet, he guided me around to face my reflection. His lips moved to my ears as his fingers deftly unzipped my dress and pushed it past my shoulders with slow deliberation.

"I've been remiss in telling you how I feel about your body," Alexander said, his breath tickling my earlobe and sending warm tendrils of pleasure cascading down my neck. "Your gorgeous cunt gets so much of my attention, but when I said your whole body was made for fucking, I mean it."

His fingers stayed hooked into the straps of my dress, preventing it from falling to my feet. Alexander's mouth drifted across my skin to the curve of my neck. He pressed a lingering kiss there, his eyes closed in reverence, and I melted against him. His eyes snapped open, and I saw wildness reflecting from them. "This—" he brushed the spot with his lips "—was made to kiss—so smooth and soft. When I'm burying my cock in your perfect cunt, I can't help myself."

He demonstrated with another leisurely caress of his lips, but this time his teeth sank lightly into the flesh, and I gasped in approval. A pleased smile curved across his face. Alexander planted kisses as he inched the straps of my dress down the length of my arms. "Long and slender. These freckles drive me crazy." He paused. "And the way they feel when they're wrapped around me, clinging to me as I ride you—*perfection.*"

The dress slipped off me and pooled at my feet as Alexander's fingers knit through mine. He drew our clasped hands over my shoulder and kissed each knuckle. "Such clever fingers. I hate when they aren't intertwined with mine, unless they're on my cock, of course."

I nodded, my teeth sinking into my bottom lip as I drank in his reflection in the mirror—his blue eyes smoldering into mine, in such contrast to his thick, jet-black hair, his lips pressed to my hand.

"Look at yourself, poppet," he ordered when he realized what I was doing.

"I want to look at you," I whispered.

"I don't blame you," he said with a smirk, "but right now, I need you to pay attention. Follow my lips with your eyes." He stepped into the space between my body and the vanity, still holding my hand, and dropped to his knees. Taking my other hand, he guided my arms behind my back, forcing me to stand straighter and pushing my chest closer to his waiting lips. He tipped his head up, catching my nipple in his mouth. I did as I was told, watching his tongue swirl around the furled tip before he sucked it in between his teeth. My breasts swelled from his attention, growing full and heavy, as he tended to each of them in term. My body ached with building tension, as he leaned back on his heels and turned to the mirror. "It's almost cliché to tell you that your tits are perfect, but they are. Full and supple. I can ever decide if I want to suck them or fuck them."

A whimper escaped my lips and his eyebrow crooked up. "Would you like that? Do you want me to shove my cock between your tits?"

I nodded, lost to his erotic suggestions. The list of places I wouldn't allow his cock had diminished to the point of nonexistence.

"Later, poppet," he promised, twisting back to trail his lips between the hollow of my breasts down to my navel. His tongue circled it as he pinned my wrists together in one hand, bringing his freed hand to stroke across the taut lines of my stomach. "Your body makes me so fucking hot, poppet. I think about it all the time, imagining how I'm going to fuck you. When we're apart, all I can think of is getting my hands on you."

He reached to my hip and gripped it tightly, kneading it with strong fingers. "I can't take my eyes off you when you walk.

Do you sway your hips like that on purpose, knowing that I'm watching?"

I shook my head. Usually, I didn't. Then again something about Alexander stole my inhibitions. Maybe it was his dirty mouth or his sinful body, but his presence brought out a wanton side to my personality that I'd never suspected I had.

"All I can think about is grabbing these hips and putting you over my knee," he continued huskily, "or holding onto them as my cock pounds you. They curve so precisely into my hands. I swear your body is fucking proof of evolution."

I closed my eyes, picturing his body dominating mine. Frenetic energy pulsed through me, pooling where his skin made contact with mine.

"Open your eyes, Clara," he demanded. His hand lightly smacked my bare buttocks and my eyes flew open. He released my other hand and cupped both of my cheeks. "I'll have to spend a whole day worshipping your ass. It's a pity that you can't see me do it, but I'll be certain to describe every single thing I want to do to it. Everything I'm *going* to do to it."

Alexander's hands slid from my rear to my thighs, and he urged them slowly open. Dropping lower, his face nestled against the tender inner flesh. "I suppose it would be too much to ask to be buried here?"

A giggle slipped from my lips and he kissed the sensitive skin in response. "I'm serious, poppet. I want my lips down here, breathing you in. Your scent intoxicates me, you know. I want them clamping against my ears as I taste you. But I need them spreading open for me, circling around me as I fuck you."

Yes, please.

"You know how I feel about this." Alexander's lips moved up, his words whispering across my swollen sex. "Your cunt was made for me. It's so tight it just squeezes my cock when I'm inside of you, draining every drop from me.

But you know that. You know you have a greedy cunt, don't you? I want you to see. I'm going to fuck you with my tongue, so you can see how fucking beautiful you are when you come."

His tongue licked through the lace of my panties up the length of my seam, drawing hungry gasps from me. He pulled back. "Watch, poppet."

Plunging between my lips past my thong, he ran his tongue over my cleft, landing on my clit. He pushed my legs open wider, so that I could watch him in the mirror. It was too much, seeing him between my legs, watching as his tongue stroked and sucked, but I didn't dare turn away. My hands tangled in his hair, holding me to him as my hips ground flagrantly against his mouth.

My muscles contracted, tension tightening them, with each lash of his tongue. I watched as my eyes slanted dreamily and my teeth bit into my lower lip. My chest moved with shallow pants of anticipation as a film of sweat spread across my skin. I no longer wanted to turn away, I'd lost my reservations to Alexander's meticulous mouth, and I bucked against his talented tongue.

I was so close, but my body craved more. "I want to see your cock inside me."

Alexander's hands tightened on my thighs, digging into my skin, adding the edge of pain to my pleasure, but he didn't relent. Instead his tongue flicked powerfully against my clit before his mouth settled over it, sucking it into his hungry mouth.

I forgot my request as I came undone, my eyes locked with the girl in the mirror. Her ecstasy mirrored mine—mouth wide, cries spilling from her lips as she unapologetically fucked Alexander's mouth. Bliss washed over me, splintering over the brink, as I clutched his body to mine.

"Had enough, poppet?" Alexander asked, kissing the hollow of my thigh.

I shook my head, unable to speak, as I released him and caught myself on the vanity.

Alexander rose and moved behind me, unbuckling his jeans as his eyes watched mine in the mirror. The crown of his cock stuck up over the band of his boxer briefs, and I licked my lips.

"Do you want this?" His eyes hooded as he fisted his rigid shaft.

I did, but I wanted more than that. Alexander had shown me that he wanted all of me. His desire wasn't limited to my sex, and mine wasn't limited to his either.

"No," I whispered, aware of the risk I was taking. "I want your body."

His image stilled behind me as he took in my words. "You don't want that, Clara."

"There's no part of my body you don't want, right?" I waited for him to nod. He did so stiffly, but after his exhibition he could hardly deny it. "There's no part of your body that I don't want."

"Clara—" he began, but I shushed him.

"I felt the scars. I *know*," I spoke delicately, unsure how he would react to being reminded of that night. I could only trust my instinct. "And I want you. All of you, X. Your body—*all of it*—makes me so fucking hot."

A tenuous smile tugged at the corner of his mouth as I repeated his own words back to him. He couldn't argue with me, but uncertainty glimmered in his eyes. Alexander stepped out of his pants and kicked them toward the bathtub. His boxers followed, putting his magnificent cock on display. But my eyes were locked to his as his fingers gripped the hem of his t-shirt. I smiled reassuringly, and he drew it slowly up his torso, revealing the muscular slab he'd only recently allowed me to touch. I kept my face blank as the first scar came into view. Alexander hesitated, still watching me, as though any moment I might change my mind.

"All of you, X," I repeated.

He tugged the shirt over his head, releasing a ragged breath as my gaze raked over his body. The scars snaked angrily across the left half of his ribs and up across his pecs. Raw and white, they'd faded some with time, but they were impossible to ignore. I stifled a shudder. I'd known it was a serious accident, but knowing and seeing proof were completely different things. It must have been a miracle that he survived, and yet the worst damage had been done to his soul.

There was nothing standing between us now, and when Alexander's hands grabbed my hips in a fierce hold, I parted my legs. I ached to feel him move inside me. I needed it. *We* needed it.

"Take me," I whispered, "and don't be gentle."

His hand dropped out of sight and a moment later, his broad crown nudged inside me. Alexander pushed his cock cautiously into my cleft, pausing as I flowered over him. Then his hands were on my hips, forcing me down until I engulfed his thick shaft. Despite my request, his hips rocked with slow, deliberate strokes, allowing my body to adjust to his delicious girth. His hands slid across my stomach, circling and tightening across my torso as his thrusts deepened. Dipping to my neck, his teeth caught the curve of it, latching on as he continued to piston his cock until he was buried to the root against my sex.

I wanted to see him, all of him, as he fucked me, so I bowed forward, pulling free of his hands. Sinking forward, I clutched the counter, gasping as he penetrated deeper. His eyes shut against his reflection, but I drank in his lean form as he drove into me.

He was beautiful, and he was mine. The scars of his past

didn't scare me, they drew me to him. And he needed to know that.

"Open your eyes, X," I commanded in a strong, sure voice. He had shown me how he saw me, and I wanted to return the favor. "I want you to see what you do to me. I want you to see what I see."

Alexander's eyes flew open, blazing with wildfire, and the pain shining in them stole my breath away. I pushed against him encouragingly and his pace increased. His fingers caught my hair and tugged it back, yanking up my neck so that my gaze was fixed to his. And when I couldn't look away, he plunged hard into my drenched sex, impaling me on his cock. I cried out, pleasure wrenching through me as he continued his merciless onslaught. Our sights were locked on each other as the first surge quaked through me. I fought to keep my eyes open as the pressure mounted, aroused by the sheen of perspiration glistening across his carved body.

"Don't stop," I begged. "All of you. Give me all of you."

A groan vibrated from him as he poured into me, flooding me with hot gushes, and I shattered, bursting against him with a rapturous cry.

Collapsing against the vanity, I rode out the after-tremors, but Alexander continued to pound into me, moving with slick, desperate thrusts against my sensitive walls.

"Alexander," I pled, but he didn't stop.

"Need...need..." he grunted, his voice distant as he drove tirelessly into me.

I recognized the fire burning in his eyes—saw his need to control, and I trembled as my sex swelled, smarting at the endless stimulation. The veins on his neck pulsed, a guttural noise escaping his lips as he came again. But he didn't slow. He was lost, chasing the demons of his past with visceral, animalistic need.

Wresting away from him, my sex swollen and full, I turned and folded my arms around his shoulders.

"Brimstone," I whispered, not only for my benefit, but for his as well. He thought he could outrun the past by controlling the present.

"I need to be inside you," he gasped, but I shook my head.

This moment was too raw—too fresh—to ignore.

His head dropped to my chest and he gathered me in his arms, lifting me to sit on the counter. When he finally looked up, the flame was gone from his eyes, and I saw through him, even as his gaze pieced me. We were stripped to one another, unguarded and vulnerable. He tenderly positioned himself against my battered entrance, pausing as his eyes asked permission. No longer hesitating, I sheathed myself to his root, knowing there was no other choice.

Neither of us moved.

Neither of us spoke.

But we clung to one another motionlessly, woven together through shared pain and united by unspoken promise. We were defenseless, exposed, naked, and we could only face it together.

CHAPTER TWENTY

Sharing a bathroom with Alexander proved to be nearly impossible. I couldn't keep my eyes off of him, and he couldn't keep his hands off of me. I dabbed some lip-gloss on as Alexander lounged in his boxer briefs against the wall. Seeing him so relaxed around me—no longer hiding his body—meant more than I could express. I watched him in the mirror, drinking in his lean, muscular form.

"If you keep looking at me like that, I'm going to have to take you back to bed." The playful tone in his voice made my toes curl.

Yes, please, I thought. Then sighed. I was already half-dressed in my skirt and bra, and I didn't have time to spare if I was going to get to the office on time. "Don't even think about it, X. I'm going to be late already."

"I warned you that I'm a man who takes what he wants," he purred.

Before I knew what was happening, I was up over his shoulders as he carried me to my room.

"Put me down!" I swatted his ass. "I'm late."

"Stop fighting me or you won't make it in at all," he promised me, a dark gleam flickering in his eyes.

I couldn't help wishing that he would make good on that threat.

Alexander dumped me onto the bed and then dropped to his hands at my feet. Stalking up my legs, he caught the hem of my skirt in his teeth and dragged it past my hips. My teeth sank into my lips, a low moan escaping me as his bare chest grazed across my flesh. Despite the slight padding of my bra, my nipples pebbled into tight beads at the contact.

Would I ever get enough of him? Of this? I couldn't fathom it, not when my body still responded with uncontrollable lust every time he touched me. But now there was the edge of something deeper, something beyond the physical, when he touched me, and my chest ached as my emotions flooded through me.

Alexander's hands shoved my thong to the side and his clever fingers delved between my folds as he stroked in and out of my swollen cleft. "See, poppet? You're still dressed."

I forgot how to speak as his thumb massaged my clit.

"Although this bra is vexing," he said, his voice hoarse. "Your tits belong in my mouth. Don't they, Clara?"

A sob of pleasure racked my body at the thought, tightening my muscles as my body coiled, nearly frantic for release, but Alexander stilled. I rolled my hips, desperate for his fingers to continue their ministrations, but he refused.

"Clara?" His mouth skimmed along my jaw, sending tingles down my neck.

"Yes!"

He met my affirmation with the plunge of his fingers, dipping and twisting deftly as he rubbed my clit. My body heated, a thin sheen of sweat developing across my skin, and I arched against him, grinding my hips against his powerful hands as my orgasm wrenched through me in violent spasms.

Alexander brushed a sticky strand of hair from my forehead and kissed me softly. I was little more than a puddle under him, boneless and sated. It was impossible to consider going to work now.

A knock at the door startled me out of my stupor, but Alexander shushed me and pressed his lips to mine. The second knock was more insistent, and he relented, helping me to my feet and tugging down my skirt. By the time I'd pulled on my shirt, my unexpected visitor was hammering on the door.

There were only a few people who had the access code to our building and it wasn't hard to guess which one of them was banging down my door. Sliding through the living room, I reached the door, stopping to momentarily compose myself—and mentally prepare. My mother flew into the flat, a stream of incoherent babble bursting out of her. Despite her distraught appearance, she was put together in pressed linen slacks and a matching jacket. I waited for a moment, but then I realized that she wasn't going to stop talking without intervention.

"And your father has been on the phone all morning, trying to get it taken down before you—"

"Mom, I know about the story," I butted in.

"Of course you know about it," she snapped. "Your photo is on the cover of every paper in London. He's just trying to do a little damage control."

Damage control. I knew exactly what she meant by that. My parents had been controlling damage to their reputations for years. It was the nice way of saying bribing and threatening. I'd experienced being at the damage control center before, but now that I was an adult, I wasn't having it. "I'd prefer that you let me handle this."

"You?" she scoffed. "Clara, darling, you aren't thinking clearly. Your father—"

"Doesn't need to worry about this," I cut her off. "I have things under control."

She looked as though she seriously doubted that, but she wrapped her arms around me, squeezing me until I gasped for breath. What was meant to be a comforting gesture only left me in pain—as usual. When she finally released me, I glanced nervously toward the hall.

I needed to get her out of here.

"I'm fine, Mom, really," I promised her in a weak voice, ushering her toward the door.

"That's what you said before. When did you start seeing Alexander again? Don't try to deny it! Your appearance with him at that ball has been all over the internet." She wagged a finger at me, stopping only when she realized what she was doing. Clearing her throat, she straightened her silk scarf and changed direction. "We have people who can help you spin this."

"I don't think that's necessary, Mom." A flicker of movement in the hall caught my eye, and I realized my bedroom door was no longer shut. Grown woman or not, I didn't need the drama Madeline would unleash if she found Alexander had spent the night with me. "All I really want is to finish getting dressed. I need to be at work in less than hour."

She continued, oblivious to my attempt to get her out of the flat. "I called Lola this morning, and she thought that we might try—"

"You called Lola?" I asked, not bothering to hide my disbelief.

"She's going into PR and she's very savvy about social media," Mom reminded me.

"She's twenty-one and she's had fifteen majors since she got to university!"

"Lola is set on public relations," she said, completely dismissing my objection.

"You know what?" I strode over to the front door. "I've got this. I don't need you or Lola or Dad helping me out."

Mom wavered, tentatively stepping forward, her eyes fixed on the door, before she burst into tears. "You're cutting me out of your life, Clara. You know how dangerous that is. Does he even know? Have you spoken with him since the story was leaked?"

I wasn't sure what made me angrier: the idea that she thought this story would affect how he felt about me or that she didn't have my back. I'd worried enough about his reaction to the revelation, and Alexander had surprised me, even if it had taken all night for him to convince me it didn't matter. Now my mother, the person who was supposed to show me unconditional love and support, was standing before me and confessing that she thought I was damaged goods.

"He knows." But it wasn't me who finally answered her question. Alexander stepped from the dark hallway into a beam of morning light shining through the living room window. He had on the worn jeans and t-shirt he'd worn over to my house, but there was no doubt of his authority. It dripped from his voice and radiated from his confident bearing. Alexander was all man, and his stance dared anyone to question that. "You must be Clara's mother. I'm pleased to meet you, Mrs. Bishop."

Alexander offered his hand, but she didn't move. My unflappable mother was frozen to the spot.

"Mom," I prompted in a quiet voice. "This is Alexander."

She looked from him to me and back again, then launched back into her diatribe. "Well, I'm glad she told you. Relationships must be built on honesty. Don't you agree, Alexander?"

"Of course." He nodded, flashing me a small smile.

"I think it would be best for all of us, particularly Clara, if we had someone attempting to contain this story. I'm sure you agree with that as well." She clicked her manicured fingertips together as she spoke.

"Unfortunately from personal experience, I can tell you that it's very difficult to control what they publish, whether it's true or not," he said wryly.

Mom's lips pinched into a scowl, and she shook her head. "We have to do something."

"I can't promise anything, but I do have my best man looking into the circumstances behind the story," he told us.

I balked at this information. I'd told him I didn't want him to get involved. "You shouldn't be dragged into this."

"This happened because of me. It's the least I can do." The words simmered from him like a pot on low boil. Maybe Alexander wasn't handling the uptick in my publicity as well as I thought.

"Thank you." My mother lunged at him, catching him in the same awkward hug I'd been victim to earlier, and I shot him an apologetic smile over her shoulder. She broke away from him and patted his shoulder. "It's so nice to see Clara has found someone."

I cringed internally, trying to keep the smile plastered in place.

"We'd love to take you both to dinner. Do you have plans tomorrow?"

"Mom!" I snapped. Of course, she'd manage to pry a social obligation out of him immediately.

"I'd love to," Alexander said.

"You'd what?" I asked in shock.

Mom ignored me, looping her arm through Alexander's and strolling with him toward the door. "I'll arrange everything. You don't have any food allergies? I'll call Clara with the details.

Harold will be so excited," she said, not pausing once for confirmation.

I followed them and opened the door for her, nodding enthusiastically as she continued to plan out loud. Five minutes later, I shut the door. Sagging against it, I dropped my head and took a deep breath. "I'm sorry about that."

"She seems to be a bit of a handful," Alexander said with a smile in his voice.

"I can get you out of this. Don't worry about it."

Alexander's smile faded into a frown. "I don't mind going to dinner with your parents."

"Are...you...sure?" I asked in a strangled voice.

"Stop staring at me like I need a straight jacket. Unless," he paused and regarded me with a dark expression, "you don't want me to go dinner with your parents."

"No!" I yelped, surprising him as much as myself. "Of course, I do, but I understand if you aren't comfortable."

"Isn't this what boyfriends are supposed to do?" he asked. "Meet the parents. Charm them. Earn the privilege to debauch their daughter."

Hearing him use the term boyfriend sucked the air from my lungs, and I stared at him, unable to speak.

"Is something wrong?" he asked, running his fingers through his tangled black hair as the worried, tired look he wore so often returned to his face. "Did I do something to upset you?"

I swallowed against the raw feeling in my throat and shook my head. "Nope. I just don't deserve you, X."

"You don't," he agreed, his voice growing husky. "No one deserves to put up with me."

I placed a finger over his lips, pressing close to him. "Don't say that."

"Where did you come from?" he whispered. "Who sent you to save me?"

I had no answer for him. There was only one way to comfort us both, so I crushed my lips to his. In a flash, he was in control, parting my mouth and plunging his tongue into my mouth. I lost myself, tasting him, reveling in him. My desire grew to an insatiable craving that rippled through my body and pooled between my thighs. I wrapped one leg around him and circled against him to relieve the intense pressure building inside me. Alexander's arms closed around my waist and he broke away, breathing heavy and hot against my neck.

"You have to get to work," he murmured. "Unless..."

I licked my lips at the suggestive tone in his raspy voice. "Unless?"

"You want to call in sick and let me show you what a good boyfriend I can be."

It was a tempting offer. Too tempting. "Sorry, X. I can't play hooky on my third day of work."

He let me slide off him, stepping back to give me space. But the distance did nothing to calm the desire swelling in my body.

"Tonight." It wasn't a question. It was a promise of things to come.

"Tonight," I repeated, feeling the hours of separation as acutely as the small distance between us.

"I put together the graphics we discussed yesterday," Bennett announced, stepping into my workspace.

I looked up to meet his eyes, grateful that at least he could still look me in the face after yesterday's tabloid fodder. Shuffling a few files on my desk, I found the list we'd concocted the day before and checked off the completed task. "I'll work on pulling together the statistics on availability of clean water and child mortality."

"Can I just say how grateful I am to have someone helping with this? I have to be honest, I'm still in shock that Isaac Blue chose to work with us." Bennett dropped into a chair across from me. His oxford was wrinkled and there were bags under his eyes.

"Things a little rough right now?"

"Two little girls are a lot for two parents to handle, and I'm all they have," he admitted. "I can't help thinking that I'm screwing them both up."

I leaned forward and touched his sleeve, feeling a wave of sympathy at his confession. No one who cared as much as Bennett could be screwing up. "You aren't. You just have your work cut out for you. If you ever need someone to come over and watch them, let me know."

"I wouldn't know what to do if I had a night off. I'd probably work."

I laughed at this and shook my head. "No work. That's the deal."

"So what do you think so far?" He spread his arms. "How's your first post-university gig?"

"Good." I blew a thin stream of air between my lips.

He raised an eyebrow, leveling his gaze to mine. "That was very convincing."

I hesitated, uncertain whether I should bring up all the drama in my personal life. Bennett seemed content to leave all that shit at the door, but I had to accept that my relationship with Alexander might complicate things. "Well, I haven't met anyone else in the office yet, and no one seems eager to introduce themselves."

"I think they're intimidated by you," he said honestly.

"Me?" It was the most preposterous thing I'd ever heard.

"You're kind of a resident celebrity."

I covered my face with my hands and dropped my head to my desk.

"Hey," he soothed, "it'll pass and then nobody will even remember you dated what's-his-face."

"Nice try," I croaked. "They'll still have seen his texts to me. They'll still remember I'm the girl with the eating disorder."

I'd been through this before at my high school. It was impossible to ignore the dissecting gaze of your peers as they assessed your figure and how much you ate for lunch. I'd run away from it then, but that wasn't an option anymore. I didn't want it to be.

"Then show them that you're more than all that." Bennett stood and waved me out of my chair.

We spent the next hour going from desk to desk, shaking hands, and sharing small talk with the staff of Peters & Clarkwell. There was no way I'd remember half the names that had been thrown at me, but I was grateful to meet my co-workers. I could only hope that it laid to rest some of the office rumors about me.

The remainder of the day passed in a blur of reading environmental resources and taking notes in the hopes of impressing our celebrity client. I knew little about Isaac Blue outside of film posters and movies, and a quick internet search turned up a lot of speculation on his private life. I couldn't help but feel for the guy even though no story mentioned a commitment to the environment. Popping down to Bennett's office, I stopped in the doorway.

"So did Blue's publicist say why he's so interested in starting this campaign?" I asked, adding, "I'm just curious."

Bennett leaned back in his chair, folding his arms behind his head, and gave me a grim smile. "She sold me on his deep commitment to the cause, but if I'm honest, I think we're being hired to reform his image."

That's what I figured. I might know what it was like to be tabloid fodder, but I wasn't exactly psyched to invite more drama into my day-to-day life. And Isaac Blue was clearly trouble.

"I guess we should just be happy that he wants to help," I said, edging out the door.

"I'll take what I can get!" Bennett called after me.

As I returned to my desk to wrap up my final notes, already thinking about how I'd be spending my evening—or rather who I'd be spending my evening with—a glowing redhead bounced up to me. She held out a card, and my heart skipped as I took it from her.

"Victoria?" I asked with a sheepish smile, hoping I had the right name.

"Victoria Theroux," she confirmed. "But call me Tori."

"Thanks, Tori." I wasn't sure what else to say, so I shuffled my feet.

"Was the guy who delivered it available?"

"Um, I don't know. What did he look like?" I asked, a bit taken aback by the question.

I managed to keep the shock off my face as she described Norris. "I don't know," I admitted with barely-concealed amusement, "but I can ask."

"Sorry," she said, fanning herself. "I have a total daddy complex. It's terrible, but you'll get used to it."

A laugh escaped my lips, but this only seemed to please her as she broke out in a wide grin. Maybe I was going to make more than one friend here.

"We should get lunch sometime," I said. I was eager to have more friends in London, and from my brief interactions with Alexander's friends, I didn't think I was going to find any there. Plus, the idea of having a girlfriend who wasn't obsessing over her wedding sounded fantastic.

"Awesome! I know a fantastic fish and chips place," Tori agreed with a genuinely warm smile. "Some time this week."

"It's on."

"I know where you work, so don't think you can back out."
She shot me a wink and floated back to her desk. I made a
mental note where she sat, trying to attach the face and name to
the spot.

As soon as I was back at my computer, and after a quick
check to make sure no one was watching, I tore open the envelope and read Alexander's note:

Poppet,

This isn't a love letter. The thought of a moment passing
without having my cock in you is too much to bear. I want
you to know that I've spent the day imagining my hands on
your body, my fingers rolling across your nipples. Imagining
your perfect breasts arching as I fuck you with my tongue.
While you're saving the planet, I'm replaying the whimpers
that escaped your sweet mouth the last time you came and
plotting how to hear them again.

And I will hear them tonight. Whisper my name now,
Clara, because tonight I want to hear you scream it.

X

I exhaled shakily, realizing I'd held my breath as I read, but I
knew that didn't account for the dizziness swimming in my
head. That was just his effect on me. *The X effect*, I thought
wryly.

Inhaling, I did as he commanded.

"Alexander."

CHAPTER TWENTY-ONE

CoCo was the last place my mother would have picked for dinner. She told me so herself, and that was exactly why I chose the comfortable seasonal bistro in Notting Hill. Despite boasting some of the best upscale comfort food in London, it also had private dining rooms. Private and unpretentious? Just what I needed to relax.

Notting Hill on a balmy June evening felt like another world. The hectic chaos of London didn't extend to the sleepy neighborhood that could somehow be packed with people and still feel laid-back. I pointed out shops that I wanted to stop in with him sometime as we strolled down Portobello Road, and we lingered at the few stalls open late on a Wednesday night, thumbing through old books and antiques of questionable worth. But as Alexander and I finally made our way to the restaurant, my nerves kicked in.

It wasn't that I didn't want to introduce him to my family. I loved my family, even if that wasn't always easy. And I knew that I couldn't keep him away from them for long, especially if I was going to be on the cover of a goddamn tabloid every other day. The fact was that things were complicated. My mother was over-protective and over-opinionated. My dad was a little better, but he always gave in to her. And I wouldn't put it past Lola to spend all night flirting with Alexander—or trying to, at least.

Not to mention that Alexander and I didn't have a typical relationship, and I could never be certain if he would suddenly shut me out.

"You're quiet," he said, and I realized we'd reached CoCo without saying a word.

I glanced over at him and a possessive ache burst across my chest. He'd gone out of his way to give me a night of normalcy, dressing in worn jeans and a white button-down that skimmed his lean form. His eyes were hidden behind aviators with a Yankees ball cap for extra cover. None of which camouflaged his strong jawline peppered with second-day stubble or the roguish curve of his smile. While the ensemble offered plausible deniability if he were approached, he couldn't disguise his luscious sex appeal. I knew it wasn't the kind of thing a boyfriend typically wore to meet the parents, but then again, Alexander wasn't a typical boyfriend.

"Actually, I'm tired." I wasn't exactly lying. My body hadn't adjusted to waking up early for work yet or to my newly implemented nocturnal activities.

"I feel like I should apologize for keeping you up half the night," he said, drawing me close and kissing the top of my head, "but I'm not sorry."

His arrogant smirk tugged at me until I was smiling too. "And I won't be getting any sleep tonight either."

"Hot date?" he asked.

"The hottest."

"Anyone I know?" Alexander's hand wandered to my tail-bone, his fingers drumming lightly.

"I would say you're on intimate terms." I ran my tongue over my lips and blew him a kiss.

"You need to rest." He was sincere, but I suspected his valiant selflessness wouldn't last long, until he added, "I'm sending you home alone tonight."

A vise-grip squeezed my heart, and I fought to keep my tone playful. "But I owe you sexual favors."

"And what did I do to deserve that, poppet?" he asked as the familiar, wicked glint of lust returned to his sky-blue gaze. "Tell me so I can do it again."

"You might not be saying that after dinner." I reached for the door, but Alexander caught my hand, pulling me against him.

His index finger traced down my cheekbone, over the bow of my upper lip and came to rest on my mouth. "Have a little faith. I can be quite charming when the situation requires it. I am a prince after all."

"Prince Charming, huh?" I raised my eyebrows. "I don't remember him having a dirty mouth and an insatiable sex drive."

"He kissed the wrong girl," Alexander whispered, moving closer until his lips hovered over mine. "Or maybe 'happily ever after' is only code for multiple orgasms."

"The Brothers Grimm have nothing on you." I teased, but I swallowed at the thought of Alexander and a happily ever after.

Alexander spotted the telltale slide of my throat and winked at me. "Wait until I tell you my theories about *riding* off into the sunset."

"Behave." I smacked him on the shoulder, trying—and failing—to look serious.

"I love it when you get riled up. It makes me think of spanking your pretty, little ass." His eyes hooded as he spoke, and a shiver of anticipation ran down my neck.

"Well, well, well," an amused voice interrupted our banter. "Can I get in before he mounts you on the spot?"

I looked over Alexander's shoulder, startled to find Lola watching us with an entertained grin. As usual, she was dressed to the nines in a skin-tight pair of fire red capris paired with a breezy linen tunic that showed off her toned arms. She shouldered her bag and sauntered over to us, thrusting her hand out to him.

He hesitated before he took it, glancing over at me with a questioning look.

"Alexander, this is my sister, Lola." I tilted my head toward her with a tight-lipped smile. "Lola, allow me to introduce—"

"Oh, I don't think that's necessary," she said as she held his hand. "It's lovely to meet you. Clara has told me *absolutely nothing* about you."

Alexander tipped his head politely but drew his hand back quickly. The crackling intensity that had hung between the two of us shifted to a heavy tension now that my sister had joined us. I couldn't be sure how much of our exchange she had overhead, but judging from the haughtiness on her face, it had been enough. The last thing I needed was Lola making tonight any more awkward.

I struggled for something to say to break the ice, but it was no use. The nerves that Alexander had managed to vanquish returned with paralyzing intensity. Just as the moment grew painfully uncomfortable, he stepped forward and opened the door, gesturing for us to enter.

"Ladies first." He flourished his arm across the threshold, and I bounded inside, grateful for his diplomacy.

"Ohh. A gentleman," Lola cooed, following me through the door. She eyed him as she passed, not bothering to hide her calculating look. As always, she was the cool one—self-possessed and in platform sandals that made her nearly his height. The few people waiting near the entrance watched her as she strode confidently forward to the maître d' to give our name.

"She seems like a...handful," Alexander whispered as we were guided to the second floor's private dining room.

"Mmhmm." That was the nicest possible way to describe my sister. Lola was a force to be reckoned with most days. I could only hope today wasn't one of them.

But luck hadn't really been on my side lately.

By the second round of cocktails, conversation had slowed to a halt among our small group. Mom had insisted on waiting for my father before ordering, and he was over an hour late. The dining room, which had been decorated with a staggering number of clocks, attested to the fact. I sipped my Bloody Mary, hoping that getting tipsy might pass the time, but dozens of second hands ticked at the same rate all around me. Any other evening, I would have found the eclectic, if somewhat quirky, decor charming. Tonight it only accentuated the nausea churning in my stomach.

"I don't know what could be keeping him," Mom said, apologizing again and checking her phone.

"I'm in no hurry," Alexander said serenely, but the hand stroking up my thigh told a different story. He definitely had other things on his mind.

"We should order," I said as the clocks around us struck eight. My fatigue, coupled with low blood sugar, was wearing through my already fragile patience.

"Let's give him a few more minutes," Lola suggested, sipping her cocktail. "Tell us how you two met."

"Pick up the Daily Star," I snapped, unable to contain my ill mood any longer.

Lola gave me a reproachful look, her red lips pursed over her drink. She looked exactly like my mother as she did it. "I want to hear it from the source."

I opened my mouth to tell her off again, but Alexander stopped me.

"I was stuck at another boring party, trying to hide out," he said, "and then this beautiful girl showed up and started telling me off." His hand caught mine and raised it to his lips, but I caught his cocky grin before he kissed my knuckles.

My mother's eyes widened, a small gasp escaping her lips. Sometimes I wondered where the ambitious, bohemian feminist I'd seen in pictures had disappeared to. Mom had attended Berkley. She'd fought to get a fledgling company off the ground. Now she thought a woman approaching a man was scandalous. If she thought that was shocking, I could only hope Lola would keep what she'd overhead between Alexander and me secret.

"Clara!" she said, scolding me as she had when I was a little girl.

Alexander chuckled and set his drink on the table. "No, I deserved it."

"So why did you kiss her?" Lola burst out.

"Now that is a long story," he said, his grin on glorious display now, "and seeing as it didn't make the papers, I'm going to keep it to myself. But I will tell you that I spent the rest of the day trying to find out who your sister was. She kept a low profile at Oxford."

My mother sighed at this. "She's not very social. I did my best, but sometimes nature has other plans."

"I find her company intoxicating," Alexander said in the low voice he usually reserved for whispering indecent thoughts in my ear. "I want her all to myself anyway."

Mom's eyes flashed to mine, gauging my reaction, and I tried to look nonchalant, turning my attention back to my drink. She had her concerns about my relationship with Alexander, but that wouldn't stop her from jumping to conclusions.

"Aren't you coy?" Lola murmured. She regarded him for a moment, as though he'd issued a challenge.

Alexander dismissed the comment with a shrug, waving to the waiter peeking in at the door. No doubt the poor server was beginning to question if we'd ever place our orders.

"Are you ready?" the man asked. His eyes darted around the group, but I couldn't help noticing that he skipped over Alexander as though he was intimidated.

I couldn't imagine having that effect on people. It was hard enough to be scrutinized by the public. Something I'd recently learned myself. How much worse was it to have people fear you? Alexander didn't seem fazed by that kind of attention though. He didn't even notice it as far as I could tell. Of course, that was part of what made him so formidable: how he carried his power with such candor. It wasn't an affectation or a show. It was his birthright.

"Can you bring us this evening's appetizers?" Alexander asked. "We have another guest coming, but I can't allow these ladies to wait any longer."

I thanked him quietly, grateful that he had been the one to defy my mother's dinner gag order. Alexander leaned over and kissed me. The soft brush of his lips was tender and protective—a reminder that he considered it his job to watch out for me. My eyes closed instinctively, waiting for more, and my mother cleared her throat.

"I read up a little on your company, Mrs. Bishop," Alexander said, changing the topic quickly.

"*Former* company," Mom said. "Let's not talk business."

"She gets enough of that from Dad," I explained.

"That's true," she said with a rueful smile. "At least, it used to be."

The offhand comment struck me as odd. My mother had always been supportive of Dad's start-ups and ideas, even though none had proven as successful as the dating site they'd sold during the internet boom. But now the pride that usually accompanied business inquiries was markedly absent, replaced by an indifferent tone that was laced with bitterness. I checked the clocks again, wondering where my dad was this late. Something was going on with my parents. I couldn't put my finger on what exactly, but things were off.

Lola leaned forward eagerly, more than willing to fill the awkward silence. "Tell us about growing up in a palace!"

"Don't they have books devoted to that?" Alexander asked.

"They do," she admitted, "but I hear that the reality is quite different. Although I am a sucker for happily-ever-afters."

Her eyes flickered to mine, and I sucked in a steadying breath, keeping my face blank. She had heard Alexander's and my conversation, and I was going to pay for that later. For now, I tittered with forced laughter.

"It's not as exciting as it sounds." Either he hadn't picked up on her none-too-subtle hint that she'd been eavesdropping earlier or the man knew how to bluff.

"Bollocks!" she cried. "I bet you've been all over the world and that you grew up riding horses and hunting foxes."

Alexander's mouth curved up, his eyes growing distant with memory. It was obvious that Lola had hit upon something. "I suppose I did. It's rather boring really. Dinners with foreign dignitaries. Riding lessons. Although I've never enjoyed hunting."

"I'm a member of PETA," she informed him. "I don't approve of hunting."

I scowled at this tidbit. Evidently her concern over animal welfare didn't extend to her leather shoes and handbag.

"Unfortunately, it's a tradition in our family. I'm not particularly interested in it either." He paused, and this time when his eyes glazed with memories, he laughed. "Actually, when I was eight my father told me I was going on the hunt for the first time. I was incredibly excited. I'd had riding lessons before then, but I'd never been allowed to go with the men."

It was the first time he'd spoken of his family and childhood with such lightness, and I listened with rapt attention. Alexander's past was a heavy burden on him, so to see him smile over a memory made my heart burst. I couldn't help but wonder what might be different if he hadn't endured so much tragedy and loss early in life.

"I couldn't sleep the night before," he continued, "so I crept to the stables to brush my Arabian in preparation. Anyway, I'm in there with my horse and I see this red fox locked in a cage. I couldn't believe it. The second I saw him, I remembered all the hunts I'd watched begin at my family estates, and I realized we were going to hunt *him*."

We were all silent, hanging off his every word as he added, "So I did what any eight-year-old kid would do, I hid him."

"Oh my god!" Lola exclaimed, fluttering her lashes. "Where did you put him?"

"I didn't really think it through," Alexander explained with an uncharacteristically sheepish smile, "so I took him to my bedroom."

"I bet your parents loved that," my mom said dryly.

Alexander paused, a pained look flashing over his features. It vanished nearly as quickly as it had appeared. Only one of his parents would have been present for his act of vigilance, and I could imagine his father had found it less than amusing. "My mother," he said slowly, "would have, I think, but my father did not. In fairness though, I did make one, tiny mistake when I brought him inside."

"Which was?" Lola prompted. She was swept up in the story, making her look much younger than her age. Apparently the X effect extended outside the bedroom.

"My sister let him out of the cage," Alexander confessed, spreading his hands innocently. "It took the staff two days to trap him, *but* the hunt was cancelled!"

"So you were the hero," I said.

"That's one way of looking at it." He shrugged and sat back in his seat again. "I doubt the staff thought so."

We laughed at this, and I drank in Alexander's full-bodied laughter. It was the first time he'd mentioned his sister Sarah casually, and I wondered if he'd even realized he had done so. He'd made it clear that she was off-limits, implying it would only cause him more pain if I pushed him to speak of her. But was avoiding her memory helping? It seemed a shame for him to forget the happier moments the two shared.

The arrival of my father delivered Alexander from having to entertain us further, and a glowing warmth settled over me as I watched the two shake hands and exchange introductions. But one glance at my mother's face immediately dampened the mood.

"Again, I am sorry," Dad said, taking a seat beside my mother. "Have you been waiting for me? You should have ordered!"

"I called you," she said frostily, not bothering to disguise the recrimination in her voice.

"I got caught up at the office," he explained. "We get such terrible mobile service there, but I should have found a phone and called you."

My mother didn't reply, even as her posture stiffened. My stomach flipped over at her obvious resistance to my father's apologies.

For once, it didn't seem like my mother was being delicate. It felt like she was being strong.

THE STRANGE BEHAVIOR OF MY PARENTS OCCUPIED MY thoughts as we rode back to my flat in the Rolls Royce. Dinner had gone off without incident, but her aloof attitude had lingered throughout the evening. Mom had said something offhand about Dad's work last week on our lunch date, but I'd dismissed it. Now it had reared its vicious teeth again, and I had to figure out what to do about it.

My father had been obsessed with investing in new start-ups. He had stock in dozens of companies, but nothing had fulfilled his desire to build something of his own. He'd sold *partner.com* because we needed the money, but also because he expected to build another successful company. Nearly twenty years of investments and ideas later, his only claim to fame was the still popular dating site. Mom had encouraged him, so what had changed? I wasn't imagining the rift between them.

"Clara?" Alexander said. His hand slid between my legs as if to coax me from my thoughts.

Tonight was supposed to be about us—our relationship—and I'd spent the evening analyzing what was going on with my parents. Maybe I was avoiding the obvious. Alexander and I had our own issues to deal with. It was a lot easier to worry about someone else's marriage.

"Sorry, X." Swinging my legs up, I crawled into his lap.

"Something's on your mind." He didn't ask me to share, and the message was clear: no pressure.

It was unlikely he could help me figure out what was going on with my parents, but I appreciated that he was here. "I was thinking about my parents. They barely spoke to one another."

"And that's not usually the case?"

I shook my head. I couldn't quite articulate what was bugging me. "My mom tends to be a little high maintenance. She was definitely giving my dad the cold shoulder."

I shrugged it off and wrapped my arms around Alexander's neck. I'd been so preoccupied with my parents that I'd almost forgotten that I had him all alone. Shifting, I straddled him, brushing my body across his in invitation. The contact stirred my blood, sending it to pool in my core.

Alexander traced the line of my décolletage with his index finger, and my breasts swelled under his touch. My nipples tightened to beads, anticipating his attention, and I rocked against him as desire engulfed my senses. He caught the nape of my neck and pulled me forward, his mouth slanting over mine as he captured my lips. His breath was hot, laced with a lingering tinge of liquor, and I licked across his teeth, savoring the taste of him.

"I owe you sexual favors," I purred, my hands going to his belt buckle to free his thick erection.

Alexander groaned, his hands sliding to cup my jaw as he held my lips to his in a languid kiss that left me breathless when he broke away.

"Come to the country with me this weekend," he breathed.

Time alone with him, outside London and its shameless paparazzi? "Do you even have to ask?"

"I'm not asking," he said, a smile playing at his lips. "I already told them you would be there."

I froze. "Them?"

"My family."

"You want me to spend a weekend in the country with your family?" I asked.

"There will be some friends there as well. Edward has invited a group."

If that was meant to reassure me, it failed miserably. "X—" I began.

"You said anything," he reminded me. "I said that I wasn't asking. I expect you to be there with me."

"Don't you want to spend some private time with them?" That was a reach, and I knew it.

Alexander cocked an eyebrow, aware that I was getting desperate for excuses. "The only person I want private time with is you. Three days apart is too long. I need to know you're being taken care of."

"I can take care of myself," I reminded him.

"You can get dressed." His hands dropped to my hips and skimmed lightly down them. "You can eat and drink and sleep, but you won't have everything you need." Alexander rolled his hips against my groin. My sex clenched as his erection ground into me.

"You raise a good point," I panted, running my tongue over my lips.

"Do I?" he asked, his words raspy as he continued to circle under me.

"Mmhmm," I moaned, losing myself to the lurid motion of his hips. "You owe me."

"I thought you owed me sexual favors," he said, a devilish smile coming over his face.

"I promised that before I found out I'd be dealing with your family for a whole weekend. Let's call it a draw, X, or you'll be repaying me for a long time." But as desire pooled between my legs, thrumming through my clit, I knew it was a lost cause.

"Oh, poppet." His mouth cruised leisurely across my collarbone as his hands strayed under my skirt. "I am more than happy to be in your debt."

He hooked his thumbs over the band of my thong and tore it cleanly from my trembling sex.

"You know there are finite resources in the world. You might spare a few pairs of panties."

Alexander flipped me onto the seat, moving between my spread thighs. "I'd love to hear more about your panties," he said with a smirk, "*later.*"

CHAPTER TWENTY-TWO

The country house was actually a sprawling forty-room estate nestled over one hundred acres of private land. I'd been to mansions before, but Norfolk Hall surpassed them. It belonged to an entirely different time and place. Spires stretched to the sky, and the facade had been painstakingly refurbished to approximate the sixteenth century original brick. There was a stable and tennis courts on the grounds. Inside, marble floors, priceless art and polished mahogany bannisters perfected the imposing manner. I felt like I'd been invited to stay in a museum. It was too much to absorb at once, and that wasn't just due to the estate.

I'd dreaded the idea of dealing with his father over the weekend. The King hadn't bothered to hide his feelings regarding our relationship. When we arrived, I discovered it was so much worse than an awkward family gathering. Alexander's family was here, along with over a dozen of their *friends*. I'd met a few of them at the ball, and I hadn't been eager to see them again.

Particularly Pepper, who watched with distaste as Edward

made the introductions to a number of older family members present for tomorrow's hunt.

This weekend was turning out to be exactly what I'd hoped to avoid. Stupidly, I'd believed I might get a chance to speak with Alexander's father in private. I thought maybe if he got to know me, he might reverse his opinion of my relationship with his son. But I couldn't see how that was going to happen with this many people around.

We'd arrived so late that dinner had been served already, and by the time I got to my room, my stomach was grumbling. Grabbing a protein bar from my bag, I took a look around. I had to admit, albeit grudgingly, that my room was spectacular. Complete with a four-poster bed and a sweeping vista of the English countryside, the only thing it was missing was Alexander, who had been placed in his own bedroom across the estate.

A printed schedule of activities rested on my pillow, and I rolled my eyes as I realized someone had planned every moment of my stay here. Right now I was supposed to be in the Billiard Room for cocktails. Tomorrow I had brunch with the Queen Mother.

"But when will I find time to kill myself?" I asked the empty room.

Play the game, I ordered myself.

Ten minutes later, I happened upon Alexander in the hall. He'd changed into a three-piece suit as jet black as his hair. The result seethed with heart-stopping sexiness. I wanted to clench my fingers in that silky hair and feel him through those perfectly tailored slacks.

"Poppet?" It was more than a question, it was an invitation. A smooth, seductive smile carved across his face as if he had read my mind.

I sighed with longing and shook my head. It wasn't fair that he had this effect on me.

Alexander pressed his index finger to my lips. "Save those for me."

"I'm not allowed to sigh?"

"Oh, I insist that you sigh," he whispered, leaning in to nuzzle my neck, "and whimper and moan when I'm *fucking* you. I demand it. I'm a selfish man and those noises belong to me."

"I'd be happy to comply," I purred, running my hand down his chest, catching my fingers on the button of his jacket.

He drew away and adjusted his cuffs. "Don't tempt me or we'll never make it to our scheduled appearance."

"So I'm not the only one with a printed itinerary?"

"Unfortunately not." He crooked his arm. "To the Billiard Room?"

"Yes. I was lost," I admitted as he offered me his arm.

"I would have found you," he promised, but the accompanying smile was tight-lipped. He had been on edge when we left London, and I watched as the tension settled back over him.

The Billiard Room was steeped in the stifling tradition of the past—oak-paneled walls decorated with mounted stag heads and stuffed pheasants. Jonathan occupied the bar, his sleeves rolled up and his attention focused on plying his companions with drinks. The women he was tending to swiveled to watch me. I recognized the redhead from the ball: Amelia. But the other girl was unfamiliar. Both their faces remained impassive, regarding me with cool indifference.

I'd dressed down for the evening in a sleeveless, navy-blue maxi dress and, upon entering, immediately wished I hadn't. Alexander stepped through the door without hesitation, grabbing my hand as he passed, and led me into the dimly lit room.

"An hour," Alexander promised me. "Do you want a drink?"

I shook my head. The last thing I needed was to lose my head around this group of *friends*. My only solace was the absence of Alexander's father and grandmother. I hadn't been formally introduced to everyone in the room yet, but as far as I knew, only Pepper truly had it out for me.

A man dressed in livery appeared at the door, his gaze sweeping across the group before landing on Alexander. He crossed to him, speaking in a low voice that was lost in the clamor of conversations around us.

Alexander gripped my arm. "I need to attend to something. Edward will look after you."

He was gone before I could protest. I stared dumbly around the room, noticing the wicked glances the girls at the bar were sharing at Alexander's sudden departure.

"Come over here," Amelia called, waving me over. The invitation was coated in sugar, much too friendly to be genuine, but I couldn't spend the whole weekend hiding from them.

Jonathan slid an empty tumbler onto the bar. Between the careless wave of his blond hair and his blue pinstriped vest, he looked as if he'd stepped out of an old movie. And when he spoke, his words dripped with the golden boy charisma that ensured him a constant supply of new bedfellows. "What's your poison?"

My thoughts flashed to Alexander. He'd asked me the same question at Brimstone, and my answer was still the same.

"Oh wow, you've got it bad," Amelia said, sneering at my dreamy expression. "Give her a gin and tonic. Clara, allow me to introduce my sister Priscilla."

Priscilla flashed me a smile with too much teeth. She had the same red hair as Amelia, but her fair skin was covered in a veil of freckles. "I've heard so much about you."

She didn't bother to hide the implication in her voice, but I forced a grim smile. "Don't believe everything you read."

"Oh, I don't bother with tabloids," she said, "but Pepper has been talking about you for weeks. Alexander tells her absolutely everything."

"I doubt that," I said serenely. She was trying to bait me, but I wasn't about to bite.

Priscilla shrugged her thin shoulders and sipped her drink. "Oh, Jonathan, use diet tonic. Clara watches her weight."

I wasn't certain if there was a punishment for slapping a princess, but I felt like I'd be doing a public service. Someone caught my wrist before I'd even realized I'd raised my hand to actually do it.

"I'll take that," David said, releasing my hand and reaching for my drink. Without a word, he maneuvered me away from the vipers' nest. "That was a close one."

He handed me my cocktail, and I took a deep swig of it, too angry to speak. When I was finally calm enough to regain my faculties, I turned to him. "How did you know I was going to hit her?"

David cracked a grin. It spread across his elegant, chocolate skin up to his coal-black eyes. It was a genuine smile, and I relaxed a little more. "I spend most of my time trying not to hit them myself. I guess I've developed radar."

"So tell me, David, are you some type of masochist?" I asked, laughing when his eyes widened at my bold question. "Why else would you choose to spend time with these people? They're like the Royal Brat Pack."

"I have my reasons," he said with a shrug, not offering to elaborate on what they were. "And they need me to up their cool factor. Somewhere along the line, they got the idea that hanging out with a black guy meant they weren't just entitled wankers."

"Is that right?" I snorted as I swirled my straw in the clear liquid.

"It's what they believe."

"So why are you really here?" I asked. Maybe David had a nihilist streak, but I couldn't see anyone putting themselves through the torment of spending time with these people without a damn good reason. And I was dying to know what it was.

"Hasn't he told you?" Pepper slithered over and draped herself over the back of my chair. Her golden curls bounced free, brushing over my neck. "Don't be shy, David. Maybe Clara can give you tips on finally nailing down a prince."

I looked at David quizzically, but his eyes were trained on the venomous blonde. "Don't try to be witty. It clashes with your stupidity, Pepper."

"At least I'm not a—"

David stood abruptly, knocking my drink onto my lap. "My apologies. Excuse me."

I swiped at the ice-cold liquor, brushing it from my skirt before it could soak completely through.

"Shame about your dress," Pepper said. "At least it was hideous."

I glared at her but clamped my mouth shut. It might be smart to keep my enemies close, but it was even better to keep my mouth shut around them. I had no doubt every word I uttered to her would be distorted and used against me. Edward watched from across the room. Despite the concern written on his face, he didn't put down his billiard cue.

This evening was turning into a nightmare, and if I was going to survive the entire weekend, I needed to pace myself on the drama. Exiting the room quickly, I realized I had no clue how to find my room again. I would have to track down Alexander and pull him away from his urgent business.

My footsteps echoed in the empty hallway. Not even a sliver of light seeped from the closed doors that lined the corridor. Passing each, I listened for Alexander, pausing when I finally heard low, angry voices. I crept toward them, concealing myself in the shadows. It wasn't that I wanted to eavesdrop, but I suspected that my intrusion wouldn't be welcomed.

It took my eyes a moment to adjust to the room's darkness, and when they finally did, I realized that it wasn't Alexander and his father. It was Edward and David. Not wanting to interrupt their argument, I turned to leave just as Edward lunged forward, grabbing David's face and crushing his mouth to his own. My confusion froze me to the spot even as comprehension dawned on me.

I pressed myself to the doorway to stay out of view. How had I not seen it? My mind replayed David and Pepper's nasty exchange, and Edward's reaction to his departure. I'd wondered why David had stayed around when he clearly loathed most of his companions. Now I knew: he was as stuck as I was.

David pulled away from Edward. "Enough! I'm tired of this game."

"This isn't a game," Edward said, taking a step toward him.

David backed away, shaking his head. "You're flirting with those sniveling bitches and running around pretending to be a playboy. You may not think you're playing a game, Edward, but you are—and from now on, you're playing alone."

"David, wait!" Edward called, catching up to him and grabbing his arm.

"Take your hands off me," David warned.

"I'm sorry that it has to be like this." Edward released his arm. "I wish it were different. I love you."

David ran a hand over his closely cropped hair. "That won't work this time. It's not enough anymore. Wishing gets you nowhere. If you want things to be different, then change them."

"You know what I'm dealing with. If Alexander—"

"Waiting around for your brother to solve your problems isn't changing things," David said harshly. "At least, it isn't changing things with me."

Edward brushed a finger down David's cheek and shook his head sadly. "Tell me what to say."

A rustling noise behind me drew my attention away, and I whirled around in time to catch Jonathan and Priscilla approaching. I stepped into the doorway, blocking them from entering the room. David and Edward would see me, but something told me that their relationship wasn't common knowledge. I knew what it was like to be under the scrutiny of the Royal Brat Pack. Whatever was happening with them, they deserved to work through it privately.

Priscilla swayed on her feet, clutching on to Jonathan as she giggled. The two stopped as soon as they saw me.

"Excuse us," Priscilla hissed. She attempted to push past me but lost her balance. Jonathan caught her waist and held her upright.

"What's going on, Clara?" Jonathan waited for me to explain why I wouldn't let them past. His gaze darted from me to the door, his pupils as black as a snake's in the dark.

I had to think of something quickly, but my mind stuttered to a halt. "Do you...have you...seen Alexander?"

"She's like a lost puppy," Priscilla said with a snigger.

"Hush, Pris," Jonathan admonished her. He smiled apologetically, but his eyes remained cold. "I'm sorry to say we haven't."

I'd delayed them long enough to buy Edward time, and I could only hope he had used it, because I wasn't sticking around to deal with the drunken tart. Breezing past them, I offered a simple goodnight. Behind me I heard Pris whisper, "Off to bottom Alexander."

A smug grin carved across my lips. I knew I wasn't imagining the edge of jealousy in her tone.

But as soon as I was free of them, I was left to ponder what I'd stumbled upon. Did Alexander know? Did anyone? I understood why David was angry, but I think I knew why Edward had kept their relationship a secret. The gossip. The tabloids. The assumptions. I was all too familiar with what it was like to be linked to a Prince of England. Still, Alexander had claimed me as his, not hiding our relationship. How would I feel if I was still his dirty secret?

My stomach flipped at the thought, and I realized I had my answer. As difficult as things sometimes were, I wouldn't have been able to cope with it.

It was an impossible situation: being torn between love and reality.

I FINALLY FOUND ALEXANDER IN THE LIBRARY WITH HIS father. Hesitating at the door, I tried to decide if it was better to knock or wait for them to finish. Alexander had disappeared to speak with him over an hour ago, and from the sound of their discussion, he wouldn't be finished any time soon. Alexander's grandmother Mary watched the exchange stoically, hands folded serenely in her lap. I had no doubt that she was analyzing each of Alexander's statements for later dissection.

"You have responsibilities," Albert lectured him. "Clara is very pretty, but you can't make life decisions based on what your dick wants."

Alexander folded his arms over his chest. "This is the twenty-first century. Clara is well-bred—"

"She's American." Mary said the word *American* as though it tasted rancid on her tongue.

Alexander glared at her, his lips thinned, and she shrank back under his primal stare.

Albert continued, ignoring the exchange between his mother and son. "You need to be prepared to assume my role—"

"Are you planning to retire?" Alexander asked dryly.

"I do not approve of your flippancy," Mary chided. Her nose tipped up as she spoke.

Albert rubbed his temples, his voice growing somber. "There are situations that you need to be briefed on, and yet you're busy screwing that—"

"Choose your words very carefully," Alexander warned him, rising from his seat with clenched fists. "She is precious to me."

I'd spent enough time lurking in the shadows tonight, and I was tired of it. I rapped once on the door and stepped inside.

"I'm going to bed," I told Alexander, ignoring his family. I thought of David as I spoke. I was tired of the games too, but I wasn't ready to walk away.

"I'm coming with you." Alexander crossed the room and took my hand. The light contact crackled with suppressed electricity. We'd both spent the evening defending ourselves against attack, and I knew that the bond we shared had seen us through it. I longed for his hands on my body, for the reassurance of his demanding, but attentive, touch. Judging from the protective way he stood between me and his father, he felt the same need.

"We are not finished speaking," Albert said.

"This conversation is over," Alexander said in a firm voice. "I'm not debating this with you any longer. I've made my decision."

Albert's eyes slid over me as if estimating how challenging of a problem I was to him. A chill cascaded down my neck, turning my blood to ice under his unflinching stare. But in the end, he only said, "Goodnight."

CHAPTER TWENTY-THREE

My fingers twisted together as I hesitated in the hall. Alexander had headed to his room to change this morning, and I was surprised by how nervous I was about brunch without him. The hair on the back of my neck stood up, awareness sliding over my body, and I turned to find Alexander watching me from a doorway.

"Have you decided to run?" he asked.

I looked at him, confusion swirling through me. After last night I'd considered it, but Alexander had persuaded me to stay with methods that were likely illegal in several countries. No, I had decided to weather this weekend. It would be over soon, but I knew that there were going to be issues to deal with when we got back to London. For now though, I crossed my arms over my chest and shook my head.

"This—" he ran his fingers down my silk, garden skirt "—needs to come off later."

I'd chosen a simple white blouse and skirt because they looked appropriate for brunch, but I'd deliberately worn the pale green skirt for the way it billowed as I walked. That, combined with its shortness, was sure to catch Alexander's attention.

"Cancel the hunt and you can take it off now," I promised in a husky voice.

"I'll only be gone for two or three hours," he said, running a hand down my bare arm reassuringly.

"That's long enough for them to eat me alive," I pointed out. I tugged at the hem of my skirt.

"I'm told they're serving sandwiches," he said, "but I'll remind them that they have to answer to me if anyone upsets you."

I nodded, not reminding him that I could take care of myself. He probably just wouldn't like the consequences.

"You've got that wicked gleam in your eyes, Clara," Alexander said softly. "What are you thinking?"

"Nothing." I stroked a hand down his chest, leaning in for a kiss. But he pulled back.

"Something tells me that you're going to be fine." He sighed and took my hand, pulling me toward the dining room. "Try not to be charged with treason."

I wasn't making any promises.

The men going on the hunt had gathered, and as soon as they saw Alexander, the teasing began. Jonathan clamped a hand on his friend's shoulder and shook his head. "You're going to let that fox get away, Alexander." Jonathan's gaze swiveled to me and he grinned. "Although it doesn't look like you're hurting for tail."

I shot him a thin-lipped smile. He might not remember what he did to Belle, but I did, and he wasn't going to charm me into forgetting, especially not with locker-room humor.

Pepper entered the dining room. Her hair was up in a demure bun, and while her electric yellow dress hugged her willowy figure, it still fell just below her knees. Her gaze slid up and down me. She didn't bother to hide her smug dismissal of me as the Queen Mother appeared behind her in a loosely fitted, linen pantsuit. Her appearance distracted Pepper, who began to immediately kiss ass.

I stifled a gag over the obvious and false flattery. Did Pepper really think she could get to Alexander through his grandmother? That just proved that she didn't know him at all.

Alexander caught me around the waist, pressing a kiss behind my ear that sent a ripple of excitement tingling through me. "I will see you soon, poppet."

And then he was gone. Pushing my shoulders back and my chin up, I took a seat at the table. Edward appeared in the doorway, and his grandmother balked at him. "Aren't you joining the men?"

"Hunting doesn't appeal to me," he said, stepping into the dining room. "I was on my way down for coffee."

I knew I liked him.

"Join us," she said, patting the table next to her. "We'll have tea."

"I would love to, but unfortunately I need coffee. I'll see you for dinner though." He pecked her dutifully on the cheek and ducked back out before he could be entreated again.

Mary turned toward me, a tight smile on her face. "I'm afraid that this brunch might not suit your tastes."

"I'm not picky." I dropped my napkin, smoothing it over my lap.

"We don't eat a lot of American food," she said with an edge of apology, although there was an edge of something cutting under it. "I wasn't certain what they served for brunch."

I bit back the retort that tried to tumble from my lips. "English breakfast will be fine."

She waved that off. "Too many sausages. I've ordered something much lighter. I hope you don't mind the absence of meat."

"I'm sure Clara will have plenty of meat later," Pepper said in a sweet voice as I choked on the sip of water I'd just taken.

I cocked an eyebrow at her. Who was being immature now?

Thankfully, the staff appeared before the claws came out, placing platters of finger sandwiches and egg tarts before us. Everything smelled wonderful—buttery and rich—and my mouth watered impatiently. As Belle had drilled me, I waited for my host to choose her food first. I didn't feel the same etiquette applied to Pepper Spray.

"Don't wait for me," Mary admonished. "You girls look like you're wasting away."

I bit my lip to keep any hateful words from spilling out.

"You know that I have to watch my figure, Mary," Pepper said. "But you're right to be concerned over dear Clara. We must be certain she's eating."

My eyes narrowed. "That's really none of your business."

"They printed it in the Daily Star. It's everyone's business." It was Mary who spoke, her dark gaze regarding me like a hawk. "If you're going to keep company with my grandson, I'd advise you to remember that you have no secrets, young lady. Every mistake you have ever made is news. Just as every decision you make from this moment on will be." A grim smile curved onto her lips, as if to say *welcome to the family*.

"You'd do well to share that bit with your friends as well," Pepper added, but her haughty smile suggested that I was too late for that.

Who had she been talking to? I pushed aside my curiosity, realizing that it didn't matter. Right now my survival depended on getting through this brunch.

They wanted me to retreat. They expected me to as they circled around me, squawking and flapping their wings, which meant it was the last thing I would do. "I'll be sure to pass along your advice."

"Be careful," Mary continued, smothering a scone with Devonshire cream. "You never really know who your friends are."

I sipped my tea deliberately, peering at them over the cup's rim. "I imagine that *you* don't."

AFTER A *DELIGHTFUL* BRUNCH, I RETIRED TO MY ROOM under the pretense of reading, but I couldn't concentrate. The morning meal of double entendre and backhanded compliments had exhausted me, and I wished once more that I were back at my flat, having a low-key weekend with Alexander. But I recovered when there was a knock at the door and bounded toward it.

I forced a smile when I opened it and discovered Norris. "Good afternoon."

"They're on their way back, Miss. Alexander sent me ahead to ask you to welcome them."

I didn't need further persuasion. Tugging on my boots, I followed him outside as the hunting party arrived. Alexander steered his horse toward me, a riding crop clutched in his hand.

I raised my eyebrow, nodding at the instrument.

"Father insisted. Of course, if you know what you're doing, you don't need one," he said with a shrug. He lorded over me, looking regal on the powerful Arabian.

"I could have used one this morning," I admitted and his lips twitched.

"I suppose it would have its uses," he said in the slow, sexy voice I loved. Alexander held out a hand, and I looked up at him in surprise. "Come."

I'd waited all day to hear him say that, and I couldn't keep myself from raising my eyebrow suggestively. His mouth curved into a mischievous smile. After spending the day saying all the wrong things and constantly apologizing for myself, the sight of his sinfully beautiful face made my mouth water.

"I'm wearing a skirt," I said as the breeze caught its hem, whipping it slightly too high so that my bare thighs were revealed.

As ready as I was to run away with him, I wasn't exactly prepared for riding a horse, and everyone was bound to talk about us while we were absent from the house.

"Believe me, I noticed." Alexander swung a leg over the saddle and jumped down, pulling off his helmet to reveal his sexy mess of jet black hair. He looked magnificent in his riding breeches that hugged his muscular calves and did nothing to hide his tight ass. "I need to get you away from these bloody people. I want you all to myself."

"Where are you taking me?" I asked, dropping my hand in his. Skirt or not, I would go anywhere he led me.

His voice lowered, since more than a few curious eyes were now watching us. "You're asking the wrong question."

"I am?" I blinked my eyes at him in mock innocence.

A growl rumbled in his throat as he took in my act, and I could see the wheels turning behind his crystal-blue eyes. "You should be asking *what I'm going to do to you.*"

My mouth went dry, and I waited for him to continue, too caught up in the heavy sexual tension crackling between us to find my voice. I craved the reassurance of his touch.

"Ever heard of the term *saddle sore?*" he asked with a wicked grin that made my pulse rev in expectation. "If I don't ride off with you right now in front of all these people, tonight they're going to wonder why you're walking so strangely."

Oh my...*yes, please.* "So the ride is an alibi?"

"It's all part of what I plan to do to you." His arms wrapped around my waist, and he drew me roughly to him. I stumbled into his arms, my head swimming with the heady cocktail his presence always created. When he brushed his lips over mine in what was for him a fairly demure show of affection, all the reasons that this was a horrible idea vanished. A moment later, he hoisted me onto the saddle. It was large enough to allow me to ride sidesaddle, but then I remembered what he said about keeping up appearances, and I shifted my leg so that I was sitting normally, my feet dangling above the stirrups. I pushed my skirt safely under my rear so as not to show off my bum to half the Royal Family but also to avoid chafing against the leather. He handed me his riding crop but passed off the rifle he'd carried during the hunt to a nearby gamekeeper. Alexander mounted the horse, taking the reins with one hand as the other held me firmly against him. I settled into the embrace, relishing his warmth and the hardness of his body against me, although even as I relaxed, a steady thrumming built inside me at his nearness.

"Alexander!" Albert strode toward us, his mouth set in a grim line. He'd spent the day riding a horse, but not a single strand of his slicked hair was out of place. Despite his composed appearance, his son clearly had him ruffled. "We have guests."

"*Clara* is my guest," Alexander said in a disinterested tone. "I'm taking her to see the grounds. We'll be back for dinner."

Albert's cold gaze flickered over me, no doubt noting my inappropriate riding attire. Alexander might be able to fool the other guests as to his intentions, but it was obvious his father saw through to his son's true motives. "I expect you to be properly dressed at the table."

He turned on his heel and left without another word, but behind me, Alexander tensed after the minor altercation. A pattern was beginning to develop. I only wished I could see all the pieces at play, so I might understand both of them a little bit more. That would take time, but with Albert actively sabotaging me, how long did I have?

"C'mon," he said, and without asking for the riding crop back, we began to move at a steady clip. I clutched the crop in my hands as we moved into a canter, and my body rocked against his, the saddle bruising into my thighs as we rode faster across the estate. When we were out of sight of the main house, Alexander slowed the horse until we came to a halt in a stretch of flat land. Miles of unbroken countryside lay before us. Grassy hills, hay bales and weathered trees stretched across the gray, spring sky. The air was fresh, warm but pure, and I breathed in deeply, filling my lungs. But I was too dialed up to calm down.

"Beautiful," I murmured as Alexander's arms encircled me.

"Yes," he said in a husky voice. I could hear the desire in it and my core clenched, remembering his earlier words.

"You have me all alone," I reminded him. "What are you going to do to me?"

Alexander chuckled at this as his lips skimmed down the back of my neck. "Not yet, poppet."

I was already primed for him, my lust a combination of arousal and distress. Alexander's arms tightened around me as if he sensed my anxiety. Being with him allowed me to forget that I didn't fit into his world.

"You're unhappy," he guessed.

I hesitated before finally nodding. "I don't belong here."

"Oh poppet." Alexander let out a long sigh. "Neither do I."

The resignation of his confession twisted my heart. He had no choice. The lottery of birth had placed him into this family, and even I couldn't see a means of escape.

"But," he continued, "you are wrong about one thing. You do belong *here* with *me*."

I swiveled around recklessly, mashing my lips to his, but despite the urgency rushing through me, he slowed the kiss until I breathed only because he did.

"So are you going to take me for a roll in the hay?" I arched an eyebrow in invitation.

"I'm planning much more depraved things. And I'll start by..." His words trailed away as his hands slid under my skirt. My clit pulsed with his proximity, recalling the last time he'd employed his very talented fingers. But he didn't probe in between my legs, instead he stopped on the band of my lacy underwear. "You are such a tease in this little skirt. I've had blue balls all morning thinking about your barely covered thighs. Do you know what it's like to spend the whole day hiding an erection from half the monarchy?"

"I can't say that I do," I baited him. My breath hitched at the thought of his hard cock in those pants. I wiggled my butt back teasingly, bumping against his groin and discovered he wasn't lying.

"Exactly," he growled against my ear. His hands twitched violently and then ripped through the delicate lace of my panties. I moaned as he removed them, the shredded fabric scratching across my slick sex. He made no move to touch me further, even as he shoved the remains into his jacket pocket. Lifting my skirt so that the wind whispered across my bare ass, he whistled appreciatively.

"This gives a whole new meaning to bareback," he said, and I could hear the smug smile in his voice.

It did indeed. I was exposed—deliciously so. The leather was smooth against my soft flesh and I felt wanton—ready for him to take me. But he didn't. Instead he urged the horse on. The first few steps were slow, and the leather seat slapped gently against my clit, leaving the saddle wet with my desire. The sensation startled me, vibrating through my wound-up nerves and setting me on the very edge. But even as Alexander increased our pace to a full gallop, his hand hot against my belly, I didn't fall over it. My need built in me, overwhelming my senses until I was humming with want. I squirmed in his arms in an attempt to encourage his hand to slip further down, but he held me steady, completely in control of my body *and* its release.

My only solace was the stiff bulge that pressed against my backside. He was as aroused as I was, and soon—when he stopped his sweet torture—he would be inside me. My sex swelled at the thought, and tiny ripples of anticipation trembled through me. All I needed was his touch to push me over.

We rode for what felt like an eternity, and I fought the urge to touch myself to end the torment. I knew he would never allow it, but mostly I wanted Alexander to undo me. Simple masturbation no longer held any appeal to me—not while this sinfully sexy man was pressed against me. I needed his cock, his fingers, his tongue. My pleasure belonged to him. When I could take no more, I shifted in the saddle and laid my head back, imploring him to stop. He slowed enough that he could lift his hand to my face to softly stroke my cheek. "Yes, poppet?"

"*Please.*" No longer racing along at a furious clip, my desire filtered through my blood, winding every nerve in my body into taut bands.

"Please what?" His mouth twisted in pleasure, betraying that he already knew.

"Please, stop. I...need...you." The words were choked, still so foreign to the girl who never asked for what she wanted. Alexander had told me once that I would beg for him, and he was right. I'd been begging him since the first time he touched me.

His hand dropped to my neck, wrapping around it with a light but firm grip.

"Say it, Clara," he commanded.

"I want you to fuck me," I said in a voice barely over a whisper. I felt any moment I might burst into flames if he didn't touch me, but it was this tension controlling my body that made it difficult to even speak. I could think only of his lips on mine. His flesh against mine.

Alexander paused. "Want or need?"

I swallowed against the raw desire building in my throat and continued my plea. "I need your cock. I need you to fuck me until I can't take any more. *Please.*"

He didn't speak as he dismounted the horse, but when I turned to follow suit, he stopped me, pushing apart my legs until I was spread before him. His eyes grew heavy as he trailed his fingers down the soft skin of my thighs, but his hands traveled no further. I was merely on display to him, and he studied me as a connoisseur of art might regard a painting or a sculpture, worshipping the work before his eyes.

I forced myself to breathe deeply, afraid I might come from the intensity of his gaze alone, locked as I was under it until he snapped out of the reverie and helped me down. As soon as my boots hit the grass, he was on me. Lips crushed together as our hands tangled in hair and clothes. I tugged off his jacket, throwing it to the ground before his hands caught my wrist and he shook his head. He drew my arms up and pinned them together with one hand. I didn't fight against the raw, predatory instinct that rolled off him any longer. Instead, I submitted to it, nearly overwhelmed by my desire for him. With his other hand, he shoved down my skirt until it pooled around my ankles. Then he yanked open my blouse, a few buttons popping off in the process. Later, when I had to go back to the house wearing no panties and missing buttons—that would be a pain in the ass. Right now, it set my body to smolder as he tugged my breasts free from my bra.

His head moved down, capturing my breast and sucking my nipple deep into his mouth. I gasped as he flicked it, teasing me with his tongue, and I felt my other nipple pebble in anticipation. He shifted his attention to its furl, and I wished there were more of him—that I could feel the heat of his breath on every bit of my body. Alexander continued his playful assault on my breasts until they were swollen and heavy and my knees grew weak, threatening to betray me. But he caught me and *tsk*ed in my ear. "Not yet, poppet."

I moaned as his words whispered across my neck. He could make me come with his voice alone, but he wouldn't. Alexander was generous with his pleasure, but it was always on his terms. Today he had made it clear he was going to push me to the height of ecstasy, push me until I broke—and I wanted nothing more.

I needed it like I needed him.

He released my arms, and they fell to my sides, my muscles burning and weak. "Take off your bra."

I did as I was told, my eyes fixed on his beautiful face. I imagined running my tongue along his chiseled jaw as I opened the buttons that had escaped his massacre. As I shrugged off the bra, I focused on the scar over his left eyebrow, remembering how he'd sighed as I touched it. I was still learning how significant that moment had been between us. Those brutal scars that he once thought marred his perfect body only made it more beautiful. They reminded me that this god before me was a man.

Releasing the last remnant of my day's ensemble to the ground, I stood before him stripped down to my boots. The June air was warm on my body, even under the shade of a nearby tree.

"I have half a mind to set you back on that horse and watch your tits and ass bounce across the countryside."

My eyebrows shot up. I couldn't hide my exasperation as the thought. "I have something else I'd rather ride."

A smirk carved across his face. He knew he'd gotten to me,

which meant he also knew he could drive me to the very brink
of sanity with his torturous teasing.

"You get off on this, don't you?" I asked. "Nearly driving me
half-crazy until you fuck me?"

A darkness flickered in his eyes as he considered my question. "I do, poppet, which is why I should take you over my knee
and smack that sass right out of you."

I couldn't contain the tremor of pleasure that shuddered
through me at the thought of being bent over his knee. I would
never have allowed any other man to do something like spank
me. I probably wouldn't have allowed them to even mention it,
but in the short time I had known Alexander, his dominance
had consumed me, taking me to the brink of too much and never
past it. And now I was desperate to have his hands on me in any
way I could.

"In fact..." His voice trailed away as his eyes landed on
something behind me. I didn't dare to turn, uncertain if I
wanted to know what had caught his attention so fully.
Alexander took my hand and brushed a kiss across the top. "I
need to know that you trust me."

"I thought I had proven that already," I said. After what
we'd experienced together, I thought it was obvious. "I've never
been with anyone like I've been with you."

"I assumed that much." The cocky tone was back in his
voice. "That doesn't mean you trust me."

"Do you trust me?" I asked as boldly as I could while
standing stark naked in the middle of the countryside.

Alexander's eyes grew distant, and I wished I could take it
back, but instead of growing cold and hard as they had when I'd
stepped over the unstated boundary that separated us before,
this time they flashed, filling with fire as he nodded his head. "I
think you're the only person I've ever trusted."

I forgot to breathe as the bare, vulnerable side of Alexander flashed before my eyes. It was gone in an instant, replaced by the rakish, handsome man he usually showed the world, but I'd seen through his disguise once more. He'd asked me the question first and it lingered still, dancing in the smoldering flames of his irises.

"Yes," I whispered, knowing he needed to hear me say it. "I trust you."

His answering smile wasn't the arrogant grin that usually melted my panties, it was quiet and serious. The victory in it was present, but it was not full of self-satisfaction. He did trust me, and I'd given him that which he craved the most: control. I'd given my body, my mind, and—I realized with a pang—my *heart*.

"Do you remember your safe word?"

I nodded, feeling slightly embarrassed that there was a need for one, but Alexander had pushed my body further and further since I'd submitted to his darker desires. I'd only been able to do it because I saw his compulsion to protect me. "Brimstone."

"Turn around and face the tree," he commanded.

I did as I was told, and he rewarded me with the contact I so desperately craved. His hands swept up my sides, encouraging my arms to rise over my head, allowing him access to me. I braced myself against the tree as he pressed against me. His riding clothes scratched gently across my bare skin, making me ache for the touch of his skin against mine. For now, I relished the roughness of his probing fingers as they caressed my abdomen and trailed around to my backside, leaving paths of fire in their wake. Then he pulled away abruptly.

"Close your eyes."

I squeezed them shut and waited for him to return for what felt like an eternity. I was barely conscious of the rough bark digging into the flesh of my wrists or the slight soreness from my stretching limbs. When he finally came back, I felt his presence even though he didn't touch me.

"Spread your legs," he ordered me, and I obliged, my body viscerally recalling the times he'd commanded me to do so before. "That is a fucking beautiful sight."

His hand clamped over my sex and a low growl rumbled through him. He tempted me with his contact but offered no reprieve from my desires, even as I felt his own jabbing against my bare ass.

"Your cunt is so wet for me," he rasped. "Feel how wet you are."

I dropped a trembling arm between my legs, and he caught my hand, pushing it against my throbbing, swollen sex. It was slick, heavy with lust, and ready for him. Despite myself, my fingers found my clit, but he pushed my hand away. "None of that."

I whimpered at the chastisement, the potential pleasure welling up in me until I thought I might burst, and when he moved away, leaving me to feel abandoned and desperate in my need, I thought for a moment I might cry. My safe word crept onto my tongue, and I fought the urge to say it. He had asked me to trust him, revealing for a moment the wounded man he was beneath the veneer of arrogance he wore like a well-cut suit, and I was powerless to say no to his request.

I bit my lip and waited, ready for whatever he might give me.

The first lash bit against my clit, vibrating through my body and making me cry out. It wasn't painful, merely unexpected, and it wasn't enough to push me over the cliff my body clung to. Cold leather rubbed across my seam, and I realized Alexander had found a purpose for the riding crop after all. Then the smooth rod was gone. I held my breath until it cracked lightly against my backside. The sting seared across my tender flesh, raising goose bumps along my skin. Alexander's hand rubbed the spot with soft strokes, dissipating the remaining heat left by the whip, even as the flame kindling between my legs blazed into an inferno. He continued his massage, and I realized he was testing me, waiting for me to give the word that would urge him on or deliver me from him.

"More," I moaned.

Alexander stepped forward and pressed a kiss to my neck—a simple gesture of gentle reassurance before he stepped back again. This time I heard the crop cut through the air before it smacked against my other cheek. The lash was more forceful but still controlled, even though my knees buckled at its impact. I cried out his name in affirmation of my pleasure.

"Wider, poppet," he demanded, a dangerous note tucked into the words.

The crop pushed between my legs again, rubbing deliberately before it whipped against my clit once more. The bundle of nerves sang with longing. I was so close, but I knew this couldn't satisfy my growing need. The orgasm mounting in me felt hollow. It wouldn't diminish my craving. Only he could do that.

"I need you," I cried as the crop snapped against my sensitive bud again. Alexander stilled behind me, so I continued, "I need you inside me. I need you to fill me."

"Are you sure, poppet?" he asked, but even as he spoke, I heard his zipper.

I managed to nod despite the lightness swimming through my head. Alexander intoxicated me. Without his touch, I forgot how to breathe. He had become the center of gravity I returned to after being stretched past my limits. I needed that haven now more than I ever had. Not just because he'd taken me to the very brink of pleasure, but because here, amongst his family and friends, our connection felt tenuous. I yearned for him, coveted him.

His finger dipped into my sex, and I relaxed against him.

"You bloom for me like a flower," he murmured against my ear. The finger disappeared and the empty sensation returned, but it evaporated as I felt the thick crest of his cock nudging against my entrance. Even though I was practically dripping for him, I braced myself for the initial stroke—the one that always walked the line between pain and pleasure.

"I need to fuck you, Clara," he growled, his breath hot in my ear, and his cock twitching between my legs. "I don't know if I can be gentle."

I wanted all of him.

The angel and the demon.

The heaven and the hell.

He was my curse and my salvation.

I answered without a second thought. "Don't be."

Alexander groaned at my words, one hand wrapping fiercely around my belly as the other pushed his cock inside my trembling cleft. Despite his warning, he stilled for a moment. His now free hand brushed the hair from my neck, pushing it over my shoulder and holding it there, so that he could crush his body closer to mine. And then without further warning, he slammed into me, igniting a surge of flames that burned through my sex. His hand tangled in my hair, tugging me to him, yanking my head back until his lips captured mine. He continued his tireless assault as he guided my quivering legs down against his hard quads. I was nearly sitting on him, his powerful legs bent to allow him deeper access as he stroked against my velvet walls.

The self-control I'd fought to maintain crumbled a little with each thrust, abandoning itself to the fulfillment I so desperately craved. Alexander broke our kiss, releasing my hair so that

I could lean into the tree as he drove his cock toward a furious climax.

"Come for me," he ordered, and I unraveled around him, my limbs tightening and then softening as I shattered into him. He broke over me like a wave across the shore, pulling me out to sea and stealing away my breath as I drowned in his power. As I drowned in him.

As the final fragments of pleasure swirled through me, his pace increased. He had taken me to the brink and let me fall over while maintaining the rigid self-control he clung to, but now his cock thickened and pulsed in my sensitive channel as he poured into me, flooding my sex with hot semen.

"Clara. My Clara," he groaned as he came, and I heard the truth in my name on his lips. He was as lost at sea as I was.

We were both drowning.

CHAPTER TWENTY-FOUR

I lay in the grass, spread naked over Alexander's jacket while he tightened the saddle for our ride back to the estate. The sun blazed overhead, and I lounged lazily in its heat. I was in no hurry to return, especially given our current state. Half-dressed with his chest bare, his dark hair tousled from fucking, Alexander looked like a god, and I was enjoying the view. Despite the slight soreness from the rawness of our encounter, my core tightened as I caught sight of his unbuttoned pants, and I couldn't help but want him again.

Alexander turned and narrowed his eyes, sauntering toward me like a panther stalking his prey. I beckoned him with my finger, sighing as he lowered over me, holding himself in a push-up without touching me. I couldn't complain because it showed the rigid discipline he'd developed over years of military service, as well as the chiseled muscles. I couldn't resist running my fingers down the length of his abdomen, the tips of which practically vibrated over his packed abs.

His eyes hooded as I caressed his forbidden zone. "You were giving me a come-hither look."

I arched against him, brushing my nipples across his flesh.

They responded immediately to the contact, beading tightly, and I bit my lip, imagining teeth nipping across the sensitive tips. "That's a shame. I meant to give you a come-fuck-me look," I purred, arching higher so that my sex made precious contact with his groin. He was hard again, and my legs parted instinctively for him.

"Now I see the difference." He groaned as my hands stole to his fly and freed his cock. If it weren't for its warm, pulsing veins, it could have been mistaken for marble. His body belonged to a different time. It was a work of art that belonged in a museum, and it was all mine. Reaching further down, I urged his sac free, cupping it gently and then giving it a playful squeeze.

"Christ, I love it when you play with my balls." His head dipped away from my mouth, finally finding my breasts. He covered my nipple with light suction, increasing the pressure until I felt it between my legs, which tightened instinctively, urging his cock to find its home.

But I wasn't done yet.

"I want to suck you off," I whispered, and Alexander stilled.

"If you do that, I'll only be able to fuck you longer." He rocked his body against mine, so that his cock slid in and out of my grasp, poking into my pubic bone. The gesture felt like the promise of good things to come.

But I couldn't ignore that the sun no longer shone directly over my head. "How long do we have?"

"Not nearly long enough to satisfy me. I want to fuck you in the twilight and under the stars and as the sun rises."

"Yes, please," I said, licking my lips at the thought.

"You're so fucking hot for me, poppet. Do you know what that does to me?" Alexander pushed off of me. Kneeling between my legs, he fisted his cock, displaying its magnificent length. "You've got such a greedy cunt. All I want to do is fuck it. Fuck it hard. Fuck it slow. I want the absence of my cock in your pretty little cunt to feel abnormal. It belongs to me, and I'm going to take care of it as often as I can."

My sex clenched at his words. I wanted to please him. No, I *needed* to, because his fulfillment had somehow trumped my own, but I didn't know how to say that to him. Instead I scrambled to my knees, dropping to my hands, and ran my tongue along his shaft. Alexander's hand caught my hair, and he urged me up to a kneeling position with gentle force while he stood. His hands stayed in my hair, stroking my head softly as I licked his cock. Catching his balls on my tongue, I sucked one gently into my mouth and rolled it around until his hand clenched my hair more tightly, then I released it and focused on the other one until he urged me back.

"I'm going to fuck your mouth now."

Before he could push his cock past my lips, I was on him, my mouth settling over him. I hollowed my cheeks, sucking and tonguing him with long strokes, and Alexander held back, allowing me to pleasure him. My hand gripped his cock, stroking him hard, urging him toward release.

I drove my mouth down his shaft, hollowing my cheeks as he spurted against my throat, relishing the heat of his seed until he stilled. Alexander's eyes remained closed even after I pulled away, pleasantly surprised to see his erection hadn't diminished in the slightest. When he finally looked at me, I felt scorched to the bone.

"My turn," he said in a gruff voice.

He laid me back, pressing my legs open with his hips. But he didn't move inside me, despite my pleas. Instead he dropped a trail of kisses down my abdomen, stopping to whisper against the hollow of my thighs. "Do you know why I use the wax seal on the notes I send you?"

I nodded my head, even as I tried to understand why this was important right now. "So they remain private."

"That's the practical reason." He paused, drawing his tongue along the crease and making me gasp. "The crest is an old family one."

"I had no idea they were so official," I murmured, growing warmer as his mouth hovered so close to my clit that I could feel his breath on it.

"Traditionally," he continued, his fingers pushing into my seam and parting the delicate tissues, "red was used in correspondence to the church."

I thought of the red wax seal Alexander had employed, and my blood heated from a mixture of embarrassment and arousal.

Alexander paused, shifting his attention from my swelling sex to meet my eyes. "You are my religion, Clara Bishop. Sacred. Lovely. I want to worship you."

His mouth dropped to my cunt, and my breath caught as his tongue flicked across my clit. He teased my bud with soft, quick brushes that sent small ripples of pleasure through my body. When I didn't think I could take any more, he settled over the sensitive spot and sucked hungrily. His finger probed my entrance, and I relaxed wider, welcoming him. He pushed another finger in, fucking me with long, deep strokes as his tongue swirled over my clit, and I came undone, shattering to pieces under his skilled assault.

"You taste so fucking good," he purred, trailing his tongue along my slit. It was too much for me to handle, and I shuddered, clamping my legs against his head instinctively. He rose to his knees, his hand fisting his shaft, and stared down at me.

I barely had time to register the contact before he'd pushed into me again.

"I can't," I moaned, my body not yet recovered from the earth-shattering orgasm he'd just given me.

"I say you can," he growled. My sex responded with shock, not ready for more stimulation, as he moved slowly in and out of my cleft. Alexander's thumb found my clit and expertly stroked the sensitivity to excitement. I flowered for him and he sunk deeper inside me. "Put your legs over my shoulders."

I obliged, stretching until my ankles hooked over his shoulders. Alexander groaned as his hands found my ass, gripping it tightly as he thrust into me with delicious slowness. I was on the verge of spilling over, and I caught my lip between my teeth trying to make the exquisite pleasure last longer.

"Wait," Alexander ordered me. "I say when you come this time."

He slipped out of me, and I cried out at the absence of him. He shushed me as he stroked his crown down the length of my seam. "I love watching your eager, little cunt opening for me."

I whimpered as he rubbed his cock along my sensitive lips.

"Tell me what you need, Clara."

I watched him through my hooded eyelids, his spell making me feel as though I was drugged. "You."

"You have me."

I wiggled against him, encouraging his cock back to my cleft, but he continued to brush it over my sex without entering me, using just enough pressure to make me incoherently excited without letting me climax.

"I want your cock," I moaned

"I had to make sure you were ready," he said, stroking his head along my swollen mound until I was nearly breathless. "I needed you relaxed and wet, so I can fuck you hard."

"Please," I whispered between pants.

Alexander thrust inside me without hesitation, pounding with supernatural speed and force, spurring me toward the edge. My hands groped for something to grab onto as he continued his unrelenting assault. They tangled in his dark hair, and I held on as his cock drove me toward another orgasm. Despite his ferocity, it built slowly, flickering and smoldering in low but powerful waves of fire through my whole body until I ignited under him. I splintered into a wildfire that blazed to life and came screaming his name just as he did, jetting into me with hot, potent jets.

He collapsed onto me, and my arms wrapped around him, cradling him against me. I didn't want this afternoon to end.

"I could do that for the rest of the night." His words were hot and urgent against my neck.

"Let's," I agreed.

I felt his lips curve into a grin as he brushed them over my skin and rolled off me and onto his side. "I love that your body is so needy. It's quite the challenge to keep your beautiful cunt satisfied."

"It's only needy for you." I gasped as he dipped one finger into my drenched slit.

"Yes, that's right, poppet. Only I can give you pleasure." His finger twitched inside me as his eyes gazed hungrily into mine. "And I will give you more tonight after dinner."

I closed my eyes and pictured Alexander taking me on the large four-poster bed in my room. "Promise?"

"Everything I say to you is a promise." There was a raspy edge to his voice as he spoke, and I reopened my eyes to meet his. "When I say I'm going to fuck you, that's a promise. When I say I'm going to make you beg, that's a promise. And when I say this beautiful cunt is mine, that's a promise."

His lips captured my mouth, and he proved he was telling me the truth as he fucked me senseless one more time.

. . .

Alexander tucked his jacket around me as I did the best I could to get my blouse to close. There was no use. I looked like I'd endured a good fuck, and with the heat still in my cheeks, I didn't care who knew. I was drunk on his mere presence. That would be obvious to anyone who saw us, but it was more than our physical encounter that lingered in my heated blood. This weekend had proven over and over again that the connection between us was real.

I was in love with him.

I no longer had any doubt of that, but I couldn't be certain that feeling was reciprocated. I heard it in the way he said my name and felt it in the way he touched me—in the soft caress before he fucked me blind. I replayed the afternoon tryst in my head as we rode back to the estate, for once content with the silence that had followed our previous lovemaking. Was it lovemaking though? I searched my memories for more hints, more clues that I wasn't alone in this state. Surely the fact that Alexander hadn't pumped me and dumped me like the other girls he'd been photographed with in the papers was proof. He'd even brought me here, amongst his family and friends, which had to mean something. Of course, everyone here hated me, so maybe that wasn't reassuring after all.

By the time we rode into the stable, I felt half-crazy. How was I supposed to figure out a man who couldn't—or wouldn't—open up to me anywhere but in the bedroom, or in today's case, against a tree? We had a connection. For now I had to trust him with more than a riding crop. I had to trust him with my heart.

But as the memory of our wild afternoon stole into my mind, I was distracted from my more analytic musings. Just the thought of his virile, masculine body was enough to make me forget all my worries. But we weren't alone here, and I couldn't act on the desire slowly filtering through me.

I was in such a haze that I barely registered dismounting.

The appearance of a stablehand finally snapped me out of it, and I tugged Alexander's jacket tighter. His hand stayed on my back, reassuring me, even as my cheeks burned as the stablehand gawked at my appearance. The man quickly recovered, averting his eyes and offering a gruff good evening to us both.

Alexander held my hand as he guided me to the veranda nearest my guest bedroom. I tried not to obsess over the small gesture, even though I was sure I would later. For now, I delighted in the strong, firm feel of his fingers woven with mine. Then it was gone. He held a finger to his lips and peeked inside, gesturing after a moment that it was safe for me to enter. But he caught me in the doorway, pressing me against the frame and kissing me roughly, his tongue sliding forcefully into my mouth. I was consumed, melting eagerly against him. My hands sought the firm abs that lay hidden under his shirt, and I ran my hands down them, my fingers lingering on the jagged scar that he tried so hard to hide. Alexander's breath caught, aware of my touch even on the scar tissue. He seized my hand as he drew away and shook his head.

"No, Clara," he warned.

I blinked against the tears welling in my eyes at the harsh rebuke. Two steps forward. Three steps back. I had my answer: we weren't moving forward. How could we ever possibly do so when he hid so much from me? Forcing myself to look away in attempt to hide the pain twisting through me, I gave him a rueful smile. "I'll see you at dinner."

"Clara—don't." He refused to let go of my wrist, and when I pulled against his hold, his grip tightened. "Not here. Not in this place. I can't explain it to you."

"Try," I snapped, my frustration showing.

"I can't." His eyes had grown hard, but for a moment, they smoldered to life as he met my gaze. "It's not you, Clara."

"It never is." I was tired of the constant back and forth when all I wanted was to know where I stood with him. "I thought after this afternoon—"

"You need to change for dinner, poppet," Alexander stopped me. The abrupt change of subject stung as much as his dismissal of me. I couldn't help thinking this was about more than wanting me to be presentable to his family and friends. How could I ever be what Alexander needed? No wonder they all judged me. We all knew what I lacked—not only the pedigree, but the calculated indifference that could be flipped on like a switch.

"Maybe I should just go home."

"No." Another command.

I raised an eyebrow at him. Was he totally incapable of separating his need to dominate me sexually and personally?

He paused, as though measuring the best way to respond to my obvious resistance to his demand. "I want you to stay, but I'll understand if you go. I'd leave if I could."

"Then leave with me," I pleaded. Whatever secrets this place held, they were destroying him.

"It's not that simple, Clara." The weight of six years of exile showed in his blue eyes. "I can't run from this. Not anymore. But there's something you should know."

I waited for him to continue, knowing everything depended on what he said next.

"If you run, Clara. I will follow you."

MY DECISION WAS MADE BEFORE I REACHED THE HALLWAY. Clutching Alexander's jacket closer to me, I breathed in his scent, willing myself to believe I could put up with the secrets and the strange double life I'd found myself in. Leaving him felt like an impossibility. I'd lost myself to him completely, and now all I could do was steel myself against the scrutiny of his world.

I felt her eyes on me before I saw her, and when I turned, she was indeed watching me, her lips curled into a sneer that did nothing to mask her beauty. I tugged self-consciously at the jacket and made a beeline for my room.

"Oh my, was there an accident?" she called after me.

I stopped, my resolve hardening at the venom in her words. I couldn't run away from Pepper Lockwood. She'd insinuated herself into Alexander's life, and even though I couldn't understand for the life of me why anyone wanted her around, I knew she was here to stay. "I need to get dressed for dinner."

"You might consider showering as well." She wrinkled her nose. "You smell like cheap sex."

"A smell I'm sure you'd recognize," I said with a smile.

"Clara, dear, stupid girl, do you still think you can play this game?" She walked toward me, her thin arms braced against her chest as she appraised my appearance. "You think we're eating you alive. I can see it in your eyes. You look just like that poor fox they loosed this morning, hopeful but terrified. But I'm here to tell you: we haven't even begun to feast on you yet. We're not even past the appetizer course."

I swallowed against the rawness mounting in my throat. I couldn't let her get to me, and I certainly couldn't let her see me fazed. "I know you like your games. Surround a weaker creature and call it sport, but there's something you need to know: I'm not the fox."

"You aren't the hunter either." Pepper's nostrils flared as she spoke. I'd hit my mark. She wanted me to roll over, but I was no longer willing to wait for her to pounce.

"Neither are you. Neither of us *belong* here, Pepper. But the one that gets to stay is the one he *chooses*." I emphasized my words carefully, hoping she'd take my hint, but she remained unmoved.

"And you think that will be you." She giggled at this, tossing her blonde curls over her shoulder, the essence of poise and femininity no matter how much pressure I applied.

"I'm the one sharing his bed," I said without missing a beat.

"You're the one he's fucking. Did he take you out to a field?" Her eyes travelled once more over my disheveled form. "You think if you let him shag you like an animal, he won't get bored?"

"Trust me—" I tilted my chin up in a show of a pride "—he's not bored."

"Not yet." Her words were clipped as she shrugged off my bravado.

"And you're the one who can keep him interested?" I guessed.

"There are expectations for Alexander. A whole country's expectations. That means a lot more than some piece of ass he picked up for fun. Alexander knows his time is running out. That's why he's *slumming*."

"Slumming?" I actually laughed at this, ignoring how it echoed through the hall. "Pepper, *dear, stupid girl*, you have the name and the connections, but don't ever forget that I have a trust fund that could buy your family three times over."

Pepper's eyes rolled back against her perfectly fake lashes. "Discussing money is so crass."

"People who have none usually think that," I said. "But that's what is in this for you, isn't it? Validity for your old family name. A chance to prove your titles and history still mean something to someone. To anyone."

She took a step back as though I'd struck her, and this time there was no doubt I'd hit my target. "And what do you have to offer? You're only a little girl who got rich on internet dating."

I blinked at this, unable to fathom how this couldn't be obvious to her. How could these people be so incredibly broken that they couldn't recognize the one thing a person craved? The one thing a person needed? It could only be the lack of it that accounted for their utter ignorance on the matter.

But my silence inspired her, and she laughed once more. "Wait—*love*? You think you can give him love! I knew you were delusional, but that's actually pathetic."

I'd never actually considered punching someone before. At least not seriously, but I thought about it now, my hands curling into fists at my sides. "My relationship with Alexander is between him and me, and your opinion isn't welcome. So please feel free to shut the hell up."

"Believe what you want," she said with a dismissive wave of her manicured hand. "But consider this a friendly warning: Alexander isn't capable of love or true emotion, and he'll only destroy you. You're already drowning in his darkness, Clara, and someday when he has to face himself and the man he will become, he'll need someone at his side who can't be pulled under."

And she believed she could be that person. Maybe she was right. I'd seen the darkness she spoke of flashing behind his eyes, felt it when his dominance took over. Could he ever be happy without breaking me further than I was already broken? But she was wrong about one thing. Alexander felt things, even when he allowed his darker emotions to cloud his perception of reality. That passionate loathing that he felt toward himself and his place in the world proved he did feel, perhaps more acutely than any of us. A woman like Pepper couldn't understand that. She couldn't see that light could bring him out of his prison. The realization felt like a weight had been lifted from my chest—only to be anchored to my feet. While I didn't believe him incapable of love, I wasn't certain I was strong enough to be the person to show him that. I'd walked through the valley of the shadow myself and I was not unscathed.

"Maybe," a soft voice said from a nearby alcove, startling both of us, "you should listen to the lady and shut the hell up, Pepper."

Edward emerged from the dark recesses, neatly attired in a vest and tie, no doubt dressed for dinner. His glasses were perched on the top of his head, indicating he'd been reading, but his hair was mussed up as though he'd been anxiously ramming his fingers through it, and I spied tired, bluish circles under his eyes. I was little embarrassed to think he might have been here the whole time. Still, he seemed in support of my suggestion that Pepper should back the fuck off.

"Lady?" The word rolled out of her mouth drolly. "I suppose it takes one to know one."

Edward exhaled a long *can-you-possibly-be-serious* sigh. "How very witty. I'm nearly positive that you must be the reincarnation of Shakespeare himself with insults like that."

"Don't be so intellectual, Eddie. Men don't find that attractive," she advised, clicking her nails together as she spoke.

"Clara." Edward strode toward me and offered his arm. "Allow me to see you to your room."

"Gladly." A mixture of relief and disgust and confusion swirled through me. As soon as we were out of earshot of Pepper, I added, "I think that went well."

"I suppose that depends."

"On what?" I asked. "How much did you hear?"

"All of it," Edward admitted, his eyes flitting to me briefly. "I saw you and Alexander, and I wanted to give you some privacy."

"And then you left me to defend myself against Pepper Spray?" I smacked his shoulder.

"Pepper Spray? Have you nicknamed us all?" His mouth crooked into a grin. "Am I Queen Edward then?"

Now it was my turn to feel sheepish, even as I shook my head. "You are Nice Edward Whom I Don't Want to Kill."

"Something about the way you said that makes me think there are others on your hit list."

"Only the Royal Brat Pack." The answer slipped out before I could even consider how childish I sounded or whom I was talking to. I had no doubt that he could guess to whom I was referring, and after what I'd witnessed last night, he might take my dig rather personally. I chewed on my lip, waiting for him to drop my arm or laugh, but he did neither.

"Another excellent nickname. I've never come up with something so fitting before myself."

I couldn't help but take his response as an indication that he wasn't offended. "What names have you given them?"

"Assholes. Wankers. The usual," he said with a shrug.

"I want you to know that I don't think David—"

Edward's demeanor shifted immediately, and I was reminded that he was Alexander's brother. Without a word from him, I knew to drop it.

"About that," he began.

But I held a hand up. Now it was my turn to save him. "You don't have to say anything. My lips are sealed."

"So I don't have to buy you off?"

My mouth fell open until I realized he was joking, and I shut it quickly. "No," I said dryly. "As you know, I'm a woman of means."

"So I heard." His answer lacked the snappiness of his earlier comebacks as his eyes faded into thought. "It's a well-kept secret. Not about me. About him. I don't want to see him hurt."

I'd spent the last day enduring derision and condescension. Edward didn't have to elaborate on what he hoped to save

David from, but I couldn't help but wonder how David felt about it. It was a difficult line to walk openly being here with Alexander. How hard must it be for David?

Taking a deep breath, I forced myself to be brave as I opened the door to my room. "Do you want to come in?"

"I'm not sure how Alexander will feel about me being in your room."

"Somehow I don't think he'll mind."

"I have quite the reputation, you know." But he stepped inside.

"That's why I'm not worried."

"Yes," he said, "because a gay man is only ever in a woman's room for innocent reasons."

"You aren't going to steal my underwear, are you?" I teased, shimmying out of Alexander's jacket.

Edward's eyebrow shot up as he took in my blouse.

"Wardrobe malfunction." I opened the armoire, hunting for something appropriate for another stuffy dinner.

"Whatever he did to you, I hope it was worth ruining a Donna Karan."

"It was," I promised him as I continued to riffle through the clothes I'd brought. I had thought I was over-packing, but being stuck around Pepper and her brat pack made all my clothing feel dated or casual or cheap.

"Go take a shower," Edward suggested, pushing me toward the en suite.

"I can't find anything to wear. There's no point. Maybe I'll go like this and give the whole rotten bunch of them heart attacks."

"It would certainly weed the line of succession a bit if you did that," he said, shaking his head bemusedly. "Don't worry about your clothes."

I stared at him as he began to poke through my dresses. "Are you going to pick out an outfit for me?"

Edward's back was to me now, but I saw the laughter rolling through him. "Oh *poppet*, there might be some unfair stereotypes about gay men out there, but our sense of style isn't one of them."

CHAPTER TWENTY-FIVE

An hour later I was fully clothed, my makeup perfectly applied, and my hair curled. I tugged self-consciously at the dress Edward had chosen for me. I'd bought it at Belle's insistence, and it was far from my usual style. The satin skirt rested a good eight inches above my knees, and the lace fabric of the top draped over a nude slip. I looked positively naked under it. It wouldn't take much to imagine my breasts as the thinness of the fabric left no room for a bra.

"You're sure you don't have some tape," Edward said as he swept my chestnut locks over one shoulder, eying me analytically in the loo's mirror.

"Not all of us carry a fashion emergency kit," I said drily as I stared at my reflection, trying to decide if I could show my face in this ensemble.

"More's the pity. Oh well, Alexander will like it." Edward winked, grabbing my hand he spun me away from my self-analysis and whistled. "You have excellent taste. Your closet is a gay man's dream."

"Want to play dress up?" I asked seriously. It was a safe bet that Edward's trim body would fit into some of my clothes.

"Oh no, I like to see beautiful women in dresses, but I don't swing that way," he assured me. "Christ, can you imagine what the family would think of that? They lucked out and only got a mild case of metrosexuality to deal with."

I laughed along with him, noting that he was rocking a tweed vest, horn-rim glasses and carefully polished wingtips. It wasn't the careless, sexy look of his brother, but rather a carefully articulated sense of taste all his own. "I wish I could claim I bought these clothes, but I had help."

"Personal shopper?"

"My mother has tried for years to dress me like a nice British aristocrat. I'm sorry to say I'd rather be in jeans and sandshoes," I admitted, sighing in remembrance of my university days. "My flatmate took me shopping."

"Your flatmate has excellent taste then." It was clear from his tone that Edward's interest was piqued.

"You might know her actually: Annabelle Stuart."

If Edward knew about the Stuart family scandal he didn't let on, he simply shook his head. "I'm sorry to say I don't, but I would love to. If we make it out of here alive, we should have tea."

"I would like that." Now that I'd made a friend in Alexander's inner circle, I wasn't letting go. It was nice to be around a member of the royal bunch who didn't have his head stuck up his ass, which was something I couldn't always say for Alexander, and I found Edward's openness about who he was to be a refreshing change of pace. Edward had as much reason to be coy as Alexander, and yet he'd already opened up to me.

"Uh-oh. I see those wheels turning," Edward said, interrupting my thoughts before they spiraled further into despair. "This is all you need to know. You look fantastic. The skirt isn't too short. We're likely to be treated to a viewing of Pepper or

Sandra's ass tonight. Believe me, this is nothing in comparison. This is sexy and sophisticated."

"Just like Pepper," I said with a sigh.

"That girl may look like sex on a stick..."

I raised my eyebrow at hearing this come out of his mouth.

"I have eyes, even if I'm not buying," he said with a shrug. "But no one has ever mistaken her for *sophisticated*."

"I did." I chewed my lip as I remembered my first impression of the statuesque blonde. If I were being honest, part of me would kill to look like Pepper. The other part of me just wanted to kill her.

Edward grabbed my hand. "Pepper is intimidating, not sophisticated. The difference between the two is very subtle, but don't ever forget that. She's all bark and no bite."

"I hope you're right about that." I couldn't help but think that Pepper might be more dangerous than Edward or Alexander believed her to be. There was, after all, a difference between attacking and circling. She hadn't done more than expose her fangs so far, but that didn't mean she wasn't planning a strike.

"After tonight, she'll know who she's up against. You're a badass, Clara Bishop."

"I am, huh?" I laughed at his pep talk. It was sweet of him, but he didn't really know me. The girl who had to remind herself to eat. The girl who had let her ex push her around. The girl who made excuses for everyone.

"You have to be. Alexander wouldn't be interested in you if you weren't."

"I get the impression Alexander is pretty interested in anything with two breasts and air in her lungs." I'd never spoken this fear out loud to anyone. I'd hinted at it with Alexander, always laughing off the mentions of his playboy ways in the press. The closest we'd come to really discussing his sexual history was when I confronted him about Pepper, but I'd always been as eager as he was to avoid the subject of his many girl-friends and flings.

"Don't say that." Edward shook his head, his eyes sad. He rubbed them with the back of his hand. "I'm not the only one who's been forced to keep up appearances."

"Really?" I tried to sound casual but failed miserably. There was so much I didn't know about Alexander's life before me, and I couldn't quite contain my curiosity. Alexander occupied my thoughts constantly. He'd become a compulsion I couldn't deny, and yet there was so much I wanted to learn about him.

"I'm not saying all the stories are fake. But some of them have been embellished," Edward assured me.

"And why do you think he's here with me?" I asked, searching his brother's dark eyes for any clues that would lead me to the answers I so desperately wanted.

"Because he likes you," Edward said quickly. "I heard Pepper tell you Alexander was incapable of love."

"Is she right?" I whispered, suddenly afraid.

"I hope not. I remember a time when my brother played with me as a kid. How he'd come in when I was sick and look in on me. I never knew our mother and our father—well, you know how he is, but Alexander took care of me..." His voice trailed away as though there were more, but he didn't speak again.

"But?" I prompted.

"That was before Sarah died."

"So this is who he is," I said, a note of finality ringing in the words. I'd known that. He'd told me that, but somehow I'd thought things could be different. Didn't every magazine and self-help book ever written warn that wasn't possible? And yet, here I was, trying anyway. I waved off the concerned look on Edward's face. "Don't worry about it."

"You look like I kicked a puppy." Edward's hand tangled in

his hair. He looked so much like his brother in that moment that my heart jumped. "I shouldn't say this, because I know better than anyone what it's like to get your hopes up only to have them come crashing down, but I think Alexander is capable of love. You don't just lose that ability. Whatever is preventing him from getting close to someone is all due to him not wanting to."

It was the last thing I wanted to hear, and I turned away so he couldn't see the pain on my face. Alexander didn't want to love. That was the real problem, not that he was incapable of it. How stupid was I to think I could fix him? That if I loved him it would be enough? I choked back a sob and took a shaky breath.

"Here." Edward handed me a pair of Yves St. Laurent black pumps. They were at least an inch higher than any I'd worn, even the ones Belle had talked me into for the ball. I wrinkled my nose, unable to hide my obvious distress at adding even more leg to this ensemble. I was beginning to think Edward and Belle were part of a large conspiracy to turn me into a fashionista.

"Trust me," he continued. "I saw how you spoke to Pepper. You are one sexy bitch, and it's time to show those brats what you're capable of."

"And I need five-inch heels to do that?"

"You need your look to match your attitude."

"I have an attitude?" This was a surprise to me. A memory of Daniel screaming that I was spineless flitted through my mind, but I pushed it back into the dark recesses I kept those thoughts imprisoned in.

"You do. I saw it this afternoon." Edward wrapped an arm around my shoulder and guided me toward the mirror. "And I hate to say it, but Pepper is right. They haven't even begun yet—those wankers downstairs or the leeches on the corner. They're going to come after you, and they're going to come for blood. You need to show them that you are a woman to be reckoned with, and please start with Pepper Spray."

The woman reflected in the mirror wasn't a sexpot, although she could be. The short hemline, the fuck-me pumps, and the crimson lips definitely pointed to that, but when I looked closer, I saw what Edward was saying. I stood taller not just because of the heels. My shoulders were back, my eyes were fierce.

"She doesn't look like someone who should be fucked with," I said out loud.

"No, she doesn't!" Edward let out a whoop. "If you're going to enter this world, Clara, and let me be clear, I'm not saying you should, because only the truly insane would want to be part of this fucked up family, then you have to start playing the game. Think of it as chess."

"Chess with backstabbing and sex," I said, my mouth twisting into a wry smile. The girl in the mirror did the same and I took a step back. Sarcasm looked different dressed like this. Instead of a simple defense mechanism, it was all condescension and judgment. Suddenly, I understood why Pepper always looked like she'd just walked out of the pages of *Vogue*. It was all part of her act. It was part of the girl she was pretending to be. Although it was possible that she'd been pretending so long that she had actually become the heartless bitch I knew and loathed.

"Exactly." Edward dropped a kiss on my forehead. "Last piece of advice?"

"Yes." I took a deep breath and nodded that I was ready for it.

"When you see them, when you walk by them, when they laugh behind your back—with every step you take, just think *murder*."

My eyes widened with surprise and this time I choked back laughter. "Murder?"

"Trust me. Just the word—although if you have a particularly active imagination, I suppose you can imagine how you'd do them in," he added, his mouth curving into a grin.

I raised my eyebrows devilishly. "It would be very royal of me."

Edward's eyes sparkled, watching me take my first few steps in the sky-high heels. They were a bit shaky, but I soon got my bearing.

"Do you run?" he asked as we entered the hall.

"I used to run every day at Oxford, but lately I've been getting other exercise," I answered, blushing. "How did you know?"

"Believe me, anyone standing behind you can tell. If Pepper acts up, just kick her. I can't imagine that waif could handle those legs."

I blushed at his praise, peeking down to discover he was right. My legs didn't just look long, they were shapely, and with the addition of my stilettos, I didn't merely tower, I reigned. "I could kiss you, you know."

"That's likely to be the only action I get this weekend," Edward said, straightening his jacket as we strolled, arm in arm, toward the formal dining room. I was pretty sure we were late, but at least I would be entering with a prince—and wouldn't look like I'd just been rollicking in the countryside.

I hesitated to push for more information. How far could I press Edward before he closed himself off to me? But then I remembered that was how Alexander acted. The fact that Edward had brought it up meant he wanted to talk about it. Had I spent so much time with Alexander that I'd forgotten how normal people acted around each other? What it was like to confide in a friend? If so then I needed a dose of reality, stat. "Where's David?"

"He headed home for the weekend. He couldn't handle anymore after..."

"I shouldn't have darted off last night," I said, realizing it had been me that had sent him running for the hills.

"No!" Edward stopped me, a pained look flashing across his elegant features. "Believe me, we both knew you wouldn't say anything. My father is another story. We've never come out to him, but he suspects and he managed to make his opinion known several times this weekend."

"That's unfair. Does he think all your male friends are your lovers?" I asked.

"Doesn't your father think the same thing?" he asked pointedly.

"Touché." I sighed, feeling a twinge of empathy. I knew what it was like to have parents butting into my love life. "It still doesn't mean he should pry."

"Father brought up the Defense of Marriage Act fights going on over in America. Let's just say he made it clear where he stands on the issue."

"That's terrible." Without thinking, I linked my hand with his and squeezed.

"You're late," a gruff voice interrupted us.

"Alexander." Edward gave me a quick look before dropping my hand. "I was just escorting your lovely girlfriend to dinner."

Suddenly, I was thankful the hall was dark, so that they couldn't see me blush. As much as I'd hoped to hear someone call me that, I wasn't sure how Alexander would respond to someone casually using the term.

"I can handle that." Alexander offered his arm with a questioning tilt of his head, his eyes flickering between me and his brother. I rolled mine in response. The *last* person he needed to be jealous of was his brother. Edward nodded before continuing into the dining room. But when I took Alexander's arm, he paused, his gaze raking over me. "In this light, you look naked."

Despite the tension that still hung in the air, I giggled. More light wasn't going to help with that. "We're late for dinner, X."

Alexander opened the door, sending a scrap of light into the hallway, and sucked in a breath when he saw me more clearly.

"What are you wearing?" he whispered, his voice a seductive mix of fury and lust.

Something about his reaction emboldened me further. It was what I'd hoped for—to show him that try as he might in the bedroom, he couldn't tame me in public. I cupped his chin, realizing that in these shoes I could look directly into his face rather than up at him. "I wore something sexy for you."

He hesitated as if he were trying to piece together what I was up to. "You always look sexy to me."

I liked this newfound confidence, and I felt it slipping away with each questioning comment out of Alexander's mouth. Before he could speak again, I planted a firm kiss on his lips. His hands on my ass informed me that I'd managed to distract him.

"Christ, this is short," Alexander said, sliding under my silky hem to cup my bare cheeks. "Suddenly, I'm not hungry."

I took a deep breath, willing myself not to fall under his spell. I wasn't doing the walk of shame into that dinner, not after my run-in with Pepper this afternoon. "*I'm* ravenous."

I swayed on my heels as I pulled away from him, and Alexander caught me, immediately drawing me back to him. His body pressed against mine, his erection nudging against me through his pants. I was tall enough in these that he could push me against that wall and take me with my feet still on the ground. A dozen exciting new possibilities flashed through my head as heat grew between my legs, but I shook them free, smiling at him in the dark, unsure if he could see. "Oh X, don't you know that good things come to those who wait?"

"Screw waiting." But I'd already wiggled free of his arms when his hands attempted to move under my skirt again.

"Delayed gratification, X." I skidded a little as I sauntered back toward the dining room door. We were really late now, but I took my time, swinging my hips with each step. I didn't let myself stop even when Alexander called out my name. Not when I reached the doors and he told me to wait. Instead I pushed them open and stepped into the light, never letting the smile fade from my lips.

CHAPTER TWENTY-SIX

The dining table stretched down the length of the cavernous room. Its occupants, clad in dinner attire, sat at formal place settings. The crystal sparkled, the silver was polished, and all eyes were on me. I stared over their heads, which wasn't hard considering they were all seated, and made my way to the two seats vacant at the end of the table. Daring to look at the other dinner guests, I found Pepper glaring at me with cold rage frozen on her face, her blue eyes casting icy daggers. I raised one eyebrow at her as I passed.

Game on, Pepper Spray.

As I reached my seat, the low murmurings of the dinner party grew to a buzz. I chanced a glance around the entire table this time, unsurprised that a few people turned away from my direct gaze. Everyone except two. Jonathan Thompson's cocky grin made him look as though he were in on some secret joke. I forced myself not to roll my eyes. And at the head of the table, Albert sat watching my late arrival with practiced stoicism.

I nodded my head in deference to him, feeling only slightly guilty for being tardy. Mostly because I would have been on time if it weren't for his two sons. Not that I really had any regrets about how I'd spent my time this afternoon.

A server stepped forward to pull out my chair when the dining room doors burst open. Alexander strode quickly toward me, throwing a cursory nod toward his father's place, but his eyes never left mine. I was dimly aware that the server was waiting for me to sit, but I couldn't move. The whole room had faded except for Alexander. The suppressed fury on his face said it all. I was his, and he was reasserting his claim to me. He didn't need to speak, I already knew his expectation, so I waited. He reached me, dismissing the server curtly. Taking his place behind the chair, he held it for me. "Clara."

My name was sex on his lips, and in it I felt the cocktail of possessiveness and lust and confusion that he felt. I sunk into the chair as I sunk back under his command. Alexander hastily took the chair next to mine, and I reached out under the table to place a tentative hand on his knee, but he knocked it away.

"Nice of you to join us, Alexander," Albert boomed.

Alexander's gaze stayed glued to me as he replied, "I had no idea I was a necessary aspect of your meal. You certainly didn't need to wait for me. I'm not a fork."

I swallowed, realizing that Alexander's need to exert his masculinity was no longer limited to me. It was as if my little show had augmented his craving for control. He was out to prove he was in command, which meant things might get ugly.

Albert's jaw tightened. "If you're finished with this display of machismo, I'd like to eat dinner."

"So would I," Alexander said, and I heard the words he didn't say: *I have somewhere to be.*

I could see his need to fuck me reflecting in his eyes. But if Edward was right, his brother might need to hear the word *no* every once in a while. I wasn't positive that Alexander wanted a real relationship, but he had brought me here. He had claimed me in front of his father and everyone else. That had to mean something. However, I also knew that he didn't know the first thing about having a relationship. With my limited experience in this area, I was only certain of one thing. I had to prove to Alexander—and everyone else—that I wouldn't tolerate games.

Peeling my eyes from Alexander, I turned toward my plate, suddenly grateful that the glass of wine at my place had already been filled. As I reached for it, I met Edward's amused eyes watching me. I'd been too distracted by Alexander's dramatic entrance to notice that I'd sat right across from his brother. At least I had an ally close by, especially with Pepper too close for comfort. She stared at Alexander expectantly as if she was trying to cast a spell over him, but his concentration couldn't be broken.

"Doesn't Clara look fabulous, Alexander?" Edward asked, steepling his fingers.

"She's a bit overdressed for dinner, don't you think?" Pepper said, butting in. The rest of the brat pack snickered around her on cue. "Or under-dressed, depending on how you look at it."

"Jealousy doesn't suit you." Edward ignored the evil look she cast toward him and picked up a butter knife, which he twisted thoughtfully in his hands. "It makes your complexion look all green. Clashes with your dress."

"We all know you're an expert on the subject," Pepper said, but she'd turned her angry face to me. "I saw that dress at Tamara's. I had no idea you had even heard of her. I thought she was a bit more exclusive."

"She can't be terribly exclusive if you know who she is," I said without missing a beat.

Alexander blinked beside me as though he was only now hearing the conversation between me and Pepper.

"I'll have to speak to her," she said.

"When you do, give her my love." I had never heard of

Tamara. I'd never met her. Belle had picked this dress out for me. It was purchased with my own money though, and I knew one thing. On Monday I would be in that boutique cleaning her out of every size six dress she had in stock. There was no way I'd let Pepper win, even if it was only at shopping.

"I will." Pepper smiled sweetly, and I returned the gesture as the soup course was placed in front of us. It smelled delicious, all creamy with toasted croutons floating on top. I raised my soup spoon, reminding myself to be graceful even as my stomach growled. Across the table, Pepper pushed her bowl away with distaste. Despite my hatred of her, my stomach flopped at the gesture. I had no reason to suspect that Pepper shared that in common with me, but it was a warning sign. She reached for her water, laughing at a joke as she leaned closer to Jonathan. I slurped the soup from my spoon and continued to watch her as the conversation around me picked up. Everyone was chatting, except Alexander and me. Maybe I just wanted to distract myself from his coldness and that was why I was seeing behavioral patterns that weren't really there. Maybe Pepper simply didn't like soup.

I took a few more spoonfuls before I placed my napkin on the table to signal that I was finished with it. If it was anything like I expected, I'd be stuffed by the third course if I didn't pace myself. But when I looked up, Pepper was watching me, a calculating look in her eyes. I turned toward Alexander, but he continued to eat.

Dropping my voice so we couldn't be overheard, I said, "I'm sorry."

"For what?" he asked stiffly.

"You seem upset."

Alexander's eyes flashed up to meet mine finally, a bemused smile on his face. "We still have a lot to learn about one another, Clara. I wasn't upset—" his voice lowered "—I was turned on. I didn't think I could stop myself from throwing you across the table and ripping off those shameless excuses for knickers you're wearing if you touched me again."

I blinked at this, my perception of the situation adjusting to this revelation. How hadn't I seen that? He needed to reestablish dominance, which for Alexander meant sex. That's what he had been thinking. Confidence ballooned in my chest at the thought. He wasn't angry with me. He wanted me. Because I looked hot. Because I drove him crazy.

"Maybe you should," I said, unable to stop myself. I wanted the delicious ache between my legs to grow, knowing that it would go unfulfilled for another hour or two, so that by the time we were alone once more, the moment he took me would be worth the build up.

"Don't tempt me, Clara. A man only has so much restraint." His lips twitched though, and I could see him imagining the scene: the reaction of the entire dinner party as he threw me across the linen—glasses shattering, forks clattering—and shoved his hot, thick cock inside me. I couldn't help squirming at the thought. Alexander spotted my fidgeting and smiled wider. "Soon, poppet."

I trembled at the thought, forcing myself to focus on the next course as it was served. But I could only pick at my salad, too distracted by Alexander's gaze, which continued to burn through me. When the third course arrived—leg of lamb served medium rare—Alexander grinned as they placed my plate in front of me.

"Eat up, Clara," he murmured. "You'll need your strength tonight."

My eyes closed, drinking in his words, my fork hovering over my meal. My mouth watered, but it had nothing to do with the heavenly scent wafting from the food in front of me. Alexander

should be given a special commendation for building anticipation.

"I do hope you aren't having an episode." Pepper's voice
pulled me from my fantasy.

My eyes snapped open to find a shameless smirk on her
face, her eyes gleaming with mischief that I knew was far from
innocent. I took a bite, chewing it slowly and making an *oh-my-
god* face as I swallowed. Pepper sighed disgustedly at my
orgasmic performance.

"I was so surprised when I found out about your little problem," she said in a voice that carried over the other conversations
at the table. Inwardly I cringed, but I forced myself to keep my
head held high. "Usually women with eating disorders are
thinner."

My mouth fell open, shocked that she'd not only bring this
up at the dinner table in front of a huge group of people, but that
she'd actually say something that heinous. If she had wanted
attention, she now had it. Not surprisingly, Amelia and Priscilla
tittered with nervous laughter at her little show. The King said
nothing, but his mother dabbed at her mouth with a napkin, not
concealing her disgust. But was that distaste leveled at the person
who deserved it—or at me for being flawed? I couldn't be sure.

A few seats down, Edward folded his hands on the table.
"Pepper, be careful. Your bitch is showing."

"Edward," his father admonished him.

"Oh, you aren't deaf," Edward replied, shooting his father a
sharp look over his horn-rimmed glasses. "You're just pretending
to be oblivious to what's right in front of your face."

"Something you count on," Pepper threw in, scathingly.
The comment hit its mark, and Edward clamped his mouth
shut.

My mind spun with so many things I would like to say to

her that I couldn't decide on one. I had expected her to attack me, but the heartless taunts directed at Edward pushed me over the edge. He'd called her out and she stepped over the line. Did she have any clue the damage she was doing to the fragile relationships he had with everyone at this table? My hands trembled with rage as I watched Edward pretend to ignore her. If anyone didn't belong at this table, it was Pepper.

The table fell into a silence, and I finally dared to look at Alexander, who hadn't spoken. As soon as I saw his face, I understood why he hadn't come to our defense. Veins pulsed along his neck, his jaw tight, his lips thinned into a straight line, and his knuckles had gone white from clutching his silverware. He was employing his considerable self-control, and I wasn't certain I wanted to see what would happen if it faltered.

Pepper obviously didn't share my concern.

"You should probably get your *girlfriend*—" she spit the word out, making it clear what she thought of giving me this title "—some help before her eating disorder gets her on more tabloid covers."

By now the shock had worn off, and I couldn't hold back anymore. "Pepper, I can't help noticing you haven't touched your plate or your salad or your soup. The only thing you've had your mouth on is that rocks glass. I'm happy to lend you my doctor's name after I finish eating."

Beside her, Edward bit back a smile, but Albert threw down his napkin. "Enough of—"

"You don't get to say enough," Alexander said in an even voice so deadly calm that it raised the hairs on the back of my neck. "Not if you watch as she's slandered."

"Don't be melodramatic," Pepper said, but I saw her throat slide as she swallowed nervously.

"You're here as a guest of this family," Alexander reminded

her, "because of Sarah. I'm now rescinding that invitation. I'd like you to leave."

Pepper stared at him, eyes wide as saucers, as the entire table erupted into conflicting opinions on Alexander's etiquette.

"This is my house," Albert said, knocking his fist against the table.

"And surely you stand by your son's request to have a fair-weather friend removed from our table," Alexander said loudly to match the volume of his father's voice. "Unless Pepper is here at *your* invitation."

The implication in Alexander's words was clear, and his father's nostrils flared. Pepper and Albert? It couldn't be true, although it would explain a lot.

Albert gave a terse nod of support to his son, before rising and exiting the room. The mirth was now completely stripped from Pepper's face as she stumbled to her feet, her eyes flashing to her companions as if she expected one of them to come with her.

"Pris?" she mumbled, her eyes pleading.

Pris opened her mouth and then shut it again, giving Pepper an apologetic smile. Pepper lifted her head, shooting one more withering look my way as she did, and marched from the room without another word.

"Finish your dinner," Alexander said softly.

I swallowed and stared at my plate. My appetite was gone, replaced by a pit in my stomach that was quickly filling with dread. Around us, the others picked at their food and no one spoke. Everyone too lost to think of anything to say.

"*Now*," he added in a more commanding tone, keeping his voice lowered so that only I could hear.

I took a bite and another, but I didn't taste anything. Pepper might be gone, but I felt eyes watching me, looking away as soon as they were caught. Eating became an act of rebellion. I would show them they were wrong about me. There was no glory in it though, only the hollowness of regret. I wished I had never come here.

When I was finished, I stood and nodded toward the head of the table. "The meal was delicious *and* enlightening. Please excuse me."

I rushed from the room, exiting out the door that the servers had brought the food through. I moved so quickly that I nearly ran into one carrying a large platter of decadent looking desserts. I muttered an apology without stopping.

I need to get out of this house.

It was my only thought as I dodged the staff in the kitchen, spotting a back entrance in the process. Pushing open the door while the cook gawked at me, I stumbled onto a back patio. The sun had faded, leaving only the remnants of twilight in the sky, and I breathed in the evening air, trying to steady my heart and my thoughts. Turning back, I stared at the estate. It sprawled behind me, and I marveled that with its spacious rooms and grand arches, I could barely breathe inside it as though the walls were slowly moving in on me, crushing me so quietly that no one could hear me scream.

The back door opened and Alexander stepped through. Without a word, he strode toward me, grabbed my hand and pulled me along after him. When we'd moved outside the view of the kitchen windows, he yanked me to him.

"Alexander—"

But his finger flew to my mouth, silencing my protest. "I won't apologize for her, Clara. I won't waste any words on her."

"I have a few that wouldn't be wasted on her," I said, but my voice quivered, betraying that she had managed to get to me.

"Poppet." The endearment was soft as he took my face in his hands. He brought his lips to mine so slowly that I felt the electricity building between us. It exploded as our mouths met in white-hot passion. Alexander ravaged me, and the message was clear as his tongue plunged possessively inside my mouth, catching my own and sucking it into submission: I belonged to him. Nothing mattered but what he said. That might have scared me with another man, but with Alexander it set me free. I'd spent my whole life seeing myself through a funhouse mirror, but Alexander's possession had clarified that warped vision, allowing me to see myself as he saw me.

I was limp under his domination, clay to be molded for his pleasure, knowing that when I gave myself to him, I'd experience more pleasure than I could have ever imagined. Alexander broke the kiss, stepping away, and I swayed, unbalanced without his touch. He sensed this and took my hand, placing it over the stiff bulge in his slacks. "This is what you do to me."

My fingers flew to his belt buckle, but he pushed them away.

"No, Clara. When I say," he reminded me. "Right now, I want you to turn around."

My face flushed as desire pooled in my core, imagining Alexander fucking me right here. I did as he said, and Alexander pressed a hand to the small of my back, guiding me a few paces forward until we reached a stone balustrade that wrapped around the veranda. He pushed me gently against it, bending me over the railing. I faced the house, unsurprised to see the windows of this section dark.

"When I saw you before dinner," he murmured, brushing my hair over my shoulder to whisper in my ear, "I wondered where you'd left your skirt."

I giggled nervously. "I like this dress."

"Oh, I like it, too," he said. "I like that I can do this."

His hand slipped easily under my skirt and between my legs.

"I must admit I didn't like sitting next to you, so close to this

—" he cupped my sex through the lace of my thong "—so close to what is mine, knowing I had to wait for it."

"Antici...pa...tion," I breathed, drawing out the word.

"That's exactly what I had in mind, poppet." His fingers drifted under the negligible fabric, sliding smoothly between my lips. "Do you want to step out of these for me?"

I sighed, my eyes shut as I relished the sensation of his long, rough fingers gliding wickedly between my seam. "You're giving me a choice?"

"It's come to my attention that we have finite resources on Earth," he repeated my earlier jibe, "and that I should spare a few pairs of panties."

"How forward-thinking of you," I said, hitching my thumbs under the straps of my thong and wiggling them until they fell at my feet.

"I think you'll approve of my planned call to action." Alexander bent and retrieved the lacy scrap at my feet. He brought it to my lips and urged them open, stuffing them into my mouth. "We're so very close to the kitchens, and I want to keep all those sexy little noises and cries of yours to myself."

I whimpered against the fabric in my mouth, as a hint of perfume and muskiness flooded my nostrils.

"I'm actually jealous, poppet," he said, his hand caressing down my throat and coming to rest at the nape of my neck. "I'll bet you can taste that sweet, little cunt of yours on those panties, something I've been dying to do all night. I suppose I need to do something about that."

Alexander pushed me farther over the bannister until my feet dangled slightly in the air. He stepped between my legs, spreading me before him, my short skirt providing no resistance. His hand stayed firm on my neck and his other one massaged down my bare ass until one finger slid down my crack, pushing me open for his greedy eyes. I protested feebly against my makeshift gag as his thumb circled around the soft, pink pucker he found there.

"Relax," Alexander ordered. "You belong to me, Clara, and I want you. All of you."

My eyes clenched shut as his thumb pushed against that forbidden place. I had never wanted something like this, but I was powerless to his touch. I needed to give all of myself to him. Trusting Alexander meant opening myself to him even when it scared me, although I couldn't deny the sweep of pleasure as he drew his finger in and out of me in slow, careful strokes.

"I'd like to take your ass, Clara," he said in a voice that warned me not to protest. "Remember it is mine, and I will claim it when I choose to."

He increased the pressure of his massage until the lace caught my moans.

"Not tonight," he said with a finality that left me panting with desperation. "You aren't ready, poppet. But you can't deny me my desire to play with you after you teased me all night in this poor excuse for a dress. They're scared of you, you know. So different, so confident. You've unraveled them just as you've done to me."

He didn't stop as he spoke, rather he pushed in and out faster until I clung to the railing, holding on as the first waves of pleasure broke across me. Alexander slipped two fingers into my cleft, increasing the pressure and filling me abundantly as he stretched me past my boundaries. He fucked me slowly until I cried out, overwhelmed by the new sensations that swelled in me. The panties muffled my exclamations, and I bit down on them.

"I love that little cry of yours. It sounds so helpless, as if you're begging me to rescue you. Do you want to come?" he asked in a raspy voice that sent goose bumps shivering across my skin.

I nodded, unable to speak. The world around me was a blur of darkness and light. I was lost to my pleasure, lost to the sensations crowding into my body, rippling out like tiny emissaries to warn of an oncoming storm. And no matter how overwhelmed I was, I clung to the edge, never wanting this moment to end.

Alexander removed his fingers, drawing a gasp of displeasure from me as he left me aching and pulsing with need. But he immediately dipped down, running his tongue agonizingly slowly along my swollen lips, stopping to attend to my throbbing clit with long, drawing pulls. Then, without warning, his thumb pushed inside my rear, driving me over the precipice as my orgasm surged through me in powerful crests that broke across my body and rushed over my skin. It was too much. It was everything.

But Alexander continued even as my legs clamped against his head and I called out for him to stop, although I wished he never would.

He finally released me, only to rise and press his body against mine. "I need to be inside you." Alexander pulled the panties out of my mouth. "Ask for it."

My legs shook under me, and my sex pulsed, tender and swollen. I couldn't handle any more. I was too sore, too tired to stand. "I...I can't."

"Wrong answer," he breathed, and I heard his pants unzip.

"Too much," I whimpered.

"Poppet," he soothed me, even as his cock slipped between my legs, pressing hot against my sensitive flesh. He waited, poised at my entrance. I bit my lip, trying to control my body's urge to open for him as he stroked his crown along my seam. I wanted to believe I could still say no to him, even as my body shifted from overwhelmed to excited at his restrained touch.

Alexander pressed a kiss to my shoulder as he continued to persuade me with his perfect cock. I dropped my head back, losing myself momentarily to the temptation, and when I opened my eyes, I saw her.

Pepper was frozen, watching us from an open balcony door. Our eyes met and I allowed a wicked smile to creep across my face. Her gaze stayed icy, but it was clear she couldn't look away. I closed my eyes and lost myself to Alexander once more. He was mine and soon she would know that.

"I need to feel you, X," I murmured to him. "Your skin on mine."

The stroke of his cock stopped, although it stayed wedged against my sex. I relished the tiny pops as he unbuttoned his shirt, and a moment later, Alexander wrapped an arm around my torso. He brought my body into contact with his bare chest, only the thin lace of my dress lay between us, and I could feel his warmth radiating across my skin.

"I want your cock. I want you to fill me," I moaned loudly, melting into him, even as he bent me forward and entered me with a powerful thrust that drew a loud gasp from my lips.

Alexander's hand slid from my belly to my breast, plumping it through my dress and sending more moans to my lips as my nipple beaded in response. I felt Pepper's eyes on us still, but I didn't care. I was lost to Alexander—lost to his touch. In that moment, I belonged to him and I knew that when it came to his pleasure, the answer would always be yes.

"I'm going to come inside your beautiful cunt." A groan punctuated his words, and my core clenched, tightening around his cock like a coiled wire. "Christ, you're milking me. You want me inside you, don't you? You want me to pour inside your cunt, because you know it's mine."

"Only you," I gasped as my limbs tightened.

"Only you," he repeated. His words flooded through me, and a thready cry escaped me as I felt the hot lash of his seed. I shattered into a million pieces that rained over me, drenching my body with pleasure that soaked into my blood.

It was too much and my knees buckled. Alexander caught me, sweeping me into his arms and cradling me against his bare chest as he carried me into the house. My eyes flickered to our audience, but she was gone. She'd gotten the message.

I sighed with relief, resting my head against Alexander's shoulder and breathing him in. I belonged to him, *but he was mine*.

CHAPTER TWENTY-SEVEN

The room was spartan, save for a bookshelf and a few framed pictures on the desk. I did my best not to gawk at the family photos of Alexander with his mother and sister. Alexander watched me as I looked at one of the portraits.

"She was beautiful," I murmured as I studied the photo of Sarah on her horse.

He nodded stiffly. "She loved to ride horses."

"What happened?" I asked in a soft voice. There were still walls standing between us, and more than ever, I understood how much we needed to tear them down.

"Clara, I honestly wish I knew." He spoke sincerely, and my heart ached for his loss and his confusion. The guilt had broken him but facing it might allow him to finally heal. "I remember flashes. That's why I continued to invite Pepper to events."

He told me this with some hesitation, so I forced an encouraging smile onto my face. As much as I hated Pepper, I'd track her down myself if she could give him the answers he needed to move past the accident.

"I was drinking and my sister showed up. She was underage, and I yelled at her for being at a bar." He struggled to remember, and I placed a reassuring hand on his shoulder. "For some reason we left. I don't remember much after that. And what I do remember, I can't burden you with."

"Nothing between us, X. No secrets."

"I remember how slippery her blood was on my fingers. She sagged like a rag doll. I remember the heat of the fire as it blazed across my skin, but I couldn't leave her there, even though I couldn't carry her." His eyes had grown distant, fading to another place and time. "I was so scared that I didn't even feel the frame of the door in my side. I'd been impaled, but I wouldn't leave her, so we burned together."

I choked back a sob and nodded, trying to stay strong for him even as my imagination painted a gruesome picture for me. "And Pepper?"

"She'd been flung from the car. Broken bones," he said. "If she remembers more than me, she's never admitted it."

"X, what happened was horrible." I brushed back an inky strand of hair from his forehead. "But it wasn't your fault."

"Why don't you see the monster when you look at me?" he asked. "Everyone else does."

"They don't see you like I do." My words were faint as I gathered my courage. "They don't love you like I—"

"I'm sorry," Alexander interrupted my confession. "I just need a minute." He staggered to the bathroom and locked the door behind him.

You scared him away, my critical side admonished me. I pushed the thought away, refusing to believe it. If Alexander said he needed a minute, I would give it to him.

I didn't go after him. He would come back out, and I needed time to digest what he'd told me. The physical details of the accident were public knowledge. But why couldn't he remember anything?

A knock on the door pulled me away from my thoughts, and

I opened it with some trepidation. Albert's eyebrow raised when he saw me, and I knew what he was thinking.

I bowed my head to him as he entered. Albert paced the perimeter of the room, pausing to pick up the photograph of his wife and young daughter. Taking a deep breath, I moved closer to see this one. Elisabeta's Grecian beauty was even more pronounced in the personal snapshot, her dark waves whipping across her glowing skin as she hugged a young Sarah to her chest. Sarah was a miniature version of her mother but with pigtails and dimpled cheeks. Somehow the photo had managed to capture them so vibrantly that when I looked at it I felt as though I had known them.

Of course, in a way, I had through Alexander. They lived in his memory, and I had faith that one day they would no longer haunt him. Instead, he would remember only the good times. That's why it was so important to help him find the answers he needed.

"Elisabeta was an ideal royal wife," Albert said, running his hand along the edge of the polished frame. "She was modest, loyal, and above all: *deferential*."

I pressed my lips together to keep my thoughts about this to myself. I'd seen how Albert treated his sons. I could only imagine how he treated his wife. Had she deferred to him to keep the peace? Or had she been trained to submit entirely to her husband?

"Many people believed our marriage was arranged for us, but it wasn't," he continued. "Her family sought asylum here when Greece exiled their monarchy. She was thrown into my circles, and to be honest with you, I fell in love with her the first day we met."

I wasn't certain why he was sharing this with me, but I nodded encouragingly.

"My wife was brought up amongst the aristocracy. She

knew what to expect. She knew her role." He placed the frame back on the desk and turned to meet my eyes. "Do you understand what I'm saying to you?"

"Your wife was groomed to be Queen," I said softly, but I couldn't bring myself to add the rest of his message. *I was not.*

"I hope you see that this isn't a personal vendetta against you, Miss Bishop. I could even sanction a relationship between you and Edward, but it's my duty to look out for the interests of the monarchy." His words were crisp—clean and concise—but they still sliced through me, cutting me to my very soul. I bit back a gasp of anguish.

"I'm not Edward's type," I said coldly, and the chill of my words shivered through my skin. I wrapped my arms around myself, wishing Alexander would return.

"And that proves my point," he replied with a congratulatory tip of his head. "*Appearances* are the key to the Royal Family's survival. Think of how the story would solidify my sons. Edward steals you away from his older brother. Alexander would make a suitable match, and what happens behind closed doors would be your business."

"Are you suggesting I marry your younger son so I can be his brother's mistress?" I asked the question aloud because I thought hearing it might make help me comprehend the King's suggestion. Instead I felt more confused than ever.

"The second thing only a Royal would understand is *sacrifice*."

I choked back a laugh at this. "How is lying and cheating and hiding a sacrifice?"

"I never said it was. I'm talking about sacrificing happiness, about sacrificing selfish desires. Alexander believes he wants you now, but if he gives up his title—his birthright—do you think he'll thank you in ten years?" Albert caught a strand of my hair and rolled it between his fingers. "He won't. Consider this: what

about you? How will you feel in ten years? But what if you sacri-
ficed your concept of happiness now and settled? In ten years,
when he's lost interest in you, you'll have a title and a life."

"I can't believe you would honestly think that I would do
that to either of them." The shivers had grown to tremors, and I
clutched my arms protectively. How could he believe I was
capable of that? And why would he believe that I saw it as a
viable alternative to being with Alexander?

He paused for a long moment, regarding me with tired eyes.
"You might as well know then that expectations are in place for
Alexander."

"You've made that clear." I couldn't control the amount of
sarcasm in my tone, and I didn't care anymore.

"*Marriage* expectations."

The addition of that one word instantly changed my
perspective. My mouth went dry as I struggled for something to
say. "You mean...?"

"It's long been expected for Alexander to marry within the
Royal Family. In fact, a match was secured when he was a child.
He doesn't speak of it much, but he certainly knows about it."

Albert could have stabbed me directly in the heart and it
would have been a less painful shock. My knees buckled under
me, but I forced myself to stay upright. Albert expected to win
this round with a bombshell. I wasn't giving up so easily.

"You're his toy," the King said, wiping invisible dust from
his sleeve. "And when he tires of you, he'll get a new one.
There's nothing you can do to secure your place in this family."

"Has it ever occurred to you that I am not looking for
marriage?" I asked, hoping he hadn't caught the break in my
voice. "Or a place in this family?"

Albert laughed at this. "All women are looking for marriage,
whether they know it or not."

No wonder he had such insane ideas about marriage. He

didn't even view women as people. I turned away from him, as
his barb fanned my simmering rage into flames.

Alexander filled the doorframe, watching our conversation
from the bathroom with controlled interest, but as I neared him,
something dark flashed in his eyes, warning me away from him.

"I see that since you couldn't sway me with your threats,
you switched tactics."

"We both know how this ends," Albert said, keeping his
gaze level with his son. "The tart's quite pretty, but you aren't
serious about her. Why do more damage to her reputation?"

His words stripped away all pretense of civility. Albert radiated the same primal power as his son, but the King's dominance was laced with bitter prejudice and apathetic cruelty.
Behind him, the picture of his wife beamed up at him. Had she
loved him enough to overlook this? Had she not seen it?

Or had her loss simply turned a charismatic man into a
domineering one?

"You know the expectations," Albert continued. "I've given
you far too much latitude since you returned, but it's time to
accept your role in this family."

"I know," Alexander said in a stiff voice.

My mouth gaped open as I tried to process his response. A
mask of resignation fell over his features, his eyes turning to icy
sapphires. Their fire had gone out, replaced by something cold,
unreadable and hard. His jaw was set and he looked past me out
the window. The awareness that usually accompanied his presence fled my body as numbness crept through me.

This man was a stranger to me. I didn't know Alexander at
all. Despite the shock dulling my senses, this realization twisted
my heart until I couldn't breathe for fear it would snap in two,
and I would crumble to pieces with it. The bond I'd felt
between us since that night at Brimstone faded in and out of my
perception like the signal of a black box lost at sea. It had

survived when nothing else had, and even as I searched for it, desperate to find that connection, I felt it slipping away, fading from my grasp under the turbulent waves of anger and sadness crashing through me.

The pressure in my chest increased as tears welled in my eyes. He'd warned me away, knowing that a relationship wasn't possible. He'd known that there were other expectations for him. He had told me that he wanted to fuck me. Alexander had promised me pleasure, and he'd given me that, but there had always been an expiration date to his offer. Except somewhere along the line, I'd forgotten that, and that's how I'd made the one mistake I couldn't take back. I'd fallen in love with him.

How stupid had I been to think he had fallen with me?

"I should leave you two," Albert said, breaking the silence that stretched across the room. "Good evening."

As he shut the door, my fingers closed over a book on the shelf next to me and I hurled it. It cracked against the door and fell to a heap on the floor. I stared at it, tears rolling down my cheeks. Pages had twisted and bent, the spine split neatly in half from the force of my throw.

Broken.

Misused.

Abandoned.

My knees buckled and I dropped to the floor as well. Alexander flinched, but he didn't move. A part of me that I hadn't even known existed—the part of me that expected him to take me in his arms and comfort me—died. It was all true. I'd ignored all the warnings I'd been given to guard myself against him. I'd even ignored my instinct that he would break me.

And he had.

He had done everything they said he would do. He'd done everything *he* said he would do.

So now there was only one person I could count on. Myself.

The agony of his rejection clawed through me, slicing me open and leaving me to bleed out slowly. But I'd been broken before. It was this alone that allowed me to finally gather the strength to push to my feet. I swayed once, catching myself on the bookshelf, but I stood. I stood despite my sorrow and confusion. I stood when all I wanted was to lie back down and waste away.

I stood.

And that alone made me strong enough to give Alexander one last piece of myself.

I drew in a jagged breath and stepped before him. He gazed coolly at me, remaining distant and removed, and waited.

I wanted to touch him. I longed to trail my finger across his beautiful jawline or run my hands across his shoulders. I'd never imagined that in this moment I wouldn't be able to—*that I wouldn't want to*—touch him.

Trembling with tears as I opened my mouth, I forced him to hear the words he'd tried to run away from. "I love you, Alexander."

His eyes closed, and for one beautiful moment, the distance between us faded. I felt my proclamation wash over him, saw it take hold of his body, watched him shift.

I watched him break for me.

But when he opened his eyes again, the hardness remained. "That wasn't part of our arrangement."

I had expected this reaction, but actually hearing him say it crushed me. A sob wrenched through me, and I fled the room. I wouldn't let him see me cry.

Never again.

The tears fell hard and fast, tremors racking through my body as I staggered to a recess in the wall. Crumpling to the ground, I broke down. I could have been there for minutes or hours or days. Time had ceased. I didn't care if the sun rose again or if the world halted on its axis. Nothing mattered.

I succumbed to darkness as pain pulled me under. I had trusted him, I had given myself to him, and he'd destroyed me. Just like he told me he would.

Hands lifted me from the darkness and cradled me tenderly, but when I opened my eyes, I was still in my nightmare. Edward held me with steady arms, carrying me back toward my room, whispering small words of comfort that did nothing to alleviate the agony ripping me apart.

Forcing myself to speak, my words catching on parched lips, I stopped him. "I need to leave."

"You should rest," he suggested in a gentle voice. "I'll take you to my room if you want."

But I shook my head. "Please. I need to go home."

"I'll make the arrangements," Edward agreed, not arguing further. "Clara, you don't have to tell me, but what happened?"

"I fell in love with him," I said, my words brittle and unwanted on my parched lips.

Edward didn't speak, but his arms tightened around me. We both understood that sometimes love wasn't enough.

CHAPTER TWENTY-EIGHT

I turned the key over in my hand, still trying to decode its meaning. But its existence was as unfathomable to me as Alexander's absence from my life. Two weeks later, and I was still trying to convince myself that I had done the right thing. There'd been no word from him. No phone calls. My only contact with him was on the cover of whatever tabloid he'd landed on each day. He certainly wasn't sitting at home and forcing himself to eat and get dressed every morning. He hadn't forgotten how to breathe without me. In fact, the only indication I had that he regretted what had happened in Norfolk was this brass key.

Belle poked her head into my room and found me curled up in bed. "You can't go."

"I just wish I knew what it meant," I admitted, my fingers closing over the notched blade as I wondered once again what it opened.

Belle was right though. The only thing I knew for certain about this key was where it came from. It had arrived mid-week in a cream envelope sealed with a red wax stamp that set my heart racing. But there had been no explanation included. No apology. No plea for another chance. The envelope had simply contained this key and a notecard with an address and tomorrow's date scrawled across it.

I didn't have to look up the address, because I recognized the name of the quiet street in Notting Hill. What I didn't know was what waited for me if I went there.

There was no doubt that Belle wanted me to stay away because she was angry with Alexander. But the real reason I couldn't bring myself to go was because as long as I stayed away, the key could open anything. It was pathetic, and I knew it. Still, that small sliver of hope was my lifeline.

"What would you do if you saw him?" she asked, coming to sit next to me.

I shrugged, blowing a thin stream of air through my lips in an effort to steady myself. I'd not yet reached the point where I didn't want to cry at the mention of him. "Maybe I'd ask him why," I said in a small voice. "Why he kept seeing me? Why he doesn't love me?"

Belle draped her arm over my shoulder and hugged me close. "Do you think he'd actually tell you?"

"Probably not," I admitted. "I feel so stupid for thinking it meant more to him, too."

"Uh-uh," Belle clucked. "Falling in love isn't stupid."

"It is when you always choose the wrong man," I said.

"You're human, Clara, and you've made mistakes in the past. But I saw how cautious you were after you left Daniel. If you chose Alexander, there was a reason for it," she said softly. "Maybe you can't see that right now, but you will someday. And even if he's too dense to realize what he had, remember that he helped show you that you are strong. Stronger than you thought."

"I wish that lesson hadn't been quite so painful," I croaked as the tears I'd been fighting broke through.

Belle kissed my cheek. "You're strong enough to survive this."

I hoped that she was right. It felt as though I'd walked through fire that stripped my skin and left me exposed.

Raw.

Vulnerable.

Walking, eating, existing—every moment was agonizing. I didn't feel strong. All I felt was this perpetual cycle of despair. Each morning I remembered that it was over, and my heart shattered again. I spent the day gathering the fragments and trying to piece myself back together. Maybe Belle was right, and I would survive this. Maybe the piercing anguish would fade into the dull ache of regret. But I knew one thing: there was no getting over Alexander.

"I didn't even see it happening until it was too late. I mean... I guess you never know when you're making love to someone for the last time." I couldn't quite shake the regret I felt over how we'd spent our final moments together.

"It's cruel," she agreed.

Opening my fist, I held out the key. "What do I do with this?"

"You know how I feel about it," she said, "but how do you feel?"

"It's like I'm clinging to it. As long as I don't go, it can mean whatever I want it to."

"That's no good, darling."

"I know," I whispered, "which is why I need to go."

How could I explain to Belle that I still felt Alexander's hold on me like the tug of an invisible string? I was bound to him, even as each passing second frayed the edge of that connection. Now all I wanted was to sever it and break free of him. He'd made it clear that he didn't return my feelings, but it was too late to stop myself from loving him. Holding on to hope was paralyzing me, and with each passing day, I felt the paralysis spreading like poison. It was killing me.

"Do you want me to come with you?" she offered.

I wasn't surprised that she wanted to tag along, but having a sidekick wasn't going to make this any easier. "No, I need to face this alone."

I had the rest of my life to endure alone. I might as well start facing it now.

I was in a cab the next morning before Belle was out of bed. She hadn't fought me on going, but she was worried and her concern only made me more nervous.

I'd opted for a pair of well-loved jeans and a white tank top. I had no clue what waited for me in Notting Hill, but I sure as hell wasn't out to impress anyone today. The plan was pretty simple.

Get in. Get out. Get over it.

My breath hitched when the taxi slowed to a stop in front of a gated row home.

"This it, miss?" the cabbie asked.

I couldn't get a word past the lump in my throat, so I nodded and shoved cash in his hand.

I clutched the key so tightly that it cut into my skin as I approached the house. Behind the gate, there was a garden in full bloom and a stone path that led to red steps and the door beyond. Judging from the water pooling at the edge of the walkway, someone had tended the plants recently. It was likely he or she was still here. My heart jumped in my chest, and I took a deep breath. *See if the key works before you get excited*, my rational side advised.

I dropped it twice, trying to insert it into the lock with trembling fingers. The key turned and the gate swung open, welcoming me inside the private sanctuary. Pausing amongst the flowers, I couldn't help wishing I were here under different circumstances. This place was a dream as cozy and inviting as the neighborhood to which it belonged. But right now I was too tense to enjoy it. I'd brought Alexander to Notting Hill, and the memories weighed on me, turning my favorite place into somewhere I wanted to avoid.

I'd come back though. If for no other reason than to push this all into the past. I climbed the steps, resolved to get this over with, but as I reached for the bell, I spotted a red rose tucked into the door handle. I took it gingerly, pricking myself on the thorny stem despite my care. Tears welled in my eyes and blood welled on my fingertip. There was no reason to believe it was for me, but I knew it was. Just as I knew that key was going to unlock the gate. It was the same vibrant scarlet as the one I'd worn in my hair the night of the ball. The night where everything had changed between us.

The door opened, startling me out of the web of memories I'd become trapped in. The sight of him knocked the air from my lungs, and I gasped, tying to remember how to breathe. I'd spent the last two weeks dreaming of his face, but seeing him before me, I realized those fantasies hadn't even touched on his beauty. The shock of black hair. The perfect lines of his face. The delicious curve of his jaw, the full bow of his lips, and the sapphire eyes that drew me to him, burning me with their intensity as I drowned in them.

Alexander's shirt was unbuttoned, revealing his chest and six pack. His jeans hung low on his hips. My body betrayed me, responding instinctively to the magnetic energy sizzling between us.

This was a mistake.

Whatever reason he had for asking me to come here, it had been a mistake to come. The tears fell freely down my cheeks, and I didn't try to stop them. The pressure in my chest built until I heaved with unrestrained yearning.

Alexander reached for my hand, spotting the small wound on my finger. He brought it to his lips and sucked away the blood before placing a gentle kiss on the spot. The gesture was small but not insignificant. When his arm coiled around my waist, I didn't resist him.

I couldn't.

So much for being strong, the critical voice in my head sneered.

But his mouth silenced my fears as it pressed against mine. The kiss was tender and hesitant, and his lips moved slowly. Salt mingled with his taste on my tongue, and I pulled away to discover the tears weren't mine. Alexander dropped to his knees, burying his face against my stomach.

My eyes closed, relishing the peaceful sensation that washed over me. I was desperate for his touch, even though it couldn't ward off the inevitable.

"You're thinner." His tone was measured, but I heard the edge of accusation in it along with something else that sounded a lot like fear.

I had wondered if he would catch the slightly sharper angle of my cheekbones or the tautness of my belly. The color had drained from my world when I left him, and along with it, life's flavors. I'd been relying on alarms more than I had for a long time, but I was taking care of myself.

"I'm okay," I said in a soft voice. "I haven't had much of an appetite, but I am eating."

"You can't..." he choked on the words. "Not because of me. Promise me, Clara."

His alarm caught me off guard, and I struggled not to read more into his concern. "I promise."

After a few minutes of silence, I couldn't wait any longer to understand why he'd asked me to come here. "Where are we?"

Alexander rose to his feet and wove his fingers through mine, leading me though the hallway into a living room. Now that the shock had worn off, I digested my surroundings. The home was fully furnished and artfully decorated with a mixture of antiques and clean, modern touches. A fireplace with an exquisitely carved mantle was the focal point of the living area. A plush, linen-upholstered sofa sat across from it, and the rest of the room combined vintage and contemporary into a warm, welcoming space.

"You're asking the wrong questions," he said. My core clenched as I drank in the familiar rasp of his voice. Alexander's eyes hooded as though sensing my sudden, urgent arousal, but he didn't make a move.

"Twenty questions again, X?"

He shook his head, his tongue wetting his lips as he did. "No games, poppet."

I stared around us, trying to comprehend why we were here while fighting the dizzying effect of his presence. I'd been too long without him. Now his nearness was almost overwhelming.

"Why are we here?"

"You're getting warmer." He moved close enough to me that I felt his hot, sweet breath on my face.

"Whose house is this?" I asked so quietly that he shouldn't have been able to hear me.

His mouth dropped to my ear and whispered, "Ours."

I pushed him away and stared at him, trying to make sense of what he was saying. Had he lost his mind? "I don't understand."

"This is our normal," he explained, spreading his hands. "This is our sanctuary."

There were so many questions crowding into my brain that

I had a hard time choosing one, but there was one that I couldn't even guess the answer to. "How?"

"The house is in Norris's name," Alexander told me. "I pay for it, of course, but this way we maintain our privacy."

I walked around the room in a slow circle. Alexander's eyes followed me, but he hung back as I absorbed what he was telling me.

"You mean to maintain secrecy," I said, turning back to him.

"Privacy. Secrecy," he repeated the words with a shrug as though they were the same thing.

The problem was that they weren't.

"Here we can be Alexander and Clara. Nothing between us," he continued.

"Except the secrets."

Alexander crossed to me so swiftly that I barely processed his reaction before his arms were around me. "Not between us. Nothing between us."

"Oh X," I sighed. "Everything is between us. Can't you feel it?"

"I don't want it to be." His eyes pleaded with me, and I saw the agony I felt reflected in them.

"Your father expects you to get married. He has it all planned." *And those plans don't include me.*

"I can't control what he plans, but that doesn't mean he can force me to do anything."

"Did you know about his plans?" I asked.

Alexander hesitated, and I already knew his answer before he spoke. "Yes."

Wrenching away from him, I held out a hand to warn him to stay back. "I've spent the last two weeks trying to figure out what I'd done wrong. Because I don't believe loving you is wrong."

His stance shifted, his eyes going distant. "Perhaps not for you. I stayed away because I felt it was unfair. I felt like I was leading you on."

"And this isn't doing just that?" I cried, my heart breaking all over again. I'd given him a chance to fight for me and he'd put up a wall. "Why are we even here?"

"Because I need you." He spoke harshly. His words indicting me, as if I had tricked him.

"But you don't love me," I whispered.

Alexander's hand ran through his hair as he shook his head. "I told you I don't do romance. I don't do long-term."

"What mixed signals you give me, Your Majesty." I practically spit his own words back at him. "That's a dangerous thing to do with a girl like me. What is this? A place to fuck me in? A little hideout your father doesn't know about so you can keep your tart a secret, because you can't have me showing up in the press?"

"That's not what this is!"

"Then tell me what it is," I pled, my anger faltering, "because I'm trying to understand. I really am." I was desperate to understand, because even as I stood here so close that I could reach out and touch him, I felt him slipping through my fingers.

Alexander's jaw tightened, and when he finally turned the full force of his gaze on me, I staggered back a step as it smoldered through me. "Every woman who has ever loved me is *dead*."

I broke for him all over again, shaking my head softly. "I'm sorry, X. But I'm not dead. I'm right here—and you can't make me stop loving you."

He crossed the distance between us, and I didn't stop him as he drew me roughly against him, cupping my chin firmly. "I won't destroy you."

"You already have," I whispered.

His hands dropped from me in defeat. "I never meant for this to happen."

"I know, but I'm a big girl, X," I told him. "You can't control me. You can't control who I love."

"Stop," he demanded, and I wasn't certain if he was ordering me to be quiet or to stop loving him.

I wasn't capable of either. "That's why I can't stay. I can't pretend that everything's okay. I can't pretend not to love you. I think that would hurt worse than leaving you. I'm sorry, X. I can't be your secret."

"One night," he said, his voice simmering with longing. "Stay with me one night and if you can walk away in the morning, I'll let you go."

I shook my head even as my earlier words replayed in my mind:*you never know when you're making love to someone for the last time.*

"Let me show you," he said.

Show me what? How it's going to be? How capable you are of giving me the one thing you say you can never give me? A stronger woman would walk away, but my resolve crumbled under his blazing eyes. If I left now, I would always wonder what would have happened if I had not. Going to bed with him would tear me open and rip out my heart, but the break would be clean. No regrets.

My fingers trembled as I found the hem of my shirt and drew it over my head. Alexander froze, watching me lustily as I stripped off my jeans. My bra and panties followed until I stood before him naked. "One night," I agreed. Someday he might look back and hear the truth hiding in those simple words.

Alexander swept me from my feet and carried me toward the stairs, his lips pressing urgent kisses to my neck up to my jaw as he trailed his mouth slowly toward mine. Desire ignited in my core as he captured my lips, parting them to plunge his tongue with slow, deep strokes into my mouth. My hands slipped under his shirt and pushed it off his shoulders. I ran my fingers along the worst of the scarring that twisted so close to his heart that I felt its steady beat pulsing across the tips.

He wouldn't let me say the words, but I would show him one last time.

One final night to last a lifetime.

Laying me carefully across the bed, Alexander stole over me. I tugged open his jeans and pushed them down. He kicked them off and moved between my legs, his thick cock finding its way without guidance. I gasped as he entered me with one powerful thrust. His mouth found mine again, and he kissed me, his lips lingering deliberately. Cruising lower, he trailed along the hollow of my neck down to the one between my breasts. He planted a soft kiss there before he caught my nipple in his mouth, swirling his tongue over it with languid strokes. My hands fisted into the sheets, arching against him, frantic for contact.

I needed to feel his skin against mine. One final night of connection.

Alexander's hips rolled deftly as he speared me, stretching my cleft. I moaned as he pressed harder, fucking me deeper. Then he withdrew from me, and I cried out, hungry and empty. Sitting up on the bed, he slid his hand behind my back and lifted my quivering body to his lap. His hands cradled my back as I sank onto his cock, savoring the delicious ache as I swelled around him. He filled me, and he moved slowly as I adjusted to the pitch of his shaft. It was buried deep inside me, and I circled it as the pressure built through my body.

The position was intimate, and it was impossible to escape each other's eyes and the questions they held. Alexander wasn't taking me, he was appealing to me. I felt his confusion as acutely as I felt the fevered heat of his skin. In that moment, it was impossible not to see through one another. Alexander's hands clutched my back, stilling my movement, and I understood the unspoken request.

He wanted to make it last. One final night of wholeness.

My index finger traced the curve of his face, mapping it. I brushed it over his lips, memorizing their soft fullness. My eyes met his, and I fixed the truth I saw shining from them in my mind as my hands traveled over his body, committing each inch of him to memory. I knew the darkness of parting lay ahead of us. Even as I captured this moment and its beautiful serenity, pain commingled with desire. I gave in, my feelings overpowering me, and rocked urgently against him. Alexander's arms tightened as his cock drove into me tirelessly. We crashed into one another, colliding and connecting, bridging and breaking. Each touch desperate. Each kiss pleading.

"Say it, Clara," he coaxed hoarsely.

His wish was my command. One final night of domination.

"Alexander," I breathed, "I love you."

His eyes closed as his cock spasmed against my velvet channel, pouring inside me, and I spilled over with him, unwinding in his arms. The pleasure splintered across my limbs in brilliant fireworks that fragmented as they rained through me. I rode the torrent of pleasure as I repeated those words.

I repeated them to fill a lifetime. One final night of affirmation.

Alexander didn't release me as he collapsed onto the bed, instead he entwined his limbs with mine until there was no beginning and no end to us. We lay in silence until I felt him swell inside me, and then we began to move again.

"I will never have my fill of you. I crave you, Clara. I crave your body, your taste. Without you..." he trailed away, his eyes flashing with pain. "I...I..."

And then he was pumping into me again, fulfilling me the only way he knew how, and I clung to him.

One final night of words unspoken.

I slipped silently from the bed, untangling myself from Alexander's sleeping form when the alarm clock on the bedside table read six a.m. He'd only fallen asleep a few hours ago. He'd fucked me with his mouth and cock until I was near collapse, as if he knew the moment he withdrew from me I would vanish.

We'd spent yesterday in bed, only leaving to feed ourselves before returning back to each other's bodies. But even as we laughed and lived and touched one another, I forced myself to make a thousand silent goodbyes.

Goodbye to that dirty, sexy mouth that curved so effortlessly into a smirk. Goodbye to that tangle of silky, black hair. Goodbye to his protective streak. Goodbye to the moment of deliberate hesitation before he filled me.

Goodbye to the man I loved.

I dressed quickly and found a pad of paper in the kitchen. In the end, I realized there were no words. I'd said what I needed him to hear. Anything else would just be an excuse, and I couldn't bear to leave it that way when we both knew the truth. We both saw the wall standing between us, and we both knew we couldn't tear it down alone.

I left the key on top of the paper. This home had been ours for one perfect, bittersweet day.

Stopping at the door, I closed my eyes and searched for the strength to walk through it.

"This it?" His voice startled me from my concentration, and I whipped around to face him. He hadn't bothered to dress and his body was tense, bracing for my response. I saw the torment in his eyes, and I fought the urge to comfort him.

"I'm sorry." I held my hand up, knowing if he touched me, I couldn't go through with it.

"Clara." He looked at me with a sadness that twisted through me, but he didn't come any closer. "Please."

I closed my eyes, unable to take the sight of his beautiful face, and shook my head as my fingers closed over the doorknob. "I can't be your secret."

Pushing open the door, I staggered into the crisp morning air as he called after me. I ran, but I couldn't escape the pain. I was in motion even as my world ceased to exist—even as it all collapsed around me.

ACKNOWLEDGMENTS

This book wouldn't be here if it wasn't for Laurelin Paige, who is a better cheerleader than she thinks. I stone cold love you, girl.

A big thanks to my partners in crime Melanie Harlow and Kayti McGee. Next time I'm getting a tattoo.

I'm eternally grateful to call Tamara Mataya my friend and not only because of her mad editing skills. Thanks for keeping it real and always finding the dirty joke in everything.

Bethany, I wish I could kidnap you and keep you all to myself. Anyone else would find that alarming, but I know you won't. Thanks for getting me and for always be a willing, sharp-eyed reader and editor.

Thank you to K.A. Linde for helping me with my cover woes and being enthusiastic. I think this is the beginning of a beautiful friendship.

COMMAND ME probably wouldn't be in your hands without the help of Amy McAvoy and the Truly Schmexy girls. Thank you for going above and beyond. I couldn't have done this without you.

The craziness is only beginning, Shanyn Day. I'm blessed to have you in my corner.

A special thanks to my sister, who was the first to fall for Alexander. More is coming soon! And to my husband for reading and late nights and wine and research.

And to you for reading. You're the reason I do this.

ABOUT THE AUTHOR

Geneva Lee is the *New York Times, USA Today,* and internationally bestselling author of twenty novels with varying amounts of kissing. Her bestselling Royals Saga has sold over three million copies worldwide. She is the co-owner of Away With Words, a destination bookstore in Poulsbo, Washington. When she isn't traveling, she can usually be found writing, reading, or buying another pair of shoes.

Connect with Geneva Lee at:
www.GenevaLee.com

Made in the USA
Middletown, DE
18 August 2024

59363015R00213